I LOVE THE PERSON
YOU WERE MEANT TO BE

with an introduction by Dr. Albert Ellis, Ph.D.

About her novel, Martha Wiley Emmett has written, "It is about sex and death—death by one's own hand, by another's, by accident; it is about the prison of the mind; it is about the brevity and separateness of people in contrast to the permanence and wholeness of life itself, and it is about the joy available to us despite—or even because of—that very contrast."

"This is a full-bodied yet deftly composed novel, its diverse threads relevantly interwoven . . . (the author) has given her insights engrossing fictional expressions."
—*Chicago Tribune*

"An intense and extraordinarily realistic account of a married woman's mental breakdown."
—*Washington, D.C., Post and Times Herald*

". . . more an experience than a novel. . . ."
—*Glasgow Herald*

Martha Wiley Emmett was born in 1927 and grew up in parsonages on the East and West Coasts. She received her undergraduate and graduate education at Sarah Lawrence College. The mother of three grown sons, she lives with her businessman-husband in a remodelled barn in Westport, Connecticut.

I Love The Person You Were Meant To Be

By Martha Wiley Emmett

(Original Title: Satan, Have Pity)

WARNER

PAPERBACK LIBRARY
NEW YORK

WARNER PAPERBACK LIBRARY EDITION

First Printing: March, 1971
Second Printing: May, 1971
Third Printing: October, 1971
Fourth Printing: February, 1972
Fifth Printing: June, 1972
Sixth Printing: January, 1973

Library of Congress Catalog Card Number: 63-7794

Cover illustration by Seymour Chwast

Warner Paperback Library is a division of Warner Books, Inc.,
315 Park Avenue South, New York, N.Y. 10010.

*Dedicated to the memory of
Dr. Anthony S. Votos*

INTRODUCTION

By Dr. Albert Ellis, Ph.D.

This is a truly engrossing novel: exceptionally well written, alive, suspenseful, and as realistic and personal a picture of severe emotional disturbance as I have ever read. Mrs. Emmett is obviously a housewife and a writer, but she often sounds like a professional therapist and has written a book that is incisively educational as well as fascinatingly involving. It is the kind of a volume that a professor of abnormal psychology could well use as a text and that could serve as a focal point for absorbed discussion for many weeks. For his students would, at least by Mrs. Emmett, rarely be bored!

There are many plausible theories of emotional breakdown; and two of the leading ones, the Freudian and the Adlerian, are thoroughly expounded and harmonized in *I Love the Person*

You Were Meant to Be. Because the former theory is more dramatically oriented, and is fine grist for the literary mill, it might appear on the surface that it is the entire framework of this novel. But it really isn't. When all the chips are finally down, and the verdict on the basic causation and cessation of Jane's "mental illness" is in, the Adlerian view clearly contributes as much or more to its "cure" as the Freudian "exorcism of the repressed past" (which in some ways may have indeed been helpful). At least to my prejudiced way of thinking: since my own form of psychotherapy, rational-emotive therapy, makes much more use of Adler than of Freud, and therefore seems to make considerably more sense than when, years ago, I was mainly a Freudian analyst.

Why did I change? Mainly, for the same reason that Mrs. Emmett seems to change her horse in midstream and leap from the Freudian to the Adlerian stallion. The former system is highly intriguing and challenging, especially to one who (like me) loves "detectiving" and delights in putting many little jigsaw pieces of the "mind" together, until the human "personality" seems to be thoroughly understood and correctible. But it doesn't work unless the client rationally *uses* her new insights to change her old ways of thinking. After literally years of Freudian analysis, the disturbed individual usually has considerable "understanding" of her problems, is enormously attached to (not to mention dependent upon!) her analyst, and continues to enjoy the "therapeutic" process. But too often she stubbornly resists getting better. And she often, alas, gets worse! Unlike Janie, whose analyst was methodologically flexible, eclectic, and therefore very helpful, she largely remains exceptionally prone to severe anxiety, depression, guilt, and hostility.

Because? Because, for all its complexity and profundity, the Freudian system, even when accurately descriptive, can largely exorcise past emotional pain rather than "cure" present and future leanings toward profound irrationality. Let me illustrate this point with material from Mrs. Emmett's novel. She very beautifully and artistically ties up Janie's past experiences, particularly during her early years, with her present symptoms, and thereby presumably sheds much light on their origin and causation. For example:

Jane tells us that "on the morning of the fourth day, when I awoke, I was an old man, a very very old man, with a wizened thin body and a thin ascetic face." She later discovers that this "old man" probably represents her stillborn brother whom, as a child, she thought she killed because she was jealous of him. She additionally realizes that the old man represents Mahatma Gandhi, who was assassinated on her wedding day and to whose death her father gave more attention than to her own marriage.

She also thinks, on the fourth day of her breakdown, that she is three girls. And she later realizes, in her analyst's office: "I see, see the three girls, see since earliest memories the triangle, the trio of my mother and my sister and myself, see that the rivalry between sisters for mother never stopped, because grammar school triangles, high school, college, always two best friends and me, me the central one, the leader, the competed-for, the most-loved."

Another of Janie's symptoms is her inability to

sleep, presumably because she is terribly afraid to do so; and her analyst shows her that this is because she is afraid of her unconscious, which may rise to smite her during her sleep. As she gets better, she is no longer afraid of this "unconscious," and consequently is able to sleep without pills.

Jane, throughout her life and especially during her breakdown, is abysmally guilty. Because, she finally realizes, she wanted to tell her beloved (and neglectful) father about her mother's affair and have him become enraged against her mother, the mother's lover, and Jane's sister. "He'll listen. He'll hear. And then he'll know and then he'll kill them, kill them all three, and I will be his wife."

These are a few illustrations of Mrs. Emmett's use of the Freudian method of explanation. Since all her examples *could* certainly have been true and important, let's assume that they actually were: that Jane's disturbance was related to her childhood family romance and her fear of her unconscious. Even more fundamentally, the *deeper* causes of her breakdown remain unobserved; and revealing to her these well-deduced but more superficial "causes" is likely to be therapeutically insufficient.

For, in Janie's case, why did she *originally* get —or, in rational-emotive psychology terms—*make herself* upset about her stillborn brother, her father's interest in Mahatma Gandhi, her sister's rivalry for their mother's love, and her mother's affair with a lover? The answer is that she, like innumerable other children but with greater intensity, *always* had three or four basic irrational ideas, which are part of the usual disturbance-creating irrationalities that I expound in *A Guide to Rational Living* and *Reason and Emotion in Psychotherapy*.

Thus, she felt that she absolutely *had* to have her father's unadulterated love and that it was *awful* when he didn't give her very much of it. She felt that she was an absolute villainess for being jealous of her sister and for "replacing" her stillborn brother, and that it was *horrible* that she competed with the former and had somehow magically wished the latter dead. She felt that her mother was an utter louse for cuckolding her father.

Why are these ideas irrational? Because they are derivatives of the basic irrationalities, or totally unrealistic demands on ourselves and others, that humans so frequently feel: namely, the demands that we must be perfectly achieving, completely adored, and supremely catered to. No one can consistently have these demands (or grandiose insistences) gratified; and everyone is more or less miserable when they are not. Jane (like many other disturbed individuals) had the kind of innate constitution and social upbringing—and, very likely, more the former than the latter—that encouraged her to have greater full-blown inner commands (Freud's "superego") of this kind than some of the rest of us have; and *therefore* she felt terribly guilty about her stillborn brother, exceptionally bitter at her father's interest in Mahatma Gandhi (which symbolized his devotion to "others"), unusually competitive about her mother's love for her sister, and woefully moralistic about her mother's love affair.

The heroine of *I Love the Person You Were*

Meant to Be, moreover, was born and reared with still another quality that proved to be her great downfall: she perfectionistically refused to accept herself *with* her disturbances—with her guilt, jealousy, competitiveness, and moralism. She sensed that she was putting down her father, her sister, and her mother; and she unconsciously kept condemning herself, damning herself for these neurotic symptoms. Finally, this double dose of self-flagellation overwhelmed her and she had her "nervous breakdown."

Why, it may be asked, are human beings, literally by the millions, so perfectionist and grandiose, so needful of canonization and so prone to hurtle themselves into hell? An interesting question, about which much has been written —most of it utter drivel. The simple and fairly obvious answer probably is: because they are human, because that's the crazy way they naturally tend to think. Not that they *have* to be unhappy and self-destructive, and not that they *cannot* change. But it is easier for most of them to be pretty nutty than pretty sane; and it is much easier for the Janes of the world (many of whom don't get well) to be very disturbed during most of their lives than for them to be sane.

Back to Martha Wiley Emmett's novel. Fortunately, although she frequently employs the Freudian framework, the author (like, probably, her analyst) is also sceptical of it. She devotes the first several pages of Chapter 28, in fact, to an incisive critique of psychoanalytic theory and practice when it is inflexibly practiced. Even more importantly, Mrs. Emmett is significantly Adlerian when she gets down to the fundamental alleviation of Jane's symptoms. Her book includes one instance after another of the heroine's extreme fears of failure and how these fears affect her everyday living and her ultimate breakdown. For example:

Fear of loss of love. Jane, all throughout her life, has a dire need of being loved; and she *imagines* that she will be a worthless person if she is not thoroughly, inordinately loved. She *defines* herself as a worm because, even after she falls from a horse when trotting with her father, her father perfunctorily finds that she is "all right." She sinkingly sees that "he wasn't worried about her. He cared about the others, the others, always the others, he didn't care about her." She is horrified because her father has not merely, like her analyst, fifty other patients he cares for, but *five hundred* parishioners whom he puts ahead of her. She thinks that she *needs* (not merely strongly *desires*) the undying love of her mother, sister, husband, children, et cetera.

Fear of lack of accomplishment. Jane is unusually gifted with beauty, brains, and writing talent; but whatever she has in this area is never *enough*, by her own perfectionist standards. Though others, including her actress friend, Lisa, and her husband, Ed, think of her as an "egghead" and as "brilliant," she self-critically notes: "I knew in my heart how I stood: my brain lay like a vast tract of half-developed real estate, abandoned except for a model house or two, and these I displayed as my heart and home, while I lived on the sly in a tree."

Fear of having disturbed symptoms. As noted above, Jane is terrified of her neurotic symptoms, because she views herself as being on the verge of psychosis and suicide. She is shocked at her own deep irrational desire for suicide. She is horrified (as are several other characters in the novel) by the concept of death and particularly about having a miscarriage and a dead "child." She equates, to a large extent, sleep and death; and when she gets symptoms of sleeplessness, in the course of her breakdown, she awfulizes about them mightily and absolutistically convinces herself that she cannot sleep at all without large doses of pills.

Fear of going mad. Of all the things that people are terribly afraid of, going mad is one of the worst. This fear—technically called phrenophobia—is also surprisingly prevalent when one investigates the deepest panics of disturbed individuals. Why is this so? Because the individual who thinks that she may fail at something, and would therefore feel humiliated and "bad," tends to ask herself: What's the worst, the most humiliating, thing that could happen to me?" And the answer commonly is: "Going crazy! Making a real spectacle of myself! Ending up in the loony bin!"

So with Jane. When she sees a film depicting a fictional version of Hitler's suicide, she notes that Hitler "heard no sounds except his own thoughts which were the thoughts of a madman and they were my thoughts and then he drew the knife across his throat and it was my throat, my wrist, and then I knew I would really do it, I was as mad as he had been and he had done it and I would do it, and I began to shake, the coldness had reached the center of every bone . . ."

Again, when her analyst tells her that she will get well and will forget all about her breakdown, she says: "You're lying. I'm insane and I will kill myself before you stick me in a snakepit full of crazy people like me where I'll rot forever surrounded by—"

Even Jane's therapist, for all his Freudian interpretations, finally gives her an interpretation of her disturbance which is basically Adlerian: "And before that, before the abortion, the other hospital room after your insomnia. You knew schizophrenia there, knew the agony of being caught in a dream, so from then on you had a vicious circle to contend with: sleeping meant taking a chance on insanity but *not* sleeping meant taking a chance on panic. You were tortured by the vicious circle, you felt you would become a drug addict or a psychotic, you entered a ritualistic pre-breakdown state so that you were unsurprised at the miscarriage, when you stained in Lisa's apartment you said 'There it goes' because you had willed it so, then you said 'Here it comes' because you knew you must be punished for willing it, and then you achieved a phony calm by divorcing your intellect and emotions until the split between them widened into . . . mental illness."

In other words, Jane, throughout her entire life, was mainly interested in proving her worth, her value as a human, and thought that she could do so only by succeeding at being loved and being accomplished. When she saw that she was not too lovable and not yet accomplished, she became frantic. She then realized that she might go crazy; and, viewing this as the greatest failure of all, virtually drove herself as crazy as she was afraid to become. Her unkindest cut of all to herself was her stubborn refusal ever to accept herself with flaws—and, if she must be flawless, how much worse than mere neurosis was her acute state of psychosis! So, ironically, she fell into the very state of psychotic breakdown she most feared.

As a psychotherapist, I think that her analyst was therapeutic not so much by putting the jigsaw pieces of her "mind" together as by later helping her to *combat* her perfectionistic, self-denigrating philosophy. If Jane had come for treatment to the Institute for Advanced Study in Rational Psychotherapy in New York City, I or one of my associates would have skipped the long-winded type of Freudian probing he used and would have quickly seen that her fundamental goal in life, or value system, was to aggrandize herself in every possible way: by being an outstanding wife, mother, and writer and thereby "proving" that she was worthy of living and enjoying herself. We then would have shown her, by cognitive, emotive, and behavioristic methods of teaching, that it is entirely unnecessary for an individual to "prove" anything about *herself*, even though it is often desirable for her to succeed in various *traits* and *performances*. *She*, as a total human, cannot be realistically rated or given a report card, though many of her *aspects* or *deeds* may legitimately rated or measured.

By inducing Jane to fully accept herself, her being, her aliveness, no matter *how* she succeeds or fails, and by showing her how to focus on *enjoyment* rather than on *self-assessment*, a rational-emotive therapist might have directly gotten to the very core of her heavenifying and devilifying philosophy and might have gotten there within a shorter period of time. Moreover, he or she would have left Jane, at the end of therapy, not only with an understanding of her past and present actions but also with a logico-empirical method of seeing and attacking any subsequent major irrational thinking with which she might later upset herself.

In any event, *I Love the Person You Were Meant to Be* is a gripping, marvelously true to life tale. It appears to stem from the author's personal experiences; and it details the early stages, development, and ultimate flowering of a woman's abysmal self-hatred and consequent breakdown as graphically and absorbingly as any other novel has ever done. Martha Wiley Emmett is a remarkably talented writer. Not that she would be a worthless individual, deserving of self-flagellation, if she weren't. But fortunately she wields a powerful pen. For which I am, as I am sure almost any discriminating reader will be, immensely pleased. Not many writers who know severe disturbance from the inside out have graphically conveyed its intense feeling to the rest of us. Mrs. Emmett has—and has thereby rendered a most valuable service.

"Meanwhile Goethe had been jolted by a catastrophe. A young legal attache, Jerusalem by name, whom Goethe had met, shot himself . . . At once Goethe was eager to obtain . . . full details of the suicide and its motivation . . . This supplied the spark for Goethe's creative urge. He set to work to write his own story . . . and he channeled its development into the catastrophe of Jerusalem's suicide."

From the *Foreword* to Goethe's *The Sorrows of Young Werther*

"Oh you sensible people!" I cried, but I was smiling. "Passion. Inebriation. Madness. You respectable ones stand there so calmly, without any sense of participation. Upbraid the drunkard, abhor the madman, pass them by . . . and thank God . . . that He did not make you as one of these."

"When we are robbed of ourselves, we are robbed of everything."

From Goethe's *The Sorrows of Young Werther*

PART ONE

"... O Thou, who of Death, thy lasting strong lover, didst beget Hope, fond mistress of men, Satan, have pity on my long-drawn pain ..."
From *The Litanies of Satan,* Baudelaire's *Flowers of Evil*

ONE

WHEN you are dethroned in the kingdom of your consciousness, you no longer wish to live; when you are the
slave of your brain instead of its master, lost in the land of
your own emotions, no longer friendly land but enemy,
when the you that was you has shrunk so small you can
no longer recognize it at all, then the unbelievable, the
unthinkable, the only total aberration occurs: you find
yourself plotting out your own death. For myself, the realization that I, who had so loved life, whose every desire
was supposedly satisfied, that I, who had been blessed with
every good fortune, should abruptly, inexplicably, desire
above all to cease to be, so frightened me, filled me so full
with a knowledge of my own insanity, that the original
compulsion to kill myself was compounded by a need to
obliterate such a mind as could *contain* such a thought;
I wished doubly to die. Previously, the horror of life to
me had been that it must end; now, suddenly, horror—an
abstract and far-removed and therefore bearable thing—
had been replaced by terror—not terror at oblivion but
terror at continued existence, not abstract, far-removed,
not an intellectual concept, but fear immediate and physical and overwhelming, rendering me powerless to fathom
or understand, rendering me powerless except for the rem-
nant of reason which remained, which said "Try. Fight"—
and which, triumphing, finally now, months later, permits
me to sit here writing of an irrationality which bowed me
down to nothing, wounded me irrevocably, illuminated
hideous caverns of facts formerly hidden in the abysses
of buried recollection, but which, occurring in the center
of the twentieth century, allowed me to be, at this moment, not, as I would have been at any other time in
history, a tragic memory now to my friends and family—
unaccountably, enigmatically, a suicide at the age of thirty-
one, an attractive and personable and rich and gifted and

9

much-loved wife and mother who had a miscarriage and killed herself—but alive, thinking, feeling, functioning, and, although far from whole, at least breathing again the sweet breezes of a mortality less precious but far better understood.

One day last August, a year ago, I was lying on the beach, indulging in the flotsam and jetsam of impressions which pass for thoughts in a sun-baked and half-awake head; the delicious wind nibbling my skin had sea-scent in it, salty, hinting of fish and silver-turquoise mermaids, of sails pasted pot-bellied against the horizon, and held in it sounds melted by the late-morning heat into a lullaby vaguely counterpointed with screams and with whistles, with pails scraped by shovels and with girls chased by boys across sand into surf, where the splash and the laughter, muffled by my half-slumber, seemed several worlds instead of only several feet away. The last thing I'd seen when I'd forced myself from my stupor, and, shading my eyes with my hand, had squinted at the shimmering shoreline far past the lifeguard tower to my left, had been the sight of my children kicking water at each other as they waded toward the jetty, where there were starfish to be found upon the boulders and tiny crabs and minnows imprisoned in the puddles left behind by itinerant tides. Shifting on my towel, sighing, I was aware, between brief dreamings, that I should get up and get busy, should tug myself up out of that quicksand of lassitude and make straightway for the supermarket, there to purchase the onions, the mushrooms, the tomatoes and chunks of mutton which I would need for the shish-kebab that night. But still I lay there, absolving myself from immediate action by trying to decide what drinks I would serve, and dessert; for if it turned out that, as usual, our guest was on one of his frequent diets, I would have to go easy on the ice creams and sauces that my husband and sons and I too loved so well.

Not that Roger would be anything but trim, of course; but Ed and I, as we had for ten years of catering to the man's vanity, must make sure that we committed no ca-

10

loric crime in which we might later be held responsible
for a trace of paunch upon that beautiful flat belly, a bit
of flab on that barrel chest or those Herculean biceps.
That Roger dyed his hair to conceal the gray did not
distress me; actors and actresses were my husband's business, and the artificialities essential to their trade had become as familiar to me as the fakery in Ed's, for as a press
agent he indulged in much that affronted my minister's-
daughter sensibilities. But if Roger's continual struggle
against age failed to move me, his other struggle, far from
superficial, moved me a great deal, for it was I who had
recognized it, had recognized it as somehow akin to my
own, and again that night, I supposed, I would be lending
him the equipment for introspection which he so desperately needed and so pitifully lacked.

"Mommy"—the voice of my eldest son had shattered
my meditations, my heart hammering from the abrupt ad-
justment of my mind and body from inertia to alertness;
I twisted upright and brushed from my face the spray of
sand which had accompanied his home-run arrival—
"Mommy, will you please tell Johnny once and for all he's
not magic and neither is The Martian." He turned to his
younger brother who, I saw, was lying behind me on his
stomach in the sand. "Mom says you ain't magic and him
neither."

"She didn't say anything. Liar."

"*You're* the liar. All that junk about how The Martian
tells you his secrets. Don't you know he used to tell *me*
that junk? I wised up, when *you* gonna wise up?"

"He's gonna bring me a conch shell from Mars, he
promised. You'll see, tonight when he comes to dinner—"

"He promised you something from Mars *last* time,
didn't he? And instead he brought you that same ordinary
rocket I got for my birthday. Wise up. If he brings you
a conch shell it won't be from Mars and it won't be four-
teen-carat gold and—"

"It'll be fourteen-carrot gold, he *said* so." Without looking I could tell that Johnny's chin was trembling. "Mommy, tonight when he comes The Martian is bringing me—"

"Oh, *Mother*." Bruce's voice squeaked in self-righteous

11

annoyance. "Don't listen to all that boloney. You should *hear* what The Martian always tells him and he's such a baby he *believes* it. The Martian and him's *magic,* he says. Boy, what a jerky kid."

"*You're* jerky," Johnny said; I looked; yes, the chin was beginning to tremble. "What do *you* know, jerky."

"I know you're not magic, that's what—and neither is *he.*"

"Bruce"—but he cut me off, savage with exasperation —"He's an *actor,* you little dope. He's just *Roger.*"

"I know he's Roger. He's The Martian too. He's both 'cause he's magic. Only *magic* people like him and me can be two things at *once. You* don't know. *You're* not magic."

"You little jerk. Roger's sword lands him on Mars, I suppose. Did he tell you it honest-to-God can make him disappear, huh? Back home to *Mars* when he leaves our house? *That* what you think, jerk?" Johnny was pretending to be too busy watching the swoop of a seagull to bother replying, at which Bruce, goaded into the final revelation, shouted: "It's all a trick with cameras to make him *look* like he's disappearing, that's all. It's all make-*believe.* The *Martian,* ha! Why you little baby, the day he sets foot on Mars or any other planet will be the day I—"

He broke off. A small sound sort of like a swallowed sob had come out of Johnny's throat and he was blinking a lot as he kept his eyes riveted unseeingly on the seagull. Bruce glanced at his brother and tried hesitantly to continue—"It'll be the day I . . . I . . ."

But Johnny's eyes spilled their overflow as he cried out in the anguish of a wavering faith, "The Martian's *real.* He's *magic.* Roger and me's magic and you're a big old liar."

Bruce looked at me and then back at his brother. For a few minutes, as Johnny sobbed, he chewed on the edge of his thumb and dug his heel fiercely into the steaming sand.

"Bruce—" I began, but again he cut me off, muttering, "Aw, all right, I was only fooling." As Johnny rubbed his wrists into his eyes and sniffed, Bruce added, "Okay,

12

okay, Santa Claus is at the North Pole and Superman's got X-ray vision and the Good Fairy put a nickel under your pillow when she took your tooth away and the Martian's magic and you're magic too, now you satisfied?" And he gave one loud snort of disgust—at Johnny? at himself?—as, bypassing the sand castle on which my third and youngest son was toiling at the water's edge, he dived in and swam angrily away from the embarrassment of his own compassion.

That summer Johnny didn't know how to swim; this summer he's learning. His strokes aren't strong, but they'll get stronger; he slaps at the water with his hands uncupped and sometimes forgets to kick; sometimes he feels he's sinking and in a panic he stops long enough to test with his foot, making sure he's not over his head.

Before this year, this longest year, I was positive I understood myself. My moods, my behavior—these aspects of myself I did not always fathom, but I was sure I knew who I was, and anything in my nature which was erratic, uncomfortable, unsightly, I accepted as one accepts a wart or a corn or teeth that aren't perfectly straight. My unpredictability was part of me; I accepted it. I did more than accept it, I enjoyed it, for wasn't it fun to be so complicated, so complex? Ah yes, such paradoxical contrasts in my personality—profound depths, glib flippancy—wasn't I wonderful? And my fears—the way I shrank in terror at the buzz of a mosquito or when lightning flashed cringed beneath the covers in a grisly sweat of expectation—wasn't I nuts? Ah yes, so interesting to be different, idiosyncratic, to be a writer who would write someday . . . someday when I wasn't so busy being a mother.

And then, suddenly, I found myself in astounded possession of a malignancy, a malignancy that seems more like a nightmare now, except that nightmares are brief and leave no scar. When you wake up from that deep a sleep, you can't quite remember where you are. Or who. But then if you lie there a while quietly, it comes back to you. You remember and you reject. You get up, you resume . . .

13

Yes, Johnny's doing very well indeed. And I, I too. I hardly ever panic anymore.

It had not begun like a beach day, that day a year ago. In the morning when I awoke it was raining, and even before I saw the drizzle or heard it on the roof I had known that the day would drag, drag endlessly, and that no book I could read or friend I could phone would do more than briefly quell the heavy illusion of minutes that seemed like hours, hours bereft of light. All was darkness, inside me, outside me, and I turned to Ed for comfort and he gave me what he could.

Afterwards—"Still depressed?" he said, and I nodded. We whispered; the children were still sleeping. "Weather?"

"No"—voice dull, listless—"not just that. From the second I woke up—"

"Getting your period?"

"No, dammit." Did he think everything was the body, always? Didn't he know about souls? "You wouldn't—"

"—understand." He finished it for me, easily, having heard the same complaint each time the fury gripped me —the fury to hurt, to hurt as I had been hurt—when? how?—and would never (I vowed) be again.

"Very cute," I said—darkness, darkness.

"I thought so"—and he went to the bathroom, waking the kids. And then they were in bed with me—Bruce, Johnny, cuddling up close to me, quibbling, rivals for my love—and Terry heard the noise but did not come, stayed in his crib, talking to himself, as always. Ed came back, shaven, and I said, "You woke them up. Was it absolutely necessary to slam the bathroom door that way?"

"I'm sorry, darling," he said, and that did it, the unexpected but typical sweetness, that did it—that and the two of them loving me, hating each other, punching at random across my dawn-drained body, and Terry talking, talking to himself—that did it, and I said to the boys, "Go play," and as soon as they left I burst into tears.

"Why are you crying?" Ed said. And then—"Oh, excuse me, I forgot. I wouldn't understand."

14

I lifted my head from the wet pillow. "And you call *me* sarcastic."

Stepping into his trousers—"I just hope you cheer up by the time Rog gets here."

Say, I'd forgotten about Roger! Besides, the rain was stopping, the sun might even come out in time for a picnic lunch at the beach after all. And then the shopping to be done—the day wouldn't drag after all. There, the darkness was lifting, within, without.

"Last night you weren't too chipper either," Ed said. He was doing his tie, the sun was out. "Now that you're back from shrew-land, will you kindly tell me what the hell I did yesterday to deserve another of those filthy-Philistine attacks?"

"You were late, the day was so long, the kids were squabbling—"

"If you'd turn on TV more often when they're bored—"

"Oh *yes*." I got up, put on my bathrobe, started downstairs. "TV, the panacea. If you were their mother, they'd all three be astigmatic by now." But jovial, mood changed, adding: "Don't worry, my lover. At least they never miss The Martian. Never miss a day."

Neither had I, when I was a child, listening rapt to the radio. He had first soared into my vision (as he did into yours?) from the pages of a comic book, a quarter century before, and I was among the millions who envied his feats of daring, his space-defying sword, his solar-batteried antenna-helmet buzzing and sparkling with interplanetary messages of distress, and his muscles bulging beneath the satin, sequin-sprinkled costume. Inadequately, on my Pogo stick at age eleven, I would pretend to soar from Earth to Mars and thence to smother with my body the dynamite a lunatic had placed in an orphanage on Jupiter; my magical sword a broomless broom handle tipped bright with tinfoil, I'd shout the slogan which would someday be heard—thanks to the voice of Roger Rutherford—on radio, on movie screens, on television: "The magic . . . magnificent . . . Martian!"

At breakfast, Ed mentioned that Roger's meeting with Lisa Maurice that day should net a few items in the col-

15

umns. He'd arranged the rendezvous, of course; always nicer to get two clients' names in the paper at the same time, two birds with one stone. Parroting his own publicity style, he quoted: "Lisa Maurice in town and wowing 'em along Nightery Row, but rumor's got it that a certain man from Mars has his foot in the door. Guess who?"

"Please." I thought it bad enough that he had to turn out that stuff in his office .... please, Lord, not in his *home.*

"Guess who's got his little old *foot* in the door?"— laughing, teasing me.

"Guess who, guess who." I tried to sneer, but laughed instead, unable to resist the contagion of gaiety in his face. His was one of those faces that could glow from inside like a lamp—my mother's was another—and a moth's was nothing to my helplessness. "Guess who's about to miss the eight-eleven?"

He leaped to his feet, still chewing, and with his coiled-spring nervousness—eyes blinking, head jerking, his tall thin body tensed as a warrior's for his Battle of the Buck —strode to the door with a final admonition: "Make shish-kebab tonight. Rog gave us those broiling swords for our tenth anniversary last year, let's *use* them."

As Ed careened his car backward down the long graveled driveway, swinging so sharply into the road that he almost knocked the mailbox off the fence, I remembered something I wanted to ask him, and I stepped out on the front steps a moment, hand raised hopefully, but it was too late; all that remained of him was the grating sound of gears shifting in the distance and, above the dirt road, a cloud of dust. Well, I decided, I'd buy enough food just to make sure. Lisa Maurice, in any case, was undoubtedly on a diet; like Roger, like them all, she would be starving, for sweets, for applause and for love.

On the way home from the beach—we live a mile away from the Sound in Cedarton, Connecticut—we harmonized popular songs. Terry, my three-year-old, sat in my lap, his damp and gritty little hands clamped to the steering wheel in the firm belief that he and not I was the driver. Occasionally he let out a feeble fragment of melody, but it was the other two—six-year-old Johnny and ten-year-old Bruce—who provided a choral co-operation so raucously wholehearted that I burst out laughing. Good Lord but I felt happy—happy and oh so proud, proud as a queen in my battered old station wagon crammed with wet sandy towels and wet sandy sneakers and wet sandy tan sons yodeling their throats out, with their skinny scabby-kneed legs hanging out the open tail-gate and their crew-cut heads cradled on a fat rubber raft. We were all so wet and glad and sandy and I sang like a banshee, I laughed like a fool, for I felt free as a feather in the wind.

Free? Then? That whole long year ago? No, not free, not then, not even now. I know what I know, that's all. But a feather in the wind? Yes, that I was, and am no longer ... no longer tossed upon each turbulence, flung up, cast down, a wisp without control. Now I know what I know; I feel the authenticity of myself.

It is seven, and supper has been eaten, and beds are ready for three weary heads. From where I stand I can catch a glimpse of the children's bathroom, the door open, the plastic ferry half in the bathroom and half in the hall. Beside it the rubber duck lies on its side, still dripping, and further inside, I have no doubt, a sudsy pool of soap and washrag lies upon the tiles. If I go closer I will see the little footprints going wet along the hall.

I see what I see, I feel what I feel; that is no small thing.

"Don't tempt me with *dessert."* Lisa shielded herself in mock horror from the cake I offered her and leaned forward to pluck a more sensible alternative of one small grape from the fruitbowl centerpiece. As she leaned forward in the low-necked dress Roger said, "Holy *shit."*

"What?" Lisa looked startled, glancing up at him with the eyes that so often startled others; "emeralds" was the term most often used by movie magazines, but it was more than their vivid color or their large size and Oriental shape, it was the way she used them, instinctively, adroitly, as another actress might use her voice or hands or hips or smile ... "What's the *matter?*" she repeated, and the guileless bewilderment in her eyes was the real thing this time, not, as in her many films, that calculated innocence achieved by lowering her eyelids and then looking up wide-eyed through her thick lashes like a cat through a hedge, part sensuous attacker, part prey.

"You're a freak of nature," Roger explained, with a gesture toward her ample bosom. He sipped his brandy into his satyr-smile. "Have you faced the fact that you'll be downright *pendulous* by the time you're fifty-six?"

"Till then, I'm doing all right," she retorted, unfazed by this, his latest in a barrage of insults, and I wondered if she was as perceptive as I suspected, and had already ascertained—as Ed and I knew from experience—that Roger was childishly jealous of Ed's other properties, yes, jealous in direct proportion to their degree of fame in contrast to his own. Lisa continued musingly, "Fifty-six." Then, after a moment: "Hitting fifty hasn't hurt *you* any, has it, Mr. Martian sir?"

"Forty, dear heart. Besides, it's different with men. We wear well."

They were evenly matched, all right, but I wished she'd watch out, and Ed's foot moving cautiously across the floor to touch mine told me that he wished the same. Their brief time together—at Ed's teak-and-glass Manhattan office, at the Harwyn, where they'd met with Winchell, and finally here at our house for dinner—had probably not given Lisa the knowledge that ten years of Roger had given to Ed and me: the knowledge that beneath his banter lay a gigantic vanity easily wounded by mention either of his age or of the comic-book character he portrayed.

"Mom. Dad." Bruce peeked into the dining room. "May I please sit in the kitchen and eat the garbage?"

"Leftovers," his father said. "Okay, but don't be a pig."

I added, "There's lots of ice cream left, hon."

"I just saw an old movie on television," Bruce said to Roger. "You were in it."

18

"Which one?" Roger's attitude indicated that he didn't know yet whether to be pleased or apprehensive, but chances were the latter, for Ed and I knew full well that before becoming The Martian he'd starred in one film, been second lead in several others, but that in a dozen more he had played extremely minor roles. *"Blue Mutiny?"* he said. "I starred in that one. Or *Angelica's Holiday?* I played the lead opposite—"

"You weren't the lead in this," Bruce said. "I just caught a glimpse of you in one scene. You were some debutante's chauffeur."

Ed said quickly, "Child of mine, don't you want that *ice cream?*"

"I think it was you," Bruce went on, all earnest innocent elucidation. "At least it sure as heck *looked* like you. And yeah, the heroine's name was Angelica."

There were a few bad minutes when nothing more was said by anyone; I went to the kitchen to help Bruce, and I noticed that as the others went to the living room, Ed was in the middle, like an arbitrator, one arm over Roger's huge square shoulder and the other around Lisa's unbelievably narrow waist. And then, inevitably, I heard Roger begin the rationalizing autobiography that had become imminent as soon as my son had cast doubts upon the grandeur of Rog's theatrical past.

"My family was aghast," Roger began. "I was the first male Rutherford in four generations to refute the Princeton tradition. But I stood my ground. I couldn't be a stockbroker if my life depended on it. My life depended on being an actor. I don't know how it got there but it was in my blood like a sickness."

Standing there at the refrigerator I had to smile. Even the phraseology never altered in the least. I'd heard this same tale—Princeton, stockbroker, sickness in the blood —each and every time that someone new had been added to our orbit, someone new, as now, Lisa, to whom it must be made clear at once that only the harsh hand of unkind fate had designated Roger's thespian destiny to be less than Othello at the Old Vic. Soon he was into the Greenwich Village segment of his story—the three B's:

19

beard, beans, bowling alley, he having worn the first, eaten the second, set up pins in the third to keep from starving—"my folks in Philadelphia," he said, "having cut me off without a cent." Next Lisa heard about the early days in Hollywood and his first big break as Crimson O'Connor's soldier-beau in *Look Away, Dixieland*.

"Holy cow," Bruce whispered to me. "Doesn't he ever change his tune? And he didn't bring Johnny *anything*." He dug into his ice cream, ate, then continued: "Mom, remember how Rog used to stand me up on his hand like a statue way up in the air, the way he does to Terry now? Jeez, it seemed so high up in those days and exciting." He mused for a moment on the vagaries of time. "He sure is strong. I wonder if those other actors who play those other strong-guy parts—you know, Superman and everybody—I wonder if they're strong really-truly like Rog. Mom, is anyone else so strong?"

"Well"—he was finished eating; I shooed him up the stairs to bed—"Maybe almost."

Oh, very strong. And very weak. A giant, a baby, but only Ed and I knew of the latter, for we were—Roger claimed—his only friends, only *real* friends. Once he'd said, "With most people I wonder what they want from me. Not you guys. I trust you, I'm myself with you. You haven't got me mixed up with the myth. You're used to celebrities, I don't have to worry you're chummy just because you enjoy hobnobbing with a famous face." I'd said I should think he'd be more certain of the friends he'd made before his fame, suspicious of the ones who came after. "Yes," he agreed, "but it's the other way around too. People who were just casual acquaintances before suddenly become buddy-buddy as all hell, like it's due them, like they have tabs on you because you threw an eraser in their face once in fifth grade or something. But lots of people I know now are in the same crappy strata of half-success and now and then I find one I can talk to, some other goddamn lonely bastard."

That, as I recall, was the only time he ever used the word lonely. I never heard him say it again.

20

Later, after midnight, I decided to take a look upstairs, see if—as so often happened, especially when our guests were Ed's clients—some small eavesdropper, nudged from slumber by the raucous oratory and dramatics from below, was sitting droopy on the top step, all ears and stifled yawns. But no, they were all three asleep, and as always the sight of them lying there so quiet and so minimally mine made me kneel beside their beds as at an altar, bowed down by the only form of reverence I knew—awed and humbled by the limbs, the flesh, the features, the deep breathing and the unknown dreams of these miraculous creations of mine.

From downstairs, as I knelt there a little drunken, a little weepy-sad, I could hear Roger and Lisa discussing their similar resentments, she that her studio "typed" her a "sexpot," he, of course, that his career had been "shot to hell" by The Martian. She didn't get to say much— Roger held center-stage, she waited impatiently in the wings—and I recognized the verbosity of liquor, but at least he was being witty about his predicament, witty without the usual bitterness, as he told of an incident caused by the paraphernalia necessary to sustain the illusion of floating in the moon's low gravity. . . .

"The studio technicians had put me in this contraption, this metal jockey-strap deal with ropes and junk, and I ain't paying too much attention, I'm rehearsing my lines with the script girl and arguing with the make-up man while these guys screw around with all this fuggin' ski-lift-type stuff to hoist me up for a scene where I leap at a goddamn Moon Dragon"—he waxed increasingly sarcastic—"real great scene, you can imagine, poignant as hell, I was really thrilled about doing it, had more of a challenge than Hamlet, you know . . . I figured it might win me the Academy Award . . . so natch I wasn't paying too much attention to what was going on down around my genitals when—Jesus Christ!—all of a sudden they clamp some goddamn *wire* the wrong way and damn near *castrate* me and I let out a yell they must've heard all the way from Santa Monica to Pasadena.

" 'Whatsa matter sweetheart?' the director comes over

and says to me while I'm screaming and clutching at myself and damn near fainting. 'Whatsa matter sweetheart?' he keeps repeating like a fuggin' idiot.

"So I explain to him I damn near lost my balls, I'm caught in the goddamn wire, and he's a real sadist—you know him, Ed, Christopher Pembroke, that pimply-faced prick they finally fired, thank God—and he don't give a shit about my agony, he just sees a great opportunity to ruin me with this broad him and me are both trying to make—I forget her name, played a Moon Princess in that episode, I was supposed to wrestle her away from this here Moon Dragon in the next scene—so he goes and shoos her out of her dressing room to come help me, tells her he heard she took a pre-med course once at UCLA or some damn thing, and I gotta sit there like a goddamn ass while she tinkers around in the area of my crotch making motherly Florence Nightingale noises while I—"

Ed interrupted, "You didn't make her?"

"Make her! After that, I was lucky I had anything left to *screw* with."

"What happened to her?" Lisa asked.

"The little broad? She eloped with Chris Pembroke three weeks later. Turned out she was a virgin and he married her while he was still in shock. Since then they've both been divorced and married again five times apiece."

Yes, Roger could certainly tell a story, always gross exaggerations, *r*'s rolling, always the actor's intonation and the actor's perfect timing, smoothly lush and melodious or turning pizzicato with expletives—*Jesus! God! Christ! Shit!*—giving vent to an uninhibited intensity which relied for its expression upon a vocabulary compensating in vulgarity for what it lacked in erudition.

I tried to get up from my kneeling position, but sank down again, dizzy. "Yeah," I heard Roger say, "I know what you mean, kid."

Kid? Lisa? Things were progressing. At the beginning of the evening, when they'd first arrived, he had ignored her presence completely, attempting to monopolize Ed by emphasizing all the many memories they shared, using a nostalgic monologue of recollection to shut Lisa out as

22

thoroughly as if he'd pulled the cord on a Venetian blind. But now, I suspected, his habitual lechery had won out over his resentments, or perhaps it was even more their rapport at being type-cast. Listening, I realized that yet another bond had been discovered, for they were discussing fame. . . .

"I don't mind gawkers," I heard Lisa say. "At least they're honest. You know, Rog, the staring open-mouthed, lady-can-I-have-your-autograph creeps."

"Yeah, except they rip pockets, hanging all over you. But you're right, kid, them I can tolerate at least. It's the hypocrites that kill me. Pretending they don't know *who* you are or if they do know by God *they* don't give a damn —that attitude. It's written all over their moronic faces that they don't want *you* to know that *they* know who *you* are—"

"God, yes," Lisa said. "Furtive peeks, proximity by mistake—"

"Yeah, like they have to circle the whole goddamn restaurant over by your table across the room to get to the john right next to *their* table."

"They can't hurt their pride by putting themselves on a level with the gawkers. They—"

"Yeah, they—"

But this time Lisa firmly held her ground. "They loathe the gawkers, because the gawkers' admission of a gulf between our fame and their anonymity only emphasizes it. It's pathetic, really. And funny and flattering—"

"Hell, kid, wait 'til you've been enduring it for decades, like me. Then you won't be so tolerant."

"I won't be around for decades, dear heart. Not even for half-a-one. I'll be a has-been at thirty, a senile nymphet."

She was twenty-two now, and had been shuttling back and forth between Hollywood and Broadway since she was seventeen. Ed's agency had acquired her several months before, when—in the wholesale brutality so often inflicted by performers-on-the-rise—she had fired the entire entourage whose machinations and devotion had helped her through the early struggles and had, instead, outfitted herself with only the best, as befitting her increasing success: business manager, press agent, secretary, cosmetician—all were the finest that money could buy. Not that she was "there" yet—that nebulous, indefinable "there" to which they all aspired and which so few attained—but she certainly seemed to be headed for it. Roger would never make it, Lisa might—wasn't that the crux? Yes, sitting there close together on the couch they were sitting also at a crossroads; I knew it, Ed knew it, maybe they knew it too. A crossroads, his path meeting hers on their opposite journeys—hers up, his down— where they might linger a while? exchange notes? make love? I hoped so; Roger was always searching for someone we would approve of, and this one I liked. She might be a little cruel—wasn't Roger? wasn't everyone?—but she had brains as well as beauty, and she was honest, keeping her acting talents strictly for the camera. Yes, she might be good for him, might even be good *to* him, to the Roger I cherished, as a child cherishes a doll that has always been around, and is beautiful to look at, and that would speak with truth and poetry if only it knew how.

"Janie?"—it was Roger, kneeling down next to me beside Johnny's bed—"You okay?"

"Shsh."

"Sorry"—he lowered his tone—"You okay, kid?"

I started to answer but discovered I was crying; I wiped my eyes on his sleeve and then left my forehead bent there on his arm. He stroked my head softly with his enormous hand. "What's the matter?" he said finally.

"I don't know." I didn't have to explain; he knew; moods came, they went; like a tree in a gale you could be stripped of your confidence, your gladness, your *grip*— you couldn't predict, you couldn't explain, you only could huddle and wait for the sun. "Hold me."

He held me, old friend and confessor, murmuring into my hair. "Maybe the liquor?" he said. "Lisa?"

I shook my head. "No," and then, "You know."

"Yeah, kid"—knew, of course, as Ed could never know; sweet nerve-wracked Ed who didn't understand— "Death, huh?"

I nodded; he understood; wasn't he an artist, too, with an artist's tragic vision?

Artists? Roger and I? I wonder. Perhaps he could have been; there can never, now, be any proof to the contrary, no more than there was then, a year ago, any evidence (other than his own suspicions) to support the claim. And I? Well, we shall see. I know what I know, that's all. I know that if a rouged-and-powdered lady with a lavender feather boa draped about her wrinkled neck stands on a city corner talking to someone animatedly, listening and then laughing, and no one is on the corner but herself, I feel what I feel. She is I, I am she, separated as well as joined by the instrument in my possession; and if I wield it with skill and with passion, the lady can live forever, if I wish, and I in her survival can survive.

Tragic vision? Is that what we thought we shared, Roger and I? God, what a year can do to words like those! We were pretenders, playing at emotions and labeling our pretensions with pretty words. Pride, that we had, yes, and only in our pride did we suffer. That other kind of pain, the private kind that is never paraded, deep, steady —that we had escaped, had lost somewhere en route from womb to puberty, shrugging, guilty of collusion in the loss, not mourning, not knowing it was a gem we threw away. Was it the instant we were born that we discovered we could be hurt? Did the doctor slap a bit too hard to bring the breath into those brand-new lungs? In our first upside-down bellow did we announce our vulnerability and, right side up, reject it? But protecting ourselves from grief we protected ourselves also from joy, and then to be like others (armor is not the fashion) we painted garments on the metal and achieved (almost) the illusion of being attired as others were.

We were pretenders, we were phonies, our closest approximation to pain was hurt pride, but we did not know it, knew only that something was wrong somewhere so that we could never really like ourselves; feeling phony, not completely whole, somehow vaguely detestable, we

25

detested; and it was hate, I am sure, which twisted us into our inexplicable despondencies.

But ah, we had Death. Wasn't that a true emotion—that horror, that shared revulsion? Surely that was the real thing, and, grateful for our anguish, we reveled in it—"See?" we said to each other, "I feel. I suffer." But it was only that shoddy pride again. If Roger were here how would I try to explain it? "Don't you see," I would say, "the thought of death made you into nothing. It had to do only with yourself, as did all your supposed suffering; it was a sealed heart's sole apex, no different in essence from the only feeling you ever possessed—your effect on your little world, never the world's on you. To look into the mirror of another's opinion and see yourself small, that was the next-to-greatest pain you ever knew; death was the greatest; in that mirror you were worse than small, you were nothing at all. It was the absolute indignity."

Now I know what I know; I do not have to pretend to feel.

My child is in the kindergarten camp's circus; he is the last one in the line of elephants. In his hand he holds the crepe-paper tail of the elephant in front of him; there are seven elephants in all, heavily clomping in rhythm to the harmonica music, each hanging on to the preceding tail. I am grateful he has the tail to hold, for he is blind; the mask has slipped—gray paper with enormous Dumbo ears—and he keeps trying with his free hand to push it into place, to align small holes with big new-penny eyes. In his fright and confusion he forgets to clomp, he stumbles, but he struggles on. He cannot see and I cannot help him and all the mommies laugh and clap their hands and so do I. Later there is pink lemonade.

Roger, those were pinpricks, what we felt, yes, even death—all self, all surface, all pride, all noisy reaction, like toddlers who use their booster shots to make an awful fuss. You do not say "Ouch!" when the pain is internal, deep, a part of you; when you ache inside you do not say anything at all, and, if possible, you smile and move about.

I think Ed always knew. Wisecracking, huckstering,

26

armorless Ed—twitching, temperamental, gentle, un-poetic, believer in God and Country and Family and the Singular Power of Love—I think he's always known.

Roger called the next morning from Lisa's East Coast apartment on Gramercy Park. "This girl's got a round bed and blood-red Siamese wallpaper and mirrors all over the bedroom, like a high-class French brothel, my God, she's doing this movie-star bit up right, ain't she"—with Lisa murmuring something, her head next to his at the phone, doubtless, and clad in lavender chiffon or nothing at all. But Roger wasn't calling to amuse us—not even (as would be typical of him) to let us know he'd "made" this gorgeous piece, this piece whose contours were world folklore—no, quite the opposite, something rather dis-tasteful had happened. The mail had arrived, he said, as they'd been breakfasting, and had contained this scrawled message:

"I see from this morning's gossip columns that you're The Martian's latest lay. How does it feel to lie in the arms of a traitor? Is it his money you want or his name? Listen, you beautiful whore. His money is tainted and his name was born in my brain, a brain now deprived of its creation, its product the stolen property of you and all who batten on it like filthy little leeches. I detest you all and you are doomed, doomed, just wait and see."

I must have shared Ed's premonition, for when he hung up and went to the mailbox, I followed him. The note, scribbled in red ink, was unsigned, and we held it between us to read it: *"You have betrayed me. In poverty I feed on betrayal while you dine on caviar. Be warned. Justice shall prevail."*

"Quite a coincidence," Ed said, but his casual tone was belied by the way his head kept cocking to one side, spasmodically, as if someone were tugging at an invisible string hooked into his ear lobe, and we went to the phone and called Roger back. Yes, Rog said, backhand scrawl, red ink.

"Very peculiar," Ed said, and although I did not feel frightened, felt merely curious and unconcerned, I noticed that my hands were wringing together as if they did not belong to me and all around me there was a swift intense illusion of the sound of sparrow wings. For a second I felt smothered, sparrow-smothered, and then the sensation was gone.

Hanging up, Ed turned to me and said, "What have we ever done to hurt anybody? Rog and Lisa are famous, psychos envy them, torment them—but us? Why us?"

Why us? Why sparrows? We discussed the threats for a while, then talked of Rog and Lisa, and soon we were laughing in each other's arms, exultant at our matchmaking and merrily wondering if Lisa would tell Roger about the others, the forerunners, the prince and the industrialist and the Chilean ambassador to Greece.

Self, when will you admit it?

Admit what?—hedging, hedging, still a residue of phoniness, of small indifferent lies.

Admit you stayed upstairs that evening so Roger would miss you, would come looking for you, admit you wept to keep him there with you—

But death? the tragic vision?

Stop that! You were jealous of Roger and Lisa just as Roger had been jealous of Lisa and Ed. For once Roger wasn't doting on you, leaning on your every word, soaking up your introspective brilliance like a sponge.

I felt so sad—

Phony! Phony!

No, not any more. I know what I know, I—

Well then, go on. You know what you know. Go on.

All right. All *right*. I knew he respected my mind, but that wasn't enough. I wanted more from the mirror, I wanted to see wanting in the mirror of his eyes. Till Lisa came, I thought I was winning—

You thought he was a bit in love with you?

Well, I tried to attract him, I always tried, with everyone. Make everyone notice me, shock them into awareness.

Ah! Like the next night? That party on the other side of town?

Yes, then. And all the other parties, just the same. You know . . .

The party was held in a remodeled barn. An enormous beam across the high ceiling formed the center post into a T, rough-hewn, ax-lacerated by whoever it was, some one-hundred-and-eighty years before, who'd felled the trees and stripped the bark to accommodate his cow, his horse, his hay and his oats and, subsequently, a rabbi roué in a yellow-checked vest, a flat-chested dancer with cantaloupe calves, a tweedy copywriter of deodorant ads, an abstract painter with an auburn goatee, several housewives dressed in leotards, and in the hayloft (turned into a bedroom) a drunken playwright curled upon the chintz. Someone with a banjo was singing folk songs, a Mozart opera was on the stereo, an antique cradle held a batch of *Saturday Reviews*.

"That your third?" Ed asked me. I sipped a martini.

"Yep."

"Please don't"—but of course I did, and then a fourth, and soon it didn't matter what I said to anyone, as long as it was barbed or, at the least, unique.

"Are you a homosexual?" I asked the Yale professor, and meeting with a lawyer, later, said, "Did you know Wolfe thought all lawyers stank?" Someone mentioned psychiatry and I said it was a hoax and someone else, incensed, told me I could use a bit of it, and we argued, four or five of us, on whether or not one must be neurotic to create. When I danced, I danced too close, and knew it, and didn't care. I had what I felt was a marvelous time and then we left.

"Nice antiques," I said, driving home.

Ed didn't reply.

"You think Dr. Potkin's wife's pretty?"

Still no answer, and, humming happily, waiting patiently for the angry silent chain-smoking to erupt into the customary accusations, I watched the rustic landscape blur by—stone walls, picket fences, ancient clapboard cottages under magnificent oaks that had been saplings when Cedarton was new, way back, back at the Presbyterian beginning, back before the Italians came to build the railroad that would so greatly change this place that hated change, the railroad that carried the natty Eds back and forth to Manhattan an hour away, where they could make the money to purchase the illusion that the oak was a tender sapling still, that Covered Bridge Road and Stagecoach Lane, Nathan Hale Lane and Spinning Wheel Road bore no Porsches bound for country clubs, but were commuterless still, were rural, humble, innocent, and none had heard of atoms or of Freud.

"Why?" Ed said at last.

"What?"

"Why do you do it?"

"Do what?"

"How can you do it to yourself? Don't you know who you *are?*"

"Yes. I'm a preacher's kid who married a charming, lovable, high-powered publicity mogul and has to have a few to hold her own."

"Can't you see yourself as I see you?"

"How's that?"

"Special. Fine. Sensitive. Good."

But drinks wearing off, euphoria gone—"Oh sure. You're blinded by love. And you love me because I'm your wife and you're stuck with me, you're that type, loyal, true-blue. I'm callous and bad and untalented but you don't know it, you love me. But if you didn't love me you wouldn't even like me. Nobody likes me."

"Nobody likes to be insulted, or asked nosy questions, nobody likes a little bitch who makes a play for every——"

"See? You don't like me. You love me but you don't like me."

"I want you to recognize who you are so you'll stop stepping all over yourself."

"Hurrah, big psychologist. Listen, I know myself better than you ever will. I'm a writer, I——"

"Well, sit down someday and write a story about a pretty matron in the suburbs who's a barrel of laughs at parties and forgets each time she's a barrel of laughs that at other parties she's abruptly gotten so shy and

tongue-tied she escaped to the car and hid and cried. Write
that one about our smug intellectual protagonist and then
go sell it to yourself."

"I——" but we were home and, silently, sullenly, got
ready for bed.

Bed. I tried to remember what it had been like, other
nights, happy nights, to think of bed as beautiful in con-
notation: tired in bed, tender in bed, wrapped up together
flesh-sated in bed, the sheets an envelope so private-white
for slipping into, for whispering inside of, for warming
feet in wintertime, for cricket-listening in the spring . . .
and it was autumn that I first brought a baby to my bed,
turning swollen-breasted on my side to let him suck my
milk from me, his head tucked into my armpit downy-
duckling-fuzzed and warm. Yes, beds were for sleeping
and dreaming, for waking up smiling and staring at ceilings
paisley with daybreak, happy . . . sometimes . . . sometimes . . .

But that night the bed was a continent, Ed on one coast,
I on the other, backs turned, separate, alien, our resentments rising up between us as solid as the Rockies.

It is tuck-in time and my middle child says sleepily,
"Mom, remember way back last year when I was little
I thought I was magic?"

"I remember."

"He never brought me that conch." I do not ask who,
he knows I know. "Now he never will."

I pull the sheet up, I fold it back down over the blanket
edge. He says, "Right, Mom?"

"Right"—I get up and turn off the light.

Then, in the darkness—"Mommy?"

"Yes, lamb."

"I saw God once."

"Really? Where?"

"I forget. He had a clicker on his back and he clicked
himself on and then he clicked himself off. Also, I know
about souls." I wait, he feels me waiting, feels me listening. "I've got this soul in here. It's made out of all sort of
crawly stuff that oozes out when you die. Only I'm not

going to die. Not you or Daddy either. We'll only die if we're ready and if we're not ready we won't."

"That sounds fine, good plan." Down by the brook a frog croaks, belchy, mournful; there is a breeze tonight but no moon, the willows do their hula in the dark. "Goodnight, darling. Sweet dreams."

"G'night. I love you, Mom. G'night."

TWO

I WANTED very much to have four children. I didn't know when the wish had begun, or why, but there it was, there it had always been ever since I was small and scheduled out my life in perfect detail—there it was, along with the wish to swim and sun all summer, read and write all winter—there it was, the goal, the necessity or, if you will, merely the whim—there it was. Three was fine, three was beautiful and my contentment was almost complete, would *be* complete, would come full-circle somehow when the fourth arrived—yes, four would be the daydream and the destiny fulfilled.

And now it was the seashore—my home away from home, with me and all the other tan and indolent fanatics sandwiched hot and sweaty between beach and sky, baked to a turn in the neighborly isolation of blankets and towels moated by sand—here it was that I informed my husband we would soon be six.

Of the six, we two, Ed and I, sat propped up in our green and white striped canvas beach chairs—the kind that hold your bottom just a half-inch from the sand— we sat and watched through our dark glasses our three already born, watched them clamber on the jetty which jutted out upon our left, the gray enormous boulders tapering out slightly curved to the little knot of fishermen at its tip.

We two, hand in hand, dopey and dizzy with sunshine and sea-scent, and our three sons slaphappy too, from the sound of their screaming which reached us all ecstatic on the wind . . . and there inside me, infinitesimal but living, lay my fourth, my little tiny final child, buried deep beneath my flesh and my tissue and my jet-black Jantzen bathing suit.

Ed took the news calmly; the conception, in this case, had not been miraculous. "One thing bothers me, Janie," he said. "You didn't stage it right."

"Huh?"—flailing my arms wildly to fend off a horsefly, wondering as always why insects seemed to make me their special target, invariably disregarding others to concentrate their attacks upon me, as if made ravenous by my anxiety.

"Don't you know you should be sitting in a rocker knitting something soft and pink with a mischievous but madonna-like look on your mug?"

"Oh yes, and you drop your pipe on the hearth-rug in your astonishment"—I went along with the game now, free of my small tormentor, for quite accidentally in my flailing its demise had been accomplished, and it lay now belly-up in the sand beside us, ridiculous, lascivious, its flimsy legs spread in the air—"and you kneel before me, head in my lap, overwhelmed, reverent, adoring, struck dumb with surprise and gratitude, worshipful, instantly solicitous—"

"—until at last, retrieving the power of speech, I say quaveringly, 'My dearest, you mean . . . you're . . . we're . . . can it be true . . .' "

"—banishing from your mind the guilty knowledge that a moment so beautiful could have resulted from another moment as obscene as *that*"—and I indicated the diminutive corpse beside us.

Ed laughed. "When you're prostituting your genius in Hollywood after you win your Pulitzer, do me a favor, will you? Write a movie script about a guy who says to his wife, 'Hey, didja get it yet this month?' and she shakes her head and he says, 'How long overdue?' and she says three weeks and he says, 'Well, honey, that sure wraps it up.' "

Three weeks it was for me, in fact, but I was wasting no time in lingering on the brink, I was diving right into

33

my bovine idiocy—and bovine it *would* be, of course, and blissfully obsessed, the way I always wallowed in it: great long everlastingly tentative lists of children's names, pretentiously ancestral like Winslow Gardiner or insipidly modernistic—Mark, Kirk, Stacy, Tracy. Yes, my breasts would swell and I would switch to ever larger bras with smug insouciance, I would don with anticipatory fervor the skirts and slacks engineered for maternity, my stomach sloping out through the opening taut with infant, and over the bulge would fall abbreviated smocks and boastful waistless frocks—ah yes, I would wallow and waddle and if I was lucky, not vomit.

But of course, I did vomit. Three weeks from that scene at the beach it had begun, the awful endless retching at the touch of dawn or dusk, at the smell of food or even, often, the motion of walking from room to room. I'd forgotten, of course. Nausea is not remembered nor is childbirth, except, in childbirth, for the immediate aftermath, that noisy and almost medicinal introduction across the unbearable distance between your bloody slab and his impeccable bassinet, a distance so unbearable, indeed, that you beg to hold the slippery-skinned simian little thing just a minute, and then he's close to you, his adorable ugliness bundled in a barrier of flannel that you remove, later, alone with him behind the white curtains—when half-a-day's already made remote the gritted teeth and tight-clenched fists and the moaned "No! No!" and even, once, a frantic shriek that broke through the deep-breathing even-breathing wall of your control, embarrassment canceled by agony—all that half-a-day away and therefore never having happened, you strip your baby naked and examine every blessed inch of wrinkled miracle.

"Mommy," Johnny asked. "How did God get the seed into you?" We'd given our boys the news the month before. "Bruce told me—"

Bruce interrupted. "Shut up, you little tattle—"

"Bruce says Daddy went—"

"Shut up, you little louse."

"He says Daddy went to the bathroom in you."

34

"The description," Ed said, "lacks accuracy."

Bruce said quickly, "Come on, Johnny, let's go rake the leaves down by the brook." It was October and everything was yellow and red, dying with ostentatious dignity. We were out in the backyard and I was nibbling at crackers that never seemed to help the way they should. And then across the lawn came Terry, his older brother's holster drooping to his knees, the pistol cocked in his hands against innumerable attackers. He was talking to them now, whoever they were, the garrulous inhabitants of his vivid and invisible world . . .

"I'll put a bullet fru you, I'll kill you dead, *bang*"—laughing triumphantly and then, massacre complete, becoming, suddenly, two people on a carousel—"It ith my turn, Phyllith, you awreddy rode the tiger"—all the time revolving toward us across the grass, flopping down and getting up again, the conversation unceasing—"It ith *my* turn, no it ith *mine, no mine, you* ride the *horthe,* up down *whee*"—until at last he careened into us, his holster dropping around his ankles.

"Daddy," he said. "Fix my—"

"Hello folks!"

It was Roger Rutherford, popping up in front of us with a grin and a flourish of his arms, delighted at our surprise, for we had not expected to see him until the following day, when he and Ed would be continuing on up to Hartford for some publicity stint. Then "Look who's here," he said as Lisa, too, sprang out from behind the corner of the house, voluptuous in velvet slacks, her red hair—disheveled from the drive in his convertible—garish against the yellow of her sweater.

"You look like the season," I greeted her.

"You don't look pregnant," she said.

"You mean I look nauseated."

"Are you still?"

"Just a little, nibbling crackers helps"—and I offered her one, which she took, sitting down on the chaise next to my legs, and starting to tell me in her kitten-purring tones of what they'd been doing, she and Roger, since last they'd visited us. "Remember? It was the first time

Roger and I had met—gee, it seems like more than just two months ago, doesn't it?—and Rog hated me at first and then by evening's end he didn't, remember?"

I remembered.

Ed and Roger went down to the brook—Bruce and Johnny had spotted a frog, Daddy had to help them catch it, they called, but they had not seen Roger yet, and now they saw him—*"Roger!"*—jumping up into his arms, the two of them, more than a hundred pounds of hard muscle and boy-dirt, gathered up and hoisted each on one of his upstretched arms, like babies, arms and legs flopping, laughing, screaming, and then jumping down and taking turns standing on his huge shoulders and being walked around like giants high above the ground, screeching, laughing—

Bruce was thoroughly ten today, I noticed, wasn't pretending to be eleven or twelve, wasn't bothering today, as so often lately with Roger, to be a cynical sophisticate, his heroes outgrown, and Lisa said, "Roger's crazy about your kids. Loves all kids, but especially them. He ought to have a few of his own."

"Are you two . . . serious?"—to which she said nothing, helping herself to another cracker and annoying me with a Mona Lisa smile.

"Mommy!" Bruce shouted. *"Look at me!"*

"Wonderful, darling"—watching Roger leap across the brook, Bruce on his shoulders joining him in shouting the slogan he'd made famous as The Martian: "Up into *o-o-o-or*bit!"

"Roger's in a good mood," Lisa remarked, and I nodded. She knew him that well now, too, I realized, knew, as Ed and I did, that when he could kid about being The Martian, could thrill the kids with his pretense as he now was doing instead of shying away from all mention of his role, he was in good spirits. I wondered if this time—now that Lisa had become a part of his life and, therefore, of ours—he would be the unglamorous and rather adolescent Roger we knew so well, who, dependent on us for the loving criticism which he would never request or accept from anyone else, would talk and talk and talk—oh, no verbal whirls and pirouettes such as he had employed last time to amuse Lisa—no, just putting the smelly-bare feet of his mind up on the warm Franklin stove of old acquaintance and settling down to soul-searching as someone less introspective might settle down to chess or checkers. Vulgar, ungrammatical, that he was, but sometimes—not always, but sometimes—his confidences were so poignant in their inarticulate intensity, in their tentative gropings toward and quick retreats from truth, that I understood his crudeness, for many years of acceptance had passed since my surprise when, as a child, I first learned that cow manure is what makes the garden grow.

"He's a deep one, isn't he," Lisa was saying, "the way he talks sometimes. He's on an escalator, he says, going down, and so's everybody else, everybody marooned on their private escalators going down to the grave, but turned around backwards, walking up real fast, not noticing most of the time that they're getting nowhere at all—"

She went on, talking as a person in love does—incessantly, insistently, bewitched by her beloved into believing his every thought as rare and profound to others as it was to herself—and I thought about that escalator, the one Roger and I had discussed so many times, each of us knowing exactly what the other meant, and leaving Ed out of it completely, believing him incompetent, incapable, oh a swell fella and a big success and generous to a fault, smart at business and sweet too and sometimes surprisingly astute, but of course not understanding at all about death or loneliness or anything abstract, for, after all, if he understood at all he would express it, wouldn't he? would join us in our discussions instead of making an exemption of himself whenever Roger and I started talking, as if he had a hole in his head where all the really vital questions should reside?

Lisa was continuing, "—and every once in a while, Roger says, you reach over the railing of your escalator and somebody else reaches out across theirs and if you bend real far and are real lucky, you just for a moment touch hands. That's what Rog says. He's so deep. But he's such a child too. My psychiatrist says all women, to Roger, are the mother he never really had."

Oh God in heaven, I thought, not another one of these —not another female-in-analysis, like so many of my friends and their friends' friends. Bad enough that people like Lisa *went* to psychiatrists—had so little pride in individuality, so little self-reliance, were so little offended by membership in the ranks of the dependent—but oh Lord, when they were *loquacious* about it, as she was obviously turning out to be, that was *too* inane. Yes, she was on it still—smugly ensconced in her sleek Freudian vessel, full speed ahead, the sails of her mundane brain filled with labels and phrases: repression, rejection, ego, libido. Crap! I thought. I heard her saying that her beautiful breasts were for Roger the teats denied him as a baby, heard the breathless confession of her own phobias and frustrations, conflicts and sick rituals—"So I told my analyst I can't go anywhere with my nail polish chipped, it offends my superficial perfectionism, I get in an absolute panic"—panic, schmanic, I wanted to burst out in irritation, go take your bruised-and-bleeding id and shove it up that frigid little arrangement of yours—for she felt nothing when she went to bed with men, she was telling me now, nothing, that is, except the affection which impelled her into their beds in the first place, and of course, the satisfaction that their satisfaction and admiration gave her. Oh, none of them knew, of course, she said, not even Roger with whom she tried to be so honest—no, he knew not that her sighs and her writhings, her moanings and open kisses were part and parcel of the wiggle with which she entered Sardi's, the sobs she sobbed with true wet tears on cue, the glances and the voice and the whole elaborate charade with which she made a nation lust en masse.

Oh Lord, I thought, she and all her kind, like a *New Yorker* cartoon come to life: the Twentieth-Century American Woman, self-centered, pseudo-sensual, pampered, directionless, lying on some fraud's leather couch three times a week and believing herself unique and infinitely interesting, believing that time spent with a dollar-a-minute listener was somehow an achievement instead of a weakness of the will, of the intellect, of character, a weakness she wallowed in, making a major production out of minor suffering, substituting a horizontal spouting of self-pity for the wisdom only solitary self-inspection could give her, yes, solitary self-inspection and its private shining blossom: Insight. Ah, Insight, that rare treasure with which I was so singularly blessed.

Insight? Even now I merely have the reins; they are mine now, along with the ability to hold them, use them, and I did not have them then, a year ago; but the steed itself—my thoughts, my emotions—the steed will balk, rear up, will race or turn a corner to the right when I mean left, and all I can do is try, try, try to control, to train, to understand and in my understanding to be master, or if not master, at least this: not slave.

Why was I angry at Lisa then, so angry that, excusing myself abruptly from her psychiatric tirade, I fled to the toilet, nausea violently increased? Bending over, weak and depleted from anger but unable to vomit, I berated her in my mind, berated the whole imbecilic fad and fetish that psychoanalysis seemed to me to be. Ever rebellious against fashion, I rebelled most intensely of all against this most popular of current parlor games, this expensive hobby enjoyed by the bored, those who—unable to tolerate their own unimportance—indulged in this much-sanctioned pastime to acquire the sense of superiority which they could acquire in no other way.

The fools! I thought, and in my wisdom vomited at last, and felt better at once, not knowing what it was I wished to be rid of, not knowing that my retching was a symbol and a sign, and that I stood thresholded then on a malignant year.

He is cutting the grass, my husband, who is too thin and an ardent liberal and sunburns easily and who is as much a part of me as his ulcer is of him, and intermittently as painful (to love is to be hurt). The odor of new-mown grass comes pungent through the window and will not be ignored; I close my eyes and breathe deeply, reveling in the sad-glad tightening of my throat, for I

39

know what I know: here is air, I smell it, taste it, fill myself with it, it is here and I am here, here, breathing it in,
out, in, out, all the vulnerable days of my life, my life
which is returned to me in grief.

I am brought to suffering by suffering; in pain I pay
my debt—this book—to pain.

Roger and Lisa stayed overnight. The next day they
persuaded me to drive up with Ed and them to Hartford
while the children were in school. Terry went to nursery
school, where, his teacher told me, he ignored the others,
wrapped up happily in his own busy world. Sometimes I
worried about him. Didn't we give him enough attention,
was that the trouble? Or was he just different—a brand-
new experience after the other two (Bruce, poised, proud,
excellent and competitive at everything he did—athletics,
scholastics—tall and tan and hard and lean, our Ivy
League type, and Johnny, our sunbeam, our round, smiling smart-alecky charmer, lazy, fresh, affectionate, the despair of teachers who adored him and forgave him all)—
was Terry with his unresponsiveness to anything except his
own imaginary universe just different?—tiny slightly
homely Terry with his round copper coins of eyes set
solemn into his small mouse-face—was he just different,
just new and odd and puzzling and, perhaps, an artist-in-
miniature?

Let him be all right, I thought; I did not think further
than that. I did not know I thought further than that.

On the drive up the highway to Hartford, where Roger,
as The Martian, was scheduled to perform at the annual
state sports show in the Armory, we listened while he
talked. Yesterday's mood was gone, his monologue was
bitter. . . .

"A living death, that's what it is, to be stuck with this
face of mine." He had been telling us again that his life
was destroyed, yes, he said, destroyed by the stigma of a
face which elicited an inevitable reaction in all who saw
him—"The *Martian!*"—amazement, then amusement, the
thrill and slight awe felt at his celebrity tempered and les-

sened by the foolishness of the role he played, the role he was, goddammit, stuck with—his huge fist struck against the dashboard in his fury—oh, the wearisome jokes, never varying, that he must endure wherever he went, every fuggin' idiot giggling about his magic sword that gave him the power to pass instantly from place to place, even from planet to planet—"Goddammit," he said, "I didn't devote my youth to the drama to end up in my middle age like *this*—a *freak,* a *laughing*-stock."

It *must* be serious with Lisa, I thought. He's admitting to middle age, he's himself with her the way he is with us, no falsity, brutal in the truths he throws at himself ... but no, not *quite* truthful, for whenever we suggested to him that he quit the role of The Martian, go back to more fulfilling forms of acting, he was ever ready with reasons for the impossibility of his position, was off again on the tale of his ten-year frustration—how, for over a decade now, since he had tired of being The Martian, the casting directors had laughed at him; how, when he applied for roles, they merely slapped him on the back with "Sorry, Rog, sweetheart, you're typed and that's that"— except for that time, last year, when Merrill out at Warner Brothers had taken a chance on him, had let him play a small part, hell, a *bit* part, practically, in that big war epic made from that bestselling novel, and how the studio had discovered to its dismay that his single appearance on the beach at Normandy—despite his uniform and his mud-grimed face—had destroyed audiences' attention every-where, that the essential spell of reality had been broken when they saw Roger lunging from the LST, and that the ludicrous unexpectedness of his presence there (like L'il Abner popping up as Cassius) had made someone in each and every theater burst out laughing, soon to be joined by others in the audience, the laughter then quickly peter-ing out as the action on the screen again engrossed them, but petering out too late for the subsequent scene to af-fect them as it would have otherwise—the tragedy, the piognancy of those oh-so-artistically-arranged corpses reduced almost to comedy, so needless their having died, it seemed, when The Martian in their midst might have

41

saved them all merely by catching those silly little bullets in his great big bulletproof hand.

"It must feel," I said, "a lot like a sterile woman feels —to be deprived of that function which nature made you for."

Worse than that, Roger had retorted, for does a woman *train* to receive her ovaries, study for *years* to achieve a uterus? It wasn't so much that he'd been born with a talent, he said, as that he'd worked so long and hard— at the Academy of Dramatic Arts, at Pasadena Playhouse, and then through all the years of summer stock in each and every conceivable role from male ingénu to villain, in order to develop his talent into a fine and sensitive instrument of communication—and now what did he communicate? *"God!"* Again his fist met the dashboard. "Comic-book crap to an audience composed strictly of the feeble-minded!"

"What about radio?" Ed had suggested. "You were in radio a long time ago. Your face wouldn't be seen, wouldn't matter. Couldn't you go back to it?"

"Radio! You *kidding?* Who listens to the radio anymore? Half-asleep truck drivers and illiterate farmhands or some desperate slob somewhere whose TV broke down. Besides, you know goddamn well I'm not talking about radio or any other hack-actor stuff. You know as well as I do where I'd be now if I'd never heard of The Martian."

I nodded, we all three did, but in truth I did not know where he'd be. I knew, of course, where *he* felt he'd be, but then the world is full of almost-artists whose major creations are their beautiful excuses. But all I said was, "If. *If* you'd never heard of The Martian. But Roger, you *did* hear, and you leaped at the chance."

"Leaped! Leaped! I was *starving,* for Christ's sake!"— and we heard it again, Ed and I (had Lisa heard it before, I wondered; she was being so quiet)—heard how he'd been drafted into the Army's production of *Winged Victory* during the few vital years when, had it not been for the war, he'd have been rising up the Hollywood ladder from his excellent start in *Look Away, Dixieland,* would have risen right up to the top where a bunch of

4-F fairies now sat enthroned, thanks to the chance his absence had given them—heard again how the doors had slammed in his face when, once more a civilian, he had attempted to re-enter his rightful place in some large studio's roster of rising stars. Oh sure, he'd finally made a few B movies, he said, had even received a certain amount of critical praise for the way his performance had saved the day for a certain well-known box office hit which would otherwise have been a pile of shit. But soon even the loin-clothed roles in Tahitian documentaries had no longer been forthcoming, and just then it had come along —the offer, the bait, the role of The Martian, a cash-camouflaged hook on which he'd dangled half-dead ever since.

It had been arranged between Roger and Lisa that she would spend the time with a friend of hers, an actress she'd appeared with in her last movie, who was making a personal appearance in a local theater and staying at the local Hilton Hotel. I wondered whether Lisa had ever seen Roger in his "long underwear," as he called his Martian costume, wondered if he'd have brought her along at all had she not had a person and a place to visit while he was thus occupied. My suspicions were confirmed when he dropped her off at the hotel, for I heard him warning her that he would meet her here at the hotel lobby at three o'clock when his show was over and that she was under no circumstances to come over to the Armory. She seemed compliant enough—a nice compliant girl, I thought, forgiving her her Freudian aberrations— and we left her, Ed and Roger proceeding to the Armory to get him "dolled up in that crap," as he put it, while I hurried out of town to the aristocratic hamlet of Farmington for a few moments, the town where all my kin resided, all, that is, except my parents, who had lately left for the Orient, my father to continue there his lifelong service to Christianity via the pastorate of the American Community Church in Hiroshima.

On the day my parents had left—they were to drive

43

out across the country for a visit with my sister and her doctor-husband before taking off by plane for their trip above the Pacific—I'd said something to them which came, it seemed to me at the time, from no premonition at all—unplanned, casual, unindicative of anything except co-operation in the amenities of departure. I'd said, "Now remember, if anything happens to any of us while you're away, don't come running way back here—"

"If anything *happens!*" My mother had looked aghast, her blinked-back tears reddening the rims of eyes so pale blue that the irises seemed to have joined the rest of her in a relentless fading, yes, a fading and graying and wrinkling which not even her quick grin and quick-swinging way of walking—like a tom-boyish teenager—could keep from annoying me by the pity it evoked in me, pity and irritation, not only that my pretty young mother should have permitted time to play this trick on her but that she should be so pitiless as to display this explicit picture of my destiny each time she turned her face to me. "You're all going to be *fine* while we're away," she'd said, voice tight and thin. "Why, three years, that's not so much. You just take *care* of yourselves."

"Okay, Mom. I just wanted you to know you needn't feel you have to come all the way back here in case of any . . . any . . . misfortune."

But her tears spilled out as she sobbed, "Three *years!*" —and we all stood around embarrassed, because I shouldn't have scared her, and because she was going a half-a-world away with a husband who loved only Jesus, and because however much she cried he did not care— and, worst of all, because *I* was not crying, had not cried at all about their leaving, could not dredge up a single teardrop as my contribution to the occasion, could only pat her bony shoulder and lecture myself about my lack of sentiment, my lack of feeling, all the while detesting her unrestrained emotionality as much as I respected my father's detachment—he, as always, impervious to the conventional responses in personal relationships, absent-minded, so obviously preoccupied with other thoughts as he hugged Terry good-by and said, "Now be a good boy and obey your mother," that I got the distinct impression that it had slipped his mind about Japan, and that he figured this was just another farewell before their return, as so many times before, to Farmington.

Well, they had gone, and when I lost my mind they never knew it. Ed, through those months of this past year (a year plucked out of continuity, separate, grotesque, severed forever from the reality of before and since) typed letters which I signed—I still could manage that—and they never caught on, thank God, for if they'd known they would have hurried back, and they no more than anyone else could have done anything about the glazed unseeing eyes, the vanished personality, the lost identity—cowering, confused—inside the emaciated body, the shabby, shaken stranger that had lately been their lovely, loving, lovable, laughing daughter.

My relatives welcomed me on my brief visit to the houses I knew so well—turreted, pillared, porticoed, Victorian, like the six-winged six-chimneyed parsonage my parents had left empty, which had looked back at me with such a blank blind-eyed stare from its black uncurtained windows as I passed it, that suddenly I felt their absence fully for the first time, felt like a little girl left in the lurch, felt as if they'd gone so far far far away they might as well be dead.

"Well!" my grandmother barked. "Well now!" She peered at me with her eyes that had been so sharp when I was a child, eyes filmy now and yellowed with age and cataracts. "What's that stuff, eh?" She leaned toward me, peering closer. "Your eyes, they look all black and funny."

"You mean my mascara, Grandma? On my eyelashes?"

"Land sakes you look terrible, young lady. You trying to be like those Hollywood friends of yours, eh? All painted up and—"

"Mother!"—her daughter, my aunt, sighed deeply as she reached across to the porch rail where her pack of cigarettes lay—"Can't you leave the poor girl *alone?* Here she's thoughtful enough to come visit you, surprise you, and all you can do is—"

"Humph!"—the old lady stood up abruptly from her wicker chair—"At least she doesn't *smoke*. No child of Russell's would go around looking like a locomotive, smoke pouring out of the nostrils like—"

"All *right,* Mother, all *right*"—inhaling deep, combining the exhalation with another sigh—"Russell Russell Russell Russell—"

—while my grandmother, after standing there a moment with her legs spread apart as a baby does to test itself when first learning the vertical, made her way down the porch steps to the lawn and away up the garden path, bent onto her cane, stopping now and again to poke at bush or blossom until she disappeared from view behind the scallop-sculptured hedge—

"—Russell Russell"—she had been to Vassar and France, my aunt, and now she was fifty and wore tweed suits and blue hair and talked like Katharine Hepburn; her husband ran the Winslow Boot Factory, she ran the Connecticut chapter of the League of Women Voters, their togetherness consisted of golf and Irish setters, their separateness, of boredom and her long late menopause—"Russell Russell, that's all I ever hear. She thinks that brother of mine is a saint. I guess he *is* a saint, your father, and your mother too, but oh dear, I do get *so* weary of hearing how bad I am and how good he is. Ah well—"

"And your other brothers?"

"Folger? Hale?"

"Speak of the devil!"—the voice came disembodied from around the corner of the porch, the porch which curved all around the broad white house on three sides, wide and scattered with wicker this and wicker that and with tall vases filled furry-green with fern—"Hey there, Jane"—he came around the corner—"I was just going out to lunch when sister-mine phoned the office to say you were here. To what do we owe the honor?"

"Ed's over at the Armory, Uncle Folger, publicity thing with a client"—and when he asked about Roger, and then about Lisa, I gave brief and superficial replies to match the questions, for I knew that to my relatives the entertainment world meant café society, and café society meant *nouveau riche,* and *nouveau riche* meant all those "awful little dark noisy people" who were always trying to weasel their split-level monstrosities into this pretty little oasis of antiquity. No refinement, those people, my kin were wont to remark, no embarrassment at the knowledge of not being wanted, no background at all, no proper schooling most of them—nothing but money. "What *are* they?" my grandmother had wanted to know. "Catholics? Jews? Is it the Jews or the Italians that are Catholics?"— but then, nothing my grandmother said astounded me anymore, not since my wedding, when Ed had mentioned his political beliefs, and she, leaning forward on her pearl-handled cane with a stare as at a rare sea anemone, had said, "Gracious sakes alive, I don't think I've ever *met* a Democrat before!"

Now she hobbled into view again, my grandmother, and the three of us watched as she climbed slowly to the marble birdbath atop the knoll where, in childhood winters, I had sledded to the familiar noise of Grandpa cranking his huge Franklin to a start in the garage and then driving it gravel-crunchingly around to the back of the house, to the porte-cochere, where Grandma waited elegant and imperious to be taken to the Ladies Aid Society or the monthly meeting of the board of directors of the WCTU.

"Saw your Uncle Hale last night, Jane," Uncle Folger said. Folger owned an insurance company and a Chrysler and a schooner called *Wet Dream* and in his heart of hearts he had never emerged from his senior year at Yale. His remaining hair was a salt-and-pepper horseshoe around the bare pink ape's-ass baldness of his head; he and his wife, whom he dearly loved, had long ago given up bed for Bermuda and bridge. "He'll be sorry he missed you today."

"Whiffenpoof Club?" Aunt Rachel asked. "They still allow him there?"

"He was very well behaved, much to my surprise and

47

pleasure. Besides, my dear sister, if they kicked Hale out they'd set an unfortunate precedent. What about the dozens of other alumni whose funds have *not* been exhausted? Where would the dues chairman be or the endowment fund if they took to snubbing everybody who likes his liquor?"

"Oh he's disgusting, disgusting"—she lit a new cigarette from her old one, impatiently, lips pursed beneath the suggestion of a mustache—"He's doing a very thorough job of dragging the Winslow name down and down until —"

"Shsh," Folger said. The old woman had left the birdbath with its rusty-bronze sundial, was back on the path and headed toward the house. Folger whispered, "Rachel, I must quick tell Jane what she said the other day when Hale came by—"

"What?"

"—you know, what Mother said when Hale came by stewed to the gills—"

"Oh yes! Quick!"

He leaned over to me, cigar-breathy. Grandmother was looking down past the long lawned hill to the street below; her mouth was pursed—for a moment she looked exactly like Rachel—as she regarded with disapproval the two hot-rodders racing along beside the high spiked iron fence with its WINSLOW above the gate.

"Well Jane, listen, he was stumbling and staggering etcetera etcetera and she said, 'Why, Hale, you've been eating too many oysters again. I *told* you how upsetting they can be.' Can you beat it?" He laughed, cigar held aloft as he threw back his head to bellow, and then he straightened up, spoke now in a loud voice to penetrate her deafness: "Hello, Mother. Enjoying this Indian Summer day?" She didn't reply and he added, "What's for lunch?"

"Lunch? Lunch?"—confused to see him there, not liking all this folderol of unexpected guests, she struck her cane again and again against the porch floor, stalling for time—"Why aren't you downtown?"

"Business can wait a half-hour when my prettiest niece

48

is in town. Thought maybe we could all eat together—"

"There's nothing in the house," Grandmother barked, and sat down hard, like a toddler losing balance. "Only Shredded Wheat."

"No milk to go on it?"—he was teasing her and she didn't know it and I remembered how it used to be, when nothing got by her keen glance and keen mind, when it was she who snapped commands and sarcasms while the daughter and three sons leaped to obey.

"Might be some milk, saving it for supper though."

Aunt Rachel winked at me. Her mother ate almost nothing but cereal and fruit; she spent a large part of her days and nights monitoring the multitudinous stairways and corridors of her abode to make sure all unnecessary lights were out; she wore the same dress for a week at a time, owning two altogether, and on Sunday when she went to church she added an heirloom brooch to the deflated bosom and a hat to the sparse netted hair, and the parson bowed and scraped because she lived on the income from her dead husband's capital and would leave it all to Russell and The Church.

"Come on, Jane"—Folger got up and beckoned me to follow him through the tall lead-paned French doors— "let's see what we can find to squelch the old hunger pangs."

In the dining room everything was as I remembered it: the silver tea set on the enormous eagle-crested buffet, the oval table with Grandpa's Chair before the hearth at one end and Grandmother's Chair facing it from the other end of the room where, as a little girl, I had never been able to see her at supper without squinting, for behind her the western light from the diamond-paned bay window had shone in with such furious glitter upon the crystal goblets that she'd sat enthroned in radiance, a sour arthritic matriarch with flashing spectacles.

"—not a damn thing in the pantry," Folger said, coming back through the swinging door; twenty years ago I had watched the small soft Scottish maid come through it, tray-laden at the buzz from Grandma's foot, fascinating me by her brogue and by the things I'd heard she did with Uncle Hale. "She wasn't exaggerating."

Rachel came in, heard what he'd said and laughed unhappily. "No, she just *is* one."

"What?"

"An exaggeration."

"Caricature," Folger said. "She napping now?"

"Rhetorical question," Rachel said; snores emanated from the open French doors. "Good grief, listen! And she calls *me* a locomotive."

Then there was the sound of the front door banging and footsteps along the hall and Uncle Hale came in. "Say now," he said, seeing me and the others. "If it ain't Old Home Week."

"Oh God," Rachel said, and raised her eyes briefly to heaven.

"How you feeling?" Folger asked him. We all went into the library and sat down; it smelled of old leather.

"Feel great, just great," Hale said. He looked sick and trembly, but sober. On the wall in a thick gilt frame the four small Winslows sat grouped for immortality, life-size, oil-painted against a silver brocade drape, all curls and frills and velvet knickerbockers, and with Hale, the littlest one, a sweet wee rosy-cheeked cherub, on the verge of tears from staying so long in one spot. "Just great," he repeated, and coughed. "Copper Amalgamated's up."

"Good. See Archie Potter last night after the meeting?"

"Yep, good letter he got from Ike, deserves it, all the work he's doing on the congressional campaign."

"Folger, does Jane know you got a letter too?" my aunt asked. She explained to me with pride, "From Ike."

Folger winked at me. "Impressive, eh?" And then he grinned, recalling something. "Say, Hale, Rachel, remember Father in the last campaign he ever got to fight in?" They did not mention it was Landon's; some things were never mentioned. "Boy, the Grand Old Party lost their number one man when they lost him, even if he *was* eighty."

Rachel said to me, "Remember Grandpa's scrapbook?" and I nodded, remembering it well—the page after page of Roosevelt vilification: newspaper speeches, pictures, magazine articles, all proving without a doubt that the odious F.D.R. was a villain and a traitor to his class and to his country, his wife an accomplice and his dog Fala the only animal in America who deserved to escape the benefits of Grandpa's favorite charity, the ASPCA. Yes, I remembered his scrapbook, remembered too how I had seen him out in the garden, standing absolutely still with birds on his shoulders and his hands and his head, gentle, happy; it was as if a mustached vested man in Rotary pin and pince-nez had wandered into an Assisi glen.

Hale said, "Con Edison's down."

"I guess I'd better get back," I said. Hale did not ask where to; he was coughing, and as we moved to the front door he said to me, "How's my brother Russell? Doing unto others?"

"I suppose so." We all laughed; from the gilt frame four pairs of eyes followed us along, stares never wavering, pensive, sorrowful.

"Still a Commie?" Hale asked me.

"What?"

"The good reverend. Still a Commie?"

"Socialist."

"Same damn thing," Folger said.

"Shsh"—Rachel gave her brother a warning smile, then turned it to me—"Your grandmaw would drop dead."

"Yes I know"—I smiled back; out on the porch the snoring was undisturbed—"Tell her I'm sorry I missed kissing her good-by."

"*She* won't be sorry," Folger said. My father had told me once that he couldn't recall his mother ever touching him; hers was not, he had said, an affectionate nature. "Uh, Jane," my uncle added. "This fellow you're up here with, this Martian fellow, is he . . . uh . . . Jewish?"

"Anglo-Saxon," I assured him. "Philadelphia, hoity-toity."

"And the actress?"

"Lisa? Hundred percent full-blooded Gentile, as far as I know."

51

"Oh, well good, good." The grandfather's clock in the corner chimed a melodic prologue to its single one o'clock gong. "All those kind of people aren't they apt to be ... well, you know ... all those climbers you and Ed run around with ..."

"Yes, I know, Uncle Folger." He smiled gratefully at my quick understanding, we said good-by all around, and I left them standing there in the carved oaken doorway, with my father's face on their faces as it was on mine, left them and drove back toward Hartford past the big stone church where he had preached against bigotry and smugness to no avail, those stiff self-righteous uncomprehending Protestant faces—his fine deaf relatives and their fine deaf friends—driving him at last across the seas to where, he hoped, he could, for the three final years before he retired, dedicate his life to those who might truly need and heed the message of Jesus the Lord.

THREE

BETWEEN our first and this, our second, meeting with Roger and Lisa—between, that is, the end of August last year and the end of October—four notes in all had arrived, to them, to us, identical in angry red-inked scrawl. Each time I waited for my first reaction and each time, relieved, I heard no sparrow wings; I wondered, finally, what could have given me such a nonsensical expectation.

"Guilty!" the last accusation had read. *"My soul your judge and jury, you stand condemned. Guilty!"*

On the phone, Ed and Rog, comparing messages, kept agreeing, "Weirdo, harmless, the creep will find another hobby soon."

But I was apprehensive. Not because (I decided) of the threats themselves, but because I had known for a moment a sensation which could not be explained, and because I disliked the inexplicable, had a horror, in my proud rationality, of the irrational, and because—I know this now—it was the first tremor of what was to come—as a villager can hear the deepdown rumble before the earthquake's fissure splits his town.

FOUR

THE wrong side of the tracks in this part of Hartford was, I found, an abrupt and accurate fact that I had never in all my cloistered youth laid eyes upon. No—no, that wasn't true, I realized, for there had been a time or two, when I was accompanying my father on his ministerial calls, when his mission dictated departure from the more familiar environs of his pastorate—away from the hedge-hemmed hilltop homes of church trustees and deacons, of little old ladies with ribbon-and-cameo-trussed necks, of all the influential sons and daughters of the American Revolution whose presence in the pews of the Farmington Congregational Church made it *the* right church for *the* right people. Yes, we'd driven here, I now recalled, when the streets were narrower and the cars were squarer, when this statue of Mark Twain had arched its quizzical eyebrows down at a cobblestoned circle of Colonial vintage rather than at the concrete replacement I now negotiated—a traffic rotary replete with signs which obliterated Huck Finn at his elbow and Tom leaning on his knee, the Tom I suddenly remembered so well, remembered peering closely as my father drove by, remembered noticing the stone eyes pupiled by small dark holes and the pigeons pecking at his bare stone feet.

The buildings remaining of those I remembered were no longer three-story homes fronted by long wide porches and strung together umbilically from kitchen window to kitchen window by crowded clotheslines, but were business establishments now, the porches enclosed to make more room inside for such concerns as Rippi's Real Estate and Fischel's Delicatessen, for the A.M.E. Church and D'Agnierrie's Funeral Home and the Yankee Package

Store. Yankee, I thought, ye gods!—for the only true Yankee in the entire district was immobile back there upon his bronze pedestal, one long mile away from the home he'd lived in—gabled, bay-windowed, its terraced lawn becoming my great-uncle's lawn at the honeysuckled juncture where one landscaped acre ended and the next landscaped acre began.

No, here was no honeysuckle, no history, no Yankee tradition; here was the place where the state's birth control bill got voted down year after year after year, Irish and Italian pouring into polling booths with papal decrees shining in their eyes, set on preventing the murder of Jewish and Protestant sperm.

I turned down a street deep with warehouses on either side—a sign at the statue of Twain had shown me the direction of the Armory—and passed a lot littered with tires and a shack proclaiming: AUTOMOTIVE PARTS—all the time wondering if I'd be on time for Roger's appearance, and wondering too, how the market was for diaphragms in Japan. What was it now, over there in the Orient, I mused, which would be casting my father into the depths of despondency; he'd gone through Catholics in Connecticut, segregation in the South, military bases in Lebanon, friendship with Franco and, of course, Hiss and McCarthy and the assassination of Gandhi—what now? The atom bomb, of course, had been the worst blow of all; for two days he'd locked himself in his study without food, and emerging on Sunday bleary-eyed from sleeplessness had preached a sermon which cost the parish a very wealthy retired admiral whose defection had left the extension of the Sunday School wing permanently in the planning stage. My father had recovered from the others, but this one did him in, ate away at his frayed patience for eleven years until one day the tea and crumpets stuck in his throat and now he was eating eels and rice, over there in Hiroshima, making atonement for a nation's wrong. And Mother? Oh, she was coping, as always, wretched rib of Adam, with the lifelong situation in which his dedication and depressions had imprisoned her

54

—ah, dedication and depression: the Mutt and Jeff of my father's pathology.

Mutt and Jeff. Here I was, thinking in comic-strip language as I hurried to a comic strip in the flesh, driving fast past the blocks which whispered in my memory until I swung around a corner and heard the whisper switch to a shout: *look!*

Nothing could have been less expected or less spectacular—just another old home, that's all, with the ugliest of exteriors, shingle, dingy and hideous, faked to look like brick and failing utterly, the color of dried blood—blood, how appropriate, for it was the bloodlessness which had appalled me, twenty-four years or so ago in that very house, where I had found myself face-to-face with my first corpse.

I was a pigtailed child with round brown eyes . . .

"Sit here, Janie," her father had said. The pigtailed child with round brown eyes sat on the lumpy couch and watched her father and the fat lady go past the dining-room table with its drooping-down lace tablecloth, watched them go through the archway toward the stairs, the strings of beads closing behind them again into a quivering curtain that matched the quivering fringe around the lampshade beside her. Their footsteps went up, up, and softer sounded the voice saying, ". . . but even though we was expectin' it for weeks, Reverend, it was still a shock when she went. I says to him, 'Better she's out of her sufferin',' but he just lies up there sorta listless, won't get outa bed . . ." and her father's answering murmur, kind, wise, though he had not really heard what the woman said, of course, because as her mother often explained "he lived in another world."

Well, this was another world for little Janie, this neighborhood, this house, so much so that she held her breath and then, letting it out, cupped her hands around her nose as she breathed in another cautious breath, trying to filter the air through her fingers—strange, musty air with an odor of onion and roses giving everything here as unfamiliar a touch as the oilcloth on the table, plaid and shiny, glimpsed through the kitchen door—and where was the pantry? The parsonage had a pantry as large as this parlor. "Parlor." She said the word aloud, never having heard it until a moment ago. "Sit here in the parlor, little girl, and wait for your poppa." And then the lady had turned to her father as they'd left to go upstairs: "Ain't she the spittin' image of you, sir." Poppa. And saying "ain't" for "isn't." The way the woman spoke was part of the differentness, along with the way things looked and smelled. She got up to see what other alien thing lay behind that closed door over there. In the homes of other parishioners where she had called with Daddy she had sometimes discovered wonders; several times it was places to hide—the grandfather's clock at the Hathaways', the suit of armor at the Reeds'—or collections, like Mrs. Peabody's Wedgwood so blue and white and delicate that forever after she could not look at a Wedgwood-seeming sky without feeling eight years old again and overwhelmed by beauty.

Now, alert to new wonders, she pushed open the door and there it was. Flowers, flowers banked thick against the long box and, above them, directly across the tiny room from her, so close she could reach out her hand and touch it, the white slightly smiling profile of the woman she knew red-faced and grouchy after potluck suppers at the church, doing the dishes as her husband—the janitor, Mr. Feeney—swept the hall clean of its heretic debris.

Dead.

Not gone to heaven. Not with Jesus. Not an angel. Just gone. Dead. A thing.

By the time the child backed away and pulled the door shut, sitting stiffly down again upon the lumpy couch, she knew what she had seen and what it meant, knew there was no God, knew who it was, lying cold and quiet forever without reprieve.

The Hartford Armory, huge as it was, seemed unable to contain the throngs who had come from miles around to attend the annual sports show. As I'd given the doorman my complimentary ticket he'd asked me if I was with Yogi Berra's party and I'd said no, Roger Rutherford's, and he'd looked baffled for only a moment before saying, *"Oh, the Mar*tian," and had ushered me by with the increased respect of the anonymous for those they discover to be one degree removed from anonymity, if only by association. The minor acts on the bill had already been done and the crowds were milling around the edges of the gigantic space, looking at the exhibits of guns, trailers, cameras, yachts, or having their fortunes told or their caricatures drawn. I asked an attendant where the dressing rooms were and elbowed my way to a door in a far corner, after being informed that I was just in time to see the two biggest acts—first, The Martian and The Midget, and second, most important of all, Yogi Berra. I heard a pimpled youth ask his companion, "Didja know Bill got The Martian's autograph when he came in? I wouldn't have recognized him—he had regular clothes on—"

Well, I could imagine the scene, for as a sometime member of Roger's entourage I'd seen what happened whenever he entered a place filled with strangers; camouflaged in his mundane earthman's attire he would be ignored by most and glanced at by those who glance at any very large and very handsome man anywhere, anytime, but gradually the stares of a few inevitably attracted yet more stares, and then heads would begin to turn for second looks as the rumors spread—"Hey, ain't that guy over there The Martian? Hey yeah!"—and it was then, I supposed, as Roger had made for the privacy of his dressing room, that Bill here had approached with paper and pencil in hand: "May I please have your autograph?"

I knew that such small flurries of excitement were, for Roger, better than nothing, were better than to be a nobody and get no attention at all—but I also understood how little it could sate the appetite for adulation with which Roger, like every actor, was afflicted; an adolescent's request for his autograph compared unfavorably with the kind of attention he hungered for—the respect of the literate, the slavish devotion of the sophisticated.

The kind of notice he received was more of an insult than a compliment, his expression always said, for did not the awe of children and idiots imply an audience composed totally of the same?—while those whose admiration he craved—the adult, the cultured, the erudite—looked through him as though his face were any other face, never having watched that face and form fill the TV screen each day at 5 P.M., never having hung on his every puerile cliché as the plot unfolded, never having sat hunched forward munching gum as he spun through the strato-sphere—"up into o-o-o-orbit!"—never having gasped in horror as the villain's blade flashed at his back nor thrilled to the look of stupefaction the villain wore as the hero swung around, the metal weapon breaking like a piece of toast against his impenetrable belly, merely tickling him, so that with casual disdain he laughingly said, "Tut tut, Jappho (Jappho—Supreme Potentate of the Planet Jupiter), you shouldn't play with knives, you might hurt yourself"—by his survival and his jest ringing down the curtain on yet another episode in the "Adventures of The Martian," alternately sponsored by Tupper's Gum and Sudsy-Bubbly Bath.

The Connecticut representatives of Tupper's and Sudsy's public relations departments stood with Ed and me at ringside as the trumpeter blew an announcement of the next-to-last act. The ring imitating a stage at the center of the Armory was no more than a rickety half-foot-high platform keeping out the close-packed spectators with two ropes which extended across the vast hall to the dressing-room door, making a pathway for The Martian and The Midget to enter upon; no red carpet, I noticed, and, thank God, Roger played the silver-shoed Martian instead of a barefoot Tarzan, for his path was scattered with ice-cream-oozing Dixie cups and yellowish spots of spittle.

In the dressing room a moment before, Ed had been helping Roger on with his bulletproof vest. "Just a pre-caution," Roger had laughed. "I guess you heard, Janie, what happened last year at the Kansas State Fair when some agnostic, in an impulsive attempt to test his belief, took a pot shot at me." And he'd shown me the scar on his arm, slashed across a biceps even more enormous in reality than the TV's eye revealed it to be. Just then the loudspeaker had roared: "The Martian and The Midget will next be seen in—"

"Midget?" I'd said.

Ed had scowled at me, while Roger had shoved his arms into his green sequined sleeves with sudden violence and had said roughly, "Yeah. Midget. Some new wrinkle they've cooked up."

And now, here he came, The Martian in all his magnificent splendor, sequins a-sparkle in the spotlight, antenna buzzing, sword held high, sprinting through the spittle and Dixie cups with the roped-back roar of sportsmen, TV addicts and comic-strip enthusiasts loud in his ears. The applause changed to hooting laughter as a midget waddled down the pathway after him, dressed in an identical costume, a sawed-off and bowlegged facsimile with a squashed-flat face that a horse seemed to have stomped upon. They reached the ring and the act began.

I don't remember much about the act; I had a way of going blind and deaf, temporarily, when I had to watch Roger demean himself. The Martian and The Midget joked back and forth, I dimly recall, off-color stuff, and then Roger employed his considerable knowledge of jujitsu—yes, that was it! that was the supposed comedy of it all: the incongruity of a supernatural man the size and strength of The Martian resorting to jujitsu to deal with his puny adversary. All I know for sure is that I kept thinking about Roger's brain, Roger's wasted talent, Roger's sensitivity and bitterness, and when a hairy-nostriled man near me let out a blast of beer breath and jealous invective—*"Why dontcha pick on somebody your own size, ya fairy prick"*—I fled into my memory where Roger dwelt undesecrated. . . .

We had just come out of the studio commissary, Ed, Roger, and I; it was noon and several of filmdom's cherished were wandering in and out—in hungry, out only a little less hungry after their salad and yogurt—

when Roger, who had spied Gregory Peck loping along Lincolnesque toward Sound Stage Six, had shouted out across the palm-fringed parking lot, "Hey, Greg, seen the rushes?"

"Yeah, Rog," came the reply. "Pretty fair, some cutting maybe—"

"Where Monroe upstages you, kid?"

"Yeah"—laughing—"You noticed that, huh, Rog?" and he waved once, corporeal in khakis, phantasmal in fame, before vanishing into the concrete enormity, vast, flesh-colored, windowless, that—despite azaleas and geraniums planted in profusion—remained cheerless as a cell-block beneath the smoggy Hollywood sky.

The common enterprise in which not only Roger and Peck but every other "name" on the lot was briefly involved was a short film for the Red Cross, which would be shown in theaters across the land along with requests for audience contributions. In it Roger played himself, as did the others; for the first time in many years he would appear on the screen not as a human cartoon but as a serious actor involved in a serious endeavor. Not that he would have much chance to act, for he and the others—Cooper, Kerr, Taylor, Lancaster, Monroe—were merely required to walk around in a series of appropriate locales discussing world disasters, but the very fact of his presence in the film had lent him a professional dignity which he had long lost and long mourned. He was, therefore, in excellent spirits, and as we walked the studio streets he spoke of Taylor and Monroe and the others with casual affection, as if—currently associated with them in this minor presentation—he had forgotten that it was a temporary alliance, a fluke for charity's sake, and that never before nor ever again would he work so closely with stars of such glittering magnitude. "This is my league," his shouted remarks to Peck had told us. "This is where I belong, with the cream of the crop." We passed a tribe of Indians sucking popsicles—nodding, they glanced at, and away from, Roger, unimpressed—and again, as always when on these annual business trips with Ed to his West Coast clients' studios, I was amused by the disparity between the two reactions: Out There, the fascination with the famous, In Here, the indifference and, even, the disillusionment. The extras kept passing—cowboys, cancan dancers, flappers, a Chinese mandarin—and none stared, none cared, inured by continual proximity to Roger and all his peers.

Crossing through an alley lined with hunks of movie sets—plaster boulders, half a tugboat, cardboard sky—we came to a huge open space where dozens of graduating collegians lounged on the ground or on benches set up behind the cameras. Here and there an extra's robe lay open in disarray and then I could see beneath the austere black the more familiar uniform of Sunset Boulevard: tight jeans, T shirts, belts with hammered silver buckles bought on sprees in Mexico. Suddenly the megaphoned voice of the director made pause the motion of Cokes to lip and hands upon the gin and poker cards. . . .

"Okay, okay, let's try it again, come on everybody, we'll take it again from the middle of the commencement speech."

Mechanically, for the tenth or maybe the twentieth time, the graduating class rose from their various methods of time-killing and stood before the psuedo-brick university façade. On its balcony Spencer Tracy faced them, properly attired as their president, and as a voice called out *"Lights! Camera!"* the retinue about him fell back, out of camera range, leaving the star poised intently for the final *"Action!"* and he leaned forward on the podium and said, "But now, my dear young friends, those days are behind you. Before you the future looms—"

"Cut! Cut!"—and it happened again, the inevitable interruption, the flaw, the fly-in-the-Celluloid-ointment, as a plane approached overhead, low, loud—and as the director sank down in disgust into his canvas name-placarded chair under the overhanging boom, a hundred tasseled mortarboards bobbed again toward Cokes and poker games, while above the pilot banked his plane toward San Fernando Valley, oblivious of the curses being uttered in his wake.

"There's Boone," Ed said, and I spotted him in the

crowd, the young co-star, robed, tasseled, separated from his fellow graduates by two yards, a doting retinue and several million dollars. "I have to talk to him," Ed said. "Meet you guys later back at the dressing room, okay?" And Roger and I proceeded down the street which became, after one more block, a row of tenements.

No social dramas of the poor being currently in production, the street was empty, save for a stagehand who had selected this decrepit cranny in which to have his solitary siesta; he was lying back on one of the many identical brownstone stoops, his head on the top step, mouth open, and we stepped over his moccasined feet without waking him. A sagging knotholed fence had a familiar look—Our Gang Comedies? gangster sluggings? love scenes between Sicilian immigrants? poignant shots of hungry children raiding garbage cans?—and across the manholed street, squeezed between a pawnshop and a delicatessen, a shabby chapel stood ready for yet another of those final scenes of Mass and sweet redemption which would send the audiences sniffling from the theaters, chastened by an afternoon of sorrow in the slums.

"I played a scene here once when I was just starting out," Roger said. "I was a young hoodlum with lousy parents—a drunk, a prostitute—and I got shot. Jesus Christ"—he gazed around—"I remember it all now, I remember that role, yeah, I bled to death right over there" —and he went and stared down at the spot; was he thinking that if he looked hard enough he could bring it back, the catsup-blood, the youth?—"Boy, that was a good part, a part I could feel, really *feel*, in *here*." He clutched his stomach with both hands. "The director wanted me to underplay it, but when I got to that line, that line I died on, with my one arm raised just a little like a kid asking a question in school, Christ, when I said that line I couldn't keep my voice from shaking and the tears ran down my face—I couldn't *help* it, I *felt* it, I *was* that kid."

"What line?"

"The director let it stay. Said it was all right, tears and all."

"What was that final line? Do you remember?"

"Of course I remember. Just four words. 'Why was I born?' That's all."

We had paused by the corner tenement; before us lay an open lot, prop-littered, and I saw a guillotine against a palm tree's withered skirt. I said, "Do you like playing raw realism? Or do you prefer classic tragedy? Or sophisticated comedy? Or—"

"Goddammit, Janie, that's not fair."

"What?"

"That's like asking a guy with both legs in braces what he likes better, swimming or tennis."

"I just—"

"Besides, I don't know. Classic tragedy's beyond me, I'm afraid. Back at the Academy we did some Shakespeare in class, but I never did latch on to what the hell it was all about."

". . .'and our little life is rounded with a sleep'—"

"What?"

"Shakespeare."

"Yeah? Well, I guess he made sense sometimes. *That* sure makes sense."

"I figured that'd reach you. Watch out, that'll collapse under you, won't it, what's it made of, papier-mâché?" —and Roger got up from the fire hydrant on which he'd sat, and came over to me at the stoop. Above us X's were whitewashed onto the windows and a board across the door proclaimed: CONDEMNED. "There's lots in good literature that you'd understand," I said, "if you'd take the time and effort." Listen to me, I thought, the pot calls the kettle black, but as we strolled out of the slums and through the open lot into Rome, I continued, "Kafka, for instance. He shared our . . . our . . . thing."

"Kafka?" All about us fake marble declared the greatness that was Rome; the stately columns of the market place were Doric and I would have expected Caesar at any moment if, instead, a Thunderbird convertible had not slid into view, carrying a plump brown plaid-capped man who waved and shouted, "Hey, Rog, sweetheart, seen the rushes?"

The phrase must be some sort of hierarchical password, I decided, as much a requirement of their rank as was, on the underling level, the boredom and the cynicism and the whole aweless attitude which sneered at the small galaxy in their midst: okay, so you're lucky, so you made it, so what?

"Kafka?" Roger repeated. "What did he say?"

" 'The realization of ultimate annihilation casts a shadow backwards to cancel the joy of every present achievement.' "

"Yeah! He sure . . . knew, didn't he." We had come to the Forum, phonily ancient, phonily splendid, and Roger took me with him up a wide, imposing flight of steps that ended, high above, in a gold-painted canopied throne. He sat there and I sat to his side, on a golden lion whose glittering sinews, I saw, were only slightly chipped. "Where'd you read it?"

"College library. I was doing research for an English theme—Existentialist Extension of Self into Death in Essays by European Novelists Since the Seventeenth Century."

"Aw, come *off* it," Roger said. "Cut the *crap*." He threw one leg over the carved-gilt armrest. "Keep it simple, it *is* simple, it's *everything,* and *nothing*—"

"Tangible ephemerality?"—but he was looking off into the distance, past the Corinthian pillars and the palm trees and the studio gates, out beyond, past the sprawling townlessness of stucco and neon and chrome, way, way out past all this to the brown mountains flashing their jewels of pink and yellow houses where out of windows framed in night-blooming jasmine and jacaranda the sea could be seen far below discarding its double row of whitecaps like a twin meringue along the pie-crust curve of sand called Malibu.

"Casts a shadow backwards," he said at last. "A shadow backwards, huh, kid?"—and then he stood up and hugged me and let me go and we stood up there way up above everybody else and laughed and laughed. "To hell with the fuggin' shadow," he said. "I'll do it."

"Do what?"

"Get a role like that again someday. A role I can *feel*."

"Sure you will. Lots of 'em."

"Right, kid. Goddamn right"—and we stood there watching Mary Queen of Scots cross the Forum eating a hot dog and we laughed some more, both of us blind on the brink of chaos, and the sun came out and shone upon the eucalyptus trees, erasing every shadow except one.

Yogi Berra was addressing the crowd when Lisa Maurice surprised me with a kiss on the cheek. "I thought I'd *never* find you," she mumbled into my ear. "What a *mess*."

"Lisa! Roger told you to wait for us at the hotel."

"I know, I know, but my girl friend had to leave earlier than I'd expected and I got so *lonesome*. Ever been in a city where you don't know a *soul*? It's *awful*."

"This is my old stamping grounds," I explained. "I was brought up in Farmington just outside of town." But around us shushing began and I beckoned Lisa to follow me to the dressing rooms. No one recognized her; as usual, when in public, a scarf concealed her brash red hair, and she wore no dark glasses, for, she told me, they merely seemed to draw attention to her—"Ho *ho!* Dark glasses! A *celebrity!*"—but a complete dearth of comestics served her purpose, she'd found, and I was surprised at how easily she could thus transform herself from a famous beauty into an equally exquisite nonentity. The way she carried herself remained provocative, however, as did her body, contrasting oddly with the puritan-plainness of her face; it was as if this factor of her appeal was out of her control, immutable, and I imagined that someone at the Actor's Studio had once assigned her an exercise in the projection of lust—"*Be* lust, Lisa dear. Don't just pretend. *Be!*"—and she, succeeding, had never since ceased.

Lust, ha! I thought. She's Labrador itself between her legs.

We found Ed in the dressing room with Yogi's coterie and the publicity men from Tupper's and Sudsy's; I heard someone say, "The agency sure pushed the panic button on that one," and someone else's reply, "Well, that's the way the cookie crumbles"—and, feeling superior, intellectual, inner-directed, I stayed just long enough to find out where Roger was, then left with Lisa.

When we found him he didn't see us at once. It surprised and strangely depressed me to see him sitting there that way, sort of small and collapsed, as if deprived of his height, he was deprived also of his dignity, diminished, dwindled into his midget-victor's niche of freak, grotesquerie. His silly attire, skin-tight, glitter-bright, with the satin garish against his hard thick thighs and calves, transformed him into some sort of pitiful paradox: Samson the Circus Clown. That Lisa felt as I did I knew the moment I looked at her, for her expression echoed my silent question: Is that *Roger?*—and I realized again that she was not at all the glass of pink champagne the whole world thought she was. She hadn't known Roger very long, not when compared to the years that Ed and I had known him, but I knew from experience that sleeping together and waking together and the confidences in between can bind two people closer in a fortnight than a lifetime of vertical conversation.

Roger was at the end of a dark back corridor of the Armory, the walls intermittently lined with closed ticket windows and prizefighter pictures. The chair in which he sat—beat-up brown leather with stuffing issuing from slits in its sides—had been set in a doorway labeled, above, EXIT. A light bulb dangled over his head and he kept brushing away the flies that flitted around his head; it was hot and stuffy and he was sweating in his heavy padded costume. Spread along the corridor was a queue of the devoted—devoted, that is, to their hobby of autograph collecting. Roger was signing a photograph for each person, handing the slips of paper back with his world-famous grin—a handsome automaton—and the narrow hall smelled strongly of popcorn and of armpits.

Suddenly a single voice rose above the sounds of muted talk and shuffling feet. The woman to whom Roger had just handed his autograph had handed it back to him, tossed it, actually, so that it slid off the satin of his lap

66

onto the filthy floor. "Sign it The *Martian*," she demanded. "Who knows who Roger *Rutherford* is?"

Everyone laughed. Gratified that they appreciated her logic, she turned to her audience and elaborated her theme. "Roger *Rutherford*," she sneered. "Big *deal*."

More laughter.

Roger stood up. Until he saw Lisa I expected something typical of him, something casually exasperated and sarcastic like "Well, that's show biz" and then perhaps a stroll with scornful slowness out the door, away from the ugly place, the ugly people, the ugliness of self-disgust. But when he saw Lisa, saw in her face that she had seen him now as he saw himself, he sank down into the chair again, the accompanying creak comical in the sudden silence. A boy started to laugh again but stopped when, staring where the others stared, he saw The Martian's mouth go slack, his eyes go wet, and then the sobs choked up from deep inside him like pig-grunts as he sat there, head bent back, staring straight up at the naked electric bulb as if he saw some terrible prophecy there.

Lisa had taken hold of my hand; her hand was cold. And now she screamed. It was a fishwife scream, completely uncontrolled, but somehow with anger and compassion contorting her features she was even more beautiful. *"Get out,"* she screamed at the line of astounded people. *"Get out of here, you lousy rotten little bastards."*

Roger didn't seem to hear her at all or notice that, after a moment, we four were alone, for Ed had hurried in and, finally getting the people out, had shut the corridor door against further intrusion.

The light bulb still held Roger hypnotized, but his weeping dwindled as mine began, and I knew, even before I looked, that Ed was gulping too, for we are always affected by everyone and everything exactly the same way ... by everything but death.

To stop my crying I stared very hard at the EXIT sign above Roger's head, wondering where it led.

FIVE

IT WAS simply annoying the first time it happened. The telephone had rung and Johnny had answered it. "Hello?" And then, "Hello?" A pause. "Hello? Hello?"

"Who is it?"

"I dunno." He picked his nose. "Somebody listened to me say hello and then hung up."

Ed had said, "Why can't people be more courteous when they get the wrong number? And holy crud, Johnny, get a Kleenex, will you?"—turning his attention back to the New York *Times*. It was Sunday morning in early November and a fierce storm the night before had torn all but a few stubborn leaves from the leaning-Pisa-like tree, a leper-barked sycamore, which stood on our front lawn stripped and glistening now in the drizzling rain. A gray day, dreary, chill, but still it was Sunday morning, and in our happy family these hours were the jewels on the silver ring of the week. Saturday afternoon's hodge-podge of necessities was finished with—shoes soled, car washed, birthday parties attended, suits to the cleaners, bike chains fixed—and another Saturday night in Cedarton had come and gone. Saturday Night in Cedarton is almost a dirty word nowadays, of course, supposedly encompassing the typical antics of exurbia when the children have been put to bed and it is the grownups' chance to play. This time we had dined with three other couples in a house you couldn't stand up straight in if you were, like Ed, six feet tall; it had reeked of antiquity quite literally, the seventeenth-century beams giving off an odor which mesmerized one no less than the kettle hanging huge in the hearth, the spinning wheel quaint in the corner, the floor wide-planked and wobbly under your feet and sloping so extremely in spots that you walked downhill and uphill from one wing-backed chair to another. The evening had contained the customary ration of sophisticatd chitchat and serious discussion with a modicum of flirtation and inebriation and the inevitable interlude of esoteric parlor games. The hostess had been so successful in her combination of couples that Ed and I had come away with the warm feeling of having added another name or two to the little list of people we wished to see again. For once I had behaved myself, had stifled my desire to shock, to tease, and Ed was pleased. My head had gone down into his lap as he'd driven home and the steering wheel had grazed my cheek as I sleepily mumbled corroboration to his remarks on Ruth Schur's verbosity, Nicky Wright's bigotry, Carol Kenny's legs, Bill Rosen's lechery.

"You were so pretty," Ed said. "I was so proud of you."

"You were so handsome. I was so proud of you." And looking up at him, reaching up for a moment to touch his cheek, the image formed again in my mind as it did so often in these months of waiting and of daydreaming, the image of my daughter who would be, in turn, the image of her father; the boys were like their mother in their features and coloring, possessing my blond-streaked brown hair, my skin, tanned Indian-dark for all but four months of the year, my largish mouth and smallish nose and general appearance of a healthy, wholesome high-class type, the type of whom it had been said "She has good bones," before motherhood and a hearty appetite had rounded the angularity of my face, or, if someone arty were striving to define my charms—the charms I sometimes believed in with unconcealed conceit, sometimes bitterly disparaged, despairing of my plainness—the type compared to the ladies portrayed by Dutch painters of that era in which people seemed to spend their time standing around in tiled rooms looking as cleanly scrubbed as their surroundings. Yes, I was "put together nicely," receiving many a pleased look but seldom a second one, and my sons were cute carbon copies, the All-American boys of the All-American mom. But my husband—ah, Ed was a different matter, was more in Roger's league or Lisa's, was often mistaken in one night club or another for one of the handsome actor clients whom he publicized, and surely our daughter, if it was a daughter, would resemble him, would be blessed with his many sensational endowments—the radiant face, the toothpaste-ad smile, the fine straight nose, the great dark eyes, the dimples, the white white skin and black black hair that storybook heroines have so often but humans almost never—oh, she would be a lovely thing, our little girl. Or perhaps another boy? Well yes, well fine, four sons, that *would* be proud-making; that *would* be quite a crew; how Ed would preen, how female I would feel, ringed round by all my men.

Ed had turned his face quickly to nibble at my hand upon his cheek. "My wonderful wife, I adore you."

"My wonderful husband, I adore you."

"Oh God, but we're lucky, aren't we?"

"We are. We are."

"Why are we so lucky?"

"Why, oh why?"

And the passion of his happiness had entered his blood, hastening it through his body so that the lap I lay on stirred with love, its hardening answered in my own body with an echoing surge, and I raised my head and fumbled to release the telltale flesh, the swollen evidence, the instrument of our imminent pleasure. We giggled like naughty children.

"There I was," Ed said, "driving down Main Street unzipped and fully erected"—but the car swerved dangerously and he pushed me away. "Great way to get caught in the wreckage. Let's save it for later."

So we'd saved it for later, the ancient rigmarole of legalized lust, too often flattened into a pattern of action and reaction, of cause and effect, tame, stale, joyless, insipid in its imitation of the original conflagration between stranger and stranger, lover and lover, bride and groom. And yet now, as so rarely, it happened well, as if, for once, a decade of proximity were an asset in the matter instead of a detriment, giving us as it did a detailed clinical knowledge that transformed each of us into an artist, well-practiced, confident, playing upon the delicate instruments of each other's bodies without inhibition and,

70

alas, without curiosity or excitement or delight. Enjoyment, yes, affection and arousal and relief, but nowhere the pain and the passion reserved for the newly-arrived, the newly-arrived at desire, surprised and overwhelmed. And yet in the midst of our locked-together rocking, loin to loin and mouth to mouth, I was aware of something wonderful that the long-ago beginnings of our love had never known, and dimly I realized that it had something to do with time, and memories, and friendships, with innumerable shared crises and compromises and small intimate deceptions of Them by Us, and had most of all to do with the faceless baby safe and sacred within our embrace, proclaiming us creators and therefore beautiful even as the unbeautiful sounds came from our throats, the unbeautiful motions quickened, straining, straining—"oh!" —"there! there!"—so that in the gentle ebb, smiling, sated, I was reminded of the first long rising note of Gershwin's *Rhapsody in Blue* with its orgasmic peak and falling off and, too, was reminded of the bedtime tale I'd read year after year to first one boy, then another, and another, of the little train with all the toys for the good little children on the other side of the mountain, puffing up the crest and over it—"I *think* I can, I *think* I can"—"I *knew* I could, I *knew* I could."

And now, here it was, the morning after the night before, the five of us encased in rain and bathed in flame, for Ed had kindled the first fire of the season as I'd made our traditional special-breakfast-for-Sunday of French toast and sausage. We had eaten it on trays before the fireplace; the months since the previous winter seemed to have erased the memory of fire from Terry's mind, for he stared at the blaze enchanted by the leapings and curlings of color and smoke, so that I had to keep reminding him, *"Terry.* Your *breakfast,"* poking him out of his trance to get his fork away from its hovering place above his plate and up to the solemn thin-lipped little mouth beneath the long nose and inward-dreaming eyes. Bruce and Johnny reveled noisily in the picnic aura of the meal, warmed not only by the flames which painted light and shadow with flickering fingers across their flushed faces but by the gay mood in which Ed and I had awoken, pleased that after a late night our sons had let us sleep later than usual, had behaved themselves, for once not quarreling, until the deadline hour of ten had brought them screaming with impatiently delayed appetites into our bed, tumbling, tickling, shoving each other for the favored place between father and mother—"the boloney in the sandwich," Ed called the winner—and they had smelled of dust and oranges.

"Have you been wrestling in the closet?" Ed had asked, sniffing suspiciously at their rumpled pajamas. "Or stuffing yourselves with so much junk you won't be hungry?" But they were on top of him, he was a vanquished Gulliver to their triumphantly shouting Lilliputians, and I'd jumped from the fray to get started in the kitchen.

And then our settling-down-and-sighing time, Ed's and mine, full of food and anticipation, the New York *Times* piled up in front of us as the kids got dressed for Sunday School, Ed with his sports section, business section, news-of-the-week—I with my book section, drama section, magazine section. These two piles of oh-so-separate newsprint typified our marriage, I was thinking—to each his own and yet we feel together. Don't we? Don't we? And then the phone had rung. And now, a half-hour later, it rang a second time.

"I'll get it this time," I called upstairs to the boys, and said hello into the mouthpiece, receiving no reply except soft breathing. "Who's there? Hello?" But silence still and then a stealthy click.

"Dammit, that gripes the hell out of me," I said to Ed. "Once I can forgive, but *twice*. And not even an 'I'm sorry, wrong number.' Christ."

"I bet it's him. Or her."

"Who?"

"The nut. You know he's been pestering Roger and Lisa with phone calls lately instead of notes. Switched from written to spoken persecution. Now I guess he's gotten around to us again."

It had been a long time since the first incomprehensible

message of revenge had arrived. Almost three months had passed, months in which my pregnancy nausea had gradually faded until only a twinge remained when meat was cooking or someone smoked a sweet-smelling pipe. Even the Hartford trip with Roger and Lisa, a month before, seemed long ago now, and in its lack of any repetition or repercussion had acquired a make-believe quality, as if it had never happened at all. Driving down the highway that same day Roger had been his old self, not seeming to notice how strained the rest of us were, not seeming to realize that we found his intensity unnatural now, seeing in it the new and hidden dimension of the possible Roger, the piteous Roger, the Roger who could come apart at the seams right out in public that way, without any pride, with no control, and oddest of all, with no recollection.

Lisa and I, at about the halfway mark of the return journey, had found a release from the tension in a common bond; both of us, we discovered, loved to sing, to harmonize, to indulge in the intricate juxtaposition of voices which elicited in our listeners an opposition in direct contrast to our own pride and delight. "Oh Dan-ny boy, the pipes the pipes are call-ing, from glen to glen and down the moun-tain-side"—and when Ed and Roger, up in the front seat, begged us to lower our tones, we continued quietly, righteously in league against these our callous depreciators, with "Hallelujah Chorus," "Scarlet Ribbons," "Annie Laurie"—sometimes sliding around in bewilderment from one wrong note to another until, bursting into laughter, we admitted defeat and began again in another key, or, occasionally, going straight through a melody with such remarkable ease, with—we assured each other afterwards—such clarity of tone, such professional precision, such promise of eventual perfection, that we fell laughing into each other's arms on the concluding chord, silly with victory.

Everything was fine, our gaiety said; nothing had happened, nothing had changed; all's well that ends well. And besides, who could feel anything as niggling as apprehension when on either side the foliage was shameless

73

in its blatant array of orange and yellow, maroon and brighter red like...like..."A Chinese funeral," Lisa said. "Death with a festive flair."

"Yes," I said. "God, yes."

And I liked her more and more. I was beginning to understand why Roger turned his head every few moments to look at her, not smiling, not speaking, just looking at her and then away as if assuring himself of her continued existence; he was, I realized now for sure, in love. Not just with the face, not just with the figure, but with whatever it was in this flamboyant-looking creature which had already begun to kindle my respect, to inspire my curiosity, to warm me with the knowledge that a person whom I valued liked me back.

It was afternoon. The drizzle continued; the boys were beginning to be bored, Ed—his newspaper finished—to be irritable, I to feel my nausea more and to try unsuccessfully to check the depression of spirit which nagged at me as I heard the children's hilarity deteriorate into bickering, heard Ed's temper flare into snarled or shouted reprimands like some Sunday-stubbled ogre who'd never heard of quiet discipline, felt this earthquake of disaffection shake our no-longer-cozy nest so that I wished to screech, to weep, to flee. And when the telephone bell sounded through the strife I forgot about the previous calls and rushed to answer what I hoped would be some pleasant interlude—a neighbor asking our precious offspring over there, perhaps, or a friend from the city dropping by for a drink. But this time the pause after my "hello" was followed by a single word which hissed into my ear like venom from the tongue of a snake—"Bitch!" Shocked, I said nothing, and then had just opened my mouth to ask who held this unusual opinion of me when the man hung up.

"Him?" Ed asked.

"No doubt about it." I told him what he'd said. "His voice sounds just the way you'd expect it to. Bitter. Psycho. You know, like his letters."

Even if Bruce had not already guessed at the situation

74

by eavesdropping on our many whispered conversations, he would have been wise to it now, for he had listened in on the extension and now came bounding up the stairs from the playroom. "It was him, wasn't it? The guy who's cuckoo. Huh, Ma?"

"I guess so."

"Goddammit." Ed had come to the phone now, angry, twitching, his head jerking spasmodically and his eyes and eyebrows too. A nervous wreck, I thought, watching him, and, never having felt what it was like to be nervous, I felt no compassion at his suffering, but only annoyance and a perverse inclination to imitate him, to make a joke of his high-strung nature which was so opposite from my own phlegmatic one. "This has got to stop," he shouted, and muttering something about seeing what the story was with Roger and Lisa, seeing if they too were being pestered or if we were alone today in being the privileged recipients, he dialed their number in New York. Look at him, I thought, the stretched elastic band about to snap, the dramatist, the loudmouth, the lowbrow, and remembering now in my doldrums only the times when that lighted firecracker quality had brought me embarrassment —the public exhibitions of jealousy and possessiveness, the sulking erupting into senseless harangues accompanied by the almost spastic motions of his head and face—remembering this, happening so seldom and yet so destructively, I chose now not to remember that other aspect of his tension, chose now not to remember that it was this very quality of the man—the lighted fuse, the stretched elastic band, the tortured child—which had made me yearn to take him in my arms when we first met, to put his anguished head against my breast, to feed my physical peace through the pores of my flesh into the pores of his flesh until his nerves let loose their pitiless grip, his body relaxed on mine, and all that was left was the love in his eyes, the brightness of his smile, and the warmth with which he melted me, mended me, made me forget that death is all there is.

I listened in for a minute as Ed spoke to Roger—yes, Roger said, their Sabbath too had been disturbed by

75

phoned epithets, yes, he was upset, too, but take it easy, Ed boy, don't go flippin' your lid—and then I'd gone to the closet and gotten out my slicker and a pair of Ed's boots—I couldn't find mine—and had put them on as I answered Bruce's questions.

"Why does the man phone Roger and Lisa and us?"

"He's sick, darling."

"You mean sick in the head? Crazy?"

"Yes, sick in the head, but maybe not all the way insane. We don't know, darling. We can only hope that he—"

"What makes some people crazy?"

"Insanity is something the scientists are trying to solve now, darling. It's one of the diseases, like cancer, dear, that they've made advances in without yet finding a complete cure. Maybe they'll never know all the answers, but they're trying to all the time."

I stood ready at the door now, but Bruce's brow wore a deep scowl in his attempt to fathom this strange thing, this mystery, and I felt obliged to continue our conversation until his curiosity was at least somewhat satisfied. Not that I could tell him much. Mental illness. What was there to tell him about it, really? I knew so little. It was a thing which happened to someone else, never, of course, to oneself. It had happened, for instance, to an acquaintance of ours on the other side of town, a Mrs. Hahn, about whom we had said, when she was suddenly removed to a state institution after the birth of her first child, "Isn't it awful?" feeling, however, not too terribly sad inside, for it was only the tragedies with which you could identify —the kind which might conceivably happen to *you* someday—that could really touch your heartstrings. This thing, this business of being mentally ill, it was just sort of disgusting, really—oh, one shouldn't feel this way about it, of course, one should read the articles about how it's just like any other sickness and afflicts more Americans than all the other diseases put together and everyone's emotions are a *little* bit sick—why, look at *Roger,* for God's sake, and even Lisa with her psychiatrist and Ed with his temper and his twitches, even I myself with my horror

76

of death—yes, yes, but still, wasn't one more apt to shudder than to shed a tear when one thought of anything so alien to one's understanding as actual insanity? I shuddered now, but only from the cold, for I had opened the door and turned to go out.

"Bruce, when Daddy gets through talking to Roger tell him I felt like walking in the rain, okay, honey?"

But Bruce had one more question, the same one he'd started with. "What *makes* somebody lose his mind?"

He looked so worried, I had to offer some sort of reply, but I was thinking—oh Lord, of all the subjects to have to sound knowledgeable on, why didn't I listen in that Abnormal Psychology class in college? Quickly, not wanting the wind to chill him as he stood near the door, I said, "Nobody knows for sure, dear. They think it's partly genes, you know, genes? not the dungarees kind, but..."—he nodded impatiently; he was no dumb kid —"... and partly environment."

I closed the door behind me. This last word he obviously hadn't recognized, and pausing on the porch to glance back through the window I watched him go to the dictionary in the bookcase. Ah, I smiled, my scholarly darling. And then the other two appeared by the window, and pressing their faces with squashed-flat noses against the cold pane, they waited for my kisses against the glass.

Kissing the coldness, then turning toward the rain, I felt my mood change back to the morning's magic, felt so filled with gratitude for my good fortune that I tipped up my face into the raindrops to lick them like bits of nectar along my lips, and when the children began to bang on the window for attention I paused on the pathway to wave back at them—all of them now, one, two, three, making squashed funny-faces against the glass; joining in their foolishness, I danced a jig of joy in my great big boots, splashing, arms flapping like a marionette's, eyes rolling like a clown's, laughing back at their laughter and feeling glad to be alive, feeling glad with ecstatic gladness to be me.

Then when did it begin? I trudged humming through

the puddles on our muddy road not knowing I would never again walk this road as I was walking it now, never again see these trees or this sky or feel this wind and rain as I felt it now, had always felt it; for what we see and feel, and how we see and feel it, is part of what we are. And what I was that moment I would never never ever be again.

SIX

"OH Lord, not *again*," I groaned to Ed, next to me in bed, when the telephone rang. It was nine o'clock in the evening of that same rainy Sunday; the boys' edge-of-slumber singing reached my ears in an amusing polyphony of separate melodies from their various bedrooms down the hall, and I had fallen asleep just a minute before with the book I was reading open against my neck.

Reaching for the phone, I waited for the inevitable, for of course it must be the kook again with another hissed vulgarity. But no, it was a friend of mine from the city, a Grace McNulty, telling me of a tragedy which had befallen a couple she knew, friends of whom she had often spoken but whom I had never met. Their only child, she said, a daughter of twelve, had been thrown from a horse and killed instantly, her neck broken. Sleepily I expressed my shock, my sorrow, feeling sincere in what I said even though the emotion of annoyance I felt at being awakened was stronger than the emotion I could summon up at the demise of someone I did not even know. I talked to her some more, making a date to meet Wednesday at the Harwyn for less depressing conversation over cocktails, and then, hanging up and telling Ed of the tragedy, set my book aside and settled down to re-enter the sleep from which I had been so rudely removed. Ed stopped reading now, too, his eyelids "heavy at the hinges," he yawned, and we laughed at ourselves as we turned out the light, for we were champion sleepers, he and I, marveling at the acquaintances who watched midnight movies on TV or something called The Jack Paar Show. Weeknights eleven was our limit, and, as now, it was usually closer to the children's bedtime than to adults' that we fell asleep, often waking in the morning with our light still on and our books next to us on the pillows. As I nestled spoon-fashion on my side into the comfortable curve of Ed's body—my back against his chest, my bottom snuggled into his abdomen, his legs bent up parallel to mine so that we lay like a Siamese fetus—I had what I figured would be my final thought before my mind blanked out again: *please, Terry, sleep through the night,* for it was too unreasonable, too wearying, this continuance of his middle-of-the-night awakenings which should have ceased when he was still a baby; habitually, for three years now, he had awakened and babbled on for an hour or so in his bed before falling asleep again. He wasn't toilet-trained—that was mostly the trouble—and his own soaked diapers were what woke him. I could have remained undistressed if, like Ed, I merely slept through the babble, slept through the vehement dialogue of the many invisible friends with whom Terry enjoyed these nocturnal visits—no, not friends only, but deadly enemies ("Bang! I shooted you! Wow, look at you bleed!")—all of which disturbed Ed not a whit, leaving me, however, wideawake and listening with morbid attention to this odd child's imaginary homicides, and then, of late, wide-awake still after the chatter subsided, awake through several more hours before the bureau would gradually emerge into shape in the faint beginnings of dawn, at which point, more often than not, sleep in its perversity took me briefly again to its bosom, only to be wrenched awake again in a scant time by a child sliding beside me beneath the covers for a cuddle and a kiss.

But this night Terry did not awaken me; this night I never slept.

This night I never slept. Five words no more fantastic than the fingers on my hand, and yet my fingers too soon would soon betray me.

This night—oh monstrous fluke!—I never slept.

79

SEVEN

I FELT the terrible anger of the unjustly imprisoned. "Take these down," I demanded, each time a nurse entered my room. "Get me out of here."

For now that the sleepless night had ended, had become a morning blurred with exhaustion and fear, I knew only that I could not escape my bed, the bars around it preventing me in my drugged state from any recourse other than these my repeated and repeatedly ignored pleas: "Put this fence down ... please, oh please ... you must not cage me in this way," as I tried desperately and unsuccessfully to compete with the efficient routine of hospital activity all around me, my requests bringing no other result from my crisp white jailers than pleasantly adamant refusals, the kind of pleasantness and rigidity employed in dealing with a troublesome child.

They were kind, they were firm, they said I should wait and see what the doctor had to say, he would come soon. I should sleep, they said.

Sleep. Sleep. I could not sleep. I would not sleep. Sleep, so simple, so instinctive, so suddenly and strangely elusive, sleep was unachievable, was out of my reach, forever, forever.

It had begun at midnight. Ed had long ago departed into the dreams which occasionally sent his mumbling into my hair or his trembling into the hand upon my hip. I lay awake, waiting for that which never came, lay awake for the third hour now and tried to control my thoughts, but they swarmed behind my eyeballs like buzzing flies, yes, the world behind my eyes contained a disorderly swarm, and dangling down sticky from the center of my mind was a piece of flypaper—it was labeled SLEEPLESSNESS—around which collected my panicky thoughts, helpless, doomed.

80

"Ed?" I shifted, disrupting his position against me, and he moaned as he turned over on his back. "Ed?"

"Mmmm."

"I can't sleep. I try and I try and I can't." No answer. "Ed. I can't *sleep*."

"Mmmm."

"I've been lying here ever since Grace called, wide-awake. I keep getting wide-awaker all the time and it's awful, awful."

"Hmmm?"

Groping my fingers across his face in the darkness, I found an eyelid and pressed it up. "Ed! *Please* talk to me."

But he pushed my hand away and turned over with peeved, impatient abruptness onto his stomach, his face turned away from me, muttering only, "Christ, Janie, count sheep or something, baby, will you?" and I was left as alone as only one can be who steps along the edge of a nameless panic.

Oh, not that we were strangers, panic and I, but that was different . . . that panic was almost on purpose, that other panic which was perpetrated upon me by my other self, by that sadist from the outer spaces of the soul. And now, thinking about that familiar panic, it began as it always began with an initial twinge of the terror to come, and I could stop it—ah yes, there was still time, it was like the start of a sneeze, when a swift motion of the finger to the nose—pinch!—could stop it before it began —for now all that was needed was a swift motion of the mind to things concrete—to here and now, to bed and Ed, to November 1958, Cedarton—and the sensation would be severed before it was too late; but no . . . no . . . it was already too late, my mind was on its way out of time into eternity, powerless now was I to avert this weird projection of myself from the brevity of existence into the endlessness of nonexistence, and as I reached the farthest outpost of the soul—reached the state of death itself in my imagination—the word, as always at this second of unbearable perception, burst from my mouth— "*No!*"—and I sat up quickly, was pulled up, rather, by the safety valve of my sanity, rescued and rescuer, one step ahead of my advance messenger from the land of no-more-me.

They'd given me another shot just before the doctor came and now his words, the nurses', Ed's, floated all around me like an evil-smelling incense. . . .

"Asleep . . . must be asleep . . . couldn't be awake after all we've shot into her . . . physically impossible to retain consciousness . . . never happened before . . . hostile attitude, hostile to nurses . . . don't worry, we'll snow her under . . ."

I forced myself from the whirlpool which had my head at its center, a quicksand whirlpool which held my body heavy, submerged, immovable; I forced my mouth to move. "I can't click it off."

"What? What did she say?"

And the nurse's reply, "We keep thinking she's asleep until she murmurs something about how she can't click it off."

"Yes." The doctor's voice. "I remember. She said that when she phoned at 3 A.M. She kept saying that she couldn't click it off."

"Yes," Ed said. "That's when she first began to get extremely upset. Couldn't click off her mind, she said."

At three o'clock that morning I had been moving agitatedly around the house for an hour, had sat on the couch, on the floor, on every chair in every room, had knelt in the bathroom gagging into the toilet, had taken some of Ed's pills for nerves, mine for nausea . . . had tried to read, but could not read . . . to think of something besides sleep, but could think of nothing else as my curious dilemma increasingly engulfed me, for hanging down from the ceiling of my brain like a chandelier ablaze and unextinguishable was the knowledge: *I'll never sleep again.* So finally, in desperation, I'd called our family doctor, who told me that this sort of behavior wasn't like me at all, I was allowing myself to get out of control.

"It has nothing to do with control," I cried. "I can't sleep, don't you understand, I can't sleep."

"Lots of people can't sleep lots of times," he replied. "They don't get hysterical."

"I'm not—"

"You're hysterical. You're working yourself up into an hysterical fit over nothing at all."

"But—"

"Relax. You have a touch of insomnia. It's nothing. Take a sleeping pill."

"I can't. We have none. Besides, I gagged up all the other pills I took."

"Phone your druggist. Get some Seconal and insert it rectally. Two, three, four, if necessary, it doesn't matter. But get *hold* of yourself." He hung up.

Get a druggist up in the middle of the night? Ridiculous, I told Ed, when he repeated the doctor's suggestion. But he asked, "More ridiculous than what you're doing to yourself?"

"*I'm* not doing it. It's just *happening* to me." And I tried to explain it to him, tried to tell him how it was to have a trembly tree trunk down the center of me from hard heartbeat to tense gut, which, every few moments, as he stroked my forehead rhythmically, blissfully dissolved, and I would think, ah, now, now I will sleep at last, sliding like a billiard ball to drop unknowing into the dark corner pocket—but oh! how opposite from unknowing, how frantically aware when, a second later, I was cruelly scooped up—whoosh!—and tossed again onto the table with the bright light shining down. Hateful the game: pockets one could slide into, only to be snatched out at once by that merciless hand. Soon I was fearing the pockets as much as the hand—so close to peace, so false the closeness.

I called the doctor again. "*Do* something. I can't *stand* it."

He sighed, "What can I do? Put you in the maternity ward of the hospital where they can snow you under with injections?"

"Yes!" I heard Terry's nocturnal babble begin in the next room. "Yes, yes, put me in the hospital."

"Janie—"

I thrust Ed's arm away; I wished I could hit him full in the face for his lack of comprehension. "Don't you *see?* I have to go. They'll put me to *sleep.* I'll *sleep* again."

"All right." Why did he affect that perplexed expression? Wasn't it perfectly *clear* what I was saying? "All right, Janie, if that's what you want."

"It's not what I *want.* I can't *help* it, don't you understand? My brain . . . my brain . . . it won't click off, oh, help me somebody, I can't click off my brain."

For three days they "snowed me under." Sometimes I would be aware of covers being adjusted around me, of Ed's eyes wet with tears, close to my own, of my head being held as food was fed into my numb-feeling lips, of my own voice weeping, "I want to go home, I want to go home," and of the doctor's voice whispering to Ed, "Anxiety state. Symptomatic of deep disturbance. We'll see how she is after she wakes up from all this. Psychiatric observation essential. Commitment to institution probably not necessary."

Commitment. Commitment. Commitment. And bars around my bed, each time I moved my hand it struck my prison bars. Oh God oh God oh God. Not me. Not me. And still I almost slept.

On the morning of the fourth day, when I awoke, I was an old man, a very very old man, with a wizened thin body and a thin ascetic face. Here was the bed, the window, and here was the very old man and he was me and I was him. I lay absolutely still, not thinking, just being. Being—without astonishment, without rebellion, entirely without emotion and without doubt—this very old man. Then I fell from the hospital room into dreams again and awoke when the sun was full across my face, drying the dampness on the pillow next to my cheek which my dribblings had formed in my slumber. The very old man had drooled in my slumber, but the sun had barely reached the window sill when last I was awake, so time must have passed and yet time seemed somehow to have vanished, and now I was three girls. No, I thought, no,

I am *not* these three girls, I am *me*. But *we* are you, there *is* no other you, they argued. Unmoving, unfrightened, unsurprised, I felt an enormous struggle go on inside me, as if we three girls were in the dark cellar of myself and above us the trap door was closing, closing, slowly, irrevocably, shutting us in with each other forever. No! Something in me twisted free. No! Not me! And the something that knew I was me and not them, suddenly strengthened by the threat of extinction, braced itself against the trap door of my mind, pressing, pressing, and my mind opened up and I rose out into my own identity, leaving them behind, the three girls, eluding his grasp, the very old man.

I was breathing hard. I had not moved a muscle, had not blinked my eyes, but the blinds at the window beside me had been closed by someone my eyes had not seen; I lay now in shadow and in horror, breathing in rough gulps as one breathes who has battled a great battle and has only just barely escaped.

"I'm me," I whispered. "Here I am. I am me." And at that instant, as one would pick a piece of lint from one's sleeve and flick it away, I picked that tremendous battle from my mind and flicked it away from me, away, away, into the place where one's unbearables reside, and where —for some, for you, perhaps? and you?—they stay dormant or in ferment from the cradle to the grave.

As far as I was concerned, it had never happened; the last few days and nights could not have happened and therefore they had not happened, and to have the doctor send this slimy soft-speaking psychiatrist into my room would have been preposterous if it had not been so funny. "Good grief." I grinned up at him as he stood at the foot of my bed. "I've seen mountains made out of molehills before, but this takes the cake."

"What takes the cake?" he said quietly, solemnly, and I laughed out loud at the sight of him standing there so humorless and so stymied—for who could stymie a psychiatrist if not myself?

"*This* takes the cake, dear heart, this little pretense of

a dialogue we're conducting," and I laughed again, feeling at the top of my form—witty, charming, in charge of the proceedings. The long hair which had been matted for three days had been combed by the nurse and, spread out on the pillow against which I sat, made me look, the nurse had said, like Alice in Wonderland; I felt appealingly little-girlish, and yet roguishly adult, and I could feel my eyes sparkling, so full of self-assurance that I kept waiting for this character, this Dr. What's-His-Name, to start blinking stupidly as one does in the light of too bright a sunshine.

He had asked me how I felt and I had replied that I felt fine. He had asked if anything was troubling me, and I had retorted that I was troubled by the inevitability of death but that I doubted if dear Sigmund himself could remedy that situation. He had asked if I thought I needed the services of psychiatry, and I had said that I was aready deeply embroiled in analysis, had been since the start of adolescence, and that fortunately the expense of my treatment was kept at a minimum by the advantageous fact of analyst and analysand both being myself. Well, then, was I happy, he asked, and I answered sublimely so—and, he wanted to know, did I consider myself neurotic to any appreciable degree? To a degree concomitant with my intelligence, I had replied archly, and did he consider himself so? But he wished, he said, that I would just talk— just talk about myself a while and let him listen in, forget he was present, if I could, and just ramble on about my life, my thoughts, my feelings on any subject which came to mind.

"If I oblige you, sir," I said with mock subservience, "may I go home?"

"Do you want to go home?"

"Well, of *course* I want to go home. I feel perfectly okay."

"Perfectly, eh?" he said and, catching the sarcasm, I went along in the same tone for a while, saying, "Yeah, perfectly. Tiptop. Nary a care. God's in His Heaven, all's right with the world."

But he did not smile and somehow the game had

soured; I suddenly felt as sick of my own flippancy as Pagliacci was of his painted face, and I wished this idiot would give up and go away, wished that Ed would come right now and take me home. But he stood there waiting, young, callow, clinically casual, and I knew I had to get it over with, so—deciding to toss him a brief auto-biographical fantasia, a shocker of a Freudian montage to see what he would do with it—I told him that I had a pathological attachment to my sister, a sadist-masochist for a brother, an adulteress for a mother, a fetishist for a father, that I quit college when the Thetas blackballed me for my promiscuity, and that I enjoyed mushrooms, coitus and avocados, "though not necessarily in that order."

"That's it in a nutshell," I said with my best wise-cracking smile, and waited for his reaction.

"Well, I give up." He smiled back, his annoyance barely hidden, and snapped shut the little notebook he'd been holding in his hand. "Perhaps we can make another stab at this when you decide to take your condition seriously."

"Don't call me. I'll call you." I chuckled at my own cleverness—God, but it was fun to have the upper hand again—and added: "Besides, I do not know to what condition you refer, unless it be, as I said before, the ir-reparable condition of mortality."

"I believe we both know that I refer to your mental condition. I also believe you know it has quite recently revealed itself as precariously unstable."

This time my laugh was loudest of all; in the middle of it, as the psychiatrist turned to go, Ed walked in with two of the nurses.

"See?" One nurse pointed to me as at a successful chemical experiment. "Why, she's a new person." And turning to the other nurse, one I hadn't seen before, she triumphantly explained, "Mrs. Thompson here got into something of a stew during a bout of insomnia a few days ago, but we snowed her under and look at her now."

"Look at me now," I boasted to Ed, and flung my arms around his neck as he bent down to kiss me. "Take me home, please."

"As soon as you're strong enough."

"Strong enough!" Again I laughed; everything was so amusing today, I was a glass of gaiety filled so full that the least little thing spilled me over. But the next moment Ed and the nurses were the ones who were laughing as I stretched my legs, touching the floor, and they folded under me; I had no strength at all, my muscles seemed to have evaporated. "Good Lord, I can't *walk!"*—and, sinking down onto a chair, I laughed some more.

I did not notice when the psychiatrist left, and by the next day my weakness was gone and only my merriment remained. Before I left the hospital I got a Nembutal prescription from my doctor—he wrote it out on a little piece of paper—and I went home with laughter crowding my throat like vomit and with the little piece of paper clutched so tight in my fist that, upon arriving home and opening up my hands to hug my children, it fell upon the floor in a wet blue wad of blurred ink.

"Mommy," Johnny asked, as I pressed my face into the warm velvet of his neck, "where have you been?"— and then, not waiting for my answer, he was telling me of all that had happened to him in my absence, while in my mind his question lingered—"Where have you been? Where have you been?"—and my unvoiced reply, "I don't know. I don't know."

Now I knew how Ed felt, knew—in fact—how it might feel to be a Mexican jumping bean, for I couldn't stay still; suddenly, without knowing how or why, I had joined the previously abhorred ranks of the busy busy busy people. Always before I had pitied those whose stimulation came from outside themselves, pitied and scorned them, the hectic ones all around me, among whose pointless peregrinations I squatted on my sweetly solitary island of quiet introspection. Oh, I had my public side— and quite a side it was, with its artful artlessness attracting or repelling, depending upon the sensibilities of its target —but the private side was, Ed knew as well as I, the me that counted for most, the me that he loved despite the mood-vacillating dazzle of the façade.

"When I'm a reminiscent old widower," he'd said once,

"I'll always picture you like this—horizontal, with your bare feet up, staring into space with a mustache of lemon meringue."

But now—parties! I wanted parties! For three weeks every night was Saturday night, but every morning was not Sunday morning, no, no more Sunday self, only a self that began at dawn its dread of dusk, began upon waking a rigid ritual of protection against the hour when I would again be in bed—and then? Then I would sleep, of *course* I would sleep, the small yellow capsule would *put* me to sleep. Ed was drawn into the ritual, but he made no comment, merely played his part: tucking me in on the dot of the hour—not a minute before, not a minute after—winding the clock, handing me the capsule and the glass of water, turning out the light, leaving the door ajar six inches, and I would lie on my left side in the identical position in which I had lain the night before and the night before and the night before; the timing must be exact, the actions must never vary, the eyes must close on schedule and the brain click off, and this bedtime ritual, surely, would ensure my sleep, my safety, my sanity. And still the parties continued, and we saw more of Lisa and Roger in less than a month we otherwise would have in a year.

"You seem a bit different lately," Lisa said, "but I can't put my finger on it." She did not know about my "thing," as Ed and I called it; it was a change too subjective and elusive to merit a more definitive label.

"Butterfinger," I replied with a laugh. "It's very simple. My torso's starting to spread and I'm funnier than ever."

"Well, funny, yes, *très très gaie* ... but ... oh hell, *I* don't know ..."

Like a canoe, I thought, as she sipped at her fifth drink, for wasn't that the way I felt, like a human canoe? Yes, I could feel myself paddling anxiously on this side and then that side to control myself against incomprehensible currents, and oh, what nostalgia I felt for the rowboat I'd been before—beautiful sturdy rowboat one could lie down in to sunbathe, with the oars locked for the time being—

". . . you're not worried about anything, are you?" she asked. "Is that lunatic beginning to bug you?"

"Well." I might as well lie. "I can't help being a *bit* upset, of course, what with all the phone calls and then another threat note last week . . ."

"Yes, the same one we got. How do you like that stuff about the robbery we're all supposedly involved in? *Robbery,* no less. *There's* a new wrinkle."

"Besides," I said, "this business with Roger worries us too. You know, ever since—"

"Yes. Yes, I know. But except for Drake City last week he's been fine ever since. Chipper as can be." Chipper like I'm chipper, I thought, while Lisa waved with alcoholic abandon to someone across the room; we were sitting on the periphery of a party, a penthouse party given by Milton Cohn, who owned all commercial rights to *The Martian* and who, via his comic-book firm, had introduced the character to the public in the first place, twenty-four years before, subsequently going from two-bit publisher to millionaire mogul, carried up upon the famous sword as it soared out of comic books into radio, movies, television, merchandising, big business. "My poor Roger lamb," Lisa was saying, "he's even more of a mess than me," and then—tipsy, her verbal reserve decimated not only by drink but by the confidences we had already exchanged in the many preceding evenings—she began to ramble on in a confused way. No, I realized, not confused, but confusing; it was I, the sober one, who was somehow lacking in equilibrium, so that the whole scene had a Dantean quality, an inferno of laughter and chatter and swaying sophisticated forms. Everything looked the way it might through someone else's borrowed spectacles; if I were to walk, surely my step would meet the floor before it meant to, and when I talked, seldom, it was just to ask another question and to hope I'd grasp her answer through the fog. . . .

EIGHT

"WE'RE both scared, Rog and I," she said. "You, you're safe and cozy as a birdie in its nest, you wouldn't understand." Birdie? I thought. Sparrow? But she continued, "You've got a good marriage, swell kids, satisfying daily routine with no fear in it—you're typical."

"Typical?"—thinking, *no fear, no fear.*

She sipped her drink and when she spoke again she could keep neither her inebriation nor her sudden hostility out of her voice. "Yeah, typical. The happy li'l homemaker, the wholesome result of a wholesome upbringing, my God you're so happy and healthy and wholesome it sticks out all over you—shiny face, shiny eyes, shiny life —you've had it good ever since you were born, you went from adoring maw and paw to adoring hubby and adoring offspring, from one pretty suburban street to another." Her words were all blurring together. "You and Ed and Rog and me, we pal around like we're all sorta the same, all smugly ensconced at the top of the heap, the tiara of the Twentieth Century—White Protestant American Successes—but boy what a difference really, Rog and I, we *clawed* our way up, you wouldn't understand about that, would you, about desperation, the kind he and I feel, knowing that now we've managed to escape from our lousy pasts we've got to *stay* up here somehow, can't go back, known fame, glory, been fussed over, couldn't go back." She paused, waving, and our host waved back. Smiling, she belied her smile with a whispered "Prick!"

With an effort, feeling even this unsafe—might not the motion of my head increase the distortion within it, dizzy me more?—I turned and looked at Milton Cohn. I saw the small round body set into the Egyptian sedan chair like pea into pod, saw the cigar smoke curling up to the arched top which had once sheltered ancient queens on their journeys to the Sphinx, saw the squat legs stretched ahead

91

of him and crossed at the spot where a slave's black hands had once gripped the horizontal poles of the chair. I saw the thick gray hair springing out like raccoon fur between the socks and trouser cuffs, saw the canapé go into the mouth, heard the Brooklyn voice sound out loud and nasal, saw no listener flinch as bits of chicken liver were ejected from the lips. Behind him, along one long high wall, a mural stretched huge and hideous: Milton himself, seated, smiling, royal, and, around him, frolicking across the plaster, dozens of the cartoon characters which helped to fill his till, and looming largest—soaring skyward, Roger-faced—The Martian, dwarfed only by the figure at the center, pink-cheeked, paternalistic, benign. I saw it all, saw it as if I stood on a porch beside a lawn party, face pressed against the screen, looking, hearing, separate, alone. Beside me, so close I needed only to stumble once upon arising to crash through it, the plate-glass window framed a northward view of Central Park: hansom cabs in lamplight, muffled men on benches, walls and trees and island bedrock pushing through the grass, and, backdropping the lake and the paths and the hidden antelopes and carousel, the battlements of Harlem jutting castle-like and proud, their dinginess obscured by miles of dusk.

"—wouldn't understand," Lisa said.

I had not been listening, had been growing more and more removed from my surroundings, more and more alarmed by the urbanity with which these transitory animals were laughing and chatting and kicking their caskets aside, so that I had to clamp my tongue between my teeth to keep from calling out: *"Do we exist? Listen, everyone, how can we be sure we exist?"*

"—no use trying to explain unhappiness to somebody like you."

"Somebody like me?" I forced myself into reality.

"Yeah, like you. All of you." She finished her drink; she seemed angry and now I listened, carefully, for she was saying things which seemed to mean much to her but which sounded like gibberish to me. "All of you. Stoker College for Women, big deal, *big* deal. The whole bunch

92

of you always treating me like—" She stopped, beckoned the nearby waiter, regarded me with green-eyed malevolence as he poured, then drank and stared away across the room, seeming to forget that she had stopped in midsentence.

I said helpfully, "Treating you like—"

But she was having no help from me, she was having nothing from me now but the symbol that I, in her drunkenness, had become, the symbol, she said with sudden sullen clarity, of "all the snob-faced cashmere-sweatered saddle-shoed little bitches I ever shot a blob into the hot chocolate of."

"Blob?"

"Blob of whipped cream. With English muffins, of course. *You* remember, surely, it was always hot chocolate and English muffins at the break between chapel and the first class of the day." She finished her drink. "English muffins for all the English-named girls with their ... what's your name?"

"Janie Thompson."

"I mean your *maiden* name, Little Miss College Gal."

"Winslow."

"Winslow. Yeah. *Win*slow. Perfect. He'd call you Miss Winslow deferential-like when he passed you with his mop, wouldn't he, and you'd answer 'Hiya, Jimmy' as you went tripping over his pail on your way to Western Civilization."

"Who he?"

"Huh?"

"Who he with pail and mop?"

"Who he, who he, my *father,* that's who he, Jimmy the janitor. You were all just *crazy* about Jimmy, weren't you—I mean, he was such a typical small-town *character,* wasn't he, the things he said and the way he said them, why a regular *Jukes* family type—all those mountain village people intermarry till they're feeble-minded, didn't you learn that in sophomore sociology?—I mean, take his son, Jimmy's heir to the throne of collegiate ridicule, the good-looking adolescent who clipped the campus hedges, precocious in one essential area and thus become Town

93

Cocksman, he was fun for you to shack up with, wasn't he? I mean just on week-nights, of course, on the sly between Dartmouth weekends—just for a quick screw in the hay behind the funny old storybook barn. And Jimmy's wife, who ran the dinky old drug store on Main Street and whose chin warts amused you so you couldn't stop giggling into your hot chocolates—and the *daughter* of the family, oh my God, the *daughter,* wasn't *she* a little slut with her big fat un-English breasts bouncing behind the counter when she helped her ma, bouncing right in your beaus' faces when it was Saturday on campus and all you flat-chested little eggheads found out your fathers couldn't help you out *then,* could they, a raise in the good old allowance wasn't going to keep your dates' eyes offa *me,* was it?" She started laughing now and said, "English muffins. You still like English muffins? You English?" I was too surprised at her monologue to realize the question was meant to be answered, but then she said it again. "Huh? Are you? Excuse me, your *an*cestors, I mean. *Way* back, of course, *way* back."

"Yes, English," I said. "Mayflower. Pilgrims. Plymouth Rock, the whole bit." She nodded like a prophetess, much pleased with herself, and I added, "French too. Mother's side. Descended from Huguenot refugee Jacques Corbin . . . fairly recent immigrants, though. Seventeen—"

But all at once she was speaking of Roger again. "Know how many times Roger's mother was a bride? Guess, just guess."

I guessed—merely out of whimsy—seven times, for Roger and I had always been too busy discussing our souls to make mention of our mothers. But Lisa said, "Yes, seven. He told you about it, huh?"

I started to demur, to explain I had merely meant my guess to be farfetched, nonsensical, but a couple passed by, heads together, laughing, and I saw Ed greet them as he crossed the room to us. "Who's that?" I asked him as he sat beside us.

"The newlyweds. Bob and Wanda Decker. He's the one who went through that hell last year, remember?" I shook my head and he explained, "He's Cohn's lawyer, but a fairly decent guy. His first wife was a brilliant girl, quite a beauty too, and a wit, and then last year something happened to her mind. She changed completely, quiet and withdrawn, but when Bob asked her to see a psychiatrist she took a taxi up the Hudson River Drive instead and jumped off the George Washington Bridge."

"She *killed* herself?" I was shocked.

"Yep"—and he turned to Lisa, kidding her—"In your cups again, lady?"—while I stared after the lawyer, fascinated by his intimacy with disaster, his fast recovery, his insouciance, wishing I could run after him, could grip his elbow and swing him around and demand, "But why? How *could* she? Why would *anyone* do a thing like *that?*"

Some time later—ten minutes? an hour? time, too, was out of whack—Milton Cohn arose from the sedan chair and crossed the room to where we sat, pushing Roger along ahead of him like a tugboat shoving a steamer, the contrast in their heights making one a midget, one a giant. Reminded of the midget Roger had wrestled two months before, I studied Roger's face now, as he approached, to see if his mask might be slipping tonight as it had so drastically that other time, but no, as usual it was securely in place, so handsome, so confident, so magnetically masculine above his enormous shoulders that I felt bashful as he sat next to us on the floor, felt as shy, for a moment, as any of his juvenile admirers might feel. "Hi, kiddo," he said, and my shyness receded, leaving only the sensation—often experienced before but never, before tonight, so intensely—of being both participant and spectator, involved but uninvolved.

Milton Cohn called the company to silence and, standing above us with Napoleonic stance and stature, began his speech about the guest of honor . . .

"We got The Martian to fly in on us here a while, folks, in between his interplanetary duties, and I guess you who ain't seen him for twenty years or so have gotta admit time ain't done nothin' to our boy but broaden a biceps or two."

" 'Our boy,' " Ed whispered in my ear. "Rog must love

that." Then he added, "Bet a quarter we'll be hearing Shakespeare before the clock chimes twelve?" He repeated his bet in Lisa's ear and she smothered a chuckle in his shoulder, for we had told her of the ironic extremes in our host's mentality: the worship of the buck, the vulgarity, the insensitivity, and mixed with it like diamonds in the mud, the love of all things Shakespearean, and his elephant-memory for passages many a fine scholar would find obscure.

The audience, consisting primarily of his comic-book staff's upper echelon, sat scattered in the splendor of the traditional décor while Milton spoke of the search in 1934 for "a very special human being" who could bring their "fabulous new character to life," the first fabulous adventure hero for the kids to be born, he said, since Robin Hood. "No adventure character since," he said, "has amounted to anything more than a pale imitation of the great, the bold, the original concept of The Man from Mars who is invulnerable, fantastic, fabulous, a folk hero for the children of America to cling to as an emblem of strength, justice—"

"The children of America, Christ!" Roger said, and he made no attempt to keep his voice low; he too, like Lisa, had been drinking heavily. "Pretty soon he'll be dragging in God, mothers and the Virgin Birth."

Milton Cohn glanced down at him, frowned, then continued in a more realistic vein about the financial aspect of The Martian, sweeping his hand in as all-embracing an arc as his short fat arm was capable of, as if to illustrate by the lavish surroundings just exactly what The Martian had meant to him. But I was not hearing him now, nor was I hearing any more of Roger's derogatory mutterings, for I was remembering the previous week, when I had gone with Rog and Ed and Lisa to see the children of Drake City. . . .

When Ed and I had arrived at their apartment to pick them up for the trip to New Jersey, Lisa had just finished zipping up the back of his Martian costume. As she attached his antenna to his head I heard him say almost

96

to himself, "I hope I get through it okay." He looked grim.

"Is it Cohn that's bothering him?" I asked Lisa while Rog and Ed preceded us to the elevator. "Does he resent his turning this jaunt into a publicity thing?" Milton had heard that Roger would be visiting the Drake City Home for Crippled Children and, immediately, typically, he had horned in on it, hoping somehow to circumvent Ed's refusal to allow exploitation of his client's sincere altruism.

Lisa had replied that no, much as Roger disliked the idea of Cohn's meeting us there, it was something else he dreaded much more; he dreaded the visit itself. I asked why he did it, then—why, for that matter, he was always doing things like this, charity appearances for unfortunate youngsters—for through all the years this was one facet of him I had never understood. Why did he continue to do something he seemed to loathe? Had Lisa discovered the reason?

"He feels he has to," she said.

"Has to?"

"That's all he'll tell me. That he feels some kind of an obligation. Maybe he—what's that word my analyst loves? —identifies with them."

"With whom?"

"Well, I don't know, maybe with anybody who's . . . well . . . small and hurt."

Get through it okay? He managed—strutting through the wards, laughing, greeting, tossing the tinier ones up in the air, braces and all—he managed to get through the first part of the afternoon, traveling from bed to bed and wheelchair to wheelchair, followed by an entourage of doctors, nurses, Milton, photographer, us, and, finally, feebly, the few less-handicapped children who could limp or hobble or hop along in his wake. He chatted with each patient a moment, presenting *The Martian Comic Book* and *The Martian Coloring Set*. A toddler on crutches, too young to recognize him, wept when he came near, but most smiled shyly, or laughed in delight, while others, overcome with awe, turned their faces sidewards against their pillows or peeked out from the hiding-places their outstretched fingers made.

And then Roger came to a freckled boy whose twisted legs were tugged above him into the therapeutic agony of traction. The child grinned as his hero kidded him with "Howsa boy? Want to enter the freckle contest?" ruffling the curly head in his huge hand. But suddenly the boy grabbed the huge hand and buried his face in it and then, when his face emerged, the grin was gone and tears fell like a cloudburst down his cheeks. Clinging to Roger's hand he began to kiss it, kissing it all over with feverishly intense little kisses of faith and adulation, saying, "Straighten my legs, please, straighten them, please, please . . ."

Quickly a nurse hurried to interrupt the scene. "Pete," she said, "stop that this second. Now you just let go of him, do you hear? You know The Martian can't—"

But the boy began to scream, "He *can!* He *can!* You are The Martian, ain't you, mister? You *can* do it, can't you? You're magic, you can do *anything, anything,* I've seen you do things no one else can do, I watched you on television bend a crowbar crooked, *oh please, bend my legs straight, please please you know you can do it, please please—*"

The tableau was irresistible to Mr. Cohn and his photographer; they glanced at each other, nodded with imperceptible glee, and then the flash bulb went off, catching the crying child with his lips to The Martian's hand, catching the image of overwhelming homage, leaving out the frantic, pleading screams and the look of anguished futility on Roger's face.

In the same motion with which he pulled his hand from the child's grasp, Roger swung at the camera, knocking it to the floor. Then he walked away from the boy, away from us all, kept walking down through the long ward, from hopeless case to hopeless case, until—turning with a final wave of his hand in the far doorway and calling his traditional "The magic . . . magnificent . . . *Martian!*"—he whirled out into the corridor and then out

98

onto the brown winter grass, where we found him retching violently, his sequins sparkling in the late afternoon sun.

And we drove home, the four of us, without conversation, Roger hunched silent inside himself and speaking only once, when he mumbled, "Oh Christ, oh Christ." Then, looking out at the billboards and the oil tanks and the Jersey blur of houses all identical as graves, he said: "Oh Christ but it's ugly, it's all so fuggin' ugly."

And now our host seemed to have divined my thoughts, for he was speaking of Drake City and of The Martian's appearance there; it was clear that he had banished the camera incident from his memory. Around the room the restiveness of his guests was apparent in the increasing clinking of glasses, but he spoke on, standing there under the high ceiling with its center skylight, one hand on the balcony's Doric pillar and the other holding the cigar which he tapped into an ashtray held for him by Frank Tibasi. Frank was known as our host's best friend, bodyguard, private secretary, court jester; it was also known that three decades ago, before *The Martian* and its accompanying money and prestige, Frank had done his master some service which was shrouded in mystery but which—rumor had it—involved an illegality which had cast Mr. Cohn into irrevocable debt to his right-hand man.

"Well, you shoulda seen those kids!" Milton was ecstatic. "At first they couldn't believe their eyes. Then they realized it was really The Martian himself in the flesh and their faces lit up and the ones that could move came crowdin' around just to *touch* him, y'know, like he was *God* or somethin' . . . I tell you, folks, they can talk about cowboy stars and Superman and all them supposed bigmoney boys, but I'm tellin' you The Martian's still the hottest property in the juvenile field, bar none. Yessir"—he used his cigar to point down at Roger—"yessir, after all these years our boy here outranks 'em all. So, folks, how about a toast to our boy with the Midas touch?"

Only Ed, Lisa and I recognized the glitter of cynicism in Roger's eyes as he raised his glass to respond to the raised glasses of Mr. Cohn and his guests; the others saw only the charming smile, and his quiet voice matched his smile as he rose and said, "You're too modest, mine host. What about *your* contribution to the hospital? May I tell the good people about your gift to Drake City?" Milton looked appropriately modest and pleased as Roger, weaving slightly as he stood above the three of us, continued, "I'd like all you friends of our host to know that the several thousand this fine philanthropist gave to the hospital was—" he paused—"tax-deductible." He sat down.

A few people snickered; Milton Cohn did not. But it was moments like this for which Frank Tibasi was ever-ready, and he said now, "Say, boss, how about a bit of the Bard?"

I anticipated the poke of Ed's elbow before it reached my ribs, and then I heard him whisper to Roger, "The soul of a poet, our host," but Roger was busy beckoning a waiter for yet another drink.

It came in the order in which I had heard it before, a fragment of *Hamlet,* then some *Othello,* and then came a crash which shattered me out of my detachment and the others out of their bored lethargy. It was a noise out of nowhere—my heart banged with the abruptness of it— and then, when the glass fell all around us, I thought the chandelier had fallen. But looking up where the others were looking, I realized that where most rooms have chandeliers this one had a skylight, and that it now winked a big black jagged night-eye down from the hole which had been broken in the glass. Something, I saw now, had hurtled through it and dropped directly between Roger and our host, for they were both bending to pick it up. I felt the guests pressing behind me to see the rock that Roger held in his hands: a rock the size and shape of a head, with something painted on its smooth surface. A picture—I saw it now—a picture of The Martian, a perfectly proportioned likeness about five inches tall, its costume done in the vivid colors we all knew so well and the familiar face painted in complete correctness of detail as only a professional artist could have done it.

"My God," Milton muttered, staring at it as at an apparition. "It must be—"

"What?" Roger said. "What do you make of it?"

"So *that's* it," the little man said. "Well, I'll be damned. The notes, the calls, now this."

"You get threats too?" Roger asked. Mr. Cohn nodded. "So do I. Lisa, too. and the Thompsons here."

But Milton just stared at the painted rock, repeating, "I'll be damned, well, I'll be damned." And then: "So *that's* who it is."

He looked up at the hole in the skylight, then down again at the rock. There was silence in the room, suspense, trepidation, but this time I did not even listen for the sparrows, did not remember or, remembering, did not care, for I was back—involved again, curious, a *part*— and with my nebulous re-entry into the world of yes-of-course ("yes, of course"—a smile, a shrug—"we do exist") I noticed that the four of us, I, Lisa, Roger, Ed, were holding hands like children playing Farmer-in-the-Dell, like children interrupted in their game.

And then, glancing around at us dazedly out of his jowled and shock-pale face, our host spoke the name we all stood hushed to hear. "Matty Atkins," he said, and his cigar shook in his hand. "Matty Atkins, I'll be damned."

NINE

"HE NEVER belonged at Acme Comics in the first place," Roger said. "Matty Atkins was a real artist, real artists can't turn hack"—his mouth twisted bitterly and I realized he was speaking not just of Matty—"it makes them sick inside."

I could see the partial reflection of Ed's pajamaed back as he sat with Roger at the bar outside Lisa's bedroom door—the bar which semicircled across a corner of her apartment's entrance hall, on one side of it the door leading to the kitchen, and on the other side the living room with its Oriental furnishings stark and low-slung amidst the tasteful accumulation of tapestries, silk screens, jade vases, carved teak Mandarin lamps.

Ed said, "And he seemed okay in those days? Not schiz a bit?" Stop it! I thought. Don't use that word! (three girls, oh no, old man, oh no, not me.)

"Who's to say?" I saw in the glass the shrug of Roger's big square shoulder. "Maybe he knows exactly what he's doing. I wish to hell, though, that we'd been able to catch him before he climbed down."

Climbed down, he meant, from Mr. Cohn's terraced rooftop, for we had all recovered in a moment from the surprise of the sudden crash, the falling rock, and had rushed up to the duplex's balcony and out the French doors to the cold night air and the smashed skylight. No one, silence, solitude, just a big ball of a moon balanced on the seal's nose of a skyscraper—but then Ed, peering across the few feet to the adjoining building, had pointed down at the fire escape which ivy-vined its angular pattern down the brick. *"There he goes!"* Ed had shouted, and we all—Roger, Lisa, Milton, the others—surged to the wall to see the small figure scurry down the final length of ladder to the alley below, seeming smaller than a small boy from our viewpoint high above, but sending a long shadow across the sidewalk as he ran to the streetlight-bright avenue and then vanished quickly from sight.

"I still say we should call in the police," Ed said now.

"Ha. Just try convincing Cohn of that."

"What the hell's he hiding? Tibasi knows, that's obvious."

We had returned here to Lisa and Roger's place as the party had ended in haste and confusion for all but the four of us who, being the victimized, had stayed on a moment to discuss Matty with the fifth victim, our host. Sometimes lately, as now, Ed and I had taken to sleeping here at our friends' mid-Manhattan apartment while a babysitter spent the night with our sons in Cedarton. The parties were constant—I saw in the mirror the traces of exhaustion on my face—and I said now to Lisa, "I grow old, I grow old, I wear the bottoms of my eye-bags rolled," to which, surprisingly, she replied, "Do you dare to eat a peach?" No, not surprising anymore, I realized, for if I found her now acquainted with Eliot's Prufrock, it was only an additional dividend on the recent pleasure of discovering her intense preoccupation with improving herself. In this, as in her tender attention to the perfection of her flesh, form, hair, eyes, clothes, she shamed me, for she went at it with an ardor and list-making thoroughness almost amusing to those who, like myself, had never known the hunger pangs of cultural deprivation. Spinoza was on her *S* list, and Shelley and Saint-Saëns, and I did not know now—still don't know, now that she's garnered her world-wide reputation for a profundity annoyingly superfluous in one so exquisite to look upon—whether she saw her self-taught seminar as a springboard to true intellectuality or only as a more laborious cosmetic. "Look at Ingrid Bergman," she often said. *"That's beauty,* the kind that *counts,* that *lasts,* the kind that shines out *through* the face from *inside,* comes radiating out from a cultivated mind, *that's* beauty." Usually, when she admired a member of her species—actress, fashion model, society woman —her comment would be "There's class" or "There's quality"; for the number of times that she implied I myself had this nebulous asset, there was an equal number of times when she bewailed my laziness and my perversity, bewailed my frittering away of my "potential" via rounded heels and droopy skirts and mashed potatoes mountained high and cratered deep with gravy. "Flat-chested eggheads," she had labeled my kind in her harangue earlier in the evening, but she was wrong on both counts, as wrong on the latter count as Ed was when he boasted of my brilliance to all and sundry, for my literacy existed almost solely on the tip of my tongue. Ah, yes, I might label him in moments of marital disharmony a "low-brow," but I knew in my heart how I stood: my brain lay like a vast tract of half-developed real estate, abandoned except for a model house or two, and these I displayed as my hearth and home, while I lived on the sly in a tree.

"No one at Acme ever really got to know Matty,"

Roger was saying. "But one cartoonist had been over to his place for something and Cohn told me this guy said he'd never seen canvases like that. Crazy shapes, colors, but with a terrific impact. Put all his emotions into his paintings, I guess—at least from the little I saw of him he seemed like a gentle little fella, sort of screwy but pleasant."

"Can you think of any reason why he—" and Ed and Rog went on discussing it, and Lisa went on brushing her hair, but I was remembering the previous discussion, back at Milton's penthouse, where we had sobered up on coffee served in mugs on which The Martian, arched for flight, was emblazoned in solid gold. . . .

Our host had been the only one on the defensive, and rightly so (Ed said later) for what did anyone but him have to feel guilty about? Had *we* purchased the idea of The Martian for a piddling sum and made millions from it, relegating its originator to a measly salary, no percentage of the profits, and, ultimately, the ash can? Hell no, Ed had said, and granted we were all eating mighty high off the hog thanks to somebody else's bright idea, still, it was only in Matty Atkins' twisted mind that, sharing the benefits of his creation, we shared also some illogical blame.

"A grubby, money-hungry little maniac," Cohn had stormed. "Okay, granted The Martian was his baby—granted he deserved an initial payment—which he got, five hundred dollars, a helluva fair chunk, believe me, seeing as how in those days a buck was worth ten *times* as much, and he'd never had a penny in his life before, and he was goddamn lucky and he knew it, too, to sell that idea to me when nobody else, but *no*body, would buy it. I had the brains to recognize a fabulous plot gimmick when I saw one—and he'd had the brains to think it up—and he got paid and that coulda been that, legally I coulda told him to clear out then and there, but no, I'm a softhearted guy, I seen he had a wife and kid and outa the goodness of my heart I gave him a steady job—let him keep on with his baby, plot it out, draw it—and he got

104

a nice salary for that, too, but was the grasping little creep satisfied? Not him, he had to go and *sue*—well hell, okay, so he had his stupid lawsuit and he lost it, fair and square, all rights belonged to me and it was legal, and after that he was out on his ear dead broke and about time, too, about time I got rid of that ungrateful little hanger-on with his sniveling demands and his lousy blackmailing—"

"Blackmailing?" Roger had interrupted. "How could anybody blackmail *you*, Milton sweetheart, you're pure as a fuggin' *lily*, ain't you?"—and none of us had missed the quick glance which shot back and forth between Milton and Frank Tibasi before Roger continued, "You don't want to let the police in on the case, right, Milton? Supposedly you don't want the good name of The Martian smeared all over the tabloids, right? Any other reason you like steering clear of the law, huh, Milton? Huh?"

"Matty's a nut," Milton blustered. "He's a nut but he ain't dangerous. We don't need no cops. He don't scare me."

"*Any* cops," Roger said. "*Doesn't* scare you."

But Milton paid no heed to this correction, muttering as he handed his empty glass to Frank Tibasi, "All the psychos *I* get. That guy who created Superman, I met him, he's a doll, happy, satisfied, him and them guys who do Batman and Buck Rogers, they're dolls, why don't *I* get the dolls"—he glared at Roger; "tax-deductible," clearly, would long rankle—"Why in the name of God do *I* get stuck with every creep that ever crawled out from under a wet rock?"

Roger's tone was sanctimonious, his face saintly. "Ah," he intoned solemnly, "we each get what we deserve in this world."

"Yeah," Cohn raised the glass which Frank had leaped to refill. "Yeah, Rutherford baby, I'll drink to that. May you get yours, and soon."

Ed and Roger had gone down the five steps from balcony foyer to living room. Entering their living room was like "falling into Japan," Ed had said to me after our first visit here the month before, and I wondered now if any of my father's parishioners had teak or jade or ivory about, whether, to them, this apartment might not be as foreign-seeming as it was to me.

"Might make a good item," I heard Ed say. " 'Roger Rutherford is being menaced by a maniacal character straight out of one of his own TV scripts—' "

From Roger—"Try Parsons. Hopper wouldn't touch me with a ten-foot pole since you fed her that exclusive that wasn't no exclusive."

"I told you, Rog boy, my leg man goofed—"

—in what Hiroshima hovel were they now performing acts of mercy while their prodigal daughter sat around in the Opulent Love Nest of Naughty Show Biz Folk, divided by far more than seas and continents from the way of life they'd chosen for themselves? They? No, he. And chosen? No, *been* chosen, not by A Call from the Lord (as he claimed; not just claimed, believed) but by A Necessity of the Id, hooked on Service for his self-survival as another might devote himself to Business or to Baseball or to Dope.

"—sick of it," Lisa said.

"What?"

"All right, so Matty Atkins hates our guts. Okay, so we keep our fingers crossed he's all bark and no bite. We've been talking of nothing else for eight straight hours." She sighed, red chiffon rising, falling; everything in her room was red—walls, bedspread, carpeting, even the row of tiny carved-wood animals that marched between the mirror and her busy hands. "Tell me more about your sister. What's she like?"

"Like me, only more so."

"I hope I can meet her someday."

"Oh, you'll doubtless bump into her the next time you're in Bend, Oregon."

"Doubtless." She smiled at me in the mirror, then returned to her bedtime ritual. As she applied the exotic array of creams and lotions to her face—her fingers darting about the vanity top from jar to jar, from cotton puff to oily cloth, practiced, professional, putting to shame the two-second splashing of soap and water which passed for

106

my nightly beauty treatment—I thought of my sister and of her silent physician, reticent, reserved, who fled the agony of his profession's demands for a gregarious nature to communicate with creatures of water and wilderness, and whose trout and venison she cooked, whose beer she brewed and bread she baked, whose bed she kept warm through nights when birth or illness called him into the little homes of loggermen along the Columbia River, a community he served not as his father-in-law served his, but out of another belief: that civilization was hideous, that to live as his ancestors had lived was to exorcise from his awareness the outcome of their dream, that a return to family life sufficient unto itself was more than a denunciation of progress and a shunning of its group values but was somehow a small contribution to a non-existent archive. *Time? 1958. Place? America. Fact? Human unit—man, woman, children—educated, atheistic, lived solitary on twenty acres with brook, pond, forest, garden, orchard, cow, horse, chickens, rabbits, pigs, books, records, chess set. Historical effect? None. Personal effect? Maybe happiness.*

"—saw Milton Tuesday at the Copa," Ed said.

"Drunk as the proverbial skunk?"

"Natch—"

—and of course it was true what Lisa had said in her liquor-lucid analysis of my past at age eighteen: I *had* been among the saddle-shoed throng who spewed out of the chapel dors and down Main Street to the little old drug store, had indeed eaten English muffins spread sickening-sweet with raspberry jam, and although in my college town whipped cream in hot chocolate was less popular than marshmallow in cocoa, still it was true that as we hurried back up to campus for the first class of the day we *did* giggle at the village idiot we passed on the way, *did* flirt with the handsome lad of little brain who tooted by us driving the town's one dilapidated taxi, *did* bring a gap-toothed grin of pleased obsequiousness to the sexton's face as we greeted him with a patronizing chorus of "Good Morning, Pauls" and he stopped his sweeping of the dormitory steps to say, with his whistled *S* which never failed to make us giggle, "G'mornin', girls." But she was wrong, Lisa, about the cashmere sweater; that I had not owned; daughters of the clergy know not of cashmere, but I got by, I was trim and skied well and dated much and only occasionally baffled my comrades by the unpredictable moods which drew me from the campus to the mountaintop towering above the town, there to pen verses and hate death and wonder who I was and how and why—and if at such a moment the chapel bells cascaded up the hillside to prickle my skin with the chimes of my childhood, echoing across the pine-wooded peaks which blurred pale green against the horizon like a watercolor that had been touched before it had dried, then I would find myself suddenly bent over as if in pain, crippled for a minute by the sound of the bells and the sight of a sky containing no angels, crippled by a grief so intense it made me cry aloud: "Oh God! Oh God!"

And then, one late May day, I arrived home in Hartford for summer vacation and found a stranger standing on the station platform dressed in high-heeled shoes and lipstick, and with a bosom she had not possessed on my previous holiday home at Christmastime. It was my sister; she had grown up—gone the baby fat, gone the five-year difference in our ages—and by the time the sun went down on our impassioned dialogue that day I knew that I was no longer alone, that from now on my mountaintop moods would be letter-writing moods, and that whatever I wrote her she would understand, and that whatever she answered I would understand, and that our parents had produced a most joyous rarity: twins, identical twins of the spirit—our blood, our cells, our genes all arranged somehow in the two separate sperms of our father, the two separate eggs of our mother, to result in this remarkable rapport.

Oh, we had a brother—he was off in the Army somewhere; a war was on—but all I recalled of him was the amazing shade of pink his face would turn whenever he lost his temper, which, it seemed to me in retrospect, was often.

"I never knew you had a brother," Lisa said. "How come in all these heart-to-hearts we've been having you never mentioned him before?"

"He never comes to mind"—but now he did, filling it with the sound of sparrow wings, and Lisa was talking beside me and Ed and Roger too in the other room but I stood up, arm across my face to defend myself—from what? from what?—and Matty would hurt me, I was guilty and he would hurt me—and the little red radio was on—"get the news," she said—but instead the radio blared organ music, it filled the red bedroom with a terrible sound, sparrows and horror and hymns—

"What's the matter?"—she said looking up, puzzled.

"Hate it," I said.

"What?"

"That."

"What?"

"Organ music."

"Oh." She switched it off. She looked at her watch. "Well, it's ten to three."

Three! Three tonight must be the magic number. I called quickly, "Ed, it's almost three." Must sleep, must *sleep*.

Understanding, he came to me, and when we were in bed and the ritual complete—pill, light, door—he said, "Okay?" and put his hand on my tummy, on his child. I felt the fear disappear and I breathed deeply and pressed my hand on his above the place where our baby was beginning to *look* like a baby; smiling now, love-filled, I pictured it curled up tight like a funny little grilled fist, its fingers folded across its inch of a chest like—I suddenly thought—a miniature corpse in its coffin. *No!* "Ed!" I said, and he hugged me to him, but this time the fear flooded me completely, for it was three and I must sleep. And, having slept, I must awake. Must awake in the morning and be *me*.

Awaking, checking on my identity by identifying each object around me—chair, desk, window, bureau—I saw again the ivory Buddha that had been the last thing I'd noticed last night before I sank into sleep. Yes, now I remembered, I had dreamed of it, not of this Buddha but of the other, the other that had dwarfed my parents in the picture postcard they had sent from a place called Kyoto. What had happened in the dream? Someone had been afraid—who? they of the Buddha? the Buddha of them?—but I couldn't remember. So, putting my nightmare away somewhere (somewhere? where in the brain is somewhere?) I thought of my parents prior to Japan, remembered the day of my marriage, which was the same day Mahatma Gandhi died. . . .

"Russell. Come out now. You *must* snap out of it." My mother had spoken with her forehead to the closed door, rattling the doorknob slightly, her voice muted in the hope that my sister and I might not hear her, which we did, nonetheless, standing hands together in our room with the bridal and bridesmaid gowns gossamer white and yellow on their hangers and the newly arrived bouquets boxed in tissue on our beds. We could hear our father sobbing in his study down the hall.

"Russell. Let me in. Let me *in*, dear." Then after a moment: "*Listen* to me, Russell. You *must* control yourself. Think of Janie, dear. Can't you please *try* to think of Janie? Russell—pull yourself together—it's her *wedding* day."

But now instead of sobs there was a silence. Our mother must have felt this was a good sign, for her voice took on a lilting tone, optimistic, sounding against his silence like a Good Humor truck's bell tinkling outside a funeral, and she said, "Get ready now, dear, all right? The girls are dressing and the guests will be arriving soon."

But my sister and I, still holding hands, glanced down the hall in time to see him fling open his door so quickly that our mother staggered back as if struck, but this time he did not hit her, only stood tall and tear-streaked with his fine Christ face, stood there looking at her as if she were a bug, and yet through her too, as if she were not there at all.

I didn't care. I told my sister so. "I don't care"—loud,

so he'd hear it, which he did, jerking a bit as if coming out
of a trance—and mother said with great gaiety, implying
another crisis safely past the crest, "My goodness, all this
fuss about that little old man in diapers way over there in
India, why my goodness—it's a shame, of course—girls?
don't you agree? it's simply *ter*rible that somebody killed
such a . . . a . . . *good* man . . . you know how your father
admired him"—she turned again to him—"but gracious
sakes, dear, I should think on your own daughter's wedding day you could—" but now he did touch her, just a
little—twisted her arm until she cried out, then let go
and said, "All right, all right"—and it *was* all right, with
everyone saying later what a lovely wedding, what a lovely
bride, and didn't it give you a lump in your throat to
watch those two tears slide down out of Reverend Winslow's eyes as he conducted that beautiful service? A wonderful man. A wonderful family. God bless this happy
home.

Ed, Roger and Lisa had left the apartment, each bound
for some noon appointment, and I was alone, sitting up
in bed as I wrote a letter to Japan. "Feeling fine," I told
my parents—they had not been told of my hospital session—"Lots of parties, lots of fun"—and then just a small
warm gush of something beneath me, and before I felt
the wetness or saw the spreading stain across the sheet, I
heard someone say: "Well, there it goes." Then the same
strange voice, belonging not to me but coming from my
mouth, added softly, "Here it comes."

TEN

THERE it goes.
Or maybe not? "It is," said the New York obstetrician,
"in large part up to you now."
My responsibility? *Mine?* No. No. (Here it comes.)
Perhaps all was not lost, he said. The water had burst,

111

yes, and there was intermittent bleeding; still, in a fair percentage of these cases the uterus had been known to heal itself, and his examinations showed that the fetus remained in the correct place and position. The blood showed no trace so far of embryonic tissue—that was a hopeful sign. How hopeful? Hopeful enough to try, he said, although he was making no promises. These things could go one way or the other. If I could lie immobile, well then . . . we would see . . .

Calm. I was calm. It was as if all my nerves, dispensing with their preliminary skirmish, had ganged up together to go into hiding, like gremlins, leaving my body so inert as they secretly planned their all-out offensive that even more than in the former days of my complacency I was at peace, at peace in mind and in muscle, in a peace imposed by absolute necessity: to let go now, to move, to stir, even to *think,* would be to . . . to . . . kill.

Here it comes. (No, calm, calm.) But here it *comes*.

When Roger arrived at the Manhattan hospital on the second day of my three-day stay, the nurses were a-twitter like a flock of small white birds around a peacock— and oh, how he did strut, my euphoric visitor, feeling, as he said, "so fond of myself today I suspect I really *am* superhuman," and proving his self-satisfaction, indeed, by the graciousness with which he gave his autograph to the suddenly dutiful attendants who found now a succession of essential tasks needing their immediate attention in my room. Soon children, too, began to pile up in a neck-craning group outside the door, for the word had filtered across the floor to their wing of the hospital, and those that could walk had hurried to catch a glimpse of their hero. "Pied Piper," I teased him, but he was busy answering questions from the hall—where was his costume today, where his sword, without it could he just appear on the ground floor or would he be taking the elevator down like ordinary people.

"Trade secrets, kids"—laughing, walking back and forth from wall to wall, his five strides in each direction making my claustrophobic cubicle seem tinier still.

112

Micronite filter.
Mild, smooth taste.
For all the right reasons.
Kent.

America's quality cigarette.
King Size or Deluxe 100's.

Micronite filter.
Mild, smooth taste.
For all the right reasons.
Kent.

Regular or Menthol.

Kings: 17 mg. "tar,"
1.1 mg. nicotine;
100's: 19 mg. "tar,"
1.3 mg. nicotine;
Menthol: 19 mg. "tar,"
1.3 mg. nicotine
av. per cigarette,
FTC Report Aug. '72.

Warning: The Surgeon General Has Determined
That Cigarette Smoking Is Dangerous to Your Health.

"You're like a lion in a cage," I said. "Do shut the door. I feel like I'm in the zoo."

Complying, he administered several more pats to small awed heads, squeezes to small shoulders, a gay farewell to adulatory ears—"Now you just get well quick, you kids, that's orders direct from The Martian"—and sat down next to my bed in our sudden privacy. I said, "Well, why so manic?"

"Today is a red-letter day, that's why, my lass. I woke up this morning and flexed my massive chest in the mirror and there atop my neck I saw this face, this face of The Martian I'm stuck with, and suddenly the thought came to me: why stuck with? Must one in this day and age be stuck with one's face? No! So you see? A way out at last. God!"—he rose again and resumed his lion's pacing—"Why hasn't it ever occurred to me before?"

"Why hasn't *what* oc—"

"Plastic surgery! A new face! A new start! A brand-new career, start from scratch. Ha! Screw the reruns!"

Reruns, he explained to me for the fiftieth time, were the taped films of The Martian program which were shown repeatedly on television after the original series was concluded. It was this procedure that deprived him of work. "Every day at five o'clock I'm The Martian and so, as far as any other TV jobs are concerned, I'm poison." It wouldn't be quite so bad, he said, if he could at least be taping new series; at least he'd be busy, be acting, even if it was in a role he had come to detest. But this way his job was done, and although each time the series reappeared he received his residual payment and therefore had no money problems, still, he had nothing to *do,* unless, of course, he said, he were to quit acting and go into some other business, "and that, for me," he said, "would be like you, Janie, retiring from motherhood."

(Here it comes.)

Movies, of course, were out. No, it was TV or nothing, and he was poison. "Ah, screw it, screw 'em all," he said —pacing, pacing. "I'll start from scratch. I'll do the whole bit—little theater, summer stock, Broadway bit parts—until I get back my sea legs. Jesus, Janie, I've been

113

stranded on the dry land of one lousy role for so long I feel really shaky now that I'm about to get back in the swim. Shaky but free. *Free!*"

His exuberance matched my calm; it was as extreme, as inappropriate. I said, "What does Lisa think of it?"

"Oh, she was asleep when I left the apartment, exhausted from all our partying. But just wait till I tell her there's a gate in this prison wall after all, a gate I never noticed before. Me at a dead end? Me washed up? Ha! Wait till I tell her. A new face, Lisa baby, a new life—new new!"

"New pan, new man, huh?"—but he was not listening to flippant remarks, not reacting to sarcasm, did not care, either, that life and death were battling for a one-fourth finished child inside my womb.

"I love that girl, you know that, Janie? I think I'll marry her."

"Oh?" That's all I said, for he did not know I knew now who he was, did not know what Lisa had said the day before, sitting beside my bed . . .

. . . with her garish hair wound around and around into a complex nest on the top of her head. She had penciled a black beauty mark beside her dimple; it emphasized the planned pallor of her face, the cheeks creamed and powdered to perfection, the eyes not just green-irised but green-rimmed, green-lidded. Queen Nefertiti, death mask, death.

Here it comes.

"He'll never marry me," she said. "He'll never marry anybody and neither will I."

Calm. Calm. Don't move, don't stir. It all depends on me.

"This isn't the first time I've been nuts about someone and it won't be the last. You know my reputation, you knew all about it before you ever met me, so did everybody else who ever read a gossip column. Errol Flynn—he just happened to be one that got found out about. Hell, Janie, I'm twenty-two and I'm an old whore."

"Lisa, no—"

"Oh, I'm a *nice* whore. I mean I've got a good brain and I'm a real warm swell honest frank indi*vid*ual, sure, and I'm a pretty fair actress, too, but all the same I've fallen in and out of too many beds for the past half-a-dozen years to have any illusions about my qualifications for a long white bridal veil." She took out a cigarette, tapped it on my forehead and then smiled back at my smile as she struck a match. "Aw Christ, why do I tell you these things. You're too good a listener, you know that? Confidences come to you like to a magnet." She inhaled deeply, then bent her head back, the whole ornate red weight of it; I waited, watching the smoke rise from the taut white pearl-choked throat. "They're rarer than you think, good listeners. I mean ones who really *hear*, comprehend it and register it and file it away for digestion."

"Tell me about Roger."

"What don't you already know? How he swings?"

"You say he'll never marry. Why?"

"Because his mother was a bitch on wheels, that's why. And because his father left him and never came back and because none of his stepdaddies was any Father Christmas either."

"He never told me. Could you? Would he mind?"

"Well, when's visiting hours over?"

"Four-thirty."

She glanced at her watch. "That gives us time."

When he was nine, at boarding school, he saw a father hugging his son. It was the start of Easter vacation and everybody else had a place to go. When he saw the man hugging his son he backed up into the john so they wouldn't see him watching. Then, when they left, he fell down on the floor. He didn't expect to, but since he was down there anyway he stayed there a while, his cold face against the cold tiles, curled up in a ball to warm himself. Tevelman the sexton had turned up the dorm heat too high as usual and it was much too hot, so there was no reason really for him to feel so cold, all goose-pimply, just as there had been no reason at all for his knees to go limp and collapse him down that way. In a few minutes he got up—his knees locked again all right—and went down to the reception room to watch some more hugging before everyone went away. Then he was alone in the dorm, but during the holiday he slept down in Mr. Glover's apartment. Mr. Glover didn't have any place to go either because he was old and a widower and all he cared about was ancient history and chess.

"Where's your mother?" Mr. Glover asked him one day while he was learning chess from him.

"Who?"

"Your mother."

"Oh, Edythe. She's in Italy on her honeymoon." He remembered that a few years before, when she'd been on one of her other honeymoons, he'd imagined that it was something sort of holey and sticky like a honeycomb but also sort of round and white like a moon. He took a peek now at Glover to see if he looked funny the way people did sometimes when they mentioned his mother, as if they were trying to hide how sorry they felt for him, but Glover was just pulling at his mustache and squinting at his bishop.

The memory he had of falling down in the john and then playing chess with Glover was tied together in his brain with something else that always made him very ashamed to remember because it was so stupid. He'd stolen a king and a queen and a pawn after the game that day and had put them in his bed. That night they lay there next to him as he slept, silent and ivory-white and close together. He even remembered how, when he put his head on the pillow and turned sidewards to face them, the dent he made put them on a slant so that he had to make another hollow to keep them from toppling down on him. It was really stupid and he returned them the next morning before Glover could discover they were missing.

It was stupid, the whole thing was stupid, but he still remembered how pretty they were, the three of them there.

116

"When do you think you can go home?" Roger asked me. He was at the door, his head grazing the top of it.

"Tomorrow, probably. Ed'll drive me—carefully—no bumping."

"Baby may be okay after all, huh?"

"Hope so"—and he blew a kiss to me as he turned to leave and, motionless, I smiled: I had a week to go and he had half a year.

When he was ten he spent the summer with Edythe and with Manson Biggs, who was her husband then. They'd taken a place at Newport. He spent a lot of time alone; Edythe and Manson were mostly out on yachts with people. Once, though, one Saturday when it was Manson's turn to have his daughter for the weekend because his ex-wife had flown to Palm Springs for a party, the four of them played croquet together, the two children and the two adults. It would have been fun if Manson and Edythe had tried a little harder, instead of only hitting the ball through a wicket or two before going to the summerhouse to "wet their whistles," as they said. Every time they came back they played a little worse. Finally, since it was threatening rain, they'd called it quits. He and the girl his age—her name was Pamela Biggs—ran into the summerhouse when the first drops fell. They searched for the whistles their parents had kept wetting, but all they found there on the green wicker table was an empty cut-glass pitcher and two matching glasses that smelled bad in the same way Manson smelled bad when he breathed in your face and Edythe too, sometimes. He remembered that when the cut glass was on the buffet with the sun shining through it, it had glittered like mica on rocks, but with a golden glint instead of silver. He and Pamela had nothing to do stuck there in the summerhouse while it rained, so they took off their shorts and underpants to compare their pee-ers.

"You don't have one," he said.

"I do too only it doesn't show like yours." And she didn't seem to mind when he tried to find where it was inside that funny-looking place that looked all bare and

117

empty like God forgot to finish it. The only other pee-er he'd seen besides his own and boys' at school was Edythe's once when he'd walked into her bedroom without knocking. But that hadn't looked so funny, probably because of the hair.

That night he was in bed, with the rain on the roof lulling him so that for a change he didn't feel wide-awake or a little frightened the way he usually did in the dark, when all of a sudden, just as his eyes were closing, the door opened. For a second he figured he *was* asleep and that this was a nightmare, for it didn't seem real, being pulled out of bed for no reason at all by Manson, whose nose and eyes and cheeks were even veinier-red than usual. But then he realized he was really awake and that he was being shaken so hard he thought his neck might crack. It didn't but his buttons did, popping right off his pajamas when Manson tore them off to toss him bare-naked back onto the bed. He drew his legs up and ducked his face down at the same time and rolled over like a snail so that the whiplashes landed mostly on his back, but they still hurt so much that, even though being almost asleep and then being so surprised had partly numbed him, he couldn't help crying out from the pain. The crying seemed to make Manson madder. "You dirty brat," he kept saying. "You dirty brat."

As soon as he was alone again he crawled back under the covers. The first thing he heard above the sound of his own whimpering was the voices outside his door. . . .

"*Really,* Manson, that's over*doing* it. Your *riding* whip. You could've *killed* him with that."

"Wish to hell I had. Should've castrated him with it, next best thing."

"A little boy his age doesn't realize—"

"Don't give me that shit, Edythe. He's not so goddamn little."

"Well anyway, Lilly Sue always exaggerates. I bet she took what Pamela told her and blew it all up when she told you just because she—"

"Do me a favor, Edythe. Don't bore me with all that domestic crap again. I married you, not your maid or

118

your damn brat in there, and it's bad enough this marriage is a mistake, now all I'm interested in is making damn sure my daughter can visit me without that little pervert thinking he can get away with—"

"Ha, listen to the lecture by the lecher! Listen to the lecture by the lush!"

Letcher. Kastraytid. Purvurt. Those words meant nothing but the others did, Manson's first ones: "Wish to hell I had."

No longer whimpering, he thought: I wish you had too. As soon as he thought it he knew it was true. But what he felt was too terrible; it was sort of opposite from crying, what he felt, as if even now that he was no longer curled up tight like a snail he felt as if he were. As if no matter how hard he tried he could never uncurl. Never uncurl and never cry. Never again.

"I wish you had," he said aloud. The lullaby of rain had stopped. He lay awake, making a hollow in the pillow next to his head and half remembering that something belonged there. He couldn't remember exactly what it was, though.

"Visiting hours are over, Miss Maurice," the nurse said. Behind her in the hall three other nurses took turns peering over her shoulder at Lisa, and when the nurse moved away several more bug-eyed strangers were revealed, convalescent patients who would tell their visitors next day, "She's just as beautiful off the screen, maybe even more so. Awful lot of make-up, but ... well, show business. Besides, you know she ... well ... all those others and now The Martian ... *you* know, naturally she can't look like a nun."

She bent to kiss my nose. "Take it easy, honey," and she walked to the door. Easy. Calm. In a second I would be alone again. Alone to think. It all depends on me. "Sorry if I talked your ear off, but you asked for it."

"I ate up every word."

"Happy digestion, dear. Be good now." Good. Bad. Wicked. Here it comes.

I almost weep a dozen times a day. When he awakes in the night, my littlest—and he always does, always has—there are three questions he asks, as ritualistic as everything else he does:

"Mommy, am I yours 'cause you borned me?"

"Mommy, will you still be here in the morning?"

"Mommy, are you real?"

Yes, I reply to the first, the second, yes again (as far as I know) to the third. And then, fading away from the side of my bed, fading away wraithlike into 3 A.M., he gives his invariable command: "Don't go to sleep."

No longer do I ask him why I mustn't. He has told me often, always the same. "You might not come back from your dream."

He knows about that; so do I.

But I do not weep. I lie awake and think the thoughts that make (perhaps) a book. And then, when daylight comes, I write them down.

Creation stops my ears now, not the Flents of yesteryear. How well I remember the way they felt, those silly Flents, the wax pellets spread within the nooks and crannies until not a sound could reach me from the no-more-cherished world. For months their slow insertion was my nightly ritual.

And now my ritual is concentration, with pen in hand instead of wax in ears. Deafness is achieved, the words appear and *voilà!* all I feel or felt or am is captured on the page.

One hour, one paragraph—can this be happiness? Am I not a madwoman still, scribbling, hunched and deaf, immersed, insane?

No, I am back—peculiar still, an inky fool, but back. I visit in that land now only by proxy.

Oh proxy in pajamas, oh small beloved proxy, hold my hand! You see? It's real.

It took us three hours to make the one-hour trip from New York City to Cedarton. As we drove slowly around the last curve in the road before our house came into view I felt a stab of absolute terror and then Ed said,

"There they are. There's the boys," and there they were, two of them, halfway up the sycamore tree in our front yard, Bruce and Johnny, perched still and solemn on the branch like a pair of owls, their round eyes looking across the lawn at little Terry who was crying inside a tangle of clothes-hanger wire, wire which—I saw now—was supposed to be an antenna, for his brothers too were hanger-headed, but correctly so, their wires coiled steady on their brows and spiraling up, festooned with strips of Reynolds Wrap in silver-sparkling imitation of The Martian. They had not seen us yet, and Bruce yelled to Terry, "Come here. Come over here and I'll help you."

"You come down," his little brother wept. "Come down, come down"—and Bruce lunged into a long leap, his makeshift sword sweeping up as he yelled, "To Mars," landing on the hard December ground like a cat and hurrying across the dead grass to readjust Terry's hanger around his head. Ed and I watched him bend and kiss his brother's wet and dirty cheek, and then Johnny spotted us from the tree—*"Mommy! Daddy! Look at me! I'm The Martian! Lookit what I can do"!*—and he seemed to fall backwards off the branch so abruptly that Ed and I both cried out at once—*"Johnny!"*—but no, he was all right, he was hanging by his knees from the branch and we could see his upside-down face grinning at us as the antenna fell to earth beside the whittled stick that was his magic sword.

"Wonderful, darling," I called, "but please be careful" —and then as Ed lifted me from the car and onto the couch in the living room, there were the questions and answers back and forth, with Ed explaining to the boys, "Mommy has to stay very quiet for a while. The doctor says she mustn't jiggle her baby seed. So remember now, no rough stuff around Mom, I'm depending on you fellas to take good care of her," and impressed, they tiptoed to me and gave me, each one, a gentle and reverent embrace, as if I were a Dresden china doll. But soon tiring of their untouchable mother, they went to the touchable maid in the kitchen—sturdy, square, "very good with boys," the agency had said—who simulated interest now with clicks of her tongue as, serving them a snack of milk and pretzels, she listened to them boast of their friendship with The Martian. "My daddy's been with Roger—that's The Martian—while Mom was in the hospital," said Bruce, and Johnny added, "He's magic, you know, The Martian. He can't die, ever," and then there began a pretzel-pitching contest, Terry participating in the fray with loud bangings of his spoon against his glass and a repetitious echo of his brother's last words—"can't die can't die can't die" —chanting in his shrillest squeal, banging the spoon, banging it, banging it—"can't die can't die"—

"Ed." I felt a crevice in my glacier, felt a fissure in my ice. "Ed—please—" and he brought me up to bed and closed my door.

I lay still, I did not move. For a week the bleeding continued, slight and sporadic and increasingly dark, almost brown. I lay calm in my bed and tried not to think. I read a book, I read another book. While the children were in school the maid left too. I lay alone, alone, alone. No one likes me, I thought, I am alone. No one phones, no one comes to me, no one cares. Alone, alone. They don't like me, nobody likes me. And like a train on a track I tunneled through to night, where the depot was a capsule and arrival time was always 9 P.M. Take my pill, lie on my left side, plug my ears, smother the clock in a sweater on the floor, smother its gargantuan ticking, smother too the phone, accept Ed's kiss and watch him set the door ajar, then wait a moment, stifle fear, and sleep. Thus the raveling straw of ritual sustained me for a time, sustained me till the day I rose from my bed and went downstairs. I was weak, I was trembling. I stood in the living room—the children were away at Sunday School—and said to my husband, "It is dead."

He put down his newspaper and came to me. "How do you know?"

"I know."

"But how?"

"My breasts." Gone the fullness, gone the beginnings of milk for my baby, gone my baby, dead, I held its death

122

inside me, my body was a morgue. Cold, cold morgue. Cold. No tears, but trembling, trembling—cold.

Ed's arms went warm around me. "Janie . . . I'm so sorry, darling . . . but maybe it's all for the best . . ."

"Yes." Can this be Sunday, our beautiful Sunday morning? This doesn't seem like Sunday, this doesn't seem like me. Cold, oh cold. "Yes," I said. "I'm glad it's over with."

Glad. There it goes. Glad. Here it comes.

How many times can you retreat from the inevitable? From the greatest inevitability of all, from the death of the body, one retreats in every birth: infant, poem, picture, hyacinth. No, not retreats, but fights as clean as Death fights dirty, to shame Him with creation, to mitigate His filthy triumph with every tune, tree, verse, girl, boy, dawn, blade of grass.

But as for the death of the soul—the death of the soul while the body still lives—is there any retreat? Where can one go but further into the dark recesses of one's mind, back, back, back against the blackness, the labyrinthine wall. But no one knew that I was being stalked. I laughed, I chatted, back against the wall.

They phoned late the next day, Lisa first, then Roger, before they flew to California. Lisa's studio, she informed us, had called her back abruptly to confer about a movie Elia Kazan would direct for them. "It's art, really *art*," she said. "Adaptation of Faulkner." As she told us about it she sounded about to weep from happiness—"Isn't it wonderful, Janie? Ed? Are you on the extension still? Isn't it wonderful? They're going to let me *act*, really *act*"—but then her voice broke and I realized she was crying, but not for joy, no, it was Roger she was really thinking of, even as she told us her good news. Roger was terribly depressed, she said, had gone into the worst slump yet, ever since she'd heard from Hollywood that morning. He was out picking up the plane tickets now, she hoped he'd make it there and back okay, for in his despair he was drinking steadily, she said, and making all sorts of threats—threatening to destroy himself, destroy her. "He's angry at me," she said, "because I won't listen to any more crazy talk about plastic surgery. He mentioned that idea to you too, didn't he? God, isn't that the craziest, most awful—" but she stopped, strangled in a noose of swallowed sobs for a second, then spoke in a low, controlled tone of their plans: she would move into his house in Beverly Hills, he would "keep house" while she went on the dawn-to-dusk treadmill which movie-making entailed, then when she went on location to Mississippi he would come back to New York and visit with the Thompsons a while "if that's okay with the Thompsons," she said now. "Is it, Thompsons?"

"Perfect," Ed said. "I'll get some publicity rolling for then," and I said, "Wait till I tell the boys. Will they be thrilled!"

"How *you* doing, Janie?" she asked, and I told her that I'd just had a lab test which showed the baby was dead— "I sort of suspected it anyhow," I said—and that I'd be hospitalized the next day "to get rid of the remains." She said she was sorry to hear it and I said, very sardonic, "God's will be done."

More farewells, and Ed remarked, "Keep us posted, Lisa. Tell Rog to keep in touch too."

"Tell him yourself. Here he is now."

"Listen," he said. "I just came from the mailbox and here's another note from Atkins." His consonants were too cautious; I could tell he was far from sober. "He seems to have gotten on a new tack with that rock he threw. This note has got The Martian's picture too, just like on the rock—no message, just the picture, done in that same red pencil of his." Then he told us how this portrait differed from the one hurled through the skylight into the Cohn apartment. In this one The Martian stood naked; the big *M,* which was in reality emblazoned upon his shirt-front, was here tattooed instead upon his bare chest, framed in pretty curlicues of hair; except for the *M,* the antenna, and the boots Atkins had drawn with an ironic fastidiousness of many-buckled detail upon his feet, he stood upon the otherwise blank page beautiful in his nudity, but utterly ridiculous too, for Matty had penciled an erect genital and had left his famous empty grin intact upon his face, the combination of fatuity above and tumescence below rendering the crimson figure not funny or vulgar but somehow saddening in its simplicity: a madman's commentary on the human condition.

Roger had suggested we look in our mailbox, which we did as soon as our good-bys were completed, and sure enough, there it was—the drawing just as he had described it—and we stood there in the season's first snowfall looking at it, watching a snowflake settle on the red genitalia for a second like a translucent filigreed fig leaf before it melted into mere moisture and was gone. Our three sons, all hopped up with anticipation at the imminence of snowmen, snowballs, snow forts, sledding, had careened outside while we were on the phone, and now Bruce lunged into me with a hug and with fervent coaxing in which he was joined by Johnny and Terry: "Can we add a toboggan to our Christmas list? Can we, Mom? Dad? A family toboggan? It's gonna be a White Christmas. Please . . . please . . ." And now Ed did not have to remonstrate, "Watch out for your mother, watch out for the baby," because they knew, and had shown no reaction at the news, except for Johnny—Johnny, who was so soft-cheeked and soft-hearted, responding with such tenderness to the softness of kittens and puppies, of newborn anythings, of all creatures small and angora and warm and quivering to the touch—Johnny had sent a single, slow, elegiac tear down the edge of his nose, where it glistened like his stricken eyes for a minute as he whispered, *"Why* did God do it, *why?* I wanted a tiny little baby sister *so* bad"—but we had not had to reply, for it was five o'clock, Bruce switched on the television set, and at the announcer's familiar heralding of their favorite show—"And now . . . the magic . . . magnificent . . . *Martian!*"—Johnny had fallen upon his stomach on the floor, chin in hand, instantly enchanted by the magic of the man, the myth, the miracles achieved by a God who broke no promises, and his brothers, too, flopped to the floor, flanking him in jaw-dropped contemplation of a costumed Roger silhouetted against the sun—magic, smiling, strong, invulnerable.

Ed looked at his sons, engrossed with such intensity in make-believe, and he smiled, then turned his smile to me. But my hand in his was cold, like a child's who is losing her way in the dark.

When I awoke from the anesthetic I smelled coffee, I smelled cake, the odors coming callous at me from behind the curtain which separated my bed from the one next to it in my semiprivate hospital room. Not only the odors but the sound assaulted me, twisting me sick inside with bitterness, for a gay party was in progress, two voices whispering, laughing, silencing sometimes into kisses intermingled with mumblings of love, and the fragments of quiet talk informed me that a young member of the nursing staff sat in bed behind the barrier of heavy white cloth which hung shroudlike from its rungs and its ugly chrome bar—yes, ugly, for everything I could see as I lay groggy and gouged-out in the dim light was ugly, everything I heard now was ugly, the sly "Shsh! They'll hear us!" of the pair beside me was ugly, ugly—he was an interne, some slight illness of hers had made her temporarily a patient, they were having an affair, he had sneaked these sweets to her but the other nurses mustn't find out, mustn't know he was here or the goodies either, it was strictly against the rules to be partying like this after visiting hours were finished and the patients should be asleep—"Shsh! Shsh! Switch the flashlight off! Kiss me!" There rose in my soul a hatred huge and grueling like a throb of great pain, rising in my soul, rising in my throat—rising, rising—and I retched, gagging, gagging, head turned weakly to one side on the pillow that erased from my nostrils now the coffee-cake aroma, filling my nostrils instead with the stench of my nausea. The sounds from my invisible neighbors immediately ceased; the hush was invaded by the sudden crunching of paper bags, the quick, cautious dumping of coffee into sink, and then a streak of ceiling revealed its every ancient scar and scratch in the instant of illumination between the door's opening and closing. He was gone. She lay, the loved one, the sly one, alone, alone as I lay, alone and deserted in the dark. With an effort I reached behind me to press the bell for help, and then my bedside became a bustle of starched bosoms and busy antiseptic impersonal hands as a pair of nurses changed my pillow, washed my face, changed my sheets, my nightgown, for I had been lying in a lake of blood, I saw now, blood brighter than blood had any right to be, and now a new three-tiered bandage of sanitary napkins was slapped against my crotch, my crotch this time shaved not for the emergence of a sweet small head but for the swiftly scraping weapon destroying any vestige of the infant which had choked to death upon its mother's blood.

Chores finished, the nurses turned out the light and started to leave when I heard my voice say, "She . . . she . . ."

"What? Did you say something, Mrs. Thompson?"

I will tell on her, I thought . . . I will, I will snitch, I will tattle, I will tell on my sneaky roommate . . . she made me vomit, she made me bleed, she and her lover, they did it, it's their fault . . . but I said, "Please—"

"Yes? What is it?" They paused impatiently; pasted on the ceiling the yellow pattern from the open doorway formed an albatross. "Do you want something?"

"Yes. My pills. They aren't here in my drawer where I put them when I arrived. I need my pills."

"Are you referring to the Nembutal capsules we removed from your drawer while you were in the operating room?"

"Yes, yes, give them back to me, please. I need one to sleep."

"You'll sleep, don't worry, you're still all drugged up."

"No, no, I can't unless . . . I must have . . ."

But stern, adamant—"Patients are not permitted sleeping pills except on doctor's orders"—and the albatross thinned to a ribbon and then to nothing as the door slowly closed and my eyeballs, bulging up at blackness, went eggcup-hollow crushed beneath the void.

At noon the next day a man came to pick me up; I recalled with difficulty that his name was Ed; I tried to be polite. He asked me how I'd slept; I had not slept at all; I did not answer him. Something had happened in that black eternity of night that I did not understand. I only knew that I was very cold and that we had nothing to say to each other, this man and I, for he seemed a stranger, kind and loving and superfluous. As he wheelchaired me down the hall past the doctor who had performed the abortion I heard him ask a question, heard then the doctor's reply, ". . . nothing much left in there actually, Mr. Thompson, just a godawful-smelling mess of necrotic tissue"—and then the man said something else, at which the doctor remarked, "Well, get her off that stuff quick."

(Here it comes.)

It was in the car on the way home that I first realized I must kill myself. And from that moment on there was no me, for months there was no me, no self at all; a thing is all there was, a mindless thing.

(Here it is. Oh God help me, here it *is*. God help . . . but . . . where is God?)

PART TWO

*". . . O Thou, whose all-embracing hand guards
from sheer death the sleep-walker pacing the
roof's edge,
Satan, have pity on my long-drawn pain . . ."*
                                        Baudelaire

ELEVEN

"I'VE lost my mind. I want to kill myself." In the waiting
room there had been a screen, a plant, a couch, a chair,
and it had seen everything as if through smoked glass,
the thing had sat there as if it were still human, regarding the wrists above the clenched-together hands, regarding the vein which jutted up like a knot of gnarled
yarn from the tight skin of the wrist, the vein beating
blue-gray in a tiny tom-tom of rebellion, resisting the death
of the mind, the absence of the self, asserting its yes yes
yes yes against the one enormous NO that the me which
used to be me had become, become this, this neuter nothing, this thing.

"What is your name?"

"Jane Thompson." Again the voice emerged without
tone, without expression, without life, whispered, listless,
insensible. A moment before the thing had raised its eyes
from its wrist and seen the trousered legs, the watch chain,
looped gold, beneath the jacket, and, in silence, shuffling
across the floor, scrunched up inside itself with non-being,
it had followed the watch chain across the floor into another room here, where it sat now facing a desk, and on
the desk those hands, and somewhere above on the other
side of the desk the voice, his voice, he who must do
something, *do* something, help, *help,* saying, "You know

your name. How can you know your name if you've lost your mind?"

But just repeating, "I've lost my mind. I want to kill myself."

The hands on the desk moved, touched a pile of papers, moved back, and there was a ring on one finger and the fingers were square, blunt, the voice above the hands was blunt, untender, please God omnipotent, saying, "Where do you live?"

"Cedarton, Connecticut."

"How old are you?"

"Thirty-one"—describing her who used to be, who had an age, an identity, who was separate and different from this thing which spoke as the yellow reality of dandelion is from the gray blow-away puff of nothingness that drifts dead on the live green stem.

"Do you have any children, Mrs. Thompson? What are their names?"

"Yes. Three. Bruce. Johnny. Terry."

"What other interests do you have besides your home?"

"I write. I wrote."

A pause. The desk, the papers, the hands, the voice, these were the whole world, horizoned by suicide. The hands moved, they opened up in a gesture which the words repeated—"You see? Your mind is still there. You give me the information I ask for, you give it to me correctly. Your mind is still there."

"But . . . but . . . I'm so confused . . . I . . . I don't know what day it is—"

"It doesn't matter."

"It does matter, it does, it does"—voice rising now, suddenly shrill, like the broken-off edge of a scream— *"I don't know what day it is I can't think my mind doesn't work I'm so mixed-up I can't live any longer I just want to—"*

"Now now, do you see visions? Have hallucinations? Hear things that aren't there?"

"No no not yet no—"

"Do you see this desk? Is it whirling around or is it staying still?"

130

"It's staying still."

"You see? Your mind is there."

"But—I want to kill myself."

The hands moved, clasped together, the thing wished it were inside the hands, caged safely inside the fingers, surely it could fit in there, fit into that warmly knuckled absolute, it could fit, it was such a small thing, smaller than an insect, it would fit. But again the hands opened, moved papers, and the voice filled the room like the voice of God. "Why do you want to kill yourself?"

"Because I'm insane."

"What makes you think you're insane?"

"Because I want to kill myself."

A long silence, long, long, how long, who could know, it could not know how long, for time had been the first unchangeable to change, the first unbearable to be borne, the first strong solid certainty to crumble into dust ...

"Tell me. Tell me how it began."

Tell him?—but there are no words. Can a corpse describe its state? Can no-self articulate its loss? What was is no more, what is must be no more, the death of this body will be no death for the brain is dead, a breath of wind and blossomless the dandelion stem.

"Tell me."

And it tried to tell him—starting in a whisper, shrilling to that sliver of a scream—told the hands upon the desk, told how both sides of the driveway had been lined white with snowbank when the thing and its husband named Ed had come home in the car from the hospital. "I sat there without moving I was cold as the snow and stiff as something frozen in the snow and nothing was real except my plan and that was clear, clear and sharp as an icicle point, my plan was clear, I would do it in the snow, red against white, but no one would see, I would do it in the woods, far off in the woods in the snow with a razor at my wrist, red on white—"

—the hands moved, they moved across a page, the hand had a pen, it moved the pen fast, faster, the pen moved like a knife across the scab of a poisoned brain,

131

the pen tore open the scab and the words spurted out, spurted out from the silence of a three-day hell—

"—they'd never find me, the boys would never know, it would be as if I'd vanished from the face of the earth, by spring when the snow was gone the last trace of my body would be gone too, this man could marry again, a new mother, the boys could have a new mother, there was no more me anymore anyway, you see, so it didn't matter about killing it, it was dead already just the body had to join the brain, something had happened in the night to my brain, I didn't sleep they took my pills the blood was red the snow fell down the girl and her lover they were whispering they were laughing the sweet smell made me sick it was against the rules *it was against the rules*—"

—no, no, don't scream, the desk is staying still, staying still, it's staying still, the hands are on the desk, the pen is in the hands, the hands are there the voice is there . . . is it . . . the voice, is it there . . . oh . . . where . . . is he . . .

"Yes? Go on please."

—oh he's here, help please help please save help help—

"Yes?"

"—and then we went in the house and we lay down on the bed and it was the same bed and the same man on the bed but it was all so different from ever before and changed somehow and I can't explain it and I couldn't explain it so I lay quiet there and when the man smiled at me I smiled back because I knew he didn't know that everything was changed, was strange, didn't know that I was mad, didn't know about my plan, and then I looked at the clock and it was noon and then I looked away from the clock for a very long time, for an hour at least or two it seemed, and I looked at the clock again and it read nine past twelve, but that can't be right, I thought, and I told the man my voice coming out of my mouth all dead like this told him that the clock was slow but no, he said it was not slow, his watch said the same time too, so I closed my eyes for a long time, it was a terribly long time, several hours it seemed and then I looked at the clock and it said ten past twelve, and all that time like half an afternoon

132

had only been a minute, and then there were not even any more minutes or seconds for time stopped completely and my plan was very clear and I was very cold but I did not shake, not then, that was later, that was after we went to pick up Terry at nursery school, and he was next to me in the car and my hand began to swell, my right hand lying there in my lap, it got larger and larger so that I couldn't move it from my lap it was so heavy and I started to tell the man about how it was swollen but then I looked down and I saw it was the same, it had not changed, like time my hand was different only to myself, and then the plan got very sharp but I didn't do anything, I didn't say anything, I knew I must wait until I could get away into the woods at night, but in the evening the man said we would go to a movie to get my mind off of everything because I guess he saw I was so quiet and he wanted me away from the boys I guess because I did not answer them very much when they spoke because I did not hear them very well, I only saw their mouths moving, and then the movie was a fictional version of Hitler's suicide and everyone came in his room and spoke to him but he heard no sounds he only saw their mouths moving he heard no sounds except his own thoughts which were the thoughts of a madman and they were my thoughts and then he drew the knife across his throat and it was my throat my wrist, and then I knew I would really do it, I was as mad as he had been and he had done it and I would do it, and I began to shake, the coldness had reached the center of every bone and I shook and I shook and the man who is my husband took me home again—"

"Shouldn't you have been in bed? You'd just been operated on—"

"Yes, I should have been, the doctor had said I should stay still for several days, but I couldn't stay still, not with the plan in my head and time stopped, not with that motor in me that began at four in the morning and churned in my insides so that my bowels were like a baby's, I should be diapered I can't hold it in, and the motor churned in my stomach and I could not eat a bite I cannot eat a bite, the motor made me go, go, go from

133

four o'clock on, up the stairs, down the stairs, around the house, back through the house, around in a circle, out the door, riding around in the car, in a store, out of the store, go to another store, go go go go don't stop or you will you will you will—"

"How much do you weigh?" The voice. Reality. Sanity. Safety. Savior.

"In the hospital I weighed 115."

"Three days ago?"

"Yes."

"Step over here." The scale read 103. And then again the desk, the hands, the voice echoing through the vacuum of no-being. "That mean you've been dropping four pounds a day since your release from the hospital." The fingers drummed for a second against the desk. "Twelve pounds in three days."

"Yes, yes, I knew . . . my wrist . . . see my wrist"—for the vein stood up from the skin, still incessantly beating out its tiny tom-tom of rebellion, bulging up blue-gray out of the gaunt wrist from which the flesh had fled as if forewarned of the plan, forewarned of the thin and tidy slit, forewarned of the blood against the snow, the red against the white, and then it was saying, "I remembered . . . I remembered . . . at the party . . . the people . . . the couple . . ."

"Yes? At the party? You remember the couple?"

"The Deckers, that was their name and it was at Milton Cohn's party for Roger the night before the day I began to lose the baby and they were newlyweds and his first wife had lost her mind and killed herself, she jumped off a bridge, he told me, he told me—"

"Yes?"

"He told me the girl had gotten very quiet and her voice got all dead and she never spoke anymore and it was because she'd lost her mind and she killed herself. I remembered and then I knew all the more that I would really do it because Hitler had felt all separated and seeing mouths moving and like everything was all removed and that's how I feel and the wife he told me about she got just the way I am she got all quiet and changed and her voice and her eyes were dead and her body tried to get dead like her mind it got all thin by itself and now it's happened to me the same the same insane insane and I will kill myself too because I want to I want to oh I have to I will I will I will—"

"Mrs. Thompson, listen to me now." The hands are here, the hands are real, he is real, he will help, he must help, help, help save please help—"Why haven't you killed yourself? For three days you say you have wanted nothing else, and yet here you are, and you want me to save you from it. Why do you want me to save you from it?"

"Because . . . because . . . I . . . I know I'm crazy, I know this isn't me this is someone else oh I don't understand but I know this isn't me but I must but I mustn't the children the children—"

"You mustn't because of the children?"

"I mustn't because of the children, I must because of the children, *I mustn't I must*—"

"Mrs. Thompson, stop screaming, I'm right here, nothing is going to happen to you, you will get well, you will *get well,* do you hear me?" Hear you, hear you, help, but must must cannot stand this too terrible crazy crazy—but the hand came down hard against the desk and shocked the dry-eyed sorrowless sobbing into silence. "There there, that's better. Now listen. You will not kill yourself, do you hear me, you will not do it. I will not let you. I will help you and together we will beat it, do you hear?"

"Beat it? Beat it?"

"We will beat this thing."

"This thing, what is it, what happened, what's happening, why why—"

"You have a mental illness but that does not mean you must—"

"I do? It's true? This is me? I'm not dreaming? I won't wake up and be me again in a minute? Oh God! Oh no! Oh why oh how—"

"Listen to me, now stop that and listen to me now. No, you will not wake up and be you again in a minute, but you will be you and a better you again someday and then it will be as if you had indeed awakened from a nightmare. I can't tell you the psychiatric terms for what has happened because it would only be a lot of words to you and not mean much so I will just—"

"—tell me, tell me, I don't understand, please tell—"

"Well then, you've had a nervous breakdown precipi—"

"—no no not nerves it's my brain my mind mental breakdown—"

"Well, anyway, breakdown is just a layman's term for an abrupt precipitation of a neurosis into a critical stage—"

"—what critical what"—please make sense oh please make sense oh don't make sense it doesn't matter just *be* here just *be* here don't leave—

"You are suffering from a critical neurotic depression with disorientation, depersonalization and suicidal compulsions. It is a severe but curable mental illness—"

"—but it's not a depression I'm not depressed that's different that's something I always knew about being depressed, I used to get very depressed sometimes but this is entirely different, oh God so different, this is not the same at all, my mind my mind I've lost it I want to kill—"

"You haven't lost it all the way and you haven't entirely lost your will to live, your life instinct, or you wouldn't be here. You are still aware of realities, you are still aware of yourself, you talk to me and I talk to you, your mind is sick but it is not gone, it just seems that way but we will make your mind well—"

"—we? we? how—"

"I can't do it alone. You have to help me."

"—how how—"

"Promise me you will not try to commit suicide. That is the first thing."

"—but how can I promise, it comes, it comes and I can't control it because I'm not me it *happens* to me I can't help it, it comes and goes—"

"Comes and goes?"

"—yes yes, comes and goes, I can feel it coming I feel okay first you see I feel as if maybe nothing's wrong

136

after all and maybe I imagined it about my mind and I feel okay but then it starts I can feel it starting it's the way I used to get about death where I could feel myself getting into an I-will-be-dead-someday panic but when that panic came it would be partly under control and I could switch it off before it was too late when it got unbearable but now this thing happens like that and I can feel it coming and my body gets the motor because I can feel it coming and it's like the other thing the oh-God-oblivion thing unbearable like I used to get unbearable but it's different oh God it's awful awful because I can't switch it off, my brain's out of control, it's my enemy, and it just keeps pulling me in more and more pulling I can't stop it and my body starts churning because I can't stop it and nothing can stop it and then I walk fast up down all around in circles or any place just not to stay still and I bang my head on the wall bang it bang it to bang my brain away that is doing this to me and then I'm all the way in it and I can't get out and it's terrible terrible oh agony oh awful terrible unbearable unbearable and it's out of my body leaving me stone cold and it's all in my head and then I get just the opposite I get very still and all quiet and scrunched-up like a bug which is how I feel a bug or nothing at all just nothing and I curl all up somewhere in a corner and everything gets sort of unreal the children everything not real not me not them not real can't stand it crazy kill myself kill myself—"

"All right, all right, I'm here, it's going to be all right" —his voice falling like magic like a muffler of assurance on the crazy dry lifeless-sounding sobs—"How do you feel when it goes?"

"—I don't know I don't know how long I'm in it because time goes time was the first thing to go to stop it stopped altogether *stopped altogether*—"

"All right. Calmly now. These things have a pattern. I know exactly how you feel, I know how you feel now, and how you'll feel tomorrow, and I know—"

"—how can you know, you're not crazy, you don't know, you're just pretending to know, you can't understand, you're not in it only me's in it and you're not and you can't—"

"I know all about it. I *know*. Trust me." The hands were clenched. "Do you trust me?"

—trust him? trust him? but what but how—

"You must trust me. This is what we will do. When you begin to get in it—"

"—yes yes in it yes—"

"—you phone me, do you hear? As soon as it starts you phone me and we will talk. I'll be available to talk to at all times until you pull out of this critical stage."

"—pull out? when? how soon? oh when when—"

"Soon. Trust me."

"You're . . . you're . . . n-not putting me in an asylum?" —there! it was out! there, it was said, it was out, will he put this thing away, put it away, off away with the others, the others like this, the screaming ones, the crazy ones, vacant brains all cooped up together like animals away put away, screaming or silent or silent or screaming or curled up like bugs bugs bugs curled up or racing around not stopping like motors in them and churning inside and banging their heads banging banging crazy brains out on gray thick prison walls prison never get out never get well never anything else until crazy as the others crazy crazy oh God all the way crazy I'll turn into the very old man oh I'll be the three girls the very old man the three girls crazy—"You're not putting me—"

"No I'm not. I'm not putting you in any hospital now because I trust you."

"—now? what do you mean, not now? will I get worse? will you put me there later? what"—the hands are quiet like he is holding them quiet like he doesn't want it to escape wants to catch it before it escapes it's crazy he wants to catch it before it kills itself wants to put it away oh why doesn't he say something why doesn't he say he won't ever put it away—"Will you ever—"

"I can only tell you that you are not going to any hospital now. You are going home from here and you are going to phone me whenever it happens between visits and we will talk. And you are not going to kill yourself

138

and you are going to get well. And you will come here to my office in New York City for an hour each day until you are well. Someday this will all be a nightmare, you will laugh about it and then you will forget all about it, it will just be a nightmare."

"—promise me promise me"—can it trust him? can it?

"I promise." But the hands are too still. Are they too still? Is he lying?

"You're lying I'm insane and I will kill myself before you stick me in a snakepit full of crazy people like me where I'll rot forever surrounded by—"

"I'm not lying Who lied to you? Why can't you trust me?"

"—everybody lies, Daddy Mommy lies they always lie—"

"All right, we will talk about them next time, you will tell me all about it, all about everything. But now I want you to go home and try to eat and try to sleep—"

"—I sleep with a pill, until four I sleep but I can't sleep without it, soon I'll need two to sleep and then three then four and I'll get so nothing will help and then I'll never sleep and it will be like a twilight world with being half-asleep all the time and never really asleep and never really awake and before it gets like that I will kill myself because then the kids won't have a crazy drug addict mother and Ed won't have a crazy drug addict wife they can get a good new mother instead and forget about me and I can forget about me I can be dead and not have to be this thing anymore—"

"You will not be a drug addict. You will not be a suicide. You will trust me, do you hear, and you will do as I say. You must promise not to kill yourself and I will promise then to get you well. You must give me your word so that I may trust you as you trust me. That's a bargain, is that clear? *We have a pact,* you and I, yes?"

"—yes yes"—maybe, but maybe not maybe not—

"If I thought for a moment that you would break your promise, I would put you in the hospital right now, where someone could watch you every second. That is what I would do right now if I didn't trust you. But I do trust you. And you trust me, yes?"

"—yes yes"—but it is so alone, this thing is so alone in this horror, alone alone and you whoever you are you are so far away over there past that vast acreage of desk, you speak of trust but who are you that speaks of trust and promises, are you really there or does it see a pair of hands that is not there hear a voice which does not speak do you lie or do you tell the truth oh are you real—

—and the thing brought its thin cold wrist up out of its lap, it brought the tiny tom-tom up to the level of the desk top where the world began and ended, the thin wrist of the thing with its pulsating rebel of an ominous knotted vein reached itself out across that mahogany oasis in the middle of hell, reached out until the hand on the wrist touched the hand on the desk and then the hands were one hand clasped hard and warm yes it was a real hand and yes he was a real God and he was magic and he was everything and there was nothing else and no one else only this hand in a pact in a promise in trust oh help oh help oh save—

—and then its cheek was against the hand of its savior, its face was buried in the hand as if the hand were an altar, and then its lips were on the altar the warm hairy altar the please God omniscient please God omnipotent altar, and all that was missing was grief, grief weirdly as absent as tears.

TWELVE

WRITING all this is like holding an ice cube, I find; at first what I feel is solid, is cold ache-making substance, but then, as I write it out of me, it grows smaller, dwindles, melts from my grasp until all I can feel is a slight numbness where something used to be. Perhaps the numbness, too, will soon be gone.

But I must be careful. The memory which melts quickly

in my hot cathartic fingers may leave a stubborn puddle, all unnoticed, on the floor. If the linoleum is slippery, will I fall? And if I fall, will I get up again?

Image, wait . . . but no, the image yields before an onslaught of sensation, for the poet in me dies at the approach of the gourmand. Yes, I confess, gourmand; no gourmet I. I lay down my pen and take up my apron, I rest my cramped fingers upon its grease-stained gingham, from sink to stove and back again I whistle at my work.

I am worse than any dwarf who loved Snow White.

Cake and steak and buttery biscuits, tomatoes nestled in lettuce and gleaming with oil and Gallic with Roquefort or bleu, shiny creamed onions and carrots and cantaloupe, caraway rye bread and jelly and Jell-o, cherry pie, waffles, napoleons, hash. Not to mention peas and beans and Hershey almond bars—

"Pig!" Lisa once hissed at me in the Four Seasons.

What headwaiter stands in attendance upon her now? And does she still remark upon the ironies of fame? She told me once of a Ben Hecht story she'd read. A convicted man had been brought to the gallows, she said, and as someone stepped forward with white wrapper and hood, another adjusted the rope around his neck. And then the man screamed out, screamed out three words and then the same three frantic words again. *This ain't me! This ain't me!*

"That's fame," she said, "at first. And then you start to become your propaganda, and you try to remember who you used to be, and you say: *that* wasn't me, *this* is."

Lisa, who are you now? Do you have a friend, or, in the absence of one, do you have a theory: *women can't be friends?* Do you remember sometimes—when alone, none fawning—that for a while we were like sisters, and that instead of gifts we traded fragile fragments of ourselves?

And do you remember the friend that Roger had? My son has many many friends like that and they all speak with his voice. In the night they make merry together, they amuse each other so vastly, so vociferously, that at

141

four in the morning, vicariously, remembering the threat, I feel his trap door closing and I press against my pillow and I pray.

If I told you I was three girls once, would you believe me? Or that I was an old man or no one at all, unborn? If you knew about my Terry, would you care? When you read about your Roger, when you recognize your words, will you laugh, or cry, or sue, or write a small thrilled note of glad surprise that ends LM:pb?

Roger had a friend who was very tall and very very strong. He was practically a giant, and he could beat up anyone, especially people who teased other people about stepfathers or mothers who got married a lot. They had long talks, he and his friend, but mostly they just roamed around enjoying the way everyone stared, and gawked, and pointed. It was fun having a friend who was so special.

But it wasn't just that he was big and strong. He was good, too, really good and kind ... not at all like the wicked giants in fairy tales. He was so good and so special he was like ... well ... a *god,* almost.

His friend was with him so constantly that he almost forgot what it was like to be lonely. Every once in a while, when his pretending didn't do the trick—when something especially awful happened, for instance, at school or at home during the summer with Edythe—he would remember his friend wasn't real but was only make-believe. Then he would feel lonely again, and frightened, and small, and curled up like a snail. But that never lasted long; he wouldn't let it; it was too terrible. If he ever lost his friend forever, he knew what he would do. And he didn't want to do that because, well, once he was dead he might want to change his mind and then it would be too late.

But it was stupid even to *think* about that. It had been a year now since he'd even *cried.* And as for his friend ... why, they were so close they were practically the same *person,* practically.

Awaking at four in the morning, it thought: not now,

not today, mustn't today, must wait, mustn't ruin the day, mustn't ruin the day for them, for all their lives looking back and remembering mother killed herself on Christmas Day ... but ... but ... they wouldn't have to know! there's a way! ah—yes—*that's* it, *that* way they'll never know—not the snow no not red on white no, might be found that way, snow might melt too soon, but oh this is the way this is the way—now? why not why not, come on get it over with, you know you will sooner or later, come on come on oh come *on*—

—and the motor churned in its intestines and it tiptoed quick to the toilet and then down the stairs up the stairs down again, now? now? oh baubles silver in the moonlight ribbons silver in the moonlight tinsel silver in the moonlight, now? no no not now, wait, but why? why not? no no don't ruin the day for them don't ruin Christmas Day—

—well all right, all right then, but tomorrow then, well maybe then but not the snow oh no oh no you know *you* know—

—ah yes! that way no one will ever know—

—but how to bear it until then how to bear it—

"Daddy! Mommy! Just what we wanted!"—and small arms around its neck and wet kisses on its cheek and smiling its face smiling, oh make a happy morning, make them a happy morning, happy morning oh merry Christmas Day—"Say, Mom, Dad, it's the biggest toboggan in the world!"

—this ain't me! this ain't me!—

"Carols, Mommy, come on"—pushing it to the piano after the turkey, the turkey which had looked on the plate like a picture in a magazine, pretty food, glossy gravy, yellow squash, cranberries red around the tweedy mound of stuffing, pretty as a picture and as inedible, but it had touched the turkey with its fork, it had traced a double track across the squash until the fork dropped from its invisibly wounded hand, its husband killing the clatter of the fork with a quickly spoken, "You've fixed us a regular feast, Mrs. Ross."

143

And the children's voices—"Boy yeah!"—"What a cook!"—"Yummy yummy yummy yum"—

—how happy they are with Mrs. Ross, they love her meals, they love her laughter, they love her like a mother, they don't need this crazy useless thing around, they won't miss this crazy thing, its presence is already like an absence and they do not even notice, they'll all be better off oh they'll be much better off—

—and Mrs. Ross wears a white uniform, she takes care of this thing and the others, and when she leaves at night the other nurse comes, and this thing is just a piece of furniture, if you bump into it by mistake you step around it and it's just an extra thing that's in the way—

"Mommy! Come on! Carols! Play the piano so we can sing carols like we always do after Christmas dinner!"— and they dragged it to the confusion of a keyboard black and white black and white red on white blood on snow no no the other way the better way the new way yes ah yes but now? not now but later later—"Mom, let's start with 'Joy to the World,' okay?"—and it smiled and it nodded and it raised its wrists up and the vein was bigger now for no flesh at all was left against the bone, a filament of skin that's all there was, so that the vein seemed rising from the bone itself all blue and bursting through— "Mommy? Mommy? *Play* now, Mommy"—and the fingers came down all wrong on the keys with a crash that shattered a glass angel on the nearest branch, sent it down into a bright red crumpled bed of tissue paper, white on red, and her little silver halo rolled like an errant wedding ring across the floor, slower, slower, wobbling, falling, still.

"My *an*gel, my pwitty wittle *an*gel"—the smallest boy named what? Terry? bursting into tears at the demise of his favorite tree decoration but the other two boys saying nothing of the angel, speaking only of the crash upon the keys, speaking now across the blank-eyed Mommy-face to their father, who failed to shush them in time—"Daddy, *why* won't Mommy play? What's the *matter* with Mommy?"—and his quickly interrupting, "Come on, fellas, we'll play our new Santa Claus records instead," and it sat there, the thing, rigid on the piano stool, rigid with its useless fingers and its useless brain, rigid while Santa sang a song of sleigh bells in the snow.

And the watch chain and the hands upon the desk and the voice oh the voice like the voice of God—

"How was Christmas?"

How could he ask. As if he didn't know. As if he didn't *know*. "You know."

"Yes."

"But I'm out of it right now. I feel okay."

"Yes, I can see that."

"How? How can you see?"

"Your voice. Your eyes. The way you walk."

"Why when I'm in it can't I walk right? Why did I stumble over my own feet the other day when I walked in here? Why when I'm in it do I stumble over my own tongue when I talk? Why why why—"

"Someday you'll understand."

"*Some*day *some*day." Anger bubbling up. "You said I'd get better but it's getting worse. It's getting longer each time. I'm out of it now but when I get back in it, it will be longer, it was almost all day yesterday, soon I'll never be out of it again, never never, and then there won't even be enough of me left to kill myself with. You *lied,* you *lied.* I'm not getting better, I'm getting worse."

"I promised you that you—"

"No! Don't give me anymore of your promises. I'm okay right now and I'm me and I can see you for what you are and you are a fraud and a liar"—but not really seeing him, seeing still only the hands, the desk—"yes, a fraud, no more magic than that other silly psychiatrist when I was in the hospital. Why what kind of a fool do you take me for, telling me Terry is my brother. He's not my brother, he's my son, I'm not so far gone I don't know my own *son.* You're the crazy one, telling me crazy things like that and letting me drive back and forth a hundred miles a day when I can't even see half the time or walk or talk or even hold a goddamn fork—"

"You'll drive all right. Even if you can't do anything

else at all, you'll drive. You'll drive because you have to drive to get to me and you have to get to me to get well, and you have to get well because a little piece of you still wants to and that little piece is my collaborator in this production, my partner in this enterprise."

"Words! Words! Drive when I can't think! Yesterday Ed typed a letter to my parents in Japan. He used all my typical phrases, tried to make it sound like me. Then he asked me to sign it. I couldn't write my name! How can I write when I can't even read? I can't read! I look at the pages and they're black and white just like the piano keys and just as impossible to figure out. I can't—"

"Did you finally sign your name?"

"Well . . . yes . . ."

"Why? How?"

"Well . . . because I had to . . ."

"See? What you must do, you will do. I know you, I know what you are, who you are. I know what you can do and what you can't do, I know what you will do and what you won't do. I know—"

"Oh *yeah*, oh yeah, you know *every*thing, oh yes *every*thing"—liar liar liar liar liar—

And liar still and liar more when it stood in its night-gown and its bathrobe on the jetty and the moon was not so fat now as it had been on Christmas Eve and so the beach spread out only faintly seen as in a dream and it was a dream it was a terrible dream to be here and yet it must be done, it was the best plan, it would be better than in the snow, better than the idea it had the other day when it left his office and got out onto the street and walked and walked around the streets of Manhattan to pass that crazy unpassable time away, walked and walked until it began to stumble as it walked, and then it was a bug and all the taxis on Park Avenue were beetles and the beetles were bigger they could kill the little bug, oh it would have been so simple then to step into the street, just run out from the curb in time to meet a beetle in the street, to bleed away, to be nothing and not *know* it, to stop *know*ing it was nothing, to be *really* nothing—but no,

146

no this was better, this way nobody would ever know, the children they would never know, no one would know what had happened to it, the sea would dissolve it as one's shadow is dissolved by a cloud upon the sun—

—and look! a cloud upon the moon, oh Oriental sky, oh cloud-streaked moon-sky fragile and ungodly as Japanese art, Japan, there's someone in Japan who cares about what happens here? someone in Japan who cares about whether their child dies a suicide?—no! stop that now, whoever it is they're far away and they'll never know, how can they know? don't you have it all planned out perfectly?

—yes, yes, well, let's go—

—and its feet were bare but it felt no cold, bare feet on wet rocks, and snow on the bathrobe hem from walking from house to car, and how softly how cleverly it had started the car so that no one awoke, how softly how cleverly it had crept from the bed where the Ed-person slept snoring slightly, and it had taken the bottle of pills heaped full to the brim by the druggist today—two dozen Nembutal—how cleverly done to be here now safe and solitary in this 4:30 world of no sound but the sea slapping at the jetty—what? what, another sound? who spoke— what? oh *those* sounds, those *summer* sounds, oh but those are August sounds and this is winter, go away oh sounds-out-of-season, go away or it will scream you away, go away, go—

—but the voices continue—"Mommy, watch me, Mommy, I can dive in and turn a whole somersault under the water before I come up"—"Daddy, can you help me catch that crab, silly old Mommy's scared of that crab, *I'm* not scared but she is, Daddy, help me put it in my pail"—"Come on, Mommy, they can't find us if we hide here in this cave, see, the rocks hide us, shsh, they went with Daddy down the beach, they'll *never* find us now, isn't this a wonderful cave, Mommy? Don't you love playing hide-and-go-seek, Mommy, isn't the jetty a perfect place to—"

—the jetty is a perfect place to do it—now! now! go ahead, come *on*—

147

—but the summer sounds, the summer sounds, remember, remember—

—forget it forget it, they'll all be better off, that was the you who used to be, that you is dead, just the body's left and oh it is so slow to starve to death, so slow, this will be fast—just swallow them, just swallow them down quick and easy the way you planned, here on the farthest rock from the sand where the current will carry your carcass out to nowhere, you won't even know when you drown you'll be asleep when you roll into the sea, so simple so easy and no one will know, the boys won't even ask where you went, their father won't know either so he'll just say you went away somewhere and in a few days they'll forget and they'll think Mrs. Ross was always their mother and the night nurse was always their mother and then they can get a real new mother a good new mother who's not—

—all *right* all *right,* let's get it over with—

—but you forgot, oh you stupid crazy thing you forgot, you forgot to bring a glass for gulping water, how can you swallow all those huge capsules without a glass of water, oh you stupid crazy thing it *told* you to bring a glass to fill with water—

—don't blame me, *he* did it, *he* did it with his miserable goddamn magic, his filthy double-crossing magic, *he* did it, *he* made it forget the glass—

—well never mind, just jump in then, what does it matter if you know you're drowning what difference does it make—

—but it's afraid oh it's afraid to die like that—

—afraid to *die?* afraid to live, you mean—

—no no afraid to die—

—*he* did it, *he* made you afraid to die when there's no way left to live, *he* tricked you like this with a stinking little pinch of hope—

—but listen! listen! the summer sounds oh hear them now the summer sounds, perhaps it's true and maybe she will really hear the summer sounds again someday someday—

And the watch chain and the hands upon the desk and the voice oh the voice like the voice of God—

"So it was all my fault, you say."

"Yes yes, without you I would have done it I would have and I'd be out of it now out of it out of it"—but where was the anger now, where the scream which had split the solitude for a second before fading away into the salt-spray that sprinkled the thing as it ran from rock to rock, stumbling, falling, cutting its feet its feet so frozen-feeling that it scarcely felt the surf upon its ankles as it ran ran ran across the beach ran up the beach to the car—

"Why didn't you do it?"

Oh where the anger now—"Because . . . because . . ."

"Why?"

"Because I promised you. Because you trusted me. Because I trusted you"—and where anger had resided in the fiber of its being there was love, and the love was larger than fear or pride, larger than death or the wish for death, it shook the very air like a hundred thousand bells—"Oh I love you I love you I love you"—

—and again it fell in worship on the altar of his desk, its cheek and mouth again against the altar of his hand—

My sons do not play the game anymore, I notice—the game of The Martian, pretending to soar, shouting the slogan, antenna-headed, sheathed and sworded, magical and huge. They seem to have forgotten that last year they used to play it all the time; they seem to have forgotten there was a last year or a Roger.

How unforgotten the forgotten is; how Nazi-German-sounding is that word. Forgotten. *Ach, nein,* forgotten. You split the *T* and swallow thick the rest.

Roger loved words, I remember. There were a few favorites he would sometimes spring in the middle of a silence, quite out of nowhere, surprising everyone but me and Ed, and, later, Lisa. . . .

"Trollop," he would say. "Trollop o'er the Hellespont, trollop o'er the Hebrides"—and we would look up from our reading or Scrabble or whatever, Ed and Lisa and I, and see him sitting there abstracted in the black butterfly chair, mumbling happily, and we'd smile at each other and know that another link had just been forged in the chain of our foursome, another silly solid link in the circle of our friendship, which we would brandish at public gatherings, baffling outsiders, saying casually in the middle of a chat about The Theater or pastrami or The Bomb, "Trollop o'er the Hellespont, trollop o'er the Hebrides"—then going on with our conventional comments, ostensibly oblivious of the startled glances all around us.

Names he loved, names of his own devising. Us ladies he rarely greeted as Jane or Lisa; it became another essential idiocy, another link, for Roger to hail us with one of his less mundane creations, like Carcinoma Carter. The one Rog liked best, considering it, he explained, the ultimate in oral aesthetics, was Gonorrhea Lutz, although he considered Dromedary Davis and Spermatozoa Jones almost as satisfying to the ear.

Wolfe was the only writer I ever heard him mention, and he mentioned him all the time. There was one phrase that had stuck in his memory, he said, through all the years since he'd discovered that another large and awkward adolescent had felt as he did: ". . . an unfathomable loneliness and sadness crept over him." This phrase seemed to contain, for Roger, not only the melodic requirements which caused him to say it out loud, meditatively, at the most unexpected moments, but contained also the power to bring the tears to his eyes.

"Unfathomable," he would say. "Unfathomable"—eyes welling, embarrassing Ed if he was around, but always delighting me, who would leap hungrily in to join him in his Wolfean anguish.

"Perhaps not," I said once.

"What?"

"Perhaps fathomable."

But he would have none of it, rejected my bid to enter his pathos, labeled my entry bathos by swinging abruptly to the other extreme of his nature and saying to me in his most unlonely and un-sad voice, "Get me a match, Carcinoma, that's a good girl."

It is well he rejected my bid; I could not have fathomed

him, nor could I now. It is only by bits and pieces, still, by inch and grudging inch, that I can fathom all the selves that dwell in me.

There are three, I have decided, three women here behind my brown and shiny face, and I used to wonder last year (before I knew otherwise, or think I know) if these were the three that had lurked to keep me captive in my dream. Were these the three girls, merely these three disparate selves?—the morbidly introspective (with myself), the lovingly perceptive (with those I know well), the artfully outspoken (with those I would impress). The first two do not approve of number three, though she approves most thoroughly of them. Number three hates herself, she's always very sorry afterward, often has she sent number one into a tizzy, and even tinged the gaiety and strength of number two. But still the two who can't abide her cannot pull their weight; when they chide her she screams out, "You just don't understand, so go away. You're private selves, you needn't fend in public, you don't need a trademark like I do."

"You *don't* need it," Ed always says. "You *know* you don't, not anymore. Just because you *can* make 'em blink doesn't mean you *must*."

When he says that (and he's right, of course) I miss my understanding advocate. I miss my friend, The Martian, who might have been more lenient with my stubborn number three. I would have explained to him, "I must protect my faucet, don't you know? I must preserve my right to turn it on and off." And wouldn't he have nodded? Wouldn't he have understood?

But why did I never tell him about *my* sentence, the sentence that means quick grief and tears to me? It comes at me from nowhere, daytime, nighttime, and grips me by the throat. It is from the most unlikely spot, for me—the Gospel—and whenever I hear it wafting toward me I smell it wafting too, all pungent with Palestinian fruit and frankincense and myrrh: "And He grew in wisdom and stature and in favor with God and man."

Why? Why, out of all the zillion words I've read in all

my life, do these few desolate me with this sweet purifying desolation?

And why didn't I share this one with Rog? Did I—do I now?—feel through the abysmal shilly-shallying of my agnosticism that Jesus does not belong in the same semantic banter as Eugene Gant or Gonorrhea Lutz?

The only time his mother ever mentioned Jesus or God was when she was upset. Sometimes Edythe used other words too, Roger noticed, but they weren't church words. Several of them were scrawled on the wall of the school john.

In chapel each morning, of course, the church words *sounded* like church words, but that was different. In chapel everything was different, the boys all looking so solemn and quiet and clean and the headmaster droning on and on while Roger made up another chapter in the story of him and his friend. His friend wasn't merely human, he decided. He was so special he could really do things other people couldn't do. Like fly, maybe. Or maybe he had a magic that kept him from being killed, or even hurt, ever. Bullets, fire, knives, dynamite—nothing could touch him. And everywhere he went all the bad guys shook like leaves because they knew he could grab a speeding bullet in his hand and just *squash* it, easy as squashing a marshmallow.

Anyway, he found out from Edythe one vacation when she wasn't married and they spent more time together than usual that he was Episcopal. When he repeated it out loud, "*Epis*copal," it sounded sort of like a dirty word, but when he told her that, she laughed at him, and he didn't mind being laughed at this time, because she hugged him too and he knew she wasn't being mean or making fun of him this time, she just liked him. He wished she would like him more often. He figured he had more fingers on one hand than the times he could remember that she acted like this, liking him and laughing and the two of them alone.

He imagined that the Episcopal heaven looked quite a lot like the school chapel—a lot of dark carved wood, and light slanting down sort of dusty-bright and dreamlike the way it did from behind clouds in certain skies sometimes, or in Grand Central Station from away up above there over the big advertisement, four times a year, twice at Christmas when he came and went, twice again in June. In chapel the lady named Mary holding the baby Jesus in the window over the cross was made of lots of different-colored pieces of glass, more reds and purples than anything else. It was called stained glass, he found out, and then his idea of heaven got a lot of stained glass in it too because it was so beautiful.

He had a dream that kept coming back. In it Edythe was holding him like in the window in chapel and she was all little hunks of purple and red and beautiful with the light shining through. But always a crash would wake him up, his heart pounding all over him as if his blood had gotten out of his veins somehow and was everywhere at once. The crash was the stained-glass lady breaking as a rock came sailing through, making a big hole full of black angry night where her smiling face had been.

And then, in the dream, she would begin to laugh. She was all broken, just pieces of glass, and yet he still seemed to see her, laughing, laughing at him. He always awoke before he could find out why she was making fun of him, what he'd done to be so amusing and so ridiculous.

It wasn't much of a nightmare compared to some others he'd had. The difference was that this one made him *feel* worse, made him feel just about as bad, when he awoke from it each time, as anyone could feel all through the chest and still keep breathing.

THIRTEEN

AND the watch chain and the desk and the hands and the voice oh the voice like the voice of God—

"And you can't cry?"

"I try I try but I can't, if I could cry it would feel so

153

good, I never knew crying could seem so wonderful and so impossible, there's scratchy sandpaper all wadded up dry where my soul used to be all soft with tears and laughter, oh I'm crazy I'm crazy as a loon, it's only crazy people who can't cry."

"And the alarm clock? Still ringing?"

"Yes, yes, at four every morning it rings in my head with a loudness that shakes my insides into nausea and diarrhea. But for a second yesterday I didn't remember why it rang and I didn't remember what had happened to me and for a second it was all so beautiful and peaceful like a reprieve and then all of a sudden there was a click, yes a real loud click in my head, just like this—CLICK!— and it clicked me back into this thing, into the horror again with time all wrong and the motor inside and everything so strange like . . . like . . . "

—his hands wading through the papers as he waited for his patient's portrait of hell, wading through the piles of papers on his desk, the hands wading in the paper like two playful octopi—

". . . like my brain is, oh how can I picture it, like it was the place I lived, it was my living room all cozy and comfortable and now it's become a torture chamber impossible to live in like those places they stick prisoners in, I read a book once about tortures and this brain of mine is like the one they called The Box, the one that was feared above all other tortures, putting the person in a place too short to lie down in and too low to sit up in and so it's torture because there's no way at all to stay in it because each way he twists and turns only makes it worse and he can't get out even when he knows he can't stand it another minute that way, well that's how it is, like my brain was my cozy living room which I took for granted and now it's become a torture chamber like The Box but I still have to live there, I still have to live in my brain even though I can't stay in my brain and I can't stand it but I can't get out either because there's no place else to be except in my brain and there's only one way to get out of this brain this box this torture chamber box only one way and you won't let me do that won't let me or I won't let me I don't

154

know, oh I hate it when you say this is just a sickness like any other sickness, it's *not* like any other sickness, you *know* it's not, I *live* in my brain, people don't *live* every waking minute in their arms or legs or organs of their body, only that small *part* gets sick and oh God how can you keep comparing *this* to any physical sickness oh my God if every inch of my guts were riddled with cancer I would still be *me,* I'd be in terrible pain but at least I'd still be *me.*"

"Yes, you'd be you and you'd be in pain and you would not be cured. Instead, however, you are in pain but you will recover to live out your life and to live it far more happily and satisfactorily than if this had never happened."

"I *hate* you when you talk as if I could ever be glad this happened and I *hate* you when you talk as if being doomed to die is worse than being doomed to live and I *hate* you when—"

"Okay. Hate me."

—hate, hate, oh does it dare? does it dare to smash its clawlike emaciated hands down upon those octopi hands, beat the octopi until they bleed? oh gone the voice of God, hear now the voice of the liar, the fraud, the one who rebuffs, who is loved but who does not love back, who said he would help but who sits there sits there a callous and unconcerned spectator of this suffering suffering suffering—

"Go ahead, don't be afraid to hate me. It's healthy for you to hate me. I know you want to hurt me now. I know—"

—screaming—*"You don't know anything. You don't know me and you don't know how to get me well and you don't know whether or not I will kill myself and you don't know—"*

"I know that right now would be an excellent time to give you an electric shock treatment."

"What?"

"Shock treatment."

"But ... but ... that's for psychotics and you told me that I'm not—"

155

"Seriously depressed neurotics often show temporary improvement after—"

—oh God he's going to have them tie the thing down on a slab and put electrodes on its head and the currents will tear through it like lightning, lightning, terrified of lightning, have always been terrified of lightning, hid somewhere whenever storms roared nighttime into noonday—"Oh no oh no—"

"It's just that I don't like to see you suffer. The treatment would help you suffer less. It hurts me too, you know, to witness and participate in your torment."

—he reads its thoughts! It's not alone in this torture chamber of a brain, he's in here too, he's here inside with it and oh he doesn't like to see it suffer, he suffers along with it (but does he love you?) no no not yet but maybe someday maybe someday—"I love you I love you"—

—ignoring its shamelessness, its love—"And the shock treatments?"

"Must I?"—oh say not say not—

"Only if you cannot bear the torment otherwise."

"I . . . I don't know . . ."

—his hands waiting, his hands which can fill this thing with lightning, his hands which have filled this thing with hatred and with love—

"Maybe I can bear it if it stops soon. Will it stop tomorrow?"

—silence silence—

"Next week?"

—silence—

"Will it stop someday?"

"Yes. Someday."

"Do you promise?"

"I promise?"

—the octopi vanish, the altar remains—

Roger, is it the way we thought it was?

We were suspended over a canyon in Pacific Palisades, six years ago, and we were speaking of God. It was a typical Southern California morning, I recall, the mist still damp in the air at nine o'clock and the sun just a piece of

156

fog that was whiter and brighter than the rest. In the cars that passed on the bungalow-bordered road beside the canyon the ladies on their way to work at factory or office or studio all wore kerchiefs to keep the mist from their curls. A tourist bus went by, Iowa eyes staring out listlessly, and, feeling sorry that I had no fame to bring a light to those eyes glazed dull by stars' gates from which no star emerged, I said, "Quick, Rog, look up and smile," but he kept gazing down, leaning far out across the railing of the rickety footbridge to test himself for vertigo.

"What?" he said at last.

"Too late, never mind. Tourists. Wanted them to catch a glimpse of you."

"You're all heart, girl"—swinging back from the railing, swinging back to our conversation—"Do you know what I mean?"

"Of course." For I did. And I do. Yes, Roger, I try to imagine the existence of God, and I cannot; it is too much for me to manage, this concept—this concept available to so many throughout the centuries and yet denied to me, of a Being which created Itself and then proceeded to create the universe. My imagination, so adept at little things, cannot encompass this, while so much less inconceivable to me is the gulf between being alive and not being, so easily crossed is that gulf (as you since that morning have demonstrated so well) that I can well imagine not that God exists but that I do not, nor anyone else. This planet? A fantasy in some metaphysical plot. This hand? Not true. Those children playing there, who came to life from me? Not so—Bruce, Johnny, Terry—not so, not me, not them, not anyone or anything, not this pencil or this paper or the four far fabled corners of the earth. That all this supposed substance is nothing but a joke on all of us, of this I can conceive; that reality does not exist, I can imagine, but that a Maker does, I must reject.

"Why is it simpler for us," Rog wondered, "to disbelieve the fact of ourselves than to accept the theory that, being indisputably here, Something or Someone indisputably began it—"

"—and therefore oversees—"

"—and may someday remove Himself—"

"—in pity or disgust."

The nearest bungalow was blue adobe, its back lawn dropping down terrace by thin terrace to the point halfway down the canyon where the slope was too steep for even the suggestion of a yard. Looking down-canyon toward the west, we could just begin to see the surf in the glittery gap beneath the lifting fog.

"We'd better get back to the house," Roger said. Ed was in breakfast conference with another client up the road, up the road and around the corner where the bungalows gave way to mansions Moorish in design and hidden by high walls and groves of palm. "Ed said when we stopped off here he'd only be a half-hour. I hope he's ready, I'm supposed to be in full regalia for the cameras by ten."

We walked off the bridge and away from the canyon, up the street. A woman on a front porch nudged the neighbor who was chatting with her; they looked after Roger, delighted at their discovery. One was holding a feather duster, the other a market bag; both were fat; they were real. A youth passed by on a motor scooter, whistling the familiar tune of a Camel commercial; his jacket was red and he needed a shave; he was real. We saw flowers and bushes and grass and all was real. The feel of our footsteps against the sidewalk, that was real, and Pontiacs passing and Thunderbirds too, and the sudden smell of bacon cooking, that was real. The Mexican gardener who smiled at us as we approached—we laughed later when we told Ed how the fellow had done such a double-take when he really *saw* Roger—he was real. The day was real, L.A. was real, we were real.

Indisputably.

Right, Roger, oh vanished one? Right, oh gone-to-God?

One time when Roger was on the train going back to school a strange thing happened. A ragged old tramp came stumbling up the aisle, staggering and shaking his head sadly and muttering to himself. He smelled as bad as Manson used to smell—Edythe had divorced him long ago, of course—but when he stopped and looked at Roger he looked him right in the eye, which was more than Manson had ever done, or any of the others, either. *

"Someday," the tramp said, and stopped, shaking his head. Then he got it all out: "Someday there'll be no tomorrow but the sun will be shining just as bright."

A tear came oozing out of his blurry old eye and then he was gone, the smell staying in his wake a while and making Roger feel sick to his stomach.

But later that night, back at school, he realized it hadn't been the smell that made him sick. It was that sentence, what it meant, how it made him *feel*. It said something that he'd known for years and yet had never known *really* until now. After Lights Out he thought about it, fingered the sentence with his mind and felt its contours; then the feeling went too far and he sat up suddenly and said, "No!" His roommate half-awoke and turned over with a sigh and the sigh brought him back from wherever it was he'd been. He hoped he'd never go there again; it reminded him of something. Of the time he'd tinkered too much with his bike? Yes, that was it—when he'd been riding along real fast the handle bars had come off in his hands. That's what it was like, what he felt. Like that time on the bike. Only worse. It was worse than anybody had ever felt anytime. Five hundred thousand times worse.

—and it held the wheel by instinct, thinking the one phrase over and over—it kept to the center lane at forty miles an hour down the highway, held to the asphalt by the two white lines on either side, held between the lines by a thread just a thread oh ghost of a soul on the gossamer thread of the web that he weaves with his words—

"What were you thinking about on your way down today?"

"One phrase over and over"—for it had seen another movie with its husband, had seen *Oedipus Rex*, but of course it had not really *seen* it, had not seen a single scene nor heard a word, but had sat there wrestling inside itself while light and shadow shuddered the screen with flickering incomprehensibilities, until the final line had emerged from the confusion and entered its brain to become, every minute since, sole occupant—

"What phrase?"

". . . and envy no one but the dead, a dead man feels no pain."

—home from the movie, in the house among the unrealities of children, nurses—"and envy no one but the dead, a dead man feels no pain"—in bed, between Nembutal and slumber, in bed between slumber and arising—"and envy no one but the dead"—all day between arising and being dressed (kind brown hands on the hair that its trembling fingers cannot fix, on the intricacy of snaps and buttons that its trembling fingers cannot fasten)—"and envy no one but the dead"—and driving down the highway and sitting here its brain phrase-ossified to stone—"and envy no one but the dead, a dead man feels no pain."

On vacation when he was thirteen Roger saw Mr. Jeliffe —he couldn't seem to call him Martin no matter *how* many times Edythe and Mr. Jeliffe reminded him of it; he guessed it was because he'd known him as Edythe's lawyer's partner a lot longer than he'd known him as her husband—well anyway, he saw Mr. Jeliffe help Edythe unfasten her swimsuit straps in back so she could lie beside the pool to get tan without getting white marks on her chest. (That summer, to celebrate the marriage, they'd rented a place they told their friends was their "little honeymoon cottage" even though it was so tremendous he got lost once trying to find the library.) Anyway, he was just coming out of the house when he saw Mr. Jeliffe fix the straps and then he saw him do something else. Instead of just taking down the straps he pulled some more and the whole top part of the suit came down. He had never seen breasts before, not that he could remember at least, and Edythe's looked pretty much the way breasts did in pictures kids showed him at school or on statues in museums, only softer and sort of droopier too. It didn't make him feel peculiar down there the way he'd been

160

feeling a lot lately, not at first it didn't. But he stopped and sort of stepped back so they couldn't see him and sure enough, Mr. Jeliffe took a look around and then he must've figured the coast was clear because he bent his bald head down all shiny in the sun and opened his mouth and put it around the full pink nipple. Then Roger watched him sort of twist around toward her, supporting himself against the hot concrete with one hand and putting the other one up on the breast he wasn't sucking and sort of touching his fingers to the tip of it. But it wasn't until Roger saw Edythe's head go back—straight back so that her face was full to the sun with her eyes closed and her hair hanging down her back and her mouth open moaning —that he got that way down there. He got that way so bad something happened and he had to go back in the house and change into another pair of trunks.

The reason he remembered all this stuff so well was that it was the first time that thing had happened to him without his making it happen on purpose. And the surprising thing about it was that it happened like that not when he was watching a movie or something where the two people are young and terrific-looking and it's all real romantic and sexy. Instead it happened when he saw that horse-faced Mr. Jeliffe doing something disgusting to Edythe, who was his mother, and terribly old.

Well, you never could tell. If there was one thing he'd learned now that he was growing up and graduating from the Lower School to the Upper, it was that you never could tell. About anything. Especially about yourself.

Oh, another thing. He'd looked out of his upstairs bedroom window after he changed his trunks and before he went outside again and if anything had happened it sure had happened mighty fast, because there they were stretched out on their backs all nice and normal like he'd imagined the whole thing.

He hadn't though. He was too old to imagine things anymore. He remembered when he was younger, even a couple of years back, he used to imagine some dumb thing about some friend, some very special friend.

Kids were so silly, the things they could think up. He

161

was glad he was grown-up. Being a little kid seemed like the dark ages now; in fact, he couldn't remember anything about it at all; it was all a blank.

"Why's Mom always up in her room?"

"She doesn't feel well."

"What's the matter with her, why did she get so skinny and quiet, is she sick or something?"

"Yes."

"But can't the doctor come and give her something to make her well?"—hiding in its room, hiding, hearing the sounds from downstairs, listening, lunatic, terrified of those it used to cherish—

"I'm in it"—clutching the phone that held the voice, the voice like the voice of God—"I'm in it oh I'm in it I can't get out oh help help help me please me I'm all the way in it oh this is the worst this is the worst yet I'm losing my grip on what's left of me and I can't stand it I can't bear it help save me save me I'm letting go I can't help it I'm letting go—"

"What have you eaten?"—sanity, safety, savior—

"Nothing, nothing, I can't—"

"For how long?"

"All weekend, all weekend"—it was Sunday and rain had turned the snow to slush, it was Sunday and a month of eondays had passed since Sunday or any other day held life instead of death.

"Come to the city. Stay in a hotel from now on."

—whatever he says whatever he says only help only help only help—

Four o'clock in the morning on a toilet for transients, that is the time and place for suicide, while a husband sleeps in the strange hotel bed beneath the framed-in-glass picture of a hunter and his dog. Five hours before the confusion of the TV screen had exploded before it eyes in a scream that was wrenched from its mouth against its will, a scream that was pressed gently back in by the hand of its husband—"Hush, hush now, my darling, we'll call him, hush now"—but the voice sounded faint in the coldness of the phone and the watch chain was a million miles away. The hand on its mouth had been the hand of a stranger, the voice in the phone had been the voice of a liar, and now the razor was reality and nothing else was real. But at the instant the razor touched the wrist a child cried out: "But why hasn't my Mommy come home?"

—oh but it must but it mustn't but it has to but it can't—

The handsome young couple, man and wife, saw many movies on the island of Manhattan; anyone would have said so, for they entered theaters and exited, daily, nightly (time must be killed, home is a place to stay away from), and that the eyes of the woman were not the eyes of one who sees would have been evident to no one but those who had known the eyes when they had looked out instead of in.

And in restaurants the eyes rolled back when the waiter asked its order, the head rolled back and its eyes rolled back in the head because the waiter was waiting for a bug to speak when the menu was a mess of black and white which made no sense. But no one saw the head roll back nor the eyes roll back and its husband ordered the meal and the meal was very pretty on the plate—"Janie darling, please, please try to eat, just a bite or two, okay? Please try? For me?"

—for you? but who are you?—

Who are you, my husband? I see you now as I write this, across the room, reading in your chair that is yours out of habit as I am yours and you are mine; I see you, as I see you so seldom—(the new chair is seen for the week of its purchase, and admired; then it is sat in, and indispensable, and seen no more)—I see you quiet for once, still, released for a precious while from the bondage of your restlessness. Last year seems very very long ago.

They would not know you now, your cardmates on the train, your trio of the 8:11 and the 5:15. Their prankster, their loudmouth, their shark, their shrewd and nerve-

163

wracked braggart—this? This tired child their noisy crony slamming down his "Gin!"?

Commuters, agents, lawyers, shoeshine boys, butchers who save the best cut for the charmer, barbers, chairmen of the board—all those bowled over by the boyish enthusiasm of this Philistine who is my link with life—hear you the cliché to which, embarrassed, I descend:

He is good.

Oh, he connives, tells dirty jokes, shouts, yells, is often in his tempers a disgrace, he hates with a bigoted passion all beatniks, Republicans, cats.

He is good.

He cries at movies, cries like a woman, he makes love with a tenderness unbecoming to his gender, he is afraid of fisticuffs, is a coward, if war came would pull a million strings to sit unmussed and safe behind a sturdy desk, he clips his cuticles and likes the feel of silk against his skin, when cruelty is in the news, when people are unjust, when he reads of hopelessness and hurt his face goes tight with rage.

He is good.

My father would remove an *o* from good; he'd make it God and put it far up on another plane, away from money, car exhaust, desire. But I am double-*o* and of this earth, I confess to no capacity for faith. Faith in myself, in family and friends, a very few—even this amount is sorely tested every day. But I am not without my compensations ...

I have a large capacity for stringing words together; Ee has a large capacity for love. Perhaps between us we will pass (instead of faith or values) a modicum of magic, crass, unhappy, to our sons, and hope that they can learn to live with it.

There is no witchcraft in the world but talent; no magic saws the heart in half but charm.

Who are you, my husband? To others you are a dynamo, a whirlwind, a monster of moodiness, perhaps, or an angel of gaiety, a breath of fresh air, warm, sweet, or a stench of Babylonian decay, shallow, a shambles of anger, ambition, deceit. But to me you are a necessity; if you were to die or (the same thing) stop loving me,

164

would find it difficult to recognize myself, for a major portion of my identity is contained in the expression in your eyes. This is not wise, but am I owl or wife?

You even make me feel that *I* am good.

And the watch chain and the desk and the hands and the voice—"I don't think it would be best right now for you to—"

"But I *must* go home, I *must,* this way it's worse than if I'm in a hospital, this way they have *neither* parent, and I should be home because even if I'm just a thing and just a piece of the furniture at least they'd have their father with them and I can't take their father away from them any longer and I know they'd be better off if you put me away but I can't stand to be put away so I will kill myself unless I can go home."

"All right." Why are his hands so very still? "All right."

On the morning after the night it returned home a person passed its bed as it awoke. It was a small round person that resembled a child, a child of its own, but it was not the child, it was someone else. For weeks it had seen everything as if through glass; now an added element of separateness had been added, as if an invisible and insidious mist were clouding the glass. And then, as the small person stood there phantom-strange holding a teal-blue Teddy bear, the glass became opaque and mirrored back the image of itself upon the bed, but the mirror was an amusement-park mirror, a fun-house mirror, containing not a woman but a hideous distortion, a creature wild-eyed with fear, a jungle beast mortally wounded, a thing which twisted away from its image with a scream, twisted away into a cave of covers, screaming as it smothered, smothering as it screamed, twisting inside a chaos of sheet and blanket until the hands of husband and nurse pulled it free, pulled its fingers from its face scratched raw by its own fingernails, and the screams kept coming out of its face like the screams of an animal trapped and mad with terror—*"Get them away from me, get them away—"*

—the phone thrust cold into the trembling hands—the voice, rough now with urgency, oh the voice like the voice of God, commanding, "Come here at once."

—and being dressed by others as an infant is dressed and then the motion of the car as the man drove it away from the grotesquerie of phantoms holding teal-blue Teddy bears, drove it to the watch chain and the desk and the hands, the altar that it bowed down its head upon in an agony of strangulation, for a piece of grief was stuck in its throat like something it had swallowed too fast, and it was screaming in its strangled voice, *"It wasn't my little boy, it was but it wasn't it was someone else it was . . . was . . . my sister I think yes it was my sister when she was little and I wanted to . . . to . . . kill her I wanted to kill her wanted to kill them all kill all three of them yes I wanted to murder them I was filled with killing filled kill children kill kill kill my children kill my children kill my children kill them kill them kill—"*

—and then he said, "All right now, all right now," in a voice that at last held tenderness, and at the sound of the tender voice of God, at the touch oh the tender touch of God, the piece of grief was unloosed from the throat and fell to the heart, breaking it open, and by its fall freeing a torrent of tears which broke through as does an ocean at the crumbling of a dike . . .

"Oh look! look!"—raising its head, caressing its wet face stinging where tears touched the scratches—"Look! look! I'm crying! I'm crying! What happened, what did you do, I can cry!"—and no food was ever so beautiful as the taste on its lips of salt or the taste in its mouth of sobs.

FOURTEEN

ED HAS a new client, as of yesterday, when the final contract was signed. His name is Drake Armour; it used to be Harvey Schenck. I will meet him tomorrow at a party

166

Ed is giving at the Harwyn, but already, from his pictures and publicity, I know what to expect. He is big and rugged and, as Roger did, he dyes his brown hair blond. Like Roger, too, his smile and his torso are his major assets; he is, in fact, much as Roger must have been when *he* was seventeen.

So all is well, and he will play *Son of The Martian.* He was chosen from hundreds of others, his press releases tell me. (The author of the items, my husband, tells me the facts: he is the nephew of the producer of *Son of The Martian.*) Drake, the all-American boy, had no interest in a TV career until tapped for the title role in this series, the papers proclaim. (He's been around for years—kid programs, phonied-up quiz shows, long before he grew to six-foot-four he played the part of Wendy's little brother in *Peter Pan.*)

Already Ed's junk is clogging up the columns: *Who's this* DRAKE ARMOUR *who has all the younger models in a furor?* DRAKE ARMOUR, *Son of The Martian, admits he's not as thrilled about his leap to stardom as he is about the leap last June which made him high school high-jump champ of Maine. What thirtyish songstress, notorious for her youthful appetites, has been phoning* DRAKE ARMOUR *all hours of the day and night?*

Ed says that Harvey's never been to Maine.

Ah well, I wish the fellow luck. Something had to be done, Ed explains; the sponsors want to continue the Martian idea, but Roger's films won't last indefinitely. And even if they did, the audiences might rebel against seeing the same old identical episodes year after year after year.

This is a way out. The sponsors are happy, Ed is happy, Drake is happy. "I'm going to play it smart," he told an interviewer from *TV Guide;* Drake was dressed—his picture showed—in the same M-crested costume his predecessor wore. "I intend to play this role to the hilt, but not get lost in it. That's what happened to somebody, I hear"—as he said this, the interviewer tells us, a wicked wink accompanied his little joke—"but not to me. I'll take other roles on the side, or if I can't manage that, I'll quit before it's too late. I won't let myself get typed."

167

He. Won't let. Himself. A subject and an object divided by a predicate. Two that are one, divided. I wish the lad good luck.

FIFTEEN

THE week in the hospital was even more timeless than the month before had been, for the thing awoke only to be fed a few bites of food and another huge blue capsule of Sodium Amytal before sinking again into the slumber of one who must vanquish an excess of time with an excess of sleep. When—in the stupor of an occasional awakening —it remembered how it was now and how it had been and could never be again, it wept as if the tear ducts were defective, in a steady stream which only sleep itself curtailed. Everything but grief and joy was drugged away, the joy like a loving puppy's, each day when the watch chain came into vague focus beside the bed and then the voice and the hands, but joy oh joy, no desk in the way now, no hateful sturdy barrier of wood, and like a puppy it licked the hands, like a baby just learning to walk clung to the legs beside the bed, like a baby just learning to talk babbled tearfully of dreams the drugs produced, told then the dream it had always had, over and over, a repeated dream since childhood as painful and incessant as a curse . . .

"My body is wrapped tightly inside a tiny package, but my head is out, screaming, screaming, and then someone comes along with a long heavy stick and strikes at my head, again and again, trying to bang the screaming thing back into the bag, banging the live head into the package with the dead body, but the head won't die like the body, it screams and screams and he keeps hitting it, hitting it—"

"You dream of Death."

"Yes, Death."

"You hate Death."

"I hated it. I don't hate it anymore."

"You fear it."

"No more. No more. I love it, I desire it, I—"

"You embrace the enemy."

"Yes. I would embrace it if I could. But you come between us. Your voice and your hands keep coming between us."

"I separate you from your love. You hate me."

"You separate me from my love. I love you."

—the words blur, the room whirls, oblivion is royal-blue and tasteless on the tongue.

A breakthrough, he had called the flood of tears. It was as if the hideous insight into infanticide had cracked the hard core of anguish and spread it out thin, so that it covered everything more thoroughly and yet less deeply. Still a thing, existing far out on the fringe of full reality, it had graduated in identity from waterless fish to legless gazelle: now it could breathe but it could not get up from the ground. But it could drive, oh it could drive (occupational therapy, he called it; alias, Something To Do). The steering wheel within its grip, the two white lines on either side, this was the world which a watch chain held in place. Between the rides were minutes as insubstantial as the figures which inhabited them; the notes alone had substance, the notes which it wrote like a sacred journal in the moments away from the altar, reading them aloud across the desk in a listless recitative that rarely faltered now, for the stumbling speech and tripping feet had melted away with the tears . . .

"*Ritalin 3* P.M., *Miltown 4* P.M., *Ritalin 6* P.M., *Miltown and Deprol 8:30* P.M., *Nembutal and Sodium Amytal 10* P.M., *Seconal 10:15* P.M., *Sodium Amytal and Seconal 4* A.M., *Nembutal 8* A.M., *Miltown and Ritalin 11* A.M., *Deprol 12:30* P.M.*"

Ah, the pills, the pills, crutches for a crippled intellect. Sleep came in torpedoes, shiny-shelled and multicolored monsters—scarlet Seconal, yellow Nembutal, Sodium Amytal beautiful blue; the others, the opposites—the waker-uppers, anti-depressants, supposedly clearing somewhat the muddled brain—were as negligible in their appearance as in their effect: Ritalin, pale and petite; pretty pink Deprol; and Miltown, the twentieth-century American cliché, downed by the dozens to muffle a motor plugged in from sick mind to sick nerves.

In this nether-world it no longer felt "in it," felt, rather, "on top of it," as an insect exists on the surface of a pond, perilously, waiting for the caprice of current or ripple to carry it under or return it to land. Visions of self-inflicted death became less frequent than visions of itself as a child, for the brain lay stunned by drugs inside the skin-taut skull, stunned too by grief and by horror, and its only clarity was in the past, as if in this death of the present the past flared up, claiming again the brain which age had weaned away.

"—to die and be born again," he called it—be born again and, toddler-wobbly, to grope from lap to floor, from chair to stair, from door to gate, and, cooing unintelligibly, to listen very hard.

"Janie's actually our third"—her mother and the woman sipping tea from the cups Janie was not allowed to touch—"We lost one just a year before she came. Stillborn."

She must not touch the lamp; the lamp would fall; she was the center of the universe.

"It was a boy. We had planned to name him Stephen. It was a terrible blow, of course, and then when Janie arrived and was so tiny I was frantic, I was so afraid of losing her too. During the first week after her birth it was touch-and-go, she was so small and she couldn't seem to get my nipple—oh, how we prayed. It wasn't until she reached ten pounds that I finally stopped being afraid."

Stillborn. Bornstill. Afraid. Mustn't touch. Other died. Almost died. Number three.

And she was the center of the universe.

Four months before it had become, for a moment or many moments now forever undeterminable, a very old man and then three unknown girls . . . three months before it had become a thing, thirsting only for oblivion . . . two months before it had become, in all but act, a murderer, and, in all but the final irrevocable degree, lost to the world of thought and of action, of reaction, of perception and awareness, of all the finite, infinite, iridescent and inexplicable qualities which distinguish man from animal; thus, for a third of a year, it had cringed across a mine-laden no man's land between death (the enemy turned friend) and life (the friend turned enemy). Lines which had been strong and sure had wavered and vanished: the line between reason and unreason, between self and insect-seeming nothingness, between life and death and between their symbolic counterparts—sleep and wakefulness. It had screamed or had been silent (the second far worse, for in the nightmare world of madness even a scream is communication, is release, is *something* instead of the everlasting nothing of no-self); it had known the death of the soul before the death of the body—than which there is no greater suffering—and, taking now the impossible for granted (what it had become was impossible and yet it was so; thus, what it could not possibly do, it did), it drove a hundred miles a day on a highway it did not see, with hands that hurt against the wheel because starvation had stripped the padding from the palms, with a brain so barbiturate-estranged from actual danger that it drove doorless from Cedarton to New York one February day, and, when asked by the voice what had happened to the door, said without interest in such a triviality—"I was still asleep as I backed out of the garage so the car door which was open got scraped off."

"Didn't you realize it?"

"Yes, the noise woke me up."

"Weren't you cold driving here?"

"No more than usual. I'm always cold now."

Cold, too, when it went to bed each night, so that its husband commented on its goose-pimply "elephant skin," and all his hugging only increased the cold, for it came not only from bones too near the surface but from fear, fear overwhelming and inarticulate, a new fear, for the words from across the desk had entered its awareness like an echo of a knowledge it had already refused to accept . . .

"You're showing certain predictable signs of improvement, so we're cutting down now on the Sodium Amytal."

"What? Cutting down?"—what? snatching its crutches away? how cruel! how cruel!

"You're not fighting the drugs as you used to. They're starting to take fuller effect. That means you're getting better."

"What? Better? How—why—"

"You're less afraid of them, less afraid of sleep, of the unconscious."

"But—"

"Never mind. Just trust me. We'll stick with the Seconal and the Nembutal for a while, gradually reducing the dosage."

—reducing dosage, getting better, sleep less, be awake more, no no—

"I think it's time you started facing the mornings. The 4 A.M. pill may still be necessary, but not the 8 A.M. one. We'll substitute the Ritalin and Miltown at eight for the sleeping pills."

—what? be awake all morning? but how but how oh no, time doesn't pass time stands stock still—

—but that's a lie, you *know* that's a lie, hasn't time started to move again, just a little? slowly, crawling, but some?—

—no! no! sick sick Sodium Amytal sleep escape suicide—

"Is time getting back to normal?"

"No! No!"—Sodium Amytal sick sleep escape suicide—

"Don't you find you need the Deprol less frequently? Don't you feel more in touch with reality?"

—no! no! cruel! take crutches away from a cripple cruel oh cruel—

"You'll find you get a new barrage of symptoms from now on for a while, but don't worry about it. You've entered the less acute stage of your illness, when resistance begins to replace depression."

—what? less acute? no! sick! suicide!

172

It was eight whole years ago, Roger, that you and I took that long walk away from the Danbury Fair. I had forgotten it until today, for today we are going there again, the kids and Ed and I, to see all the things we saw with you and all the more things that have been gimmicked into existence during almost a decade. Is the farm still there, I wonder, the one we walked to? I will notice—when we round that final meadow-slicing curve this side of Danbury—I will notice this afternoon whether that barn, like so many others in the villages of this historic county, has been vacated and remodeled to make someone's house: shored up sturdy from beneath, patched up rainproof from above, the maroon clapboard of the outer walls untouched but the inner walls removed or added or shifted around, providing the rich-but-rustic dweller with the look and smell of old cedar while accomodating well his wife and his guests and the latest in washing machines.

You had finished your two o'clock appearance, I remember, and had, as usual, parried the speech-end questions well. "Won't you vanish now?"—it was the first request to reach you from the small-fry crowd before the outdoor stage—"Hey, Martian, what about showing us how you go to Mars?"

You had your stock reply. "Can't, folks. Wish I could, believe me, but you better take it up with your local authorities here. They tell me I can't use my sword for the time being. They tell me there's a law against magic in Connecticut."

"You a phony, mister?" hooted a derisive teenager. Ed and I, standing to the side of the crowd, were as used to this kind of reaction as you were, and sure enough, your retort to the older boy was charming and predictable, delivered with your famed engaging grin. You held up your arm. "Say kids, does this muscle look phony to you?"

There was the expected long "ooooh" from the little ones, then your parting remarks—didn't you like to call it your "morality play"?—all about what kind of citizens they should be, stalwart, healthy, eating lots of Martian Macaroni. The applause was enormous; close to three hundred photos were passed out and signed; the fair manager was pleased, telling you through the flap of your dressing-room tent that even Howdy Doody the year before had not garnered more interest. The Martian's appearance had been well-advertised; except for that ring in the loud-speaker system—he'd get it fixed right away, the manager said—the event was a success for all concerned; the macaroni firm's representative assured Ed he would keep him advised as to the measurable effect in terms of local sales.

You emerged from the tent, face grim, clothes changed. "For Christ's sake," you said to me, "let's get the hell out of here."

"Be back for the next show," Ed warned.

"Four sharp," added the manager.

"I know, I know," you said.

And that is how we came to pass the farm. And how we came to go inside the barn, where you almost choked an imbecile to death.

"Look," I'd said. "Pigs. Let's go look at them up close."

We did, watching them in the mud outside the barn, and then, seeing the farmhand push a wheelbarrow of garbage in through the barn door, we wandered in behind him to watch the pigs be fed.

"Phew!" I said. I held my nose, then laughed. "Smells like a pigsty."

But all of a sudden you spoke in anger. "What's going on in there?" you said.

"What?"

Then I saw you weren't speaking to me, but were speaking to the farmhand and pointing to the pen where a huge white hammy mother lay, her litter pushing at her for their meal. "What's the matter with him?"

"Huh?" The boy looked at you with his jaw gaping, moronic, uncomprehending. "Matter with who?"

"Him. *Him.*" But I too did not comprehend until I saw the tiny wizened piglet there, ribbed, bony. All around it, shoving it aside, the other infant pigs were eating, guzzling, grunting, playing, but this one just stood, weak, wobbly, trembling, and tried to take a step or two but failed. It

174

was all dejection, all pitiableness; it looked like a poor relation.

"He means that little piggy there," I explained to the boy. "See? The undersized one that keeps falling down when the others bump into it?"

"What's the matter with that one?" you asked.

The farmhand's mouth showed spittle at the corners when he spoke. "That one? Dying."

"Dying? Why?" you demanded.

The boy's mouth hung open as he looked up at you, then back at the piglet, then, slowly, to me and at last around to his inquisitor again. "It's got no nipple for itself, that's why."

"Why hasn't it?"

"Huh?"

"Why no nipple?"

"Dried up. Few days ago."

"Can't it go to another one? Look at that belly, there's plenty of 'em."

The boy gained confidence at your stupidity; his head went higher, he licked his lips. "Them pigs know their own teats, only'll go to their own."

I was astounded. "You mean that little one's starving because he knows the one that belonged to him dried up?"

"Yes, ma'am. Just so, that's right. He'll be dead before much longer."

"What do you mean, 'much longer' "—Roger, you were the maddest I've ever seen you—"How much longer can he stand being shoved around like that? Don't you see what his siblings are doing to him?"

Word-daunted, the boy lost his self-assurance; he stuttered, "S-s-sib—"

"The others are trampling him to death, look, he's down, he can't get up."

"Down for good now, I reckon," the boy said. "About time."

"You just going to let them walk all over him till he's dead?"

The boy smiled slyly. "No matter. He's just about dead already."

It was the smile that did it, wasn't it, Roger—that and the way the little pig stood up again just then, unsteady, bruised, as instinctively obstinate in refusing to lie down for death as he was in refusing to grasp salvation at a nipple not his own. You grabbed at the boy's arm, Roger, so fiercely that he stepped back and knocked over the wheelbarrow, garbage spilling into the sawdust around his feet. Your voice was low and choked as you said, "Get that starving pig out of there, feed him or kill him or something but get him out of there."

The boy's head went down inside his denim collar like a turtle's into its shell; he peeked out, scared, eyes saying: madman! madman! At last he managed a stuttering rebuttal. "It-it-it's o-only a p-pig."

"And you're only a bum," you said softly, grip tighter on his arm, hurting, surely. "And you're going to do as I say. Get it out."

The baffled farmhand found the courage, after a long and dribbling hesitation, to say, "This is my cousin's barn and he left me in charge. You can't just come in here and order me around, who are you"—he peered closer at you, half-recognizing, suspicious—"Ain't I seen you someplace before? You from around here?"

"Never mind who I am, just get going and—"

"But I'm in charge"—sticking to his guns, miserable, dribbling—

And now your voice escaped its controls, roared out in all its wrath and glory—"When you're in charge of something you take good care of it."

"I *do*—"

"You don't, you bum. You don't deserve to have a damn thing entrusted to you, you *bum* you"—throwing him onto the wheelbarrow, then bending down with your great hands open toward his throat, his skinny, sweaty sharp-Adam's-appled throat—"bum bum bum—"

I stopped you, brought you back to your senses with "Rog, don't, you'll kill him, he's not responsible—"

The boy fled and we effected the rescue ourselves, you and I, placing the shrunken creature outside the chaotic pen, making it a makeshift manger out of warm soft rags we found, and left it there to die.

Outside, headed back for the fair, you said, "She never let out an oink."

"The mother?" You nodded. "Mmmm, didn't give a damn." You said no more, and after a while I added, "That boy, he didn't know any better, Rog. Besides, that's the way things are on farms. He probably——"

"He was in charge, he didn't take care——"

"But——"

"I hate that bum, I hate his guts"——and that was all that was said between us until we got back to the gate of the fair. Then——flipping on your faucet——you were gay and poised and charming once again.

"Say, Rog," Ed said, concerned, hurrying up to us as we arrived. "You'll just have time to get back into your costume. The crowd's waiting. Where you two been?"

"To a farm," I answered. "To a beautiful farm on a beautiful meadow."

"Well beautiful, that's beautiful, your nice little stroll almost loused up the show."

But the show went on; the show must go on, mustn't it, Roger? That's the maxim, Roger, isn't it?

I wish you could've gone through the wringer, Roger; I wish you'd had——like me——your bout with truth. It squeezes out your scapegoats, leaves you empty; it squeezes out your dirt and leaves you clean.

I wish you'd screamed the scream that has released me: I wish you'd sobbed, "Oh God, I hate my guts!"

He was a big hit in the Upper School's sophomore play. Roger had known he was the best in the cast as soon as he started getting more laughs than the others. But it wasn't until the curtain came down to the noise of their applause and then came up again and he could see it besides hearing it——the hands clapping, the faces lit up, the love leaping up over the footlights and onto the stage like something you could *touch,* practically, it was so solid——that he felt like he was going to bust out crying.

It was really a shock, because he hadn't felt like crying

177

in years, and what's more, what was there to cry about at a time like that? Later, when he was alone after the party backstage, he tried to figure it out. He figured maybe it was because now all of a sudden he knew what he wanted to be, and it was sort of overwhelming to know what you were good at after thinking for so long that maybe you weren't cut out to be anything but a *bum* and you might just spend your whole wasted life hanging around doing *nothing*. But then finally he figured also it must've had something to do with everybody else's parents being in the audience except his; even though Edythe was in Las Vegas and he knew it would be dumb for her to fly all the way back just for something so trivial, still, maybe that's what got him so weepy his throat felt as if he'd swallowed a golf ball the whole time they were taking bows, even when he took one by himself and was so happy he felt like jumping right down across the footlights to return the embrace.

Yeah, that must've been the reason.

Funny where your thoughts could lead you, carrying you way back sometimes, even way back to things that maybe never even happened. After all, how could he remember when he'd been learning to walk; he couldn't've been more than one or two years *old*. But it sure did *seem* like a memory—him trying like the dickens to walk from one chair to another without falling down, and finally doing it, and the two giants above him clapping their hands, clapping their hands, laughing and saying things like *"Good* boy, *that's* it" and clapping, clapping, and him doing it again and again so they'd clap some more, and their faces all lit up and the love leaping at him out of their eyes—well anyway, it must've been a dream. After all, his father and mother were divorced before he was three. Yes, a dream, like the stained-glass madonna and the crash and the laughter; that dream still came back sometimes and his heart still banged when he awoke.

It didn't matter. All that mattered was now, and now was fine. He had a treasure now; he knew what it was worth. A talent was a charge; one must take care.

In the next message from Matty Atkins—again a drawing of The Martian, nude again except for cape and boots —something was missing. The penis, splendid in erection, had been removed. With its erasure went the pornographic aspect of the picture, leaving an innocent abdominal expanse marred but by the single dainty navel; tumescence obliterated, only fatuity remaining, the smile of the crimson figure seemed slightly embarrassed now instead of lewd, as if to say, "Please pardon the oversight"—knowing, of course, the loss unpardonable.

A comment on his copy of the message came from Roger, telegraphed: "Now how will I———, much less ———?" And a letter followed—Ed read aloud of poinsettias around the patio, of Beverly Hills boredom ("Lisa's off to the studio at 5 A.M., I get up at 10 A.M., she's back home and in bed by 10 P.M., and I sit by the TV with my bottle until 2 A.M."), of vague references to plastic surgery and June with the Thompsons—but in every line, Ed said, he detected an underlying element of fear.

"Fear"—that word got through, but not the others, for to Ed's listener—marooned in a separate madness— the shenanigans of Matty Atkins, the reactions of Roger or Lisa or Ed, were a part of that reality which still could be grasped only in bits and pieces, and listlessly, without interest or comprehension or response.

"—such a challenge," Lisa had written. "Working with Kazan is like"—and more, much more about her career and no mention whatever of Roger, but it heard Ed's voice clearly on one phrase: "—can only conclude from your silence, Mrs. Thompson, that you're mad at me, too busy, or deceased."

"—*deceased.*" Yes, deceased, but Ed typed a letter in Janie-style, to which the deceased affixed its signature, and if the recipient was aware of the discrepancy between her friend's customary garrulity at the typewriter and the brevity of the note received, she made no more mention of her bafflement than did the recipients in Japan. But from Oregon came one short note, in March: "Something's wrong there, I can feel it. My sister's missing, she's not in this letter she just sent me, she's far away, farther away

179

than Connecticut, and a signature doesn't fool me. I don't know what's happening but I do know my sister is strong, and whatever it is she'll fight it, and someday I'll get a letter that's as authentically Jane as this one I'm writing is Jill, and then I'll know my sister's herself again."

Fight it, yes, fight it, but not the illness anymore, no, fight instead getting well, fight salvation. And remembering how they had told each other everything, always, those two loving sisters, and how they never could again, it wept with the tears of an ancient abdication, when the tears had been stifled, and—unshed, unmelted—had formed the snail-hard nucleus of a malignancy . . .

Her mother's voice singing softly the song which belonged to her, singing it to the tiny thing she cradled with love at her breast . . .

"Baby's boat's a silver moon
Way up in the sky . . .
Baby's boat's a silver moon
Floating up so high . . ."

And the dream, not just once but coming back night after night until she began at dusk to dread the bedtime, the dream of The Three Bears entering the house and going to the rocker in her mother's room. Her mother sat in the rocker holding the baby and singing tenderly, happily, but her smile fell off when The Three Bears snatched the bottle from the baby's mouth so roughly that it broke into slivers of glass and cut the baby's face. Her mother dropped the bleeding baby and The Three Bears laughed. And Janie, awakening, lay watching the kaleidoscope inside her tight dry eyelids, listening to the song that had become, now, a part of the dawn which dawned now so differently than it had before . . .

"Sail, baby, sail
Far across the sea
Only don't forget to sail
Back again to me."

The singing slid beneath her door like a slimy lava of betrayal, of desertion, of injustice, filling her with killing, for the fourth had arrived, the fourth, the fourth, the

180

small and the sweet and the beautiful fourth, usurping forever the throne and the glory contained in two arms and a lap.

No longer did the words hold true that "it *could not* get up from the ground"; now there was a slight difference, so slight that except for the switch in symptoms, the switch, too, in the symptoms' intensity, it would not have known that one phase of its agony had ended and another one begun: now it *would not* get up from the ground.

On the night of the day that the voice of God had delivered the ultimatum, taking away the bright blue crutch of Sodium Amytal, it spent the hours before bedtime screaming into a pillow with anxiety, then clawing the wall in a nebulous desperation at the idea of getting better. Then, lying in bed, waiting for a slumber it was sure would never come, it felt its brain shift back and forth inside its head—left, right, like a marble rolled inside a coconut—and then it was asleep. But no sooner asleep than its entire being was shaken again, this time not only brain but body, as if an explosion had occurred at the base of its neck, reverberating along its nerves like a nuclear reaction of the soul. Horrified, it lay awake inside the dynamited fragments of itself until the Nembutal and Seconal combined to bring it sleep.

"Hypnogenic phenomena," he labeled the explosion the next day, offering congratulations across the desk: "Well, fine. You're off the Sodium Amytal."

"But . . . but *look* at me"—for the nurse, upon awakening it that morning, had gasped in consternation at the sight—eyes bloodshot in such entirety that the eyeballs were, quite literally, a vivid scarlet, like some macabre fiend's, like Dracula's. "Chemical reaction to withdrawal," he said, and explained no further.

Nor would he explain why its head was heavy as if filled with cast iron, or why it could not control its facial muscles, or why it kept feeling fumes rising up through it as if some evil smoky geyser had settled in its innards, fuming up to fill it full of dazed sick dizziness. He was now somehow the enemy, taking it for granted that it should find itself quite unable to swallow, so that its appetite (ever better, although it did not admit this to him) could be assuaged only by way of liquids; it lived for a month on malted milks and lemonades, growing therefore ten pounds thinner in the month and feeling very pleased that it could offer this further debilitation as proof of its continuing illness.

But "Predictable" he replied to every recital of headache, fumes, starvation, and his smugness fanned its panic like a cool breeze on a flame. His hints of further abstention from the remaining barbiturates went ignored, for it clung now to the beloved capsules not only out of fear of insomnia but out of a perversity interpreted by its consciousness as necessity.

Until the morning, no special morning it seemed, when something vague and obscurely disturbing occurred beside its bed. There were voices, a child crying, another consoling, but the drugs consumed at six to kill the morning had rendered the tableau meaningless, a blur of sound somewhere on the edge of its constant all-encompassing dream. By eleven, however—when awakened to be dressed by the nurse for the trip to the city—it had shaken off the pills' effect sufficiently to see what remained in the room of the scene it had missed four hours before. Next to it on the pillow, resting porcelain-pure within the hollow a child had made for it, was a dainty figurine; her hoop-skirted gown was of garish Woolworth green, her eyes were closed beneath her yellow bonnet, and the gilt inscription across her shoes contained the first words it had read in four months: *I love you mother.*

Later—across the desk—"I didn't know it was Johnny's birthday, I didn't even know what month it was, I still don't, I only know it's his birthday because the nurse told me when she woke me, when I asked why the little china lady was lying next to me. She said his Daddy had told Johnny that his Mommy couldn't give him a party this year and so Johnny said that instead he'd give a gift to Mommy for his birthday. So the day before his Daddy had given him a quarter and brought him to the store and the little china lady's what he bought. But when he tried to give it to me this morning before he went to school he couldn't wake me up. Usually they keep the children away from me but he begged so, she told me, that they gave in, and then he was so disappointed when I wouldn't wake up that he cried and cried and she said Bruce and Terry and Ed tried to comfort him but he kept crying even when she and Ed finally got him out of my bedroom into his own, where his presents were waiting."

—the hands moving slightly in the papers on the desk, the voice silent, waiting, the grief in its own voice clogging its throat—

"I read the words. I can read again. The words said 'I love you mother.' That's what it said, I read it myself, it said 'I love you mother.'"

—come, tears, come, oh come to these eyes that can read again, to this heart that can hurt again—

—and the tears came in a storm, as they had before, the words caught up in the storm and choked out of its throat in sobs—"She was lying there so still, the little lady. Her eyes were shut, her eyes were shut."

Through the screen of its tears it saw the steeple of his fingers pressed together, through the torrent of its sobs heard his voice—"Now would you like to start thinking about being awake in the mornings?"

—and this time it did not have to answer, for he already knew, knew that the yellow crutch of Nembutal, the crimson crutch of Seconal, had already been discarded by a china lady dressed in Woolworth green.

SIXTEEN

"WE CAN'T locate him," Milton Cohn said. He had stopped off in Cedarton on his way to a convention of comic-book publishers in Boston; his chauffeur stayed outside in the "hearse," as Mr. Cohn called his long black Cadillac. "You know my man Frank Tibasi. He's followed every lead but no Atkins. The notes are all postmarked

183

New York and judging from the three days it takes for them to reach Roger and Lisa, it can be assumed Atkins mails them all at the same time, but from where?"

"And why," Ed added.

"Because he hates our guts, that's why, what more reason does a maniac need?" Milton was an incongruity on the Early American bench which fronted the fireplace, just as he had been at his own apartment, when the Egyptian sedan chair had held the overripe melon body, the cigar-poked melon face, the voice never lowered to less than a yell.

Ed said, "I don't understand what he's got against the rest of us."

"Whatdyeh mean, the *rest* of us. What's he got against *me?*"

"Well, I guess he's got a pretty good case against you, as a matter of fact—morally, at least, if not legally."

"Yeah? Who says that, your pal Rutherford? Listen I got news for you." He jabbed his cigar close to Ed's face. "I took that Martian gimmick when nobody else in publishing would even let Atkins get his foot in the door. If it wasn't for me he'd still be pounding the pavements with those pictures of his"—he thrust his cigarless hand into his pocket, drew out a rumpled piece of paper—"instead of sending these bare-assed versions through the mails trying to browbeat the same people that gave him a break in the first place."

"I never gave him a break. I never even *met* the guy."

"You will, just wait. This filth is just the beginning"—and he opened the paper, bending forward to flatten it out on the antique cobbler's bench. "Look, he took off his clothes, then his pecker, then his arms and his right leg, now his left leg. What's he getting at? Listen, Thompson, this guy's in earnest, he's sick as hell and he ain't gonna stop at dirty pictures, not him, he's got it in for all of us."

"You mean—"

"I mean I want him locked up. Sending obscenity through the mails, that's a federal offense."

"Don't you think a mental institution would be a better place for him?"

184

"Prison, nut-house, I don't care, just so long as they get him the hell off my back."

"But I thought you wanted to keep the police out of it?"

"I did. I still do. But——"

"Why?"

"Why what?"

"Why don't you like the police?"

Milton shifted all over—his bulk against the bench, his eyes toward Ed and away again, his mouth around the cigar—then said, "Lotsa reasons, Mac. Starting way back on the East Side when a cop beat me up because I wouldn't squeal on my own brother." But the recollection seemed to make him uncomfortable, for he jumped up, squashing his cigar into an ashtray and then walking with his short-legged strut to the piano. He stood there, almost the same height standing at the keyboard as Roger had been sitting at it, and played a few disconnected phrases of Schubert as he said, "Why'd your wife scoot away at the sight of me a minute ago?"

"Why, I guess she——"

"I guess she don't think I'm a suitable high-class type to come visiting here at the country estate, huh?"

"She——"

"She looks like a scarecrow, if you don't mind my saying so. What the hell happened to her since I saw her last? She used to be nice and chubby, a real doll. Why don't these women leave off the diets, don't they know men like to feel some meat on the bones? Or are you doin' it to her, eh?"—sending a wink across the room—"You makin' her life miserable, huh? You shackin' up with some cute little piece up the street or somethin'? Yah, I've heard all about this little hamlet you got here, real quaint and rustic and everybody in and outa everybody's else's beds, huh? Hey, that reminds me, didn't I hear you two have got another bundle in the oven? That'll make how many, three, four?"

"No. We were expecting a while back, but——"

"Well, just as well. She needs a good check-up for malnutrition if you ask me."

"I didn't ask you." But if Milton heard he pretended

185

not to, playing on until Ed said above the noise, "She'll be sorry she couldn't stick around to serve you some—"

"Don't bullshit me, Thompson"—his increased arrogance of voice identifying his previous deafness as pretense— "She's sorry I've stayed *this* long. Hell, it don't bother me, I'm used to these chilly little Vassar girls and their suburban big sisters. I meet 'em when their daddies go broke on Wall Street and come crawlin' to me for—"

"No, not Vassar. She—"

"Vasser schmasser. I just—"

"And her father's a minister in Japan."

But Milton did not answer; his treatment of irrelevant remarks was not deliberate, not rude; simply, it was as instinctive as the brushing away of a fly, for that which did not directly concern him in terms of personal threat or personal profit might as well have been spoken in a strange and alien tongue. Now, splendid with rings, his stubby fingers crashed angrily across the keys, making Beethoven as unbeautiful as his rhetoric had rendered Shakespeare on that night when Matty Atkins, unknown to all below, had raised his hand to hurl the rock, which—ending the mystery of who—had begun the further mystery of why, and where, and when. And now he said, "I talk like an immigrant Yid, right? And she don't like that, your wife, that offends her and her kind, don't it?"

Ed, knowing that the one under discussion was just beyond the nearest bedroom door, listening, peeking too, probably, began to protest, but Milton interrupted, "Well, there's one thing people like her oughta get through those aristocratic heads of theirs: I'm *smart*. I may talk dumb but, man, I am smart. I mean I am *smart*. You gotta be smart to push your way up past those pushcarts to Park Avenue, and one of the ways you gotta be smart is to see gold when nobody else sees nothin'. That takes brains, Thompson, tell your wife that, that takes brains and imagination. And that, my boy, is how I latched onto The Martian, seein' a million sweet green bucks where everybody else just saw a poor cruddy slob with another crackpot daydream of how-to-get-rich-quick. Yeah, I'll take one"—and he slapped Ed on the back with one hand as, with the other, he accepted from him a Scotch-on-the-rocks. He sat down, rolling the glass between his hands and looking down into it as he drew a deep sigh, in, out, then another, untypically, almost meditatively, as if he had seen a sign somewhere deep in the amber liquid which told him that this listener could be trusted, that this listener would not be one to take advantage if, for a moment, he doffed the armor of half a century.

"I'm an old man," he said, and his voice, though still harsh, was softer and even—yes—sadder. "I'm a wealthy old man and I've gone fishin' off Key West with presidents, and if anyone asked me which is better, to be poor or to be rich, I'd tell 'em quick it's better to be rich. But not much better. Whoever it was said money don't buy happiness, he said a mouthful. It don't, but it helps. But, Thompson, it buys enemies too, and every single one of 'em can hand you some long bitter hard-luck story about how I cheated 'em or tricked 'em when alla time it was just because they was dumb and I was smart. Take Atkins. He hates my guts, and for what? For being born with a brain that can take some half-baked little idea of his and make a whole industry out of it, a whole international empire. What's all this about how he wants more money—alla time ever since I met the guy, more money, more money. Hell, the creator of our biggest rival, for instance —*he* hit the big time with one bright idea, Superman—but he's an artist first and foremost, he don't have it in him to make a big stink about money. Christ, I got the only stink-maker in the whole lousy business, what's the matter with him, don't he know he's an *artist*? Artists ain't supposed to want money, don't he know artists are supposed to live in garrets and get their kicks outa all that wonderful artistic crap that guys like me ain't supposed to understand? Hell, I'm a businessman but I know my music and my literature, and even though he's an artist he can know dollars and cents, that's okay with me—more power to him—but was he satisfied with a fair settlement, and besides, a salary? No, he *sued,* and an artist suing for cash—hell, an artist that's *that* money-mad, he ain't no artist, he's just another slick operator. So okay, he learned his lesson the hard

187

way, he sued himself broke, sued himself out of a nice easy berth, sued himself back into a garret, where he belonged anyway. And now I'm supposed to take pity on a screwed-up sponge who didn't know when he was well off and went and got himself so fucked up it sent him off his rocker."

He shook his head, amazed at the Philistine evil in the fine artistic soul, and Ed said, "Do you think he really feels the rest of us are somehow guilty too?"

"Sure, he's out of his head, he's got this mental pitcher, obviously, of everybody who's benefited even indirectly from his creation, this mental pitcher of us five sittin' around together palsy-walsy and laughin' our heads off because we put one over on him."

"Roger says he always seemed like such a nice quiet—"

"Yah yah, they're the worst, the quietly persecuted ones. I know, I had an old lady who was one of them silent martyr types, Christ Jesus what a bore! Hell, the way she acted, you woulda thought it was us *kids'* fault that the old man flew the coop." And he fell silent, staring down into his drink, into his memories.

After a few minutes Ed spoke. "I wonder what fouled up Atkins in the first place. I mean, way back, whenever it was he began to get things twisted up in his mind."

"Poor slob." Milton rose, putting down his empty glass, and went again to the piano. "I remember once he mentioned his childhood to me and I told him we had a lot in common. He knew about poverty too, only he never managed to crawl out of it. I think they're better off, maybe, the ones who never get out. They never get a taste of what it's like to live good, so they're not scared"—he played a few bars of Handel—"scared you might have to go back to that again and knowing you couldn't go back. Being nobody again, that's what I couldn't take. The rest maybe, but the being nobody"—a few more bars, Mozart, Saint Saëns, Chopin. "Poor slob. I wish I'd"—but he cut himself off, suddenly savage with shame at his own sentimentality. "All right, so I feel bad about the guy, I owe him a lot, but goddammit, all that gratitude crap, that's ancient history now, that's water over the bridge,

188

and if he's got some bitterness left he oughta learn to control it, that's all, hell, don't he know he ain't the only one with problems, Christ, we're all sick, ain't we? all sick inside, only some of us gotta keep control of ourselves, gotta let bygones be bygones, fine place it'd be if everybody went around blamin' everybody else for their own troubles. Give me another Scotch, kid, will ya? One for the road—"

Then, as Ed handed it to him, he continued in his old form—cocky, the tough-guy clinging to his bad grammar with as much pride of possession as a schoolmarm to her fine diction—"I feel a lot more sympathy for Atkins even if he is out to ruin me than I do for your pal Rutherford. Rutherford, he hates my guts too, don't he, I suppose he figures if I hadn't sold him on playing The Martian he'd be the toast of Broadway now, ha! he'd be *nothin', nothin',* he's got no more talent than two dozen other guys with big shoulders and straight noses who're jerkin' sodas right now along Hollywood Boulevard hoping somebody like me'll come along and tap 'em for stardom. Listen, Thompson, I gave Rutherford his break just like I gave Atkins his—The Martian saved both of 'em, The Martian *I* made into a bigtime name, me and me alone, *I* did it—so are they grateful? Not them. Atkins I can excuse, he's sick, he had a rotten time when he was a kid and all that, but Christ, I see red when I think of Rutherford, that great big hunk of conceit, him and his Main Line background, polo horses and all that shit, where they taught him how he's better than everybody else—yeah, he's madly in love with himself, he is—the handsome high-class Roger Rutherford—I handed him his fame on a silver platter, I made him The Martian when he was nothin' but a two-bit actor playin' somebody's chauffeur—and now *he* spits on *me*"—drink finished, striding to the door—"People like Rutherford, people like him and that Little-Miss-Wellesley wife of yours, they're the ones that send me up the wall, not Atkins. Atkins I can understand, he's my kind, he's suffered and so have I and the only difference is I was stronger so I came out on top. But Rutherford—and your wife—they wouldn't recognize suffering if it came up and

189

hit 'em in the face—people like them, they're so in love with themselves nothin' ever gets through to 'em but how superior they are. Yah! I seen 'em puttin' their fine clean-cut heads together at my party and giggling about Cohn, that funny little blow-hard, and Rutherford making with the sarcasm and playing the saint, the sensitive soul, can't stand being contaminated by the very guy who gave him his place in the sun—resenting me, pretending The Martian ruined his career when actually it gave him the only decent job he's ever had. Well"—a final observation—"as for Atkins, I took all his abuse until he started with the filth. I feel sorry for him, but goddammit, there I draw the line. A sick mind, that's one thing, but a dirty one"—and he jutted a stubby arm from the car window as his chauffeur backed him out of the driveway, extending his arm out stiff in papal blessing as he shouted out his farewell comment: "Peace!"

SEVENTEEN

ROGER, it is early morning now and in this house which, in a few moments, will be so full of raucous boy-noise, I am the only one awake. A while ago I emerged from a nightmare and now at last my heart is beating at its customary pace again, calmed by the light growing brighter minute by minute in the window, spreading cheerily to the corners of the room and banishing the shadows of night as it cannot banish the shadow of my dream. Yes, my heart beats slower, but almost too slow now, heavily, the beat of it feeling as the keys in the piano do when they are not in the best working order; if my pulse were to play a song right now, it would surely be most dirgelike and most sadly out of tune.

My child was running, running back and forth. He was shouting, my Terry, shouting and running in my nightmare as he does all day on the front lawn of our house. But in my dream there was a difference, for rather than within

190

the fence of blue spruce which in reality shuts in our yard, my youngest was at play within strange walls. They were composed of round black disks, the walls, and I knew—as one always knows in dreams—exactly what they meant: they meant he was in danger, mortal danger, and yet I felt that I was powerless to save him. The walls were made of magnet-coils, I realized: they threatened him, they tried to suck him through. I tried to move toward him, to warn him not to get too close, to stop him somehow in his wild dashing back and forth across the yard, stop him before he ran in pseudo-gay abandon to the wall, which, looming up in fatal invitation, would pull him through where I could never reach. But when finally I found my voice and called to him, he looked at me with blank eyes, those eyes which shine with the look of involvement so seldom, being too involved with the invisible. His eyes were blank and I wept, wept as I did in reality a week ago, when he brought me a dandelion husk and asked me to blow its gray ephemeral head from the stem, decapitating its fluffy substance into the breeze. I blew, it disappeared.

"Gee," Terry said, eyes full of awareness, Mommy, world. "Only a teensy breath did it."

Only a breath. I cried, after he had gone, gone back to the front lawn and the running and the erratic laughter, gone back to his other eyes and all his other selves.

Only a breath. I hold my breath in terror for my baby. Must I hold my breath for all my life and his?

I remember, Roger, one time when you and I and Lisa—Ed was raking leaves beside the road with Bruce and Johnny—were watching Terry screech around the yard. We were talking together, the three of us, and accustomed as we were to Terry's antics, we had paid no heed until his shouting became so loud that we just sat there and listened to him. He was in it deep that day (I did not know it then, did not know what "it" was) and we watched for a while in silence, watched his incessant running from one end of the yard to the other, stopping short abruptly as he neared the close-packed trees at each side, stopping and bursting from chatter into laughter, from aimless motion into sudden rigid merriment before resuming like clockwork his solitary strenuous charade. Then a neighbor-child, a little girl his age, approached our gate. At once Terry grew tense, wary; he froze. "Mommy," he called to me. "Get this person off my property."

I called back. "Can't you and Suzy play together? Why don't—"

"No! No! Get her out of here. I'm busy."

Suzy backed away and Lisa called to Terry, "Can *I* play with you?"

"No!"—answer prompt, cold—"Don't interrupt my privacy. I'm busy playing with my friends."

"My God but he's bright," Lisa said, smiling, admiring. "What a vocabulary for his age. And what an imagination!"

"Isn't it wonderful?" you said, and laughed. "Isn't it a riot?"

Roger, I wish it were wonderful; Roger, I wish it were a riot. I wish that I could watch his play and not see magnet-walls. I wish that I had never felt their hungry beckoning, then maybe I could find it funny too.

EIGHTEEN

ON HER way to school she always took a short cut through the narrow alley which separated the parsonage from the church. On one side would be the cliff of gothic-gray stone, on the other the cliff of time-streaked shingle, and above—if she bent her head way back to look—was the slim corridor of sky as blue as the color of their eyes. Of mother's eyes, of Walker Moore's, and of her sister Jill's.

The stone wall of the church did not show much gray, though, for the green of the ivy covered it almost completely, the green which, at her approach each morning, stirred slightly at first in faint premonition and then—as she passed close—shook violently as a hundred anxious sparrow wings fluttered against the foliage in which their nests were hidden. Their frightened flurry never failed to startle her, but lately it was more than mere startlement that she felt, it was a deep dark terror that sent her running from the sudden rustle all around her into the safe and sunny haven of open space at the far end of the shadowy phantom-filled chasm.

The dark in there, the quiet in there, and then the abrupt chaos all around her, the chaos inescapable and yet invisible, evident not in the sparrows themselves but in the sound and sight of the trembling ivy which betrayed them—this was what held the terror, for it reminded her of something—of what? of what?—just as the sky did with its blueness.

But by the time she reached school her heart would have calmed again, morning melting into afternoon, and not until three o'clock—the bell ringing out, the children leaping from their seats, grabbing at their books and coats and pushing-laughing-struggling through the freedom-framing bottleneck of door—would she again become aware of the imminence of the alley and of the devastating effect her presence would have upon it, of the alley shrill and shaking with the multitude erupting in panic at her passing.

Funny, though, how she never went another, nicer, way. A half-a-minute longer it would take, and all the frantic flutter and disturbance in the alley be by-passed. But no, she never took another way.

And somehow, when she found them there at home— her mother and her sister Jill and him—the daily double dose of panic she had inflicted on herself would immunize her some against the pain.

Legless, armless, emasculated, The Martian was depleted now again. An ear was gone. It gave the face an unbalanced look—Ed said he was reminded of Van Gogh— and Lisa phoned to say they thought so too. So they spoke of Van Gogh, and Kazan, and Faulkner, and Ed listened and laughed and—while it sat there and half-heard him—

reported that Janie was out and would be sorry she'd missed Lisa's call.

When she was still very little she had become aware of the way Walker Moore looked at her mother. He looked at her mother the same way her mother had looked at her before Jill was born. As if there wasn't anyone else around, or if there was, he didn't matter much. As if just looking was something more important right then than anything else in the world, like drinking in great big gulps when you were very thirsty or like eating very fast when you were very hungry. Yes, hungry, that's how he looked at her, but very happy too—sort of all lit up in the eyes—and after a while Janie realized that when Walker got that hungry-happy lantern-eyes thing, her mother did too. It made her feel sort of strange in the stomach, like riding backwards in the rumble seat of the car, and invisible too, as if walking between them would be like walking into a string stretched across between them, and it wouldn't break but would merely tighten and tug them closer together as she pressed against it.

She wasn't sure just when she knew that Jill was part of it too. Her sister's eyes were very blue, and so were her mother's, and so were Walker's, so that had something to do with it. But again it was even more what their eyes *did* than the color they were, for her mother and Walker included Jill in those happy-lantern looks of theirs, leaving Janie brown-eyed and alone on the edge of their magic circle.

"Mommy's own sweet brown-eyed baby," her mother used to say to her as she turned from her ironing to give her a quick hug or—at bedtime—tucked her in with the hands so rough and wonderful, like a sandpaper angel's. But of course, she wasn't a baby anymore, and besides, Janie knew now the difference between brown eyes and blue. Brown eyes were what Daddy had, Walker's were blue. Brown were the eyes of Daddy's daughter, blue were the eyes of Walker's daughter, brown was bad and blue was good, brown was the color of dirt, blue was the color of love.

Both ears gone, the navel-dotted torso holding up the stupid-smiling face, The Martian arrived on schedule in the mail. Where his legs were removed, and his arms, the artist had not bothered to add the single cross-lines that would have turned them into stumps; the extremities simply ended, the double drawn lines forming—instead of neatly chopped biceps or neatly chopped thigh—the look of curtailed railroad tracks, as if this suggestion of abandonment, of tentative incompletion, was necessary somehow to his scheme.

It made her feel dizzy to think about the telephone extension, made her feel frightened and yet exhilarated to know that when her mother talked on the phone here in the parsonage, all her father had to do across the alley in his church study was to pick up the phone and he'd hear what she was saying. She'd noticed before that he scarcely made a click when he came on. If the other person was talking you might hear a click, but if you yourself were talking—well, like the time she and her best friend Nancy were talking about whether or not to cut off their pigtails and all of a sudden there was her father's voice: "*I* think you ought to let them grow long enough to *sit* on."

"*Dad*dy! How long have you been *lis*tening?"—surprised, embarrassed, distressed, but more than anything else immensely thrilled, thrilled that he cared enough about her to eavesdrop and then to tease her just a bit. She hoped Nancy was noticing what a swell old Dad she had, kidding around and everything just like other people's fathers did.

"Sorry, kiddo"—that's what he called all three of them whenever he noticed his children at all—"Sorry but you'll have to let me have the line now. You've been on quite a while, you know, and Mrs. Roethke is—"

"*I* know. *Dy*ing." Somebody was always dying. Or getting in trouble. Or needing comfort, or advice, or whatever it was that people always needed ministers for so that they were hardly ever home, and her mother always talked about how he wasn't part of the family because even when he *was* home his *mind* was somewhere else.

195

"Jane." Firm now. She could imagine the way his face looked, all hard-eyed and tight-jawed, like if he clenched his teeth together any tighter they would crumble into a mouthful of ivory ashes. "Jane, we do not make jokes about Mrs. Roethke's physical condition or anyone else's. Now do as I say and get off the line."

When his eyes weren't sort of hard and scary—which happened mostly when she was "fresh" or teased Jill or when her mother did a lot of sighing and sometimes crying too about how he wasn't a good father or a good husband and that if people knew what *she* knew about him *they* wouldn't think he was so good and Christlike either— well, when his eyes weren't that way, they were the other way, her mother called it "glassy," which meant he looked right at you when you spoke and yet did not reply, even if you repeated what you were saying about a dozen times, he still didn't hear you at all. Of course he always apologized if and when you finally got through to him; he'd sort of arrive back in his eyes as if he'd been away and he'd really *see* you at last, and would sometimes even ruffle your hair or chuck you under the chin or kiss you as he said, "Your old Pop's at it again, kiddo. Can you forgive your old Pop for being such a dreamy old codger?" And of course you always *did* forgive him, because he was so nice and sad-looking, sort of *mourn*ful and really-and-truly *sorry* that he wasn't like other fathers who were fun or like other husbands who "occasionally remembered they were married," as her mother often said. Her mother didn't forgive him as easily as his children did, though; it was as if she had done so much forgiving over and over again for so many years that finally she'd run out of forgiveness and had nothing much left to give him except reminders of how im*pos*sible he was—oh a wonderful pastor, she would assure Jane and Jill and Chuck—a fine preacher, a sincere and dedicated servant of the Lord, why yes indeed, she'd be the first to admit, as a clergyman he en*tire*ly deserved the devotion and respect his congregation lavished upon him—but as a human being? as a husband? a helpmate? A companion? a . . . a . . . lover? —her sigh would be dredged up from deep inside her, and

196

Janie would know that her mother's last hesitant word had to do with the pictures in the *Saturday Evening Post* of young men and women clinging together saying things like "Oh, my darling," and had to do with the way her father always came home late in the evening after making his parish calls and then sat reading himself to sleep at his desk every night no matter *how* much her mother begged him to come to bed, and had to do most of all with the look in Walker's eyes that matched her mother's, and the way, when Walker and her mother had to look away from each other, they turned their heads slowly as if it hurt to turn, unless of course it was Jill who spoke and then their eyes took her in as if she belonged somehow.

Matty next plucked out an eye. The picture seemed to wink, and Lisa phoned from Hollywood again, and Ed remarked he hadn't heard from Roger for a while.

Her brother simply didn't enter into the picture particularly. He was four years older and he fooled around a lot with chemistry sets and also read baseball magazines and he knew the capitals of every state in order, but except for these things she didn't know much about him or have much to do with him.

Once when her father took Chuck on one of his calls to a hospital, he forgot about him. Her father left him in the lobby while he went up to visit someone who was sick or dying, and Chuck waited all afternoon but his father never came back. It turned out that he'd come downstairs another way and had continued on to his other calls.

With people besides the family her mother always laughed a lot about how absent-minded her father was, and the hospital anecdote about Chuck was one of her favorite illustrations. Janie noticed Chuck never laughed about it, though, but just got all red and lip-twitchy, and when people weren't around, her mother wasn't especially amused either. In fact when other people weren't around, her mother cried a lot. The amazing thing was that she laughed a lot too, and Janie realized after a while that her mother was a person who would've spent her whole life laughing and humming a lot and never crying if she'd married someone like Walker instead of whom she did marry. It was odd that Walker and her father were best friends, they were so different, opposites practically, yes, Walker and her father were opposites the same way her mother and father were, like black and white, like daytime and nighttime. Walker wasn't only her father's best friend, he was also his best church worker, always organizing meetings and pinch-hitting for the choir soloist and lately he'd stopped being a deacon and had become head of the trustees. He was on the building committee too; her father often put his arm around him with real affection and told him he didn't know what he'd *do* without him. Walker had a mustache bushy as Groucho Marx's only straw-colored and straw-feeling, and he didn't look at all like God, the way her father did, at least that's what she'd heard one woman parishioner say to another, one Sunday in the church vestibule after the service: "If God had a face, he'd surely look like Reverend Winslow."

Her father and Walker did a lot of discussing over in the church study, and afterward her father would go calling and Walker would stop by at the parsonage for a cup of coffee with "the preacher's old lady," as he called her mother. He teased her mother a lot about her shabby hats and no lipstick and wearing cast-off clothes rich parishioners gave her just so she could send more of their money to missionaries. But no matter what he said her mother laughed, and he made her father laugh sometimes too, which was *really* something. But once at a church picnic at Lake Mahackeno Walker caught a little minnow and put it down the front of her mother's bathing suit. Her mother had screamed and squealed and then, after her father came back from taking her into the woods to remove the minnow, everybody was laughing so hard that no one noticed her father wasn't laughing this time the way he usually did at Walker's pranks.

Janie noticed it though. She figured she noticed a lot of things most people didn't notice.

198

The mutilated Martian that was taken gingerly from the mailbox was blind, eyeless, only the nose and mouth remaining in the firm red penciled outline of his face.

And Lisa phoned and said that Rog was out.

"You ought to see a doctor," her mother said. "You're a very sick man."

—weeping, weeping, his head on his folded arms, beside the bed on his knees when his early morning prayer had been drowned away in his own tears, and mother thought the children were asleep, but one was not—

"Why won't you listen to me, Russell. Won't you please let me *try* to help you? This whole depression now about Sunday School attendance, it's just a *cover*-up, can't you understand that? Can't you get far away enough from yourself to see that when you're so upset about church things or political things or . . . or . . . starvation in Afghanistan, it's all just *excuses*. You have a . . . a . . . problem. And your . . . your . . . guilt about it is tearing you apart."

"Go away. Leave me alone."

"Listen to me. I know you so well. I—"

"You don't know me"—crying changed to anger, anguish changed to hate.

"Now Russell"—backing away, stuck now against the bureau by his tall towering body like a butterfly pinned against a pad—"don't lose your temper. In the name of God don't—"

"Don't you use the word God. What do you know about God?"

—braving it out—"I know that my God is a God of love and joy. He wants us to be happy and to love one another. He does not want us to suffer if we need not suffer or to make others suffer through our suffering."

"And do I make you suffer so?"

"Yes! Yes! We all suffer, the children and I, we—"

"Do you tell them how sick I am, tell them I'm about to lose my mind, tell them perhaps I am insane already, is that what you tell them?"

"I tell them they should pity you—"

"Pity!"

"—pity anyone who goes through life with such a heavy heart."

"You don't pity me. You pity yourself."

"That's not true, I—"

"You wallow in self-pity, you've wallowed for years."

"I've done my best to—"

"I know"—suddenly slumping, contrite—"you've done your best. You didn't know, you had no way of knowing when you married me that—"

"Now don't start tearing yourself down."

—anger returning, sarcastic-smiling—"That's right, I'd better leave that to you."

"That's not fair"—tears coming, coursing down—"I've tried to give you my love, I still try. But you don't need it, you don't want it. You don't need anything but your wonderful Jesus—"

—the slap landing flat against her face, the marks of his fingers on her cheek like a pale pink glove—

—and her crying shocked away by his violence, his crying come again in his violence, and sinking on the bed with his face bleak with shame, bleak and then buried in his hands—

—and she with her hand held to her cheek, to her face suddenly tender now and somehow satisfied, almost grateful, as if something she deeply desired had been given her —and his hand reaching out like a blind man's in the empty air—and Janie's hand across her mouth to keep her crying caged inside so they would not turn and see her in the hall—

"It's my fault too, Russell"—almost whimpering, almost smiling—"I *am* a mediocre person compared to you. I'm just ordinary and I know my chatter bores you, irritates you. I know it's me as much as your guilt that drives you crazy. It's no wonder that you turn to your work, to your books. I'm just not good enough for you, that's all, not deep enough. You needed someone who could truly share your interests, your dedication. You could be a great man if only you—"

—waving her remorse and flattery away, speaking

through his tears—"No, no, I needed you, but never mind, never mind, it's no one's fault, no one is to blame, neither of us can change but we must learn to live in harmony if we can. For the children. For their sakes."

—she sighing—"It's a little late to start pretending to them. I'm afraid they already—"

"Christ said—"

"I wish—"

"—that we must try—"

"I try—"

"—to love one another."

—sighing more deeply—"If only you could snap out of these awful blue funks, dear. Everybody worships you so, why can't you think about that instead of dwelling on humanity's problems that only *God* can solve. When you talk about what a failure you are, and about . . . about . . . suicide, it's sick thinking, Russell, terribly sick thinking, and you *can't* help yourself, you've tried and you can't, you need help, professional help—"

"I have prayed—"

"Not prayer, no, not prayer. *Treat*ment. Medical *treat*ment."

"Perhaps the Lord in His wisdom—"

"Not the Lord, not the Lord. Think of your parishioners, is it fair to them, is it honest? You preach to them of self-control, of self-respect, and then you . . . you . . . well, is it fair to preach on human frailty as if you . . . you . . ."

"—like Christ, a cross to bear—"

"—what if they knew, about your temper, your black moods, about your . . . your . . ."

"Don't mention that!"

"It's mental, it's part of your sickness, you must—"

"That's enough"—snapped back to himself again, outraged at her meddling, disdainful and dignified, dismissing with distaste this typical exhibit of her nagging, her shallow lack of understanding, her everlasting harping on inconsequentials in her dearth of comprehension of the consequential—"I think you can start breakfast now."

—but persisting, mosquito-like, swatted-at but stub-

born—"If they found out, they'd call you a fraud, they'd
turn against you, every last one of them—"

"Stop that"—putting out his hand to twist her arm, to
twist her into silence—

—but she bending sideward away from him, almost
squealing now—"All right, all right, don't think of your
self, if it's too un-Christian to think of yourself then think
of them—think of the thousands of people you've helped,
the thousands who depend on you who would feel be
trayed if they knew, who would lose not just their faith
in you but in God, in goodness—"

—but at that his hands fell to his sides stricken limp at
her words, his face went into a contortion of agony, she
had at last struck home—"In Jesus' name, I beg you
stop"—and as she went to the door, martyred, satisfied,
sullen, Janie vanishing swiftly into her own room, the
church bells rang seven and Sunday dawned clear and the
dreamers awoke from their sleep.

*Now only mouth remained, and tilted sword. All else
was gone*—"Goddammit," Milton Cohn shouted into the
phone, "No nose and no news. Tibasi can't find the guy"
—and the last of the snows had melted on the lawns of
Cedarton.

The alley where the ivy was, and the sparrows, had a
small door near one end which was the back way into the
church. Nobody ever used it much; it was easier to use the
side door only a few steps away from the parsonage porch.
But one day when Mother and Jill were downtown, she
cut through the alley and slipped in silently by the small
door.

She realized that her father was usually in his church
study Friday afternoons, working on his sermon, and
since she felt unusually full of confidence today—felt al
most *pretty* in fact and somehow more lovable after win
ning the spelling bee and then being praised publicly by
the principal for her composition on "My Idea of Para
dise"—she decided he might be happily surprised if she
paid him a visit. Ordinarily nobody was supposed to

bother him when he was working, but she figured she'd take a chance. Maybe he was lonesome. Maybe he'd be so pleased to see her that he'd set her up on his desk—push all the papers aside, and the books and the Bible and the typewriter and everything—and ask her to tell him all about the day, about the spelling bee and the composition and everything. Yes, she would tiptoe in through the baptistry—the dark dank dungeon of a place between the alley and his study, the place which lightened only slightly on Baptism Sabbaths when its concrete concavity was filled with water and the velvet curtains were pulled aside to reveal to the congregation their pastor in his long black robe and, beside him, the newly accepted parishioner who would be bent back into the water as her father repeated the words which, like the Doxology or the Call to Prayer or the Wedding Ceremony or the Funeral Service, had become so familiar to her that she could recite them all by heart: "I baptize thee, my son, in the name of the Father and of the Son and of the Holy Ghost" . . . "And now let us remember the words of our Lord and Saviour Jesus Christ, who said, it is more blessed to give than to receive" . . . "Now those whom God hath joined together let no man put asunder" . . . "Ashes to ashes and dust to dust."

Yes, she would recite to him the short sentences the principal had liked so much: "Paradise is not for Protestants only. It is for everyone who has been good and not sinned." She knew he'd like that part best, that last word especially had such a swell *sermon* sound to it; she wouldn't bore him with the rest, all about the angels playing harps. But she would ask him about the harp in her grandmother's house, there in the music room that had feather-fans all across the mantel and a piano that made a real tinkly sound when you struck the keys, like when you touched your fork to a crystal goblet. Another wonderful thing there was the album all full of pictures. Her favorite was one that showed her father when he was five years old; he had long curls like a girl and the same clothes as in her book *Little Lord Fauntleroy,* all lacy around the collar and tied with bows below the knees; and grandmother's hair was black instead of white, but her face was just as stern as always, and she sat there strict and straight and scary as a mean queen with the solemn little fellow leaning toward her so his curls just touched her big fat puffed-up sleeves. Another picture she always spent a long time staring at was taken at her parents' wedding, out on the lawn behind grandmother's house. They were standing inside a grape arbor and they looked so young and beautiful and absolutely radiant with happiness that try as she might, she just *couldn't* connect them with the two people who were her parents now.

Strange about getting old. Getting old and dying. But quickly she shut her mind against that, just the way she'd shut off her sadness as she wrote her composition, knowing that what she wrote was all a fairy tale. Heaven. God. Angels. They weren't real, but death was. Stop! She wouldn't think about it, she mustn't, it was too terrible, it was worse than anybody anyplace had ever felt about anything. Five hundred *thousand* times worse.

And now she was in the baptistry, tiptoe, tiptoe. And it was dark, so dark she stopped to get her bearings, and then her eyes adjusted to the darkness and she saw him. He was wearing his boots, the high hip boots that he wore beneath his robe at baptisms, but now no robe, he was wearing instead his regular weekday shirt, its whiteness ghostly bright against the gloom. He stood with his back to her, and she opened her mouth to speak, and then did not speak, listening instead, listening and suddenly remembering the sounds that Walker had made and mother too when they had pressed together whispering and kissing in the kitchen, had pressed together and seemed to be in pain.

The final arrival reminded Ed of the first illustration in those Ten Basic Lessons that are supposed to teach a novice how to draw the human form. Smaller oval set on larger oval, the former devoid of feature and the latter lacking all but brief beginnings of arms and legs, the picture had lost all resemblance now to anything but a very slender snowman. Gone lust, gone laughter, gone all but this: a head, a body, and above—pointing toward Mars, slender, magical—The Martian's sword, bright red, as red as blood or lipstick or an apple in an orchard in the morning.

It was the second Monday in succession that her father had broken his promise. The first time she had cried all afternoon from disappointment, not only that he was too busy but that he had *always* been too busy; but this time her grief was too great to be permitted the pleasure of tears and she carried her bitterness like a cancer under her heart, hurting, hurting, and walked across town to her grandmother's house, where the deer's head on the wall watched her stonily as she entered and the big black clock standing like a sentinel at attention relaxed into gay chiming just as she greeted her grandmother, so that she had to wait a moment until the chimes ended and the soft bong-bong-bong began its count of twelve before she said again: "Daddy promised to take me horseback riding but now he's too busy."

Her grandmother looked up from the Hartford *Courant,* laying down her tortoise-shell-framed magnifying glass. "Monday is supposed to be his free day. The Sabbath being no day of rest for him as it is for most, he should allow Monday to be his time of rest."

"That's what Mommy says, but—"

"Well, the Lord's work comes before pleasure."

"Grandma, may I look at the album?"

"Are your hands clean, young lady?"

"Yes, Grandma"—and there, after she opened the album, was the picture she'd been wondering about. "Grandma, who's my mother pregnant with here?"—and she showed her the picture.

"Land sakes! Why'd she let anybody photograph her in *that* condition"—she clucked her tongue—"What's the date say? 1925? Let's see. Mmmm. That must've been the one she lost."

"My brother? The born still one?"

"Stillborn. Yes."

"What did he look like?"

"Like all new babies, I s'pose. Like a very little very old man."

"What did they do with him?"

"What? What?"—barking it out, turning the dial of her hearing aid, impatiently cocking her caustic head—

"What did they do with my dead baby brother?"

"*Do* with him!"—these dratted questions, her expression said, how in the name of heaven does the child think *up* these fantastic things—"*Do* with him?" She picked up her magnifying glass, readjusted her paper upon her lavender faille lap, dismissing the whole silly subject with "Wrapped it up and threw it away, I s'pose"—chuckling at her grisly wit—"Now get along with you, child, go on now, child, get! get!"

But she was no child, she bled, every month for the past three months she'd bled, and sometimes—several days beforehand, usually, when the swellings on her chest were even more swollen and her dreams were stalked by the specter of death—she felt down there the way it would feel to be two pieces of Scotch tape stuck together, so that she spent a lot of time jumping sidewards with her legs wide-spread to pull the stuck feeling apart.

From her grandmother's she went along the road where she knew Chuck hid to watch Maria. Maria was the girl her brother loved, Maria didn't love him. Ah, good luck! There he was, hidden behind the hedge to watch his loved one's comings and goings from her house.

"Boo!" Janie said. "I'm gonna tell on you." Hurt him, hurt them, hurt them all.

Her brother's face flushed red. "Go away, you. Beat it."

"I'm gonna tell Maria you're here."

Redder, lip twitching, nostrils taut—"You better not, you brat."

"Aren't you *ashamed,* spying on her? Don't you know she des*pises* you?"—hurt him, hurt them all—"Everybody laughs at you, don't you know that? You're an ugly freckle-faced *drip,* that's what you are."

"Ah shut up"—starting to stroll away down the road, ultra-casual—

"And you're a sissy. You're a drippy little sissy. I could beat you up with one hand tied behind me."

No reply, hurrying away so Maria wouldn't hear, hurrying away so he wouldn't hear—

"You're *scared* to fight anybody. Even *me* you're scared of. And I can beat you running too, and swimming and climbing and everything. And I'm smarter in school and I got a dozen friends and you only got one and he's even drippier than you. Ha! The two drips! The freckle-face drip and the fat-ass drip! Ha! The two sissy drips!"

His thin back was an inadequate target, it winced and it fled but it was not enough. It was an appetizer, it did not sate her need. Monday and her father was too busy. Monday and her mother was with Jill. Monday and another promise broken. Monday and her breasts too sore to touch. Monday and another lie, another. Lies and dirt and dirt-brown eyes and blue.

It did not sate her need.

Wrapped him up and threw him away.

Mother. Walker. Lantern-eyes.

Mother, Walker, sounds of hurting. Daddy too, in pain.

Illness? Death? No!

Breasts. Blue. Busy.

It did not sate her need.

And then as she rounded the corner by the church he came down the steps, her father, and he came to her and put his arm around her. "Okay after all, kiddo. Got finished up on time. Mom's made a picnic for us. Ready to go?"

Oh he was tall, her father, and good, oh he was handsome with his face like God's! And on the bridle path she was so proud and happy as he trotted next to her—the two of them alone at last, his leg against hers sometimes as they came together, stirrups clinking, in the places narrowed by low branches—that she almost choked on her unspoken words of love. And then they were cantering, and her horse shied back, reared up—she could hold on if she wished and not fall off—she could hold on if she wished. But she let go, she fell to the ground, unhurt,

207

the horse whinnied, reared once more, and galloped off down the path toward the park.

Now he was bending over her, lifting her up in his arms, holding her—"Janie, are you all right?"—and she kept her eyes closed and felt his face so close to hers. He would lift her up, he would carry her home, he would sit on her bed and tell her that he loved her, that she was his own, his very own, and that he loved her.

She opened her eyes. "I—"

"Are you hurt?"

"I . . . I . . . don't think so."

He lifted her, set her on her feet, said, "Okay?" She nodded, and he said, "Quite a spill. Walk back and wait for me at the stable. I'll chase your horse."

"But—"

He got back on his horse, paused as she said, "But . . . I . . . I'm hurt."

"You're all right. I better hurry and catch that horse before somebody *really* gets hurt. I'm worried about"—but his voice was lost beneath the hoofbeats as he galloped away, leaving her standing there with manure on her scrawny hip and a beat-beat-beat between her legs as if her heart were stitched into the tight crotch of her jodhpurs and the unspoken end of his sentence in her mouth like sawdust—"the others." He was worried about the others, whoever they might be. He wasn't worried about her. He cared about the others, the others, always the others, he didn't care about her.

And she trudged home, all the way home, not stopping at the stable—trudged home, making no answer as Jill glanced up from her paper dolls to say, "Mommy's over at the church helping Walker with the potluck supper decorations, what happened to you, you stink"—trudged up to the bathroom and undressed and got into a hot bath, lay there planning it, planning it all . . .

—*I'll get rid of the others, there'll be just me and him, I'll get rid of them, I'll wait until he's alone in the dark in the baptistry again and then I'll go get them all, all the parishioners, all the ones he loves, the others, the others, all the others who need him, who love him, all the ones he loves, I'll have them all come in quietly so he doesn't hear anything and they'll sit in the pews and I'll go up and quickly pull open the baptistry curtain and there he'll be and then they'll go away, they'll go away and never come back, they'll go away and there won't be any others ever ever again, there'll only be me, me and him—*

—but what about mother? Chuck? Jill?—

—he doesn't love them—

—maybe he does—

—he doesn't love Chuck, he's disappointed in Chuck, Chuck doesn't count—

—all right, but mother? Jill?—

—yes, mother, Walker, Jill. Well, I know what I can do, I'll wait until mother's on the phone with Walker late at night when she's saying those things she says in a whisper when she thinks we're asleep and Daddy's working on his sermon in his study and I'll wait till then and then I'll creep downstairs and over to the church and I'll tell him to pick up his phone and then he'll listen. He'll listen. He'll hear. And then he'll know and then he'll kill them, kill them all three, and I will be his wife.

She got out of the tub, dried herself gently so as not to hurt her breasts, and opened the door.

"Well hi"—Chuck, and Vincent his friend, both pimpled, both fuzzy-chinned, both smirking—"Wanna have some fun?"

—hurt them, hurt them all—"Drips. Sissies. Go play paper dolls with Jill."

"She went out. Nobody's home. There's just us." And they grabbed her, one holding one arm, one the other, forcing her to the floor, and then one holding one leg, one the other, and her bathrobe was open, and Vincent said, "Look, hairy already," and Chuck said, "Teach her a lesson," and then Vincent laughed, "Hell, some lesson, she'll *love* it," and then while they held her and touched her something sticky got on her clenched fist and there was nervous giggling as one of them said something like "—came, now watch *her* come," but it was all a blur except the delicious agony and the screams that refused to come out like the screams in a dream and—after she had

209

struggled against, stopped struggling, struggled toward—
her brother's final words: "Don't ever tell, or else . . ."

Sometime later she entered the alley and the ivy stirred.
Her body hurt and her head was filled with confusion. She
couldn't remember, something had happened, a lot that
was bad had happened recently and long ago but she
couldn't remember, it was bad and they were bad and
she was bad but she couldn't remember—the answer was
here in the alley—

—and the ivy's stirring increased as she came closer
and all around her the green of the ivy was shaking its
fists at her and now her screams came, for the chaos she
had hoped for was upon her, the chaos she had caused had
turned upon her, and the sparrows were coming at her,
wings flailing, beating at her with their wings, eating at her
with their beaks, and diving from the ivy green and
screaming in revenge, they blotted out the sun and killed
her dead.

NINETEEN

ED BROUGHT home a movie magazine today; inside there
is a picture story entitled "The Top Screen Queens," and
directly beneath their three pictures—Marilyn Monroe,
Elizabeth Taylor, Lisa Maurice—the caption reads, "Are
They All Enamored of the Same Man?"

It is a trick, of course, a gimmick, but I read on: the
same old tired lies and fabrications, the same old well-
known facts of lovers, husbands, divorces, lawsuits, canyon mansions, hilltop hideaways, eternal triangles, nervous
breakdowns, attempted suicides. The gimmick comes at
the end, past the paragraphs of tragedy and larceny,
adultery, disaster, past the photographs of legs and breasts
and Oscars on the mantels, past the blurry timeworn
snapshots of foster homes and adolescent shyness, of Liz
on her pet burro and Lisa fuzzy-headed in her first permanent with her bobby sox drooping and her eyes blinked

shut against the glare of sun upon the bright New Hampshire snow.

The gimmick? Why, they are all three enamored of God—yes, *He* is the lucky fellow in question—they have all Found Him, one way or another, via Billy Graham, Rabbi Wise, the glib, hypnotic, chaste Monsignor Sheehan. They Are Saved.

Well, everything else in show biz is a gimmick, why not God? I turn to my husband and ask, "Your brilliant idea?"

"Hell no. I just noticed it on the newsstand at Grand Central, what junk. Not that it matters, incidentally, but Lisa's religious conversion began and ended all in one month. Last thing I heard she was on Sartre."

I put the magazine down, feeling relieved that Ed has not been responsible, feeling, nonetheless, immensely sad. The dishes are done, the children are tucked in, ahead of me is evening, night, morning, age, the grave. Lisa's evening, Nikita's, bees' evening and buzzards' and Fiji Islanders' and God's—do we exist in the evening of the world?

"Shouldn't have shown it to you," Ed remarks, face visible a moment, newspaper down.

"What?"

"I thought you'd get a kick out of that article, it's so dreadful, but now I see it's got you depressed."

"Depressed? I'm just thinking."

"About what?"

"Lisa. America. Whether or not to cut my toenails now. I wonder—"

"Hmmmmm?"

"—did my toenails get cut at all? Did you or Mrs. Ross or somebody cut them or did they just keep growing all those months and curl under and sort of break off by themselves?"

"Huh?"—inexorably, his newspaper rises, the top of it level with his nose—"When?"

"Last year"—but he is vanished, as is last year, and if cigarette smoke is all I can see of one, disbelief is all I can feel for the other.

TWENTY

IT SLEPT very little—the drugs banished, the capsules curtailed (but kept in the bathroom cabinet, dozens and dozens and dozens of them, red and blue and yellow, just in case)—and the little slumber achieved was gory with dreams, for the classic aspect of analysis turned out to be not a Viennese fairy tale but simple fact: in sleep the key.

And the key was carnage, replete with symbols of sex and with symbols of death; yes, sex and death stalked the slumber like twin ghouls, a pair of childhood horrors holding hands, and in the instant of awakening it grabbed a pen and wrote down reams and reams of dreams—one page, three pages, five pages, seven—dreams so detailed and complex, so drenched with the colors of carnage and so mysterious and yet explicit in their meaning (whether of memory or of desire) that April became a major operation minus anesthetic, became a brain-turned-inside-out. Of daffodils showing yellow above the ground it was not aware, nor of breezes growing warmer nor of any outward thing, but of nightmares it could write with a madwoman's marvelous lucidity—the unreal seen clear, the real not seen at all.

And more and more, in that month of unseen daffodils, two terrible male figures entered the dreams, preparing tortures, brandishing fearfully elongated instruments, hissing obscenities, and interspersed among their depravities wandered three girls—three girls in a crimson room, three girls in a black box, three girls of whom one was ever ignored, left behind, locked out—and always somewhere, silent and frightening, an old man would appear, a very very old man: sitting motionless on a hill at sunset, and the trespasser ("It is I") stepping across his property in a cold sweat or trepidation at discovery; sitting motionless at a window, gnarled hands in lap, the servant ("It is

212

I") spoon-feeding cereal into his mouth; lying motionless on a scarlet bed while an artisan ("It is I") lifts his death-mask from his waxen face.

"The puzzle"—he called it that now when the dreams were read across his desk—"the jigsaw puzzle. The pieces are beginning to fall into place."

"The very old man? The three girls?"

He nodded. "And if you can write your dreams and read them to me like this, why can't you read anything else?"

"I can't read, I just can't. I can't read or swallow or smile or think—"

"Soon." "Soon" was his April word; everything would be soon—spring, forsythia, sanity. "Soon. Soon."

And then one night it woke up screaming (woke at four, always at four, not a moment earlier or later, night after night for month after month, like some sadistic anti-sand-man's practical joke), woke husband, children, night nurse, woke them all with the shrill crescendo of its one repeated phrase: "Pelleas and Melisande! Pelleas and Melisande! Pelleas and Melisande!"

"Janie"—Ed shaking it, shaking it hard—"Janie, wake up. It's just a dream, honey, shshsh, it's only a dream."

And later, reading the dream across the desk: "My mother is at the pulpit reciting love poems to the congregation while a man in the first pew keeps pressing his face against the pulpit as if he thinks he can press through to where her legs are, and she is very much aware of what he is doing but is pretending not to be, and suddenly I know what's happening and I jump up from the choir robe rack in the baptistry, where I have been crouching be-tween the robes, and I run all around the church, up and down the pews, trampling across all the laps, yelling "Pel-leas and Melisande' over and over again as if I can never stop."

"What does it mean to you?"

"Nothing, absolutely nothing. I never heard of anything called Pelleas and Melisande."

"Never heard of it?"

"No. Never. Why, are they words you've heard of or did I just make them up?"

"You didn't make them up. Maeterlinck did; then Debussy used them for an opera."

"What's it about?"

"Sex. Death. The carnage caused by a child's confirmation of his father's suspicions about his wife and her lover."

"Oh. Well, I never heard of it before"—but even as the denial issued from its lips, something happened inside the iceberg submerged below the surface of its consciousness, happened inside that enormity of knowledge and remembrance which had previously permitted only a small insignificant protrusion of itself to function as logical thoughts, as concrete reasoning, as known and recognizable emotions, as—now—denial. And the thing which happened below was so basic to the form of that enormity that—losing now to the conscious mind that which had provided its internal balance for a lifetime—it was shaken to its foundations, shaken as is anything which in an instant is lightened of a burden it has come to regard as essential to its identity. And the cataclysm of that change was so total that the head containing the revelation felt split open, as if by an ax, and at the same moment that its mouth opened in a sob of shock and pain, of abrupt and intense and physical despair, it knew that Pelleas and Melisande had been engraved upon its soul for the larger part of thirty years and one.

I don't suppose it should still have the power to shock me, but it does—to walk into the den between five and five-thirty and find Roger grinning at me, so sparkly-eyed, familiar, so alive. I stare back at him across the room, watching his familiar walk, listening to his familiar voice and familiar laugh, feeling friends with him again and very close until Tupper's Gum usurps the screen, relegating him again to his daily-interrupted nothingness.

Today Ed is the one who snaps off the television set after the program, and he must be feeling about it rather as I do, for—after the boys have left the den—he says, "It's the voice that gets me most."

"Yes, I know." I think a moment. "Ed, I want a record of you talking, just in case."

"Huh?"

"If anything ever . . . happened to you, I'd want to have it, have your voice still around."

"Ain't you cheery!"—laughing, patting my can, sitting me down into a chair and squatting before me, back turned—"Scratch please, fatty."

"I mean it, honey"—obliging, scratching his back— "Pictures are okay, they capture something but not enough. I'd want most of all to *hear* you again, it would bring you nearer somehow than the pictures would."

He teases me. "You can turn out the lights and put on the record and pretend I'm still hale and hearty. I'll say things to make me seem really-and-truly alive. Things like 'All right, dear, don't nag, I *will* take the garbage out.' Think that'll do the trick?"

We laughed, but tomorrow we are going to make the records. Mine for him, his for me, just in case. We will recite poetry, we've decided, and then we will be all set: all set for the eventual separation.

For, of course, we will be apart. Not maybe, not perhaps. For sure. Apart, forever. Someday. Bright-souled sensible people would say to me, "Foolish brooder, you can cross that bridge when you come to it."

Who will come to it, he or I? Where? How?

Last year has taught me to anticipate; I do not want to be surprised again.

At April's end, Ed having been notified that the patient's progress was satisfactory and that the "danger" was past, he announced that he was taking the convalescent to Florida for a week. He had to meet a client down there, a new Rock 'n' Roller, and, he said, "I hate to leave you alone, so we'll have a few days' holiday, okay? We'll celebrate."

"Celebrate?"

"Yes. Celebrate your getting better."

"Oh. Yes." And since the happiness and anticipation in his voice required its acquiescence, it said, "That will be fun."

Fun. Fun. A word from a world scarcely recallable. And the watch chain, and the desk, and the hands, and the right word now, the true one: "Afraid."

"You're afraid to go?"

"Yes."

"Why?"

"I'm afraid I'll jump out of the plane."

"Why do you think you might do that?"

"I don't know. I just think I will, that's all."

"You won't."

"I will."

"Don't go, then."

"I have to. He won't go without me, and he has to go, so I have to go. Besides, I'm afraid of nighttime without him."

"What did you tell him?"

"I told him . . . it would be . . . fun."

"And will it be fun, perhaps?"

"I'll never find out, I'll never get there, I'll—"

"I know, I know."

Yes, he knew, but he did not know what the mirror that afternoon would do, the mirror in the store reflecting back a grotesque stranger, for Ed had said in a magnificently casual understatement "Maybe your last summer's clothes wouldn't . . . uh . . . fit you too well now."

Wouldn't fit too well now? In the full-length mirror, standing beside its husband, was something stripped of flesh, a cadaverous creature all bones and eyes—bones sharp and sticking out, eyes blank above the hollows where its two cheeks should have been. As it removed its clothes, more and more of the devastation came into view —the stringy pipe-stem arms, the ridged rib cage, the skin-taut thighs—and it saw a glimpse, as it turned away in revulsion from its unrecognizable image, of the long long braid hanging down its back to its waist like an announcement: *owner has been absent for half a year.* No womanliness, no maturity, breasts vanished as completely from the body as were all signs of age from the small pinched face—gone the laugh-lines around the eyes, gone the scowl-marks from its forehead, gone all hated traces of a double chin, gone from face and form every last familiar lineament of the woman who had worn size-twelve dresses with belts too tight for comfort, gone and come instead this sad thin wraith, this size-eight starving-child a cat would not drag in.

It sat down, stunned at the sight; sat down, breathless, sick, dizzied by the realization.

"Janie, what's the matter?"

"I feel weak. Sick to my stomach."

"Want to skip this? Maybe it's too much for you—"

"Just pick out something for me please. Get me away from this mirror. I . . . I . . . just didn't know . . . how I look. I look . . . like . . . I'm twelve years old."

He hugging the little child, the shaking-all-over now and weeping child—"I love you, my darling twelve-year-old, I love you."

The watch chain, the desk, the hands, the day of departure in a brand-new dress and its hair cut shorter—"Why do I look like I'm twelve years old?"

"Because you are."

"Because I am?"

"Because you are twelve years old. When you first came here you were no years old. Then you were reborn, remember? and became an infant with an infant's tears. And you've been growing up all this time and someday you'll be thirty-one again. Only this time you'll be *really* thirty-one, all the way through you, not just on a calendar." He paused. "But why are you sitting so stiff?"

And, stiffly, rigid with fear of the trip to come, it told him of the nightmares since the sight of itself in the mirror, the nightmares flagrant with asylum horrors, the animal-people caged in padded cells, the animal-people twisted into strait jackets, the animal-people moving about in aimless terror as it itself had lately moved about, banging their heads against walls in a desperation as nebulous and overwhelming as its own had been, mindless human beings, catatonic, paranoiac, schizophrenic, silent, screaming—and it among them, one of them, crazy as a loon, so that it woke up screaming, screaming, its screams in its dream mingling with the others' but in wakefulness pounding against the compassion in Ed's face close to its own, bending over it: "Janie, shshsh sweetheart, it's only a dream."

The way it had looked in the mirror, and the fear now of putting a thousand miles between its damaged reliant brain and the voice upon which that brain's equilibrium relied, this combination of anxieties it was that sent such a surge of fear through all its veins that now, here in his office—without thinking, without caring that this was something it had wished each day for months and months to do, had stopped itself each day from actually doing—it suddenly arose from its chair and, stumbling around the desk in an agony of shamelessness, fell trembling against the chest of a man it had never yet raised its eyes to see. He had stood up to receive the embrace and, like a wooden Indian, he received it, giving nothing back but a Kleenex which he—skilled, doubtless, from many a previous episode of self-abasing adoration—had retrieved somehow for the protection of his shirt-front from the streaming tears of love.

Where pride? His arms stayed at his side, his voice like God's was silent now, and for embarrassment-anguished minutes the only sound was the sniffing and moaning and nose-blowing of an emaciated matron bound for Florida. Somehow at last it managed to stumble back to the chair, still feeling the warmth of his body but feeling more the coldness of his unreciprocating arms, his disapproving silence. Sprawled in self-disgust, it hid its face in its hands; instead of stiffness now black shame suffused it, and when he asked, "Feel better now? What are you thinking?" (with a threat in his voice of mocking laughter, of amused reproof) it answered in a whine like a stubborn child's, "I'm thinking of the airplane hatch I'll jump out of tonight"—and it meant it, but knew, even as it said it and meant it, what a loathsome phony it was now and always had been, yes, a despicable phony who well deserved his hatred and disgust.

218

In the airplane it felt too hot, and sweated; felt too cold, and trembled, teeth clicking unceasingly; felt a buzzing under the flesh as if plugged in to an electric outlet; felt the rush of air as it fell in imagination from the plane, felt the terrible drop, the gluttonous suck of gravity against the flailing futile flesh-gone rag-doll legs and arms; felt the thud, felt death. Better death than this heat, this cold, this plugged-in buzzing of a million monstrous nerve ends on its skin; better death than leaving God a thousand miles behind. '

"Your hand's like ice," Ed said, and then fell asleep until the wheels touched the airstrip in Miami. But at the bump of the wheels against the ground, its teeth stopped chattering and from between the teeth and up from the throat came something alien and beautiful, as sweet and strange and amazing as the sobs and tears had been three months before: out of its mouth came laughter.

"Janie!"—Ed looking and listening as if a miracle had happened, as indeed it had, but gradually—"What's so funny?"

"I made it, I *made* it"—and the hand he held was warm and squeezed him back.

"*Smell* that, will you? Just *smell* that!"—springtime along the highway from Cedarton to Manhattan, Ed laughing at the maniac beside him, the maniac who kept lunging at him with sudden hugs and kisses, the jumping-up-and-down maniac with tan face hanging radiant now out the open car window into the smell of kelly-green grass and budding honeysuckle—"*Look! Look!*"

"What? Where?"

"The *sky!*"

"What?"

"Oh, my God, it's so *blue,* it's so *blue!*"

And the watch chain, the desk, the hands, the voice like . . . like God's? no . . . no . . . like somebody beloved and very very pleased (looking up at last, seeing at last the face, the features), somebody with a soft-looking big nose, hard-looking big chin, pipe propped above it in mouth no more godlike than the gray wise eyes, the gray-

specked wavy hair, the beige-and-brown-striped tie...
a physician, merely, happy to see the dead come back
to life, saying now, "Welcome back!"

"From Florida?"

—smiling—"That too."

"Can you tell by my eyes?"—he nodding, puffing his
pipe in satisfaction at the sight and sound of freedom—
"That's what Ed says, that my eyes are ... are ... different.
How are they different?"

"For the first time in a long time they are ... seeing."

"Yes! Yes!"

—grinning now, Cheshire-cat-faced in elation—"Tell
me."

"Well, we got back last night. The trip back was fine,
I felt fine, I never thought at all about, well, you know, I
only thought about how badly I wanted to see my boys,
really *see* them. And when I got off the plane, all brown
and my hair sunbleached, I felt so pretty and we'd had
fun, you see, the whole holiday really was *fun.* Just once
in the hotel I felt like before, and that was when I phoned
you, because I was so scared it was coming back when I
was so far away from you, and I'm so sorry I woke you
and worried you, sobbing and saying those things, but I
was afraid, I'm sorry—"

"It's all right, it will take you months and maybe years
to stop fearing recurrence, but go on, go on—"

"Well, we went home and there at the door was a boy
I didn't *know,* he was some ado*les*cent, all tall with legs
like a man's and a filled-out chest all muscly, and guess
what? he was *Bruce,* I hardly recognized him he's all
changed and sort of prepuberty-ish"—tell him, don't let
go, tell him—"and the other two were asleep but I peeked
at them in bed and they're changed too, Terry's face had
changed from a baby's to a boy's, and Johnny's lost two
teeth since Christmas, and this morning at breakfast they
all three ate with me and they acted a bit shy but I didn't
mind because at last I *saw* them and *heard* them, I was
*laugh*ing and *talk*ing and hearing all about them again"—
hold on, don't let go—"but oh God, they're so *shab*by,
they're in rags, I guess Ed's been too preoccupied with

me or his work or something to notice, and Mrs. Ross doesn't care, I guess, because their sleeves are way up over their wrists and their trousers are way up over their ankles and nobody's even bothered to let down the cuffs or even to patch the holes in their knees—and the house! good Lord, but it's a wreck, the couch all unsprung and the walls crayoned"—stopping suddenly—"Where have I been?"

"Away."

"Away? Where? Where?"

"In hell. In the only hell there is. In the cellar of yourself."

"Yes, but no more, no more." Tell him, tell him the rest. "So anyway, just now we drove down through the springtime and I saw it, I *saw* it, I smelled it, everything is blooming, everything is so beautiful, I'm back again, oh God oh God, I'm back in the *world* again"—tell him, keep going—"and just now we stopped by for a moment at a friend's apartment and some people were there, acquaintances, actors and actresses, and I wasn't quiet, I wasn't afraid, I didn't shrink into a bug, I chatted and laughed and kidded around and had a *won*derful time, and then Ed drove me here and he'd bought a magazine and on the way down I read it, I *read* it, I saw the words, they weren't just marks, they had *meaning,* I connected them up in my head and I was really *reading, reading* again, and then a news program came on the car radio and I *heard* it, I listened and I under*stood* it, it wasn't confusing at all and at the end of it I said to Ed . . . I said to Ed . . ."

"Yes?"

"Oh, it doesn't matter what I said, what I mean is, I said *some*thing, I mean I really *said* something, something with a thought behind it, an original articulated thought, an idea, an opinion, I was really *thinking* again, *thinking,* can you imagine?"

—smiling in quiet delight—"Yes. Yes, I can imagine."

"Oh you can't, you can't imagine, if you've never died and come to life again, it's . . . it's . . . like religion, like religion ought to be and isn't, an ecstasy of being, an ecstasy and an anguish, to be part of the world and to partake ... to partake ... oh my God, I am back, I am back, I am back in my brain, here I am, this is *me! me* again! really *me!*"—hold on, don't let go, but no, impossible to hold back the sobs any longer, the sobs and the tears like April rain, warm and pouring and a nourishment, yes, head against his desk to cry and cry and cry, the crying unchecked, unembarrassed, elegiac for the weeks and weeks vanished in a vacuum, heraldic for the years and years to come, years glorious as this moment with ... with ...

"—Renascence?" he said.

"Yes"—speaking through tears—"Renascence."

"And do you understand why you cry?"

"I cry for ... for ..."

"—for joy?"

"For joy."

"Because you're you again?"

"Oh yes, yes! Because my mind has let me back in, because I'm back in my own mind, my own heart, my own soul, my own self, my own life. Here I am, this is me, really *me!*"

And it was. And it is. Here I am. I am me.

PART THREE

*". . . O Thou, staff of exiles, lamp of inventors,
father confessor of the hanged and of them that
plot evil, Satan, have pity on my long-drawn
pain . . ."*

                                        Baudelaire

TWENTY-ONE

EXACTLY a week after he sent out the final wordlessly
eloquent message to his "enemies," Matty Atkins at last
began to carry out his threats. He started with Milton
Cohn: he killed him. It was a May Day murder—the
second hour of that month, to be precise, in 1959—and a
carving knife was the weapon used, thrust deep and clean
beneath the heart of the sleeping little multimillionaire.

TWENTY-TWO

I ENTERED my own kitchen as I would enter a Baghdad
street alone at night: alien, timorous, bewildered. Around
me were the cupboards I once had known as intimately as
these hands which had opened and closed them in the
surety of habit, of instinct, of effortless repetition, of daily
domestic routine. But gone now the surety, vanished
with the memory of forks and spoons, of where they lay
hidden, they and all those other mysteriously elusive ob-
jects—where the plates? where the cups? where all those
intricacies of culinary receptacle and instrument, and how
oh how did this handle work, this chrome complexity

which denied me entrance now into a refrigerator grown unknown as an Arabian mosque in the months of my psychic blindness.

Yes, I was me again, but the ecstasy enjoyed at my self's recapture was dissolved now in the simultaneous recapture of the responsibilities that—having used insanity to retreat from—I must now use my new-found sanity to resume. Sanity. Like the muscles of a body gone weak from the nonmotion of a physical illness, my brain in vain now made its first tentative attempts at mental steps from its convalescent bed of self-absorption, slowly, awkwardly, painfully, stumbling unsuccessfully from one roomful of realities to another: motherhood (resumed as a cripple resumes his way on canes) and wifehood, homemaking, friendship—all by nonuse deprived of spontaneity, all now imbued with magnitudinous impossibility by the residue of disorientation which hampered every small forgotten task.

Facing reality, resuming responsibility, firing the day nurse and then the night nurse (one week one, the next week the other, gradually, cautiously, like removing stitches from a scar), "picking up the thread of life again" —these were the demands which loomed like monster-large obstacles between the return of my full identity and the recognition of all the mundane unavoidable chores which that identity entailed. Yes, the sky was bluer than ever before, and more beautiful, more magic, more deeply treasured than it could ever be by those who had not dallied in hell and emerged—but beneath that magical blue was the baffling nonmagic of tables to be set, eggs to be scrambled, bread to be toasted and then buttered . . .

"I can't remember."

"Just press it down. Like this, see? And when it pops up, cut the butter like this and spread it on with the knife."

"Yes, yes, now I remember, I think I can do it all right" —but it was not only as if I were in someone else's kitchen, some foreigner's kitchen in some strange and foreign land, full of strange forgotten motions of the hands and eyes and mind, it was also as if I were standing with one foot still in quicksand and the other on dry land. The effort of that one last final tug to safety, to full sanity, was taxing all my long-lost will, my me-ness; the quicksand of insanity was strong.

So I got drunk. Mine was the self-inebriation of a frightened immigrant, rendering less fearful these first few harrowing days on the lonely Ellis Island of my soul. A pseudo-lush, I wheeled about the house, loose-jointed; like a tipsy fool, light-headed, did the wash. Dizzy, whirling gaily at the sink, I splashed the floor with orange juice and laughed.

But the watch chain, the desk, the voice no longer of God but of a friend, a friend who refused to be amused by my antics . . .

"Hanging on okay?" he asked—cold, clinical, unindulgent.

"Yessiree."

"Feel loaded?"

"Yeah!"

"You're drugged. Drugged by the necessity for survival. It had to happen, it's predictable, part of the whole pathological process. The resumption of reality took too great a toll so your unconscious decided to have a ball for a while. You'll snap out of it soon. The vacation's just about over."

And it was. Vacation's-end smote me the next morning, smote me as I lay in bed at dawn. The day ahead sat on my chest heavy, dreadful, elephantine. I was underneath, crushed, crushed, and I could not stir, could not arise, for here was a hangover to end all hangovers—not just the morning after the night before, but the lifetime after the death-in-life. Here I am, I thought, it is me, really me. And I can't do it, I can't. I can't remember how to be me. I can't remember who I was, I can't remember what I'm supposed to do.

Babyless I lay, flattened by the big gray bulldozer of dawn; babyless, empty, bereft.

"What do you mean, different?" he asked, across his desk. "Different from what?"

225

"Different from being 'it.' This is *me*, all right, like before, and this depression is a depression like before. But oh God, the *degree*, the *degree* of it."

—puffing his pipe, The Great Stone Face, The Sphinx, expressionless—"The degree?"

"I used to think I knew what a blue funk was. I didn't know. Those were play imitations of this. *This* is a depression, only *this*, to wake up each morning with it tangible on top of me like a barrel of lead, and then all day dragging myself around, scarcely able to move, knowing time stopped before and could stop again, knowing I lost my mind before and could lose it again."

"Yes, you could. That's why you're here. Not only to find out *why* it happened but to make sure it never happens again."

"I almost wish—"

"What?"

"I almost said I almost wish that . . . that . . . I could retreat to the cellar again."

"You forget how dark it was down there."

"I don't forget, not quite."

"You'll forget."

"I'll never forget."

"You will."

"Never."

But, of course, he was right. I have forgotten. A nightmare lingers, fades, and then is gone.

What a triumph it had been! It had been the high point of my first nurseless Saturday morning, nurseless, maidless, helpless—but no, not helpless, for I had done it, done what I had dreaded all the week to do, knowing all the week that when Saturday came, and with it the big test, I would fail, would flunk, would stretch my mind to huge new heights in vain . . .

It was noon now, the kids were at the "Y," Ed was at the supermarket doing the week's shopping, and just an hour before I had called out to him, "Ed! Ed, look!"

He had come into the kitchen, where I sat with my triumph on the table before me. "Yes, honey?"

226

"Look!" I held it up, the paper, the long white final exam. "I did it! I did it!"

"The grocery list?"

"The grocery list!"

"Well, well, the grocery list"—he looked over the items admiringly—"Very tidy. Very nice."

But begging for more praise, dizzy on my pinnacle of accomplishment—"Isn't it wonderful? I figured it out all by myself, all those things. I remembered from before, it all came back, I remembered. I did it all my*self.*"

"Wonderful, darling, really wonderful—"

"I was so *sure* I couldn't do it. Or that if I tried, I'd goof. But I *did* it, *didn't* I! I wrote the list! My God, I feel so *proud* of myself."

"And do you love me?"

Kissing him on his nose—"You know how much I love you."

"How much? Show me how much—"

And I showed him, and he showed me, and afterward, sprawled sated on the bed, he said, "If the kids never go to the 'Y' another time, *this* hour'll be worth the year's dues."

"Mmmmm"—thinking, I did it, I wrote it!

"I'll never forget this morning."

"Me neither." I wrote it!

"Was it good? Did you—"

"I *wrote* it!"

"Do you know you're getting some fat back? I can feel some right here. Pretty soon you'll be a big huge ninety-pounder if you don't watch out."

Forcing my mind back from its triumph, my long-lost vanity perking up its ears—"What?"

"Our hipbones didn't grate as loud this time. I think you've gained back some weight."

"Oh I have, I can tell I have. When I held the pencil I could feel a pad of fat on my fingers where there wasn't any before." Pencils! Pens! Typewriters! Life!

"I love you, Janie."

"I love you, Ed."

"Never leave me."

227

"Never, never."

"Okay, that's settled"—rolling out of bed, changing his tune—"Now get your clothes back on while I'm at Food Fair"—penis Kleenex-swaddled, shoulders passion-scratched—"And for God's sake don't forget to keep the doors locked while I'm gone."

There. It was out. Through all my days of drunkenness it had lurked, and through the hangover, but I had been too immersed in first my merriment and then my melancholy to care a fig. *Matty Atkins had murdered Mr. Cohn!* Matty was in earnest, we truly were in danger, all of us. And I didn't want to die, not anymore. I wanted to live, to be a wife and mother, write a novel a year and draw my last breath against a soft silk pastel quilt at the age of eighty-nine.

"Yes," I had answered Ed. "Don't worry, I'll lock the doors."

But now it was twelve o'clock, I was alone, and the doorbell rang. A neighbor, perhaps? A friend? I made no sound, just in case, but went upstairs to peek out at whoever it might be. Tiptoeing to the window, I felt no fear, and marveled at myself, wondering if it were simply that fear and a bright May noon were incompatible or that (as it truly seemed) I had lost somehow, along the route of my soul's suffering, a part of me that cared enough about itself to be afraid for itself. I thought: among my many departed illusions—like how individual I am, how self-sufficient, how cozy-clever-safe inside my brain—I seem to have lost the illusion of involvement, have gained instead this affable detachment—agony's farewell gift to me perhaps? And as I furtively drew back the curtain to look below at what could well be the bearer of that very special news flash we each listen for all our lives (when will I die? how? where?) I suddenly recalled what the courts call the child, who, having suffered a childhood so loveless that he can no longer feel emotion, has the terrible potential to grow up into either a hero or a menace: a child with "an abandoned and malignant heart." Was this, then, the story of the nerveless acceptance of fate I now felt? Had this past half-year afflicted me with "a callous

228

and scar-tissued soul"? Had the capacity for apprehensiveness been burned out of me by my blaze of anguish? Yes, leaving intact only a single hard core of purpose, like a sturdy blackened chimney within the debris.

Matthew Atkins, madman, murderer, could even at this moment have entered my house, might have broken in somehow and be standing behind me now, knife upraised. Perhaps. But I had known a strange and nightmare peril: the imminence of body minus soul. And I—who used to run from bugs; from thunder—felt grief and pity now instead of fear.

Then I looked down, and below on the doorstep in the bright sunshine, I saw a small slim woman dressed in pink. Peasant skirt, peasant blouse, flowered print. She glanced up suddenly at a bird-song in the sycamore and I saw her face. I'd never seen the face before, but it reminded me at once of a painting by Wyeth, the painting called *Christina's World;* in the painting only the back of the girl is shown—full-length on her elbow in the grass, gazing at the farmhouse set against the yawn of sky beyond—but surely Christina's face was just like this: thin and innocent, Kansas-prairie-pure. I hurried downstairs and opened the door. For a silent moment we just looked back and forth at each other through the aroma of hyacinth heavy in the air. I smiled, so did she, but her solemnity stayed graven in her gray straightforward eyes. Her face was more wrinkled than I had anticipated, sadder, older, the pink of her dress was inappropriate, I saw now, for her age. Yet the Christina impression remained—purity, innocence—and when she spoke, not in the accents of Kansas but of France, I was as surprised as I had been by the pain upon her pale and haggard face . . .

"Mrs. Thompson?"—so quiet-voiced I strained forward to catch the words—"I'm Marianne Atkins, Matthew's wife."

TWENTY-THREE

LETTER from Ed Thompson to Roger Rutherford:

"In both your last phone call and your telegram before that you asked that I write you not only *my* reaction to Milton's abrupt demise but Janie's reactions too. Well, naturally, I am frantic, but have been hiding same from her, which isn't a bit difficult, since, as you may have guessed, she's been having some emotional problems since that miscarriage months ago and is therefore not too concerned with mere realities such as murderers running around loose with our names on the top of their lists.

"And he *is* on the loose, all right; we have it straight from the horse's mouth, as of yesterday, when who should appear upon the scene but Madame Atkins herself, and a pleasanter little lady you couldn't ask for. Here's the story, Rog—

"Matty's after you next. He's very systematic in his madness, she says, and there's no doubt in her mind that having dispensed with Cohn he's now intent on Rutherford. Only you're not really you in his mind, and Cohn wasn't Cohn. It's all very complicated and pathological, and frankly I can't make head or tail of it the way Janie tells it (she's the one Matty's wife poured her Gallic heart out to) but Janie plans to write Lisa all about it in a separate letter, and can elaborate further when we see you, which will be next week, is that right? You said Lisa goes on location June 6, so I presume you'll appear on our front stoop that day or soon after. Keerect? If you want us to meet you at the airport, speak up.

"You can stop being worried about coming east into Atkins' territory just when he has it in for you. Janie asked his wife where she figured he might be, and she said she wouldn't be surprised if he'd begun hitchhiking across the country to Hollywood. You can wave at him as you fly over! She says he's so clever and cautious that he may well be able to avoid the police indefinitely despite her coöperation with them. She wants him caught in the worst way, for his own sake as well as ours—knows he's sick enough to wipe out the whole bunch of us—wasn't sure, she claims, until he murdered Milton, but now that he's done that, she's sure he'll concentrate on you.

"Strange thing, though, Rog. She says Matty seems to be more interested in merely disfiguring you than killing you. God only knows why. Maybe somewhere he found out about all your stupid yakking recently about how plastic surgery would fix you up just fine, revitalize your dramatic career, etcetera. No, that's crazy, how could he have heard, and what would be the point anyway?

"Isn't that a kick in the pants about Milton's past publishing history? To think that the last time I saw him alive he was piously saying, 'If there's one thing I can't stand, it's filth!' When Frank Tibasi called me up to tell us all about it, he mentioned he'd just written you too. He's sure having a field day, isn't he, now that 'de big boss' is dead? I dare say he's been bursting at the seams for years to tell people, especially since he thought we knew about his prison sentence, whereas of course I never knew a thing, nor did you, right? I was more surprised to hear he'd been in prison for a year than to hear it was Cohn he took the rap for. Isn't it ironic that poor Cohn thought the worst he had coming to him from Atkins was exposure and public disgrace? And here all the time that Cohn wanted Atkins put away to shut him up in case he knew something, Atkins knew nothing at all. I can see now how in Cohn's guilty mind Atkins' threat notes took the form of obviously being threats of exposure rather than death.

"I'm glad to hear Lisa's pleased with the *Life* spread. To tell the truth, I'm more than a little pleased myself, since I was never sure till practically publication date that the cover-picture and the full six-page spread with color were in the bag. What do you think of the cover photo? Janie and I debated whether she looks more like a well-tended corpse (upper half, closed eyes) or an asphyxiated fish (lower half, open mouth) but the only conclusion we reached was that the total effect is goddamn sexy. How do you like Kazan's comment on her acting, and Brando's and the others—I like 'she can go glandular or spiritual at will' best. Tell her to stop being so oozy-grateful about the publicity, because she knows damn well I couldn't have done a thing over at *Life* or anyplace else if it weren't already well known in the industry that she'll be *the* biggest thing in filmdom even before the movie appears, simply on the strength of the rumors and predictions. From now on she's going to need my press-agentry like Sinatra does; that's 'hot copy' you're living with there, boy. After the scenes on location in Mississippi, what next? Doesn't that pretty much wrap it up? And do you suppose she could fly up for one of the weekends you're here? We hope so because, at the rate her star is rising these days, she won't have time for anything soon except making millions and receiving Academy Awards.

"See you mid-June or before. I'll arrange some kind of police protection while you're here if you still think I'd better, despite Matty's westward-ho intentions. But under the circumstances let's trust it won't be necessary. They'll probably nab him along an Arizona highway even before this reaches you, and then we can all relax and have ourselves a ball."

I found that one—Ed's to Roger—but I can't seem to find the carbon of the letter I wrote to Lisa, the one that explained in further detail about Marianne Atkins, about Matty, about Milton Cohn and the girlie magazines he'd published prior to going legal with The Martian. Did I throw it away, weeks ago, along with the pills and the vials and the Flents and all the other small ugly reminders of my downfall? Is it incinerated along with the rest, that innocent flippant epistle? In it I kidded her about her new fame, I recall, asking her to go ahead and out-Magnani Magnani, that was fine, but please to remain unscathed by Luceglory and please, also, to prove herself unscathed by visiting us in June when Rog would be here.

Please come, I said. Pretty please?

If you had not listened, dear Lisa, would June have

been different? If I had said my please just once that time instead of twice or thrice, would Roger now be standing somewhere feeling sun and rain? No, I think it would have been about the same. The time had come; it was rope's end; the camel's back was anxious for the straw. And yet . . . and yet . . .

I wish I'd said: dear Lisa, stay away.
I wish I'd said: berate, but do not laugh.
I wish that I could write a sermon all about regret.

Ed had come in while Mrs. Atkins was still talking to me, had come bursting in radiant and laden with groceries, the kids behind him laden too with bags and parcels equal to their size. "Founders' Day!" he shouted. "Hey, Janie, parade, we forgot all about it!"

"Ed, this is Matty Atkins' wife," I said. "Marianne, this is my husband, Ed Thompson."

His jaw did not drop, nor any packages; only his voice did, briefly, long enough to acknowledge the introduction and attempt an unsuccessful handshake over the top of his arm-full barricade. "Ever so glad to meet you," he said, all charm even in startlement, smiling, breathless from the excitement of Saturday and fatherhood and all the bargains found while marketing.

"Matty *Atkins'* wife!" Bruce said. An apple slipped from the bag beneath his arm, bumped to the rug. "Matty *At—*"

Ed squelched him cheerfully. "Go put those in the kitchen before you spill the whole damn dozen. You too, Terry, Johnny, *scoot"*—the name Atkins had meant nothing to our other two, I saw; their faces were shining full of Daddy and parade—"Get going now."

"I leave," Marianne said, not moving.

"No, no, come with us," Ed said. "The parade's just beginning. Can't you stay and see the parade?"

"Oh, but I shouldn't"—she hesitated; I wondered if it was his little-boy insistence she was reacting to or more her memories of Paris, of Paris parades, continual, magnificent—"To your nice wife I have explained what I came here to explain, now I go, I must—"

"But there's *bands*, four or *five* of 'em!" Ed said, impatient now. Was this mousy little mate-of-a-maniac going to ruin his day? Was she going to keep him marooned here, playing host to her indefinite departure when there was *fun* downtown? "Soldiers! Majorettes! Historical floats! All *sorts* of wonderful stuff!"

"Well—"

"Of course you'll come," he said, dictatorial, irresistible, and bounded out toward the kitchen shouting back from the hall, "Just got to put some of these things away before they unfreeze. Only take a sec, meet you in the car."

We chose the spot we always chose for watching this annual event: a stretch of maple-shaded curb across Main Street from the Cedarton Lutheran Church. A mortuary was at our backs, shades up in welcome on the first floor, shades drawn down mysteriously discreet on the second. Were they afraid of being seen at their work up there, I always wondered? Were they laboring up there now, too preoccupied to watch the parade? Hands busy, buckets filling, were they tapping their feet to the music? I studied the upper-story shades, but no . . . no inch appeared, no pair of curious corpse-ignoring eyes.

"Find any labels this time?" Ed asked.

"No luck today," I replied, looking around on the ground, and we laughed. Three years before, on Founders' Day, I'd found the label here upon the mortuary lawn, dirty, damp and creased, but legible: FOR EYELIDS ONLY— and, in smaller print beneath, after the directions for the pasting process, the warning: *unusable for lips.*

"— so dif'rint, Mommy?"

"What, honey?"

"Why do their guns look so dif'rint?"

"Those are old-fashioned ones they're carrying, Terry. When America was fighting for its freedom our army used that kind, it was a long time ago. I think they're called muskets."

"Muffits," he said. "Muffits." Beside me, Marianne smiled.

The float went by—Revolutionary soldiers, their

womenfolk in homespun frocks and starched white bonnets, a cannon and a flag with thirteen stars—and then came a band, this one from the high school, blue and gold, boys who didn't make the football team, girls the team would never try to make. Behind the band the Masons trudged unnoticed, for their plain few were followed by the Knights of Columbus in all their glory, all gay plumed hats and uniforms and gaudy-ribboned chests.

"There's Freddy!" a voice shrilled behind us. "Freddy! Hey, Freddy, over here, we're over here!" And then, quietly exultant, a postscript wafting into the abrupt hush left by the trumpet-raucous end of a Sousa: "He saw us" —just as if they hadn't helped proud Freddy on with his splendor a scant half-an-hour ago.

"Yours is a nice town," Marianne Atkins said. "You must be very happy here."

"Yes. It is. We are."

There was a perfect breeze; the leaves on the trees were a tender green, young, untouched as yet by frost or violent wind, unknowing of elements less gentle than this soft spring day contained, this day in which the very air was a benediction, cool and warm alternating against my skin, hypnotizing, catching me like a victim in the clutch of earth and sky and flower-scent, my heart aching with awareness—*this moment! this single sweet moment in time!*—knowing how rare, how precious, how stranger-shared and yet alone, alone . . .

"Hey, Mike, good to see ya"—Ed slapping backs, laughing, screaming above the scream of fife, greeting people from train or store or long wet luncheons on Fifth Avenue, joking, poking, easily breezily renewing acquaintanceships with couples who nodded and to whom I nodded back, barriered by my shell of casual self-assurance concealing bashfulness—"Hey, Janie doll, you remember the Curtisses? The party at Shulmans? Year before last?"

"Of course. Hi."

"Hello. Lovely day for the parade, isn't it?"

"Yes, it is."

Oh it is, it is, isn't it, children? Isn't it, Marianne? And then another band was upon us, dozens of drums beating, rolling—ra ta ta ta, ra ta ta ta, ra ta ta ra ta ta ra ta ta ta —and there wasn't any other sound, only the drums, and I looked at Ed, knowing what this always did to him, to me, to both of us, together and yet separately: to him because his father had loved the sound of drums, to me because that is the way I am at parades with the day beautiful and my sons sitting along the curb all so alike and unalike and so young, like the leaves, so green.

I wept, Ed wept, my tears seeping down my cheeks while he, manly, blinked his away; I wiped mine on my wrist and said to Marianne, "Isn't it silly, I always cry at parades."

"Is not silly at all," she replied, and then, made voluble once more by our female bond of easy tears, added, "Will you explain to your husband what I have explained to you? Do you think he will understand?"

"I will. He will."

An ancient horse-drawn fire carriage trotted by, backed by a line of semi-ancient veterans; between popping army buttons the annually outraged khaki was stretched across broad bellies; this was their hour, the last excitement in their lives having vanished at Verdun. Mincing at their heels, seeming to symbolize that their heyday was behind them, came a bare-thighed prancing plump coquette performing with her lips and breasts and squeaky piccolo. And now the last of the music and marching passed up the street, past the church, bridge, bookstore, pharmacy. The parade petered out, just boys on bikes now, kidding around, showing off, swerving close to the departing crowd to scare those still near the curb, their bike wheels flappy-bright with crepe paper ribbons woven loosely through the spokes.

"Great parade, huh?" Ed said to Marianne with Terry on his shoulders, Bruce and Johnny running on ahead to where we'd parked our car down by the river bank. "Really terrific!"—his tall tense body an exclamation point of delight, reminding me of all his previous enthusiasms: powdered egg yolk for the baby! contoured sheets!

236

green stamps! Janie! Janie! Look! A soap-filled Brillo pad! Oh, purchases! Oh, merchandise! Oh, things!

"—alive," Marianne Atkins said. Ed had gone on ahead with the boys.

"What?"

"Your husband. He's so happy all the time, so thrilled with everything. He must make everyone around him feel glad to be alive."

"Yes. Yes, he—"

"You are a wife, you are the woman to your man, surely you must understand that I cannot stop loving my Matthew even after what he has done, what he has become—"

Understand? Understand that total kind of loving? No, no, I thought guiltily, I cannot understand, I am not brave enough yet to love that way; ashamed, feeling more than Marianne the loser at that moment, seeing Ed whamming along ahead of us, noisy, gregarious, uninhibited, equipped with the ready quip and the easy charm, watching his antics with audience-passersby as I'd watch a vaudeville show, and thinking, no, I'm sorry, but I must refuse to understand—

"But what you can never understand is Matthew's anguish," she continued. "That I cannot expect you to understand, no one can, it is a prison he lives in and no one has a key. Ah, I know, you must regard him as a monster, evil, you cannot feel for him as I do sadness, but still I had to tell you how it is. He is lost, he suffers, he struggles but he drowns. You so happy, so fortunate, free as that bird in the tree, how can I expect you to see how it is with my Matthew—"

—oh I see, I see, with all my foolish battered soul, I see—

We were in bed, lights out, talking; it was the night of the parade, and until now Ed and I had not had a moment of privacy in which to discuss Mrs. Atkins and her odd message of explanation. "Me, forgive," I said now. *"Me* understand!"

"She sees us the way Lisa sees us," Ed said. "Smiled

237

upon by fortune, exempt from trouble. Well, *continuez-vous*—"

—so I went on telling him what I knew, telling him what she had told me in her Gallic murmurs, looking never at me but always at a spot in the air where her memories hovered . . .

He had come from a Mennonite farm in Pennsylvania, her Matthew, had fled that stern piety for its Parisienne antithesis, had used her as did his friend Utrillo to model for his paintings, and used her too as mistress before she had made the marrage her parents wished, to her second cousin Paul. She loved Matthew all the time, but had not known he loved her too; not until later, when the moodiness began and became at last his illness, did she learn how much her first marriage had hurt him, turning him bitter not only against her but against Paul's son, born the same week the father died. Returning to Marianne when the child was two years old, he seemed to accept him, taught him to draw, took the adoring child with him on his trips through the city to paint or to visit with the other artists, or simply to sit hours at a time at some sunny sidewalk café speaking of beautiful things he had seen when he himself was young: an oriole, a violet, the shadow of a wagon patterned black against a stretch of moonlit snow. Of all the rest he seldom spoke, she said, rarely mentioning those trials which a farm boy must have felt when everything was work and God and purposeful self-righteous ugliness. It was later—after his failure grew and his strangeness, after they had married and decided to take their meager earnings and come to the States, where his art might at least bring him a commercial success if not a critical one—that the doctors had told her the rest, the doctors at the hospital from which Matthew was released three times, three times to return.

"And this last was the fourth time?" Ed said now.

I nodded, continued. In New York, Marianne had told me, her husband's serious art still found no recognition; increasingly, partly now out of desperation to keep food in their mouths and a roof over their heads, he turned to hack work, searching always for some gimmick that would bring them in enough money so that he could work only at what he loved, at the abstract paintings which became more and more violent as he did also. His gentleness was gone; when the boy's face took on the contours of his dead father's Matthew loved him no longer, seemed also not to love her. And yet, much later, when she went to visit him at the public institution, which was like, she said, "a scene from hell," he would cling to her, begging her to take him away, to take him home, sobbing of his love and at those times forgetting the other times, the times when she visited a man who did not recognize her, who sat like a stone, unmoving, with his eyes rigid and his mind sealed off from her.

"Poor guy," Ed said. "Poor woman."

Then one day, she had said, she saw on Matthew's easel a pencil sketch—the figure of a man, costumed, antenna-capped, with a sword in his hand—and through the following weeks the sketch became many sketches, all with printing beneath them. Matthew took these things daily from their cellar apartment, took them she knew not where until he came home one evening with five hundred dollars in his pocket and a vow to her that never again would they be poor. Soon his creation was famous, he himself worked steadily in the firm of the man who had bought his idea, but then his peculiarities took hold again. She heard him mutter of Mr. Cohn, Mr. Rutherford, of others who also seemed connected in his mind with some crime. He sued Mr. Cohn, lost everything, lost his money and his job and his sanity and his freedom but "never never never did he lose my love," she said.

"Why couldn't the doctors help him?" Ed asked. "Didn't they make any attempt to figure out why he—"

"Yes, listen"—and I told him how they had learned of the alienation Matthew had felt on the farm in his youth, how alienated he again felt in adulthood. Both times he had run away, run first to another country from the country to which he felt no ties, run the second time into illness to escape a family which he felt was not truly his own. Alienated on the drab loveless farm by his sensitivity and artistic temperament, alienated in his marriage by Marianne's previous marriage and the fruit of that union, he ran away both times. Prevented by fear from killing the father he hated, he carried the hate into his marriage. Then, prevented by love from killing the child whose existence declared his woman's betrayal and his own sterility, he gave birth to a cartoon creature and transferred to its real-life counterparts the hate which would end at last in murder.

"Is it not odd?" Marianne had said. "To others it was a comic-book millionaire whom Matthew killed, but it was not. It was a Mennonite farmer, a French baker—he killed not a man who won a lawsuit but two other men, one who had hurt him by killing that which he had seeded, another who hurt him by planting that seed which he could never plant."

"Seeded?" I had said.

"Yes, when he was little, his private garden. He gave it all his childish devotion, he made that one small plot blaze with the only brightness in his dreary surroundings. He planted the flowers, tended them daily, loved them; instead of friends or toys or pretty things he had the care of colors growing from the ground. But one day when he forgot to clean the chickenhouse his father found him in his garden. 'Matthew,' he said, 'you are dawdling here when your work is not done. You spend too much time here, it is against the Lord's will, you are in danger of becoming a lazy fool with this pastime which serves no useful purpose. This piece of land is going to waste with flowers when vegetables could be grown here, we will make this a cabbage patch.' And he called his other son and told him what to do; it was a game for a boy who was not used to games or play, such fun it was to trample and tear up by the roots; when it was over there were flowers broken and smashed everywhere and not one left alive, and then the colors were not beautiful but had become ugly from such a sudden and brutal death."

"I wish we had Matty around here," Ed said now, yawning. "Our yard sure could use somebody with a green thumb."

240

"Oh shut up," I said, and turned away from him, hugging my pillow.

"Aw now, honey"—attaching himself to my back, warm, apologizing for his untimely wisecrack by rubbing his chin back and forth affectionately against my shoulder —"I'm awfully sorry for him and for her but dammit I'm sorry for poor old Cohn too and for all the rest of us and I hope to hell they catch the crazy bastard before he does any more interesting sculptures with that knife of his."

"He left the knife in Cohn, remember?"—I callous now, cozy, mollified.

"Oh great, oh swell, sweet dreams, dearie"—and we laughed, wiggling together like moles into the comfortable nooks and crannies of each other, and fell asleep, facing Allah.

TWENTY-FOUR

AND the watch chain, the desk, the intensity of his silent smoke-screened listening—". . . and I'm all calm inside and sort of not giving a damn."

"Umm."

"This is the last phase, the final one, isn't it?"

"Is it?"

"Well, *isn't* it?"

"Not necessarily."

"But why? What else could there be?"

"There'll always be something else until you're well."

"But . . . I *am* well, aren't I?"

"Are you?"

"*I* think I am. What do *you* think?"—what the hell *is* he, a goddamn echo?

"I think you're far from well. I think you just feel better. A little bit of better can feel mighty good when you've been where you've been."

"Well, anyway, I'm sure in a terrific mood lately, that's all I know."

"Good."

"Why do you look so unconvinced?"

"Do I?"

"You're damn right you do"—thoroughly miffed now; can't he see I'm *fine?*—"Every once in a while your dead-pan slips. What's that expression supposed to *mean?*"

"Mean?"

"Yeah, mean."

"I'm just waiting."

"For what?"

No reply. No reply. My former Lord is very very busy with his pipe.

TWENTY-FIVE

FIRST urinary, resembling infancy more than the second adolescence that it was, my pseudo-puberty arrived and took me by surprise. I was standing in a Cedarton store trying to decide about the boys' pajamas—seersucker? dacron? penguin print or plaid?—when at the same instant that I felt the need to pee my crotch grew wet, my underpants were soaked, and running to the car I sat—past mortification, numb not so much with embarrassment as amazement—mopping my socks and the insides of my legs.

Again at home it happened, again and again—no time even to reach the bathroom a half-dozen footsteps away —and for the next day's trip to Manhattan I wore a sanitary napkin and drank as little liquid as I could.

He listened, nodded as I said, "Is *this* it? Is *this* what you were waiting for?" and when I asked when it would end he lit his pipe. I persisted. "At least tell me"—shifting, feeling nervous from the rubbing of the gauze against my genitals—"if it will get worse."

—pause, looking away—"Well, it will change."

It changed, ah yes it changed. Each time the uncontrollable trickle emerged it burned, burned not just on the tender tumescent surface but up through my glands like an electric shock, so that I bent over huddled and grimacing against the pain, the pain of pounding heartbeats in my rib cage, in my temples, in my ears, in my womb, pounding into the very tips of my toes and fingers so that my entire body felt like one deep crimson blush. In a minute or two the chaos in my veins would cease, slowly, leaving me weak and trembling; only between my legs did the suffusion persist, constantly, excruciatingly, making sanitary napkins impossible now, unbearable, for they touched me there like burlap pressed upon an open wound. But I needed them no longer anyway, the napkins, for the urinary stage had passed as abruptly as it had begun, abandoning my body to a worse and far more demanding malady: an insane insatiability for penetration. The whole lower half of me felt hungry; I wanted to beg for it, scream for it, wanted to strip myself naked and bury my fists in the hunger, twist and push and pound away the hunger, somehow somehow fill it up. Somehow, something, somebody, anybody . . .

"I know what this is, don't lie to me, I recognize this"—panic-stricken, pacing around his office like a bitch in heat, weeping, moaning, putting my forehead against the wall to cool the constant flush of too much blood—"This is nympho—"

—cutting me off, curt—"That's one word for it."

"Oh God, why? Why now? I was doing so well. Why didn't you warn me?"

"I did warn you."

"Then make it go away, please please make it go—"

"It will stop soon. You have to go through an exaggerated version of puberty again, just as you had to go through your entire childhood from pre-birth on up. It's something called uncontrolled regression."

—sitting to one side, buttock lifted, trying to ease the pressure which could not be eased, could not be appeased—"How soon will it stop?"—remembering how I'd asked this question over and over months before, when my illness first began, when it was too much death in my head

I had to bear, rather than, as now, too much life in my body.

"Maybe tomorrow—"

—and maybe not, and tomorrow came, and his euphemism fell before the unalleviated onslaught of sexual appetite, and each tomorrow was intolerable—no, no not quite intolerable (as the first phase had been, the initial agony: the strange compelling force toward suicide) for this time there were certain ways to curb the need—

—the watch chain, the desk, my passive collaborator—

"What ways?"

"Well, today, for instance, when I awoke I quickly got into a hot hot bath. That helped a little. Then I got out and put lotion all over me down there, the kind that's supposed to deaden the pain of hemorrhoids, so I figured it might help, but it doesn't. Then I sliced a Dixie cup one inch deep and put it inside my underpants. That keeps the material away from me, it creates a space of cool air, it makes it bearable. Then when I drove here it happened like I've told you, like I'm crazy down there, like it's something separate from me so that my brain knows I don't want that colored man driving the truck beside me, don't want that teen-age hood crossing the street, don't really want that pretty girl to lick the pain away, my brain knows but my body won't obey, my body's a stranger to me—"

"The way your brain was a little while ago?"

"Yes, alien, my body, betraying me, why oh why, what is it, haven't I suffered enough—"

"You're suffering a caricature of adolescent sexuality, which is not positive of its object. Your body's enduring a thirteen-year-old's lust but with a thirty-one-year-old's degree of intensity. Physically it's a continual tumescence of the procreative organs, the same as if a man had an erection which refused to go away. Psychologically it's just another step toward maturity. Be happy. After this, you're well on your way to health."

—be happy, he says, be happy when I'm shocked a dozen times a day by my desires, swollen, tender-genitaled, hungering for the touch of anyone, anything, want-

244

ing women, children, fence posts, dogs—wanting most of all the large hard men, workmen, laborers, eying them excitedly as I drive past them on the street, their arm muscles bare to the warm May sun, their shoulders above their picks and shovels shiny-wet with sweat, my stares inciting some to leers and finger signals I recall from high school, signals I do not flinch from now as I did then, do not giggle or pretend I have not seen, gestures I now understand (leaning sideward to soothe the tumult beneath me, Dixie-cupped below a powder keg) because these are the signals of filth and I am filth filth filth filth—

"I can't stand it, I have to have it, have to have them, I have to—"

"You can stand it. You stood the other. You stood the other in order to keep your existence. Now you'll stand this in order to keep your salvaged existence decent and self-respecting."

"Decent and self-respecting! A nymphomaniac!"

"Think of the women who never escape. Women who don't know they're sick, don't know there's a way out. Women who do what they have to do and wreck not only themselves but everyone they love—"

"Don't preach, for God's sake don't preach, and don't expect me to pity others when I—"

"Yours is temporary."

—pacing, panting, panic-damning—"Two weeks now, almost three, that's a long time to want and not get—"

"You get. You get it from your husband whenever you want it."

"It doesn't help, it doesn't help."

"Neither would the others. Nothing helps but time. Time. And talk. And taking it out on me."

Yes, I took it out on him, confined my fiercest hunger to the one man who'd be sure to refuse me, begged, pleaded, lay on the floor on my stomach and writhed, spent one hour in this position banging my feet so hard against the office rug (as much in anger at his adamancy as in the anguish of my lust) that for days the scabs upon my toes bore witness to my shame.

"Soon," he said. "It will end soon."

"I don't understand. If I only understood—"

"In your case, part of it is guilt. More of the same guilt that deprived you of your sanity. You feel you've 'served your time' for 'killing the baby' but a piece of you doesn't agree, a piece of you insists you owe more penance, but your brain feels too free now to take on the job so your body has taken over—"

"Oh crap."

—crap not thy savior, oh savior forgive me, oh savior please fill me, take me oh savior oh daddy devour me—

"Will you *please* be*have* yourself?"—Ed holding my wrists in an angry grip as, from the other side of our bedroom door, the noise of my birthday party (farewell, thirty-one; no tricks, thirty-two) keeps the hi-fi Segovia submerged in a cacophony of laughter, chatter, glasses —"Can't you act like a hostess instead of a slut?"

Sullen—"You can't stand it, can you. Can't stand to see me having a good time. Can't stand to have me enjoy myself."

"Go ahead, enjoy yourself, but enjoy yourself some other way besides sitting on laps and snuggling up and dancing like you're trying to win a belly-rubbing contest—"

"Can't even have fun at my own birthday par—"

"Oh boy, that's right, cry, cry now, three drinks and you're not only a flirt but a weeper, I'd forgotten—"

"Yes! You'd forgotten! you'd forgotten what it was like to have an attractive slaphappy wife! Well listen you, I'd forgotten what it was like too, I forgot for months and months what it was like to laugh and sing and dance and kid around with a bunch of people at a party. I forgot for a long long horrible terrible time what it was like to be *free, free,* and now you're gonna try to lock me up again, dictate my behavior to me again, boy oh boy how could I forget what a tyrant you are, you've been sweet and kind and loving for so long I forgot—"

"It's easy to be loving when you're loved—"

"I love—"

"You lust, you don't love anymore, you act like I'm

246

something your body wants but it's nothing to do with your heart, you *used* to love me, need me, used to cling to me when you were sick—"

"Yeah, you were happy then, weren't you—"

"When?"

"When I was sick, when I 'clung' to you—"

"It was nice, yes, you didn't act like a nut all over the place like tonight, you were dignified and quiet and—"

"—and suicidal with despair! *That's* when you were happy, when I was a bug, a cipher, your private barnacle with no brain and no personality and no—"

"—and no falling all over every man like your husband can't satisfy you—"

"You *liked* it when I was quiet and mindless—"

"Damn right, I liked it better than—"

"My God, I was in hell and you were *happy*—"

"I love you, I loved your needing me—"

"You loved my nothingness, that's what you loved, you loved the pleasant peaceful holiday from jealousy my illness gave you, you loved me silent and pathetic and no threat to your ego, you loved me imprisoned and you hate me being free—"

"I hate the way you are tonight—"

"I'm having *fun* tonight, I feel beautiful and desirable and interesting, I've felt so ugly and tongue-tied for so long and now I feel so beautiful, so brilliant and stimulating and stimulated—"

"Stimulating! stimulated! you can say *that* again! You're being drunk and disgusting—"

"You're being ridiculous and infantile—"

"I wish—"

"What? what do you wish—that I'd never gotten well? that I—"

"Well? the way *you* act? well?"

"Ha, *you're* healthy, I suppose. Hell, making scenes, wearing your idiotic suffering on your sleeve, you're *proud* of your possessiveness, you en*joy* humiliating yourself in public, humiliating me—"

"You ask for it—"

"I'm asking you to butt out! I'm no puppy dog you can

keep on a short tight leash, I'm me, I'm *me* again, it's fun to be me and you're not gonna *stop* me being me! Leave me *alone!"*

"Leave you alone tonight in bed too?"

"That too, that too—"

"Ha!"

"You wish I was still sick, don't you, admit it admit it—"

"I—"

"Admit you hate me getting to be myself again—"

"I hate the way you—"

"You enjoyed my sickness, if I could turn into a chronic depressive all my life you'd be in seventh heaven, I'd sit in a corner all like a zombie, nobody'd know I was alive, you could be the whole big fat center of attention everywhere you go and never have to worry about . . . about . . ."

"—about your attitude toward everything in pants, which makes me want to vomit—"

"Your attitude makes *me* want to vomit, you're a prude and a child and a tyrant—"

"I just wish—"

"—wish I hadn't gotten well, right?"

"For God's sake, *right,* if you want to put it that way, if tonight's an example of how well you are—right! right! right!"

And the watch chain, the desk, the all-men-rolled-in-one, bull-necked, barrel-chested, all love and lust here synthesized, sharpened, reiterated in tearful tirades of desire—

"Look at me! Look at me, I'm beautiful. Can't you see I'm not thin and listless anymore, can't you see I've grown up into a woman again? Why can't you want me, why can't you want me as I want you? I want to lie next to you with your arms around me, I want to touch you everywhere, I want you to touch me, hold me, love me, oh please please love me, don't you love me—"

"I love the person you were meant to be, the person you can still be someday when we've cleaned out all this garbage—"

"Oh God, I'm talking about love and you're talking about garbage! Listen! I want you, I love you, I think about you all the time, daydream and night-dream about you, I have the most wonderful fantasies about you, and then when I'm on my way here each day I'm always so sure that *this* time you'll see me, really *see* me, not see a a patient, not see just another mental case but a *woman,* a very special *woman,* but no, you turn cold and cruel like this and sarcastic, as if I'm not attractive at all, and you make me feel as if I might as well not have gotten my flesh back, might as well still be bony and breastless like I was all those months. Oh *please* don't treat me this way, *please* try to love me back a little, why can't you why can't you—"

"Do you think I can do you more good as a lover or as a physician?"

"As a lover, a lover!"

"I can't love you back in the same way you love me now."

"You can't or you won't?"

"I can't *and* I won't."

"Please please please—"

"You loved your father very much, didn't you?"

"I hated him, what's *that* got to do with the price of beans, he was never home and he was mean to Mommy, and he cared about Jesus and all the church people more than he cared about his own family and he was always gloomy or getting all furious—"

"—and he couldn't love you back, wouldn't love you back—"

"I didn't feel *this* way about *him*—"

"It was taboo, it was impossible, it was in all your fantasies but it wasn't allowed—"

"I love *you,* I want *you*—"

"—and your husband?"

"I hate him! I hate him!"

"Why do you hate him?"

"He liked my being sick, he's sorry I got better, he was happy when I was in hell, I hate him—"

"You don't—"

"Don't tell *me* what I don't. I hate him and I hate all this Freudian shit you're always dishing out and I hate your wife and I hate . . . I hate . . ."

"Yes?"

"I hate you! I hate the way you never speak to me by my name, treat me as if I'm nameless, like I'm a number —Appointment 1:30—just one of many, how many—"

"What?"

"How many others—"

"—others?"

"—others who love you, others you don't love back, go on, give me the statistics, how many of us do you string along, laugh at our agonies behind our backs, how many—"

"Including regular private patients, clinic cases, research and staff work at hospitals?"

"How many—"

"Oh, approximately fifty, I'd say—"

"Fifty! All in love with you!"

"Well—"

"Oh don't be *mod*est, please don't de*mur*—"

"It isn't me they love, it's—"

"—their *dad*dies, we all wanna screw our dear old *dad*dies, fuck fuck fuck—"

"Is that the first way you learned to get even with him? Threw a few four-letter words around the parsonage?"

"Fifty!"—starting to sob now—"Daddy had five hundred. At least I'm nine-tenths better off with you."

"Five hundred?"

"Parishioners. His loved ones."

"Kleenex?"

—taking it, using it, gulping the sobs in a belated attempt at self-containment—"You can't love me because you're a dedicated man, that's it, isn't it. You're invulnerable to personal feeling, you couldn't reciprocate if you tried. You're immune. You're above it all. You're dedicated to science, to helping people. He was dedicated to Christianity, to helping people. It's the same difference."

"Let us hope there is *quite* a difference. Let us hope

that *mine* is *not* an expiation. Let us hope that mine cures."

"Then you don't deny you're a dedicated man?"

"I don't deny it."

"Dedicated to just exactly what?"

—and at the question his eyes suddenly turn cold with purpose, determination erasing his customary detachment (thinking for once not of my future but his own), and as he speaks his fist comes down on the desk, not hard as if in temper, but slow as if in the manner of one who has learned to keep anger as well as compassion in control— "To know more. That's all"—quietly, fist clenched— "Just to know more."

—all right, I don't need him with his stinking dedication and his stable of worshipers, I don't need Ed either, neither of them loves me, one wants to get me well to get rid of me and the other wants to keep me sick to hang on to me, I'm not the real me to either of them, to one I'm just a name to be added to his Graduate List, to the other I'm a possession to be treasured and kept under lock and key, I hate them I hate them both—

"Janie, there's someone at the door."

"You crippled?"

"Christ, honey, but you're in a vile humor lately. *You're* up, *I'm* not, will you go to the *door,* please—"

"I don't hear anybody"—but then the knock sounded louder and, sullen, I went and lifted the latch—

"Janie baby!"

"Rog! Oh Rog! Look Ed, come quick, it's Roger!"— and felt myself all gathered up and smothered in a hug.

TWENTY-SIX

"KNOW what you remind me of, leaning there like that?"

"What?" The Martian stood by the refrigerator, dwarf-

251

ing it, his elbow upon it and, in his hand, yet another high-ball. *"What* do I remind you of, darlin'?"

"Thomas Wolfe, the way he used to write—using the icebox as a stand-up desk, remember?"

"Ah, Tom, god of my fourteenth year." It was the eighth day of June, hot, humid, and Roger wore tight khakis and no shirt. "I swore I'd grow up to be as big as him and as talented. Well"—he took a sip, and before swallowing, gargled it loudly a second, then laughed—"I'm as big."

The screen door banged and my eldest son crossed the kitchen to us; Bruce was just eleven, his walk was a combination of Knute Rockne's and the Frankenstein monster's, shoulders hunched, lunging, head thrust forward, identical to his fellows and as ludicrous, exaggerating by contrast his thistle-slim frame and baby-soft face, but attempting by this newly acquired gait to erase from Roger's memory as well as from his own the not-so-long-ago days of hero worship and piggy-back rides. "Hey, Rog." Oh casual. Oh insouciant. All men are created equal. "Your turn against Johnny." He and his brother had been playing badminton, Roger had agreed to play the winner. "Better let him win. I let him, natch, otherwise he woulda bust out cryin', the little creep."

"He beat me yesterday and I was *trying* to win." Rog put his drink on the sink, spilling it although it was less than half empty; I saw Bruce's eyes go pseudo-blank with the effort of appearing not to notice, and he began balancing his racket on his outstretched hand. Then—"C'mon, Rog, will ya?"—and he butted past the invisible tackle to his left, seeming not to care one way or another (eleven, inviolate to charm) as Roger, following him out the door, crooked his immense arm around the scrawny neck, mashing the small awe-and-sun-flushed forehead into an armpit that smelled of lemony cologne and of perspiration.

I knew that smell. For six beachcombing days now I had breathed it in (revolted, attracted, intensely aware), lying next to it on the Indian blanket beside the jetty, smelling too the whisky breath as we talked in heat-baked murmurs or lapsed into sleep or silent gazing—at the ocean, at the gulls, at the sailboats or the bold and brave who bathed in water still chilled with the rains of April. His odor had been mixed with the scent of seaweed and salt-spray the day before, when he'd carried me across the sharp stones which separated the soft white sand at the top of the beach from the dark hard sand dampened impressionable by the sea, cold and gray as newly laid concrete, where we had walked in each other's footprints and talked of Atkins' plan . . .

"—but the way his obsession grew until it included all of us, that's really weirdsville," Roger said. "Me, Cohn, that's understandable, but you? Ed? Lisa? Why—"

"Maybe again it was the childhood thing, maybe when he was a kid on the farm his bitterness extended past his family, lit into everybody around, maybe the way he became an expatriate corresponds to the way he's blaming a whole bunch of us—a couple of villains isn't enough, he needs more, needs a whole circle of people to detest."

"I can see you've been doing some pondering, kiddo" —he hugged me to him a second, then bent over to pick up a pebble and sent it skimming across the water—"What about this business of Atkins wanting to wreck my face, isn't that what his wife says he has in mind more than a desire to kill me?"

"Yes, I've been thinking about that too. Maybe the alienation—"

"Huh?"

"Well, listen. Maybe as a lonely child he wished his brother could be his friend, wished the brother were less like the father and more like himself, maybe he kept wishing about it until that day in the garden, that might've been when he finally gave up hope of ever being in anything but blood a member of that family."

"And so?"

"So couldn't it have been just the same when he grew up and got himself a new family, the same only opposite? Now rather than blood being the only bond, blood was the barrier, the cause of his new alienation. Just as he'd pretended, perhaps, that his brother was his friend until

253

he could pretend no longer, so maybe he could pretend Paul's son was his own until the child began to develop his father's face, features—"

"Ah!"

"See? If he could destroy that daily evidence of the child's paternity, he could keep on feeling love, unalienated. So when he wants to destroy your face, it is Paul's face on his son he is destroying—"

"—and his brother's soul, his father's, the loneliness, separateness—"

"Clever?"

"Clever!" We laughed, brushing against each other as we strolled along, he not noticing it, I trying not to. When he spoke again his voice had lost its spontaneity—*does* he notice it? oh please no, oh please yes—and had become suddenly forced, falsely casual. "Janie, you don't suppose it's something more logical, do you?"—he doesn't, doesn't feel the touch and the hunger, it's only me—"I mean, kid, this conjecture's all very Jungian or something, but there's probably a simpler explanation of this idea of his. I mean, maybe he heard something about how I'm considering plastic surgery, maybe he's got a cute idea how he can do the job himself and save me some surgeon's bills. I mean, Janie, it's possible, isn't it, that he figures an amusing form of revenge would be to take me at my word and change my face for me without benefit of anesthetic—"

"How could he have heard, Rog? No, that's silly"—feeling embarrassed at my feelings but even more embarrassed at his, for he was trying so hard, and failing so completely, to hide his fear behind the lightness of his tone, fear of pain, yes, of physical injury, agony, scarred ugliness—but what else? Of what was I reminded as we walked along, feet chilled by sea, heads warmed by sun? And suddenly I saw it clear—The Martian, my fourth child, my fourth meaning to me what The Martian meant to Roger, he torn now as I had been, torn between clinging and ridding himself, clinging to his rationalization even as he vowed and schemed and soothed his fear with drink —I began at last to understand.

"Hey, silent thinker"—Rog pinched my chin in his fingers and shook my head for me—"Another idea?"

"No"—you don't bombard the ill with revelations; first he must reach bottom; then, climbing up all by himself (with unloving assistance, not mine) he would have to stumble over his own discoveries as I had stumbled time after time upon mine, elated, elated as I was now, already in anticipation a-quiver at the desk, leaning across the mahogany confessional with its invisible instruments of dissection, jabbering delightedly of my latest discovery, explaining that I understood now (as I'd tried to before but could not) about Roger and The Martian, about me and my fourth child, my fourth that I'd needed as he needed The Martian, needed an obstacle, a deterrent, a scapegoat, needed The Fourth and The Martian to protect ourselves from our own failure, used the imminence of the one and the actuality of the other as Elizabeth Barrett Browning used her invalidism to Robert: "... I can't ... how can I ... tied down, shackled, I cannot, cannot ... it's not my fault."

"Janie?"—Rog was snapping his fingers in front of my eyes—"Hello? Anybody home?"

I laughed, laughed and started to hug him, then stopped, cautious (body, behave), and instead pecked a quick sisterly kiss onto his cheek, sorrowful for his shackles, glad for the lack of my own, free, free to have three children and to hell with the fourth, free to face my own failure, pink-knitted blinders removed, free to fail or succeed but to keep whichever it might be where it belonged —out of the mainstream of my life—so that, with this rueful self-appreciation that I might someday learn to perfect (discussed and rediscussed away, someday perhaps, this small extremist demon in my mind and in my flesh, these sharp erratic quirks of melancholy, flippancy, of bashfulness and errant appetite) I could become the person I was meant to be, before the armor formed across the pain of being human and afraid.

"Janie"—we were back where we'd started on the beach; the children would be home from school soon, it was time to leave—"I guess it's obvious I've . . . been . . . hitting the bottle a lot lately."

"Rather obvious, my dear, yes."

"Well, I'm not making excuses or anything, but Christ it got tedious hanging around out there with not a damn thing to do while Lisa was away all day at the studio"— I said nothing—"and it got to be a habit, you know, good way to make the time go by. Have you ever had the feeling time wasn't passing at all? that something was wrong with the clocks? . . . aaah hell, it was her too, her goddamn attitude—"

"Lisa's?"

"Yeah, you'll see, she ain't that nice sweet kid she used to be."

"You think she'll come up and see us? Think she can get away from location?"

"If she can, she will. Know why? Oh, don't flatter yourself it'd be out of friendship or anything. She'd be proving to herself her recent Great Actress tag hasn't changed her, proving it to you and Ed. Oh, not to me, she stopped bothering to prove anything to me months ago. Stopped giving a damn whether I live or die—"

"Oh now, Rog—"

"Ha, you'll see, I'm past history to her."

"But . . . she was so . . . in love . . ."

"Yeah, with herself."

"I like Lisa, I—"

"She likes you too, and Ed, as much as she can like anybody. But me she's had. Two months, that's what I give any love affair of hers. Two months, three at the most. After that—get lost, little man, get lost." Then while I was trying to think of something comforting to say, someling wise and insincere, he pounced—relieving both of us—onto another subject. "Janie, hon, why no word from you all those months? Miscarriage set you back, huh?"

"Sort of."

"But Christ, honey, that was way the hell back before Christmas sometime, wasn't it? All winter and spring you were silent as a tomb. Hell, only time Lisa ever bothered

256

to speak to me was to wonder out loud what was the matter with you. What *was* the matter?"

—the matter? what was it from which I emerged totally changed and exactly the same, what was it?—a mystery that elucidated and an elucidation that mystified? a cleansing that dirtied and a filth that cleansed? a darkness that illuminated and an illumination that darkened? do I tell him that something happened but nothing happened, that it made me care less and care more, that it fragmentized and wholed me, that it never happened and it will never stop?—

"I guess I sort of ... cracked up."

"Aw now, honey, you trying to say you had some kind of a *breakdown? You?* Come on now, kid, dramatics, exaggeration, that's *my* department. You were depressed, Ed told us, and I can see you lost a lot of weight, but it wasn't anything ... well ... un*bal*anced, was it? I mean, you weren't ... uh ... put *away* or anything, so you couldn't have been ... uh ... mentally *off* or anything. Kiddo, you hung on okay, didn't you?"

"Oh, I hung on."

"Why sure, honey, why you've always been the happiest, healthiest, wholesomest-looking creature in all suburbia, that tan and that figure of yours—hell, kid, maybe you're skinnier but you still got your *good points*, kiddo, ha ha—hell, you never looked better in your life, you look like a coed—"

"We'd better get going—"

"Hell, Lisa kept saying *I* was cracking up last winter, *me! Look* at me, do I look like somebody who's losing his marbles, huh, do I, kid?"—he picked me up in his arms, laughing, and tossed me up, then squeezed me against him—"Say, you *are* lighter. Whatcha weigh?"

"Last time I looked, a hundred and five"—put me down, oh please, put me down—

"Used to be a hundred and *thirty*-five, weren't you?"—dancing me around on the sand, cuddling me to him, laughing—"You look good, kid, you're okay, we're both okay, yeah kiddo, we're two of a kind, you and me, moody but a sense of humor, that's what saves us, huh?"—skin to skin, hot, smooth, oh no oh no, put me down—"Laughing on the outside"—he was singing the ridiculous song, holding me tight, I couldn't breathe—"crying on the inside—"

"Rog, put me down"—he kissed me lightly on the shoulder, went on with his song—"Put me *down*."

He put me down. "All *right,* lady, all *right*." Still laughing, singing, he opened up the big beach towel, the one we'd joked about when we first brought it out, for it was, as Ed described it, a "grotesquerie in terry cloth." The Martian had been merchandised and the towel was one of the many products which now bore Roger's likeness; life-size, the face was a Halloween version of Roger's —witchlike, the grin so badly printed on the cloth that several teeth appeared missing—but below the face the body was reduced to half life-size, accommodating itself to the hemmed frame of the towel, so that the witch's face sat upon a dwarf's physique. Leering in imitation of the grotesquerie, Roger wrapped it around me. He was behind me, his arms pressed against my breasts; I wanted to bend my head and open my mouth on his arm, I wanted to turn and sink to my knees before him, a beggar. But he gave me a brotherly shove and leaned down to get the blanket. "Okay, kiddo, let's move on."

—ugly glutton in my blood, be gone; demon, let me be—

When Roger came in from badminton his body was wet with sweat. I gave him a lemonade, and as he took it his hand touched mine a moment.

—oh no, oh please, go away go away—

"Mom?" Johnny came into the kitchen, followed by Terry. "Bruce says Terry can't play. He won't even let him try."

"I wanna pway *bag*impum. Bwoos tells I isn't let to pway *bag*impum."

Roger said, "Terry, you tell your brother *I* said he should teach you." Then, to me, as they left: "That Bruce still worships me, you know that? He pretends he's too old for The Martian but I can see through that hard-boiled

258

facade of his. He can't keep his eyes offa me, notice that?"

I was trying to keep my hands off of him. I nodded. I was afraid if I spoke I would moan.

Bruce sat where Lisa had sat that first night of Rog and Lisa's meeting many months before. Terry and Johnny had gone to bed, but we had promised Bruce he could eat dinner with us "grownups" this once—just he and Roger, Ed and I. It was Saturday, it had rained all day, and while Ed and I did the innumerable Saturday tasks, Roger and Bruce had kept busy with Monopoly. Talk of boardwalks and railroads had grazed my hearing whenever I passed the playroom, but toward game's end—five o'clock, Roger having imbibed steadily since noon—I had stopped in the hall to listen a moment . . .

"Your move, Rog"—his urging had a desperate edge to it, as if he'd said the same thing many times before and not been heard—

"—never know it, wouldja, Brucie? But I was, kid, I was a stringbean at your age, I got beat up 'bout a dozen times a week, until—"

"Rog, it's your move."

"—until *he* came along—"

"Rog—"

"—big? hell, he was almost seven foot, weighed in at two twenty-five, all muscle."

"Who?"

"What?"

"Who was all muscle? You know, this guy you're talking about when you were a kid, who was so strong and he did things nobody else could do and everybody admired—"

"I don't need him."

"Where is he now?"

—voice suddenly louder, drunkenly belligerent—*"Who says I need him."*

—silence, then—"I guess we might as well finish this game later. You want to take a break for a while, Rog? Huh?"—silence—"Rog?"

259

"Someday—"

"What?"

"Someday there'll be no tomorrow but the sun will be shining just as bright."

"I—"

"God, he was drunk when he said that, the old guy was staggering down the aisle, but I never forgot, ain't it funny how you never forget sometimes, kid, I wake up sometimes in the night and I just *see* it up in the air like a goddamn neon sign or something, SOMEDAY THERE'LL BE NO TOMORROW BUT THE SUN WILL BE—"

"—shining just as bright."

"*Right*, kid, very *good*." And there was the sound of a backslap, the scraping of a chair—"You're a good kid, so's your brothers they're good kids, and your Mom and Dad they're good too, good people, kid, you're lucky you got"—sudden halt, table scraping now as if knocked by accident—"Oops, sorry, kid, can I help you pick 'em up, hey, it looks like a bomb hit the United States Mint, money money all over the place—"

"That's okay, I'll do it"—voice small—

"Now don't go get *grouchy*, hell if there's anything I hate it's a *grouch*, I won't *play* with you if you—"

"Rog, step over there, will you, you're stepping on the hotels."

"I don't need any lecture from you, now listen, bud, you can't boss *me* around, see? I'm The *Martian*, see? Just watch your *step*, mac—"

"Okay, Rog, okay—"

"I'm The Martian—"

"Yeah."

"I don't like your sarcastic tone, mac. You wanna fight I'll fight, I ain't afraid of you"—abrupt hush, sound of footsteps across the playroom—"What's this thing?"

"What? Oh that."

"What's it s'posed to *be?*"

"It's sup*posed* to be stained glass, supposed to l*ook* like it. My brother made it in Sunday School, copy of the church window."

"Whatzit a *pitch*er of?"

"Oh, you know, Jesus and his old lady, madonner and child I think they call it—"

"Howdidja make it?"

"*I* didn't make it, I *told* you, *he* did, Johnny, in Sunday School. He cut holes out of a cardboard, I guess, and stuck different colored hunks of cellophane—"

—but there was a tearing sound and a silence and then Bruce's voice again, not small now, anger in it a little but mostly just surprise—"Why'd you do that?"—

—no reply—

"What didja go and wreck *that* dopey thing for? My mother thought it was a big deal, that thing. When Johnny brought it home she cried, for gosh sakes, she *al*ways cries when she sees things she thinks are pretty or when she gets proud of us"—talking fast and high-pitched the way he does when he's upset and trying to hide it, trying not to cry maybe and realizing maybe how easily things get broken, cellophane stained glass and hearts and things— "I got a vocabulary list in Language that's got two adjectives that fit her perfectly, my mother I mean, she's maudlin and she's eccentric, didja ever notice that? I guess most mothers are maudlin but I don't think they're mostly eccentric—"

—but footsteps again and the door opened and out he came, The Martian, weeping—

And now at dinner he did not speak, he toyed with his food and seemed not to hear our conversation. For Bruce's sake I hoped his tears were finished, the tears which had brought tears to Bruce's eyes too, the frightened tears of the utterly dismayed, as he'd whispered to me, "He's just a little drunk," and I had answered, "Yes, he'll sober up soon." He had sobered up, yes, but remained now so totally sober, so dismal and silent, that only the combined efforts of Ed and myself had kept the much-anticipated dinner party from deteriorating into wordless gloom. Now Bruce said: "When they were going to bed I heard Terry ask Johnny where Mrs. Ross went."

My heart quickened. The children had seemed to take the nurses' departure as they had taken my illness: for granted. For weeks I had waited with dread for this moment—Mom, why were the nurses here? Dad, what sickness did Mommy have?—but now he was continuing. "Johnny told him she left 'cause Mom got well. Then Johnny asked me what sickness you had and I told him."

He stopped, steak-occupied, as if there was no more to say; I looked at Ed, he looked at me. Roger sat like a stone, as removed from the room as if he were still among the palms and eucalyptus of Benedict Canyon or Beverly Hills.

Ed took a bite of baked potato and asked Bruce, "What did you tell your brother?"

"Well, you know, about how it took a while to mend."

"Mend?"

"Yeah, you know, the place where the baby seed came unfastened."

Somewhere Matty Atkins lurked insane. Somewhere Lisa, bathed in light, emoted. Somewhere sperm met egg and life began. Somewhere blood left heart and breathing ceased. Somewhere someone fell in love, or out. Somewhere it was winter now, snow-quilted. Somewhere past the galaxies was—what? Somewhere past the galaxies was . . . God?

Sunday it rained, Monday Rog spent at Ed's office, Tuesday and Wednesday they went on publicity jaunts, and again, on Thursday, it rained. Roger and I got drenched. We had noticed the sky darken as we sat on the beach that morning, but, tentatively gathering our things together in case of rain, we had not thought in terms of haste until the first drops fell and then, without gradual increase but abruptly, like a practical joke, the water poured down as if from open faucets.

"Christ that felt good"—we came into the house dripping water on the floor, laughing, and whatever sorrow had afflicted him five days before seemed to have vanished with this Thursday as had the sun—"Nothing like taking a shower with your swimsuit on."

"I should've had the boys wear their raincoats to school."

"Oh, this'll only last a while. Look, it's starting to taper off already." I looked, and as I looked Roger grabbed me, laughing. "Hey, good luck, we forgot to bring the grotesquerie along, here it is nice and dry." He enclosed me in the huge Martian towel. "Kick those sopping sandals off, I sw'ar I'se gonna dry you from tip to toe."

He was kneeling in front of me, mopping at my feet, my legs, and I couldn't laugh. I couldn't even speak. Wanting was a blossom in my loins, tendrils spreading, tendrils lengthening and then, tendrils begging—

—no, oh please—

"Why gal, I do believe you're a bit on the bowlegged side. I never noticed that before—"

—never noticed that before? oh yes, bowed like my mother's and see those knees? yam-knees, mother's in replica, aren't they charming? and look here, look here, friend—big knuckles, uncut cuticles, haired chin, porous nose, rimmed eyes, neck accordion-pleated when I coyly turn my head—mother's, daughter's, same, the same, the very same, my genetic inheritance inevitable—

"What's the matter, honey?"

—Ed's house, Ed's friend, Ed's wife, no, no not his wife, he wants me sick, he hates me well, I hate him, he's not my husband, I'm alone alone—

—sick? doctor? patient? patience? no, no he's busy with the others, all the others, always the others, he doesn't care, I'm alone alone—

"Janie?"

—*to hell with them, to hell with them both!*

"Honey, look at me, will you?"

—alone, no husband, no doctor, nothing but the heat of a man's hand felt by my thigh through the barrier of towel and taboos—

And then watching my own hand reaching out to Roger's head and lying there, passive, a plea.

"Janie"—and how many seconds passed between my gesture and his knowledge, or between his knowledge and its effect, I do not know, knowing only that at some moment his arms went around my legs, his face went against my breast, and a muffled baffled swept-along voice

263

said, "I'm taking you upstairs"—no questions, no hesitation, clean at least (if in nothing else) in the as-the-crow-flies directness of recognition to reaction to the sad and ancient scene upon the sheets, scene to which I was both participant and spectator, bemusedly regarding whom—myself? my mother?—yes, here they were, all the tiny terrible signs of my years and of my legacy: the skin of the fingers cracked like the dried old leather edges of my grandmother's Bible, cracked and flaking, prematurely rough, inflicting the same scratchy caresses on Roger's flesh that I as a child had received at bedtime and at times of sorrow, when my Easter duckling strangled on a string, when I didn't get to ride in the rumble seat; yes, making love to The Martian with sandpaper hands like my mother's, with breasts like hers sloping stretched-skin-marked to the old-rose discus tips, these teats three times utilitarian for the nourishment of young, three times huge and hurtful for the sweet-and-sleepy sessions through the day and through the night, the lullabying paradise within a rocking chair, three times and never four, never four, never take a chance again on four, and Roger now, mouth to them breathing hot and tongue licking sophisticate-quickly, purposefully pulling passion like pollen from these not-so-pretty flowers, the ache ranging down through me like a weight of fruit overripe to bursting—oh ugly, ugly—low bosom maternity-marked, seen now by this man as I had seen my mother's, watching her emerge below her uplifted nightie in the mornings, watching her body emerge old and despoiled by the imperfections of time and toil, of pregnancy and childbirth, of ravenous infants and the laws of gravity, of too many years and too little care—yes, breasts too soft and hands not soft enough, stomach jutting like a whore of Toulouse-Lautrec's, buttock in Roger's hand doughy-kneadable, puckered, The Cutie with the Corduroy Can. Ugly. Ugly.

"You're beautiful," he said.

"You're blind."

The passionless banter of the locally aroused, the necessary interjections before the essential injection, the utterances muttered against neck and chest, arm and breast, ear and hair and mouth, muttered wherever face can be hidden, uttered and muttered, sighing and lying, twisting and listing to starboard and port, tossed in our infamous ark—

"Oh—oh yes—"

"Baby—"

—not baby, not baby, you're not my baby, you don't lie in the crook of my arm like a jewel in its case, your head here at my breast has no hollow in the bone through which my fingertips can feel the pulse beat like a silken metronome, your head is heavy and smells of Vitalis, your eyes are closed not in the fullness of warm milk but in the emptiness of this act, I know, I know, empty and ugly and stupid and darling don't stop—

—and now no more chatter, no more play, dead earnest now, apparatus swollen bloodful, dissolved in pain the virtuoso pair, forgotten the Duet for Four Hands, gone, gone control, gone the bed the limbs the thinking the shame gone all but this this—"oh sweet Jeeesus"—Neanderthal phantoms, Neanderthal sounds—"aaaah"—somewhere over the rainbow way up high high high high—

"Hi."

"Hi."

—earthbound aliens, embarrassingly bare, comfortingly close, dampness and dead desire and where do we go from here—

"Hey, wha' hoppen?"

—laughter, tension relieved, friends again, affectionate nibbles administered to necks—

"Janie, I didn't expect—

"I'm sorry."

"*I'm* sorry."

"So we're both sorry."

"So awright."

"So awright."

"Janie, why—"

"Why why—"

"Animals—"

"Nothing but—"

"Well, that's life."

"Mmmm—"

"When do the kids get home?"

"Soon."

"How do you feel? Really."

"Like what I am."

"Baby, I'm sorry—"

"Oh, Rog, not that again."

"But—"

"All my fault."

"Don't want to talk about it?"

"Want to forget it."

"Make believe it didn't happen?"

"It didn't."

"Couldn't be helped. Too much—"

"Proximity. Inevitable."

"Yes."

"Couldn't be helped. One of those things. Life's too short. Only live once. Etcetera."

"Etcetera etcetera."

"No excuse."

"Animals."

"Could you scratch me please, Rog, over by my left shoulder?"

"Here?"

"Down. More left. Ah. There."

"How soon they getting home?"

"Three-ten."

"Twenty minutes or so. We better get up."

"Yes."

"I suppose I'll go through the throes tomorrow."

"Of conscience?"

"Yeah. Cuckolding best friend, that bit."

"Me too. The Scarlet Letter Blues."

"Are you happy with him?"

"Usually."

"And what about this?"

"What?"

"This . . . incident."

"Just that."

"What?"

"An incident."

"What's love?"

"This isn't."

"Honey, I don't understand you. You've got me completely confused. I never would've guessed that Janie Thompson of all people—"

"This is sex. *Was* sex. One-two-three-skiddoo."

"Keep it light, huh? Okay. Lemme see. Sex. Isn't that the thing Americans get so het up about? That thing a place called Cedarton's celebrated for?"

"Mmmmm. Here, catch, put 'em on, you look like a dirty movie naked in your sandals like that."

"I feel like one."

"What?"

"Dirty movie."

"Me too."

"Helluva feeling."

"Mmmm. Come on, coffee."

"Good idea."

—and that was that, except that when we went downstairs I saw the towel lying crumpled on the rug where he had dropped it, wet, grotesque, showing between the folds the grimacing head and a twisted-sideward torso, legless, like the malformed creatures wheeling themselves along the street whom I used to pity as I passed them, and whom I do not pity anymore.

TWENTY-SEVEN

THE letter from Ed arrived during his half-week in Mississippi. He had gone down to work with Lisa between takes; they were formulating some personal publicity plans to fit in with the studio's arrangements for the usual pre-release press coverage on the film. The timing—as far as the four of us were concerned—was perfect, for Roger was in Canada appearing (in costume, of course) at a carnival in Quebec, and the day that he flew south to New

York would be the same day Ed and Lisa flew north, for yes, the director had decided he could shoot around her for one weekend—crowd scenes, Brando's solo takes—and I got busy preparing our agenda: the Schubert Theatre Friday night, a few friends in Saturday night, and between evenings, an intensive daytime schedule of other-people's-houses for the boys, so that our foursome could catch up on our friendship in uninterrupted garrulity.

The letter was a complete surprise. Ed usually phoned me when on business trips, but not since honeymoon days had he taken pen in hand to tell me of his feelings. To the upper right of the hotel stationery he had written "Between midnight and dawn" and, a bit lower to the left, merely: "Wife!" Then came five pages of his large familiar scrawl—the penmanship of an extrovert, I'd often proclaimed, lip curled—and some of what he said I'd heard before. Some, but not all . . . .

"I'm glad you're back from wherever you were. Don't believe me if you don't want to, but it's true. I never knew a person could be as desperately lonely as I was when you were at your sickest. There must be nothing else in the world remotely like it—to be with someone you love but to share no thought, no emotion, to exchange scarcely a word for months. Everything but your body had died, and there wasn't much left to that either. Mostly, besides the personality that makes you so uniquely *you,* it was the eyes that were gone. Whenever I looked into those blank eyes and they looked back and yet didn't look back at all, not seeing me or caring, I was so overcome by desolation that soon after the beginning of it all, way back in December, I entered my own minor illness to escape from your major one. You didn't know about it, and maybe I shouldn't tell you now, but you seem so obsessed by the idea of my resenting your return to the land-of-the-living that I feel this will convince you of your error. I'm jealous of you, sure. Sometimes my jealousy is a torment. But it is never *never* desolation, and I'll take torment over desolation any day.

"I saw your doctor. Just once. That single hour set me

268

straight on so many things that I consider it the most valuable hour of my life. Except for the hour I met you in, up there in the sky between Dallas and Denver.

"I told him that I couldn't take it. That living with you in that condition was making me even lonelier than if you had actually died a physical death. Told him that I was terribly afraid you would never 'come back,' or that if and when you did you'd be different, changed. I told him that I could feel myself getting detached from it, blotting it out of my feelings. I told him that only once in a while did I really look around and see what was happening to our family—the boys in clothes too small for them and sometimes ragged, sweet Johnny beginning to be a disciplinary problem in school and doing poorly in his work, Bruce having constant nightmares and constant quarrels with the nurses, Terry showing increasing signs of insecurity and confusion as to who was his mother and who was not. I told him that I'd always been a nervous wreck and a compulsive dynamo of activity but that now I was getting twinges of listlessness and that I knew this was dangerous, since I'd read somewhere that any complete departure from one's normal temperament is the symptom to worry about.

"Then he told *me* a few things. . . .

"He said I must be your strength. He could only do so much, he said, and I must do the rest. I said I'd never felt less strong in my life. Then he said something like this, Janie: 'Your wife has enormous strength and courage. Otherwise she would have taken her own life by now. It is only her tremendous will power which is keeping her on this side of psychosis, of schizophrenia. She is clinging to her almost-vanished identity because she remembers just enough of her former self to suspect her own potential for the future. If you can help her bear the present, your future with your wife will be a far finer thing than it could ever have been had she not suffered this tragedy.'

"At that last word, Janie, I busted out crying. Me! And as I cried I poured out the story of our life together.

"This was way back at the beginning, so I guess you hadn't had a chance to tell him much about us. He seemed

269

interested to hear about the way we met, a mile high, and about how I married you real soon before I was even out of my teens. He even seemed interested in hearing about my life before I met you and there was one thing in particular he sort of 'latched onto' . . .

"You know, I've told you about it, about how from the day I was five and had my first corner-of-the-block shoe-shine stand, all my relatives heard the reiterated refrain from my mother: 'Mark my words, my boy'll be a rich man someday.' You know I told you how proud I was to be a small entrepreneur—selling magazines door to door, selling frozen custard summers at Coney Island—but I've never told you before about my terror. Because you see, Janie, the family which continually praised me and predicted my financial success put not a healthy drive into me but a fearful one. I was always thinking, 'What if I *don't* get ahead. What if I disappoint them. If I don't become what they expect they'll stop loving me.' I felt forced toward success as the only way of fulfilling my parents' prophecies and thus retaining their respect and love.

"Well, your doctor was interested in this because you, Janie, had a similar problem, he suspected. Since you were little, people had praised your imagination, your articulateness, your poems and your stories. But you had to have four children (this too a neurotic drive, he told me; maybe someday you can help me understand it) and you always felt that *then*, after you'd accomplished the four kids, you could set about accomplishing the other; you kept telling yourself, procrastinating, that *then* you'd do it, when you had time—write the masterpiece, satisfy the expectations, earn the admiration which your childhood had taught you could be earned in no other way.

"But this pathetically similar motivation which should have been a bond divided us. I was your rival, your sibling rival, because emotionally you had never matured into a woman, a wife. And when I was first, won the 'goal' my family had set for me—my own publicity business, the right friends and the right house and the right street in the right town, prestige and money and the whole Golden Boy

270

bit—it unnerved you. 'He's done it, now it's *my* turn, now *I've* got to do it, got to keep up, got to show everybody, must reach *my* goal.') And so, losing your fourth meant not only death, murder, guilt, God knows what else, but meant *Write! No More Stalling!* But your mind did more than stall. It vanished.

"Hell, honey, this is all just one item in your illness, ridiculously oversimplified. It's just that I feel now that I know you so well, understand you and love you more for it, and yet there's so much that I don't understand and never will. For instance, during the hour we got on the subject of sex. Well, he said that you, me, all of us neurotics, have the present mixed up with the past. With you the neurosis got so severe you lost all distinction between the characters of your childhood and the characters of here-and-now. And he mentioned that if you were ever to be unfaithful to me, it would not be *me* you'd be betraying because it would not really be *you* committing the adultery. You'd be reliving someone else's role to punish that person, he said, and at the same time you'd be punishing two male figures who (as he put it) 'soil her dreams now as they once soiled her body at puberty.' He added that these two hated males might seem to you at times to be others—husband? doctor?—but that we'd be only substitutes.

"Well, my darling, here comes the sunrise. Within an hour or two the cameras will be a-grinding. Maybe I can catch some shut-eye before I go over to location and try to arrange some candid shots of Lisa that are *really* candid. She's dying to see you again, says she loves you even if you *are* a brain-picker who knows more about her than anyone has a right to know. I warn you, though; the weekend's apt to be a mighty strained affair. I guess it'll be the Finale for Lisa-Rog. As far as she's concerned, at least. The mention of his name brings naught but a sneer to her beauteous pan. As for her and the assistant director, everything you've been reading in the papers is true. In fact, the most torrid account would be an understatement! Poor Rog.

"Okay, hon, just wanted you to be prepared for the

weekend. Also, wanted you to know you've got a great doctor there. He was right about everything. He told me I could bear your illness and be your strength. And he was right again when he promised you'd pull through fine. He was right when he said the effect on the kids would be temporary and that they'd snap back as soon as you did. So I can't help but put my trust in him, as you have all these months, and believe with him that starting soon our marriage is going to get 'beautifuller and beautifuller,' as Terry would say."

Roger and I—over coffee, after the act—had spoken of the weather, of yesterday and of tomorrow, of movies and of Lisa and of Faulkner and Kazan, until finally, inevitably (as I fiddled the spoon in the sugar bowl, he fiddling with the cream), he remarked, "It's like death, isn't it."

"Sex?" At once we were on the same beam, companions in opaque analogy. "Yes, you mean—"

"—the uncontrollability of it, the giving in to mysterious forces, the one consciously accepted and unconsciously unaccepted, the other consciously unaccepted and perhaps unconsciously accepted—"

"Yes!"—ah kindred soul, ah intrepid weaver of hypotheses, metaphors, paradoxes, ironies, ah Ed-opposite, Ed-betrayer, ah screwer of mothers, my children's, your own—

"But more than that, Janie, this kind of sex is like death because the act itself is so trivial compared to the . . . the . . ."

"—ramifications of the act."

"Ramifications, yes, that's what I meant."

"What's death? Wham—pfft. What's sex? Wham—pfft. But in each case that little so-what of an instant sets off endless tremors—"

"Shadows. The shadow backward—remember, Janie? And from the other, a shadow forward—"

"—yes, from one little wham-pfft a shadow of apprehension beforehand, lying all over everything like a shroud, from the other little wham-pfft a shadow after-

272

ward, of necessary deceit discoloring everything like a layer of dirt—"

"It will bother you?"

"Lying to him? Of course, I hate lies. I've got honesty in me like a disease, oh not the phony shock-'em kind any more but the real peel-it-to-the-core kind. I think I was as starved for stark bleak unadorned truth in my childhood as poor Matty was for beauty. I—"

"But you will?"

"Lie? Of course." I noticed Roger's relief, heard the faraway screech of brakes grinding the school bus to a stop down at the corner, I hurried my words, coffee cooling, forgotten. "Rog, what did you . . . what did you . . . think . . . right afterward . . ."

"Of Ed. I thought about how jealous he is of everyone who's ever around you, except good old trustworthy me."

"Mmm, I know, but he's always so suspicious of my fidelity anyway that I console myself with that handy old chestnut, I might as well be hung for a sheep as a lamb."

"And was the sheep worth it?" I didn't reply and he said, "Well, kid, was it?"

But I just laughed (not wanting to hurt him, not Ed, not anyone ever again) and through my laughter he gave my question back to me, asked me what I'd thought, upstairs a few minutes ago, and I told him I'd concocted a fine line for some future tome: "They fell apart like the two half-shells of a cracked egg, emptied, moist, dripping."

"Poetic as hell," he said, and laughed, and the boys marched in, ravenous, adorable, and ate and ran out again, baseball-gloved, followed by Roger. "Hey wait up, you guys," he yelled, and ran away from fallen swimsuit straps and breasts one has no claim to, away into the rainwashed air and sunshine, escaping the clutching shadows, backward, forward, escaping the comic fact (oh Madonna, keep it comic) of beds containing not one Mom but three.

There's no use pretending I don't get a kick out of it. I do. Whispering the magic words to the airport gate attendant ("meeting Lisa Maurice"), being drawn respectfully from the cramped crowd of waitees to the special privilege of open sky and engine roar beyond their roofed plebeian corridor, standing between the sibilant breeze of their whispering ("who is she? is she somebody? she must be *some*body!") and the stronger gale of the plane propeller wash as it turns to a halt, scanning the small square windows for their faces, Lisa's, Ed's, and remembering—as I stand there skirt-swirled and ponytail lifted westward like a weather-sock by the wind—the days and nights I stood there uniformed, capped, silver-eagled at the breast, before I knew that a passenger would marry a stewardess and become the father of my children, before I knew how sick I was or how gifted, before I knew that my life would be splintered down the center, and repaired.

She was beautiful, she stood at the head of the steps and smiled, smiled for the newsmen on the asphalt and the public behind the glass, smiled into the cameras and their owners' shouted demands: "This way, Miss Maurice" . . . "Hey, Lisa, move forward a little."

From plane to private waiting room was a shambles of the fans' babbling and rude shoving, but between Ed and me her smiling face was like the eye of a storm, calm amidst the fury. I remember thinking: this bores her. And then remembering: fame is far less exciting than the anticipation of it, and far more annoying—who had said that, Roger?—yes, and now as the quiet of the VIP Room suddenly enfolded us I said, "Roger got in from Canada a half-hour ago and phoned here to LaGuardia that he's coming straight here from Idlewild. He should be here any second."

Then, from Ed: "Lisa, should we show Janie now or wait till later?"

"You mean that thing?" I pointed to the large object, oblong, flat, that Ed was carrying under his arm; it was brown-paper-wrapped. "I was wondering what that was. A scrapbook of this week's publicity items on you, Lisa, perchance? I've personally seen at least two dozen."

"Nope, guess again." But as I stood guessing Lisa grabbed me and kissed me on both cheeks. "You *louse* you. Why'd you go incommunicado all those months? You

274

decide to drop the Janitor's Daughter from your Friendship List?" I felt uncomfortable in her embrace, then realized why: it seemed phony, her enthusiasm and her chastisement, like the queen saying just the right thing to please the commoner. But again she hugged me, and then, holding me away at arm's length, serious now: "It was pretty bad, huh?" I nodded. The compassion on her face seemed so sincere that suddenly I felt guilty, suspecting that it was I who had always indulged in the play-acting, not she, I perhaps who wrongly saw in her the discomfort I felt, feeling out of my league, a "nobody," feeling thirty years peel away in the ever-increasing glamour of her presence so that I was a child again and cowering before the grandeur of a grownup.

I reached for the package, trying in my motion to hide my shyness, but abruptly the door opened and there was Roger. I heard just three words emerge in an excited squeal from the babble behind him—"*Martian's going in*" —and then the door closed and there were the four of us, alone, smiling uncertain smiles of concealed apprehension in the first few seconds of silence, and then all starting to talk at once, and stopping, and laughing, and, after another moment, bursting out in a chorus again, a simultaneous explosion of inanities, like a bit of Laurel and Hardy nonsense, farcical, idiotic. But the element of farce was just what we needed—it was a catharsis, somehow, dispelling the self-conscious mood we seemed to be in, each of us too aware of what had happened to himself and the others in the interim, of what had happened to Milton Cohn, and, perhaps, of what might happen to us or between us before our brief reunion came to an end—and we fell upon each other's laughter as one grasps at straws, finding everything we said so funny, so charged with irresistible hilarity, that in our gaiety we completely forgot what waited behind the door; as we opened it the flash bulbs startled us out of our laughter, even Lisa, who was so used to it, gasping a little in surprise.

As we moved along—were pushed or carried along, rather—down the corridor and up the ramp to the main lobby, I was reminded of an ant stampede; how similar it was, this scene, to the swarming of ants upon some small stray piece of food: Lisa the prize, submerged in the fame-ravenous nibblings and clawings of creatures subhuman in the callousness of their curiosity, clambering over each other for a better view, snatching at her clothing, jabbing papers and pencils so close to her face that above her wavering smile the beautiful eyes kept blinking, blinking—and I saw that I had been correct in my recollections, for her eyes *were* bright green, an unbelievable green, and I wondered again how it must feel to know that your slightest glance can startle, entice, arouse.

"Goddammit"—it was Roger, shoved against me, muttering, and suddenly I realized that it was not the shoving alone which was upsetting him, realized also that his breath was strong with liquor.

"What a mess, huh, Rog?" I spoke loud above the surrounding clamor, and he nodded curtly, but only I knew to what mess I referred. It was an invisible mess, it was inside of his head, and I'd recognized its existence in the same moment that I had found myself comparing the fans to ants and their target to a morsel of food. "Lisa the prize," I had thought, not "Lisa and Roger." And Lisa it was, not he but Lisa, Lisa alone, and he knew it—knew too, as did Ed and I (exchanging looks as Roger's muttering continued, and as, several times, he pushed back at those pushing him aside to better their glimpses of Lisa), that the occasional calls of *"The Martian!"* peppering the solid shouted sound of *"Lisa Maurice!"* were strictly the high piping voices of children, like a loyal sprinkling of kindergarteners assembled in his behalf.

The newsmen had succeeded at last in separating us sufficiently from the crowd so that more pictures could be taken. I saw at once that, despite Ed's pseudo-casual attempts at manipulating both Lisa and Roger into the spotlight, the photographers were not planning to co-operate. After several shots of the two of them together, someone shouted, "Lisa, could we take a couple of you without—uh—"

"The Martian! The Martian!" his small-fry constituents

screamed helpfully, thrilled, oblivious and thus undis-
mayed by this blatant downgrading of their hero.

"—without Mr. Rutherford"—someone finally remembered his name.

Quickly Roger stepped aside, smiling; I wished they'd
both stop smiling so hard; won't someone notice, I
thought, won't someone besides me and Ed notice how
gruesomely *false* those grins are? But I needn't have worried, for when I next spied Roger—out of camera range,
signing his name for a dozen gaping kids—the smile was
gone, *all* pretense was gone, and the manner in which he
handed back his signatures was so abrupt that I signaled
to Ed, and he interrupted his conference with the AP
reporter ("Is it true about Lisa and her director? True
she and he will undertake an independent production of
Anna Karenina? Is it true that she ... Does she ... Will
she ...") long enough to rescue Roger from his admirers,
or rather to rescue them from Roger, for he looked as if
he'd soon use one of the pencils not to sign but to stab.

Finally it was over, we reached the car, drove out of the
airport and onto the highway toward Connecticut. At
first the conversation was cursory, stilted—"How are the
boys?" "Fine." "How's Mississippi?" "Great."—but by
the time we reached the Whitestone Bridge it was clear
that Roger's recent trip to the bathroom had included yet
another trip to the bar. He became loquacious, slurring
his words, and from Westchester to Greenwich and on
fifteen minutes more to Cedarton, the three of us sat in
silence, boredom and pity, listening for perhaps the
twentieth time to the tale of how the star her*self* had insisted on Roger for a *key* part in the very *o*pening scene of
Look Away, Dixieland and how, if only he'd re*fused* and
held out for the top role or nothing at *all,* he'd be *some*-
place today, instead of ... of ...

"Of where?" Lisa's voice was brittle.

"What?" He turned and looked at her vaguely, his eyes
dreamy with Scotch and self-deception.

"I said *where* would you be?"

"Where when? What—"

"Oh God, never mind." She looked away from him,

out the window. "How lovely the dogwoods are. Christ, but the East is marvelous in the spring. In autumn too. The West can't hold a candle. Remember, Janie, how the trees looked last fall when we drove up to Hartford for that—that—"

I interrupted her mercifully. "I remember. I even remember what you said. 'Like a Chinese funeral. Death with a festive flair.'"

"I hate dogwood," Roger said, mumbling, slumped in his seat. "Hate trees, *period*. Hate *flowers*."

"Naturally." I wished Lisa would ignore his drunkenness, but she went on. "Naturally you hate anything that *grows*. That's something *your mentality* stopped doing at the age of fifteen."

He slumped lower. "Why don't you shut up. Thass all, just shut your fuggin' mouth."

Ed's hand left the steering wheel, found mine, pressed it. Strange, I thought, how the bickering of another couple can sound so vile; one's own quarreling never seems so bad, so senseless, so undignified; only when one is uninvolved, objective, can one comprehend the ugliness of love-gone-sour; and only when one is too young—a child, too concerned, uncomprehending—can one be not just disgusted, but threatened—not merely embarrassed, but shattered into bits.

"Well," Ed said after a while. "Here we are." And after the getting out, and greeting the boys (here at last Lisa ignored, Roger as always the king), and—shoes off, feet up, boys unglued from Roger's side and sent to play outdoors—settling down to whatever the weekend might bring, Lisa opened the package they'd brought.

"Do you like it?" she asked.

"I . . . I *think* so. Ed? Do *you* like it?" Usually he had no great tenderness for abstract art, and this was violently abstract; the canvas was a bold conglomeration of colors and shapes. I didn't know which way to hold it.

"Here," Lisa laughed, setting it right. "This way."

"Whether I like it's beside the point," Ed said. "Don't you notice anything?"

"I don't notice anything," Roger said; already a glass was in his trembling hand.

"Nobody asked you," Lisa said.

I looked it over. "What should I see?"

"Look, honey, here." Ed pointed to the lower left-hand corner. "See?"

Now I saw. What had seemed a squiggle became a name. Matthew Atkins had signed his name in red.

"Where on earth did you *find* it?"

"We found it on Jackson's Left Bank," Lisa said. "Just happened to come across it in a street art display."

"We?" Roger was staring at her, ignoring the painting. "We?"

"Yes. We."

"You and Ed?"

"No, not me and Ed, you through quizzing?"

"Who was with you?"

"With whom I was is none of your business."

"Screw whom. Who—"

"Screw you."

Ed stopped them. "Come *on,* folks. Let's play together nicely." And turning our attention back to the canvas— "Sure went wild with the brush, didn't he. It's crazy but I like it. I don't know why but I do. What I know about modern art could be contained within the anus of a gnat, but I've got a feeling this is good. I mean really *good.* The guy's got it. Or rather, had it."

Lisa's head was to one side, her eyes narrowed as she studied it. "I've been trying for days to figure out what it's supposed to represent. Carl, my costumer on this pic and a good artist, told me to quit trying, said if the guy wanted to tell a story he could go to Russia. He said if I feel it, that's enough. I don't know. Janie, do *you* feel it?"

"Yes." Roger was in his own world now, weeping, all tears and no sound, his head bent back against the chair and his eyes closed.

"Me too," Ed said. "But what the hell does it mean?"

The three of us regarded it in silence for a moment or two. Then Lisa said, "It looks like a garden, sort of. In a trampled-on kind of way. Doesn't it, Janie?"

"Yes." Everywhere the flowers were broken, everywhere the blood ran red. "Yes it does."

TWENTY-EIGHT

"HELL no," Lisa said. I had asked her if she was still seeing her "head-shrinker"; the two men were in Ed's room, getting ready—as were we—for the theater. "You were dead right about it."

"About what?"

"Psychoanalysis. It's all a hoax. Just like you always used to say."

"I did?"

"All those thousands I spent, and for what? I should have listened to you and saved myself a big waste of time."

"You're not . . . happier?"

"Happiness! What *are* you, somebody from the *Reader's Digest?* An advance scout for Norman Vincent Peale?"

"I just wondered whether—"

"I was a mess before, when I was a small success with sex appeal. Now I seem to be on the verge of being a big success with egghead-appeal, so I'm less of a mess. If I feel better inside, it's because realistically I've got more to feel better about, not because some quack yakked at me for five years."

"Maybe the quack-yakking helped to quell the mess so you *could* do more, maybe the mess-quelling came first and *then* the success, the improved insight and ability to communicate that insight through your acting—"

"Ah, come off it, Janie. Why try to sell me a bill of goods you wouldn't buy yourself? Psychoanalysis is for the birds . . . no, not the birds, I'll be more specific . . . it's for creatures who prefer crawling to walking, it's for cripples who got that way on purpose and enjoy every minute of it."

"You think so?"

"I know so. Listen, it's dead, Freudian analysis, dead and soon-to-be-buried, ask anybody who knows and they'll tell you, it was a noble experiment but it failed, it failed on me, failed on everybody I know who ever tried it, and you know why? I'll *tell* you why . . . I've thought about it a lot, 'cause I was damn disappointed in it and I wanted to make damn sure I understood my disappointment."

"You seem to have an increased passion for self-understanding. Can't you credit that to your analysis?"

"No, I can't. While a person's being analyzed they get older, I got five years older, but was it the five years or the headshrinking that matured me? Hell, I could've spent the five years on a *safari* and I'd still have gained that maturity. Don't you see? Analysts take credit for accomplishments that Time should take the bow for. I know myself better now? Inspect my motivations more? Sure, and a kid when he's nine knows how to tie his shoelaces a helluva lot better than he did when he was four."

"You sound bitter."

"Ah dammit, Janie, it's just I get so sick of these li'l pals of mine out there on the Coast who make a profession out of Maturity. *You* know them, New York's as full of them as Hollywood—these bores who parade around pityingly tolerant of The Great Unanalyzed, as if they're the only adults in a world of children, the only sighted amidst the masses of the blind."

"You're more articulate than you used to be."

"Oh, I'm a lot more of lots of things, and it's very pleasant, I like self-confidence, but it didn't arrive in a flash of weepy recollection on a leather couch, it arrived in the approbation of critics, the applause of the VIP's, the sensation of being pointed out as Lisa Maurice who can *act,* not as Lisa Maurice that pair of tits who screwed her way to stardom."

"And your analysis—"

"Honey, my analysis was wonderful at the time, remember how I used to rave to you how wonderful? Boy, when you're lonesome and disgusted with yourself it's great having someplace to go every day that's guaranteed to invest all your dopey little insignificant thoughts with solemn significance, it takes away that feeling of futility and gives you a jim-dandy routine with a jim-dandy goal, it's lovely, you've got someplace to go that's not too superficial, like a beauty parlor, or too complicated, like a library, it kills time but gives you the illusion of a vital occupation, you tell yourself a mere time-killer couldn't be *that* expensive. And oh, how delightful it is having somebody who's just as interested in you as you are, it's irresistible, why my God, I *still* feel cheated when I wake up from a dream in the morning and realize nobody wants to hear about it, there I am stuck with that marvelous unique crammed-full-of-traumatic-goodies treasure which *he* would've listened to, reveled in, entered upon a transport of analytical exultation with me, intense, emotionally involved— So what happens now? I get up and go to the set and re-mark to the script girl that I had this dream last night, see, in it I was all bare in the Kremlin and this spider with my father's voice was screaming at me—so do you know your lines today, the script girl says. Dammit, Janie, do you see my stockings?"

"Here"—handing them to her where she sat on the corner of the bed, watching her roll them up and then resume her talking, watching and listening as I adjusted my earrings, winding the tiny knob, feeling it too tight at first on the tender silky lobe, too loose, and then, just right—

"Oh, you get to know yourself better, sure—some memories pop up from nowhere, you feel some surprising emotions and resentments and stuff like that you didn't know you had, and that's something, it has a certain amount of permanent value, especially if you're a creative artist or trying to be, where the exposing of your psyche to public view is part of your job—sure, the more complete and authentic the psyche the better the job, that I'll grant. But those two other temporary factors that seem at the time so wonderful—the place to go, the person avaricious for your every thought—the abrupt loss of those two is hard to take, some people *can't* take it, they refuse to, they go on being analyzed forever and ever, and the analyst co-operates because he's as loath as the analysand is to admit defeat, to admit he knows as well as she does that her life has *not* improved, she *hasn't* acquired a new personality or a new lovability or a new career or a new set of glands, she hasn't acquired a goddamn thing except a bad habit and a stupid crutch. But say they quit —run out of money or their husband's patience or something—so they quit, and *that's* when they become superior bores, the ones I mentioned before that drive me up the wall. That third factor—the permanently valuable one of better tools for introspection—they *use* that instead of *utilizing* it, do you know what I mean?"

"Well—"

"Take this guy I know out at the studio, film cutter, I used to give him a lift home and we got to talking. He expected psychoanalysis to provide him with some magical improvement—with, at the very least, some new quality with which to win the esteem of his fellows—and instead he found himself in a state of deprivation, stripped of his former rationalizations, expected by his doctor and his little orbit to demonstrate tangible results, swelleroo mental health. Formerly he at least had the illusion of being special, special if only in the enormity of his suffering, but now he must face reality, and the reality is his mediocrity —exactly the universal curse from which he had hoped his analysis would release him. So what does he do? How does he survive in the imminence of a depression even worse than the one which sent him into analysis in the first place? He takes that very same self-knowledge that made him into Just Another Wounded Ego, just another cipher propelled along the Track of Life by the same damn drives as everybody else—he takes it and uses it as a replacement, uses *it* as the special quality with which to shine at gatherings of pseudo-intellectuals, substitutes *it* for the illusion of differentness and superiority left behind on the couch."

"All right, but how about you? You're *utilizing* it, your new knowledge, unconsciously maybe, but it's there in your acting for all to see, you've got a new—"

"I've got a new nothing. I got lucky, is what I got. I've been a good actress since I was fourteen, mixed-up psyche

283

or no mixed-up psyche, only nobody could see past all these remarkable outer attributes of mine—"

"Now they see."

"They see, they've acknowledged me, I can take each day because each day's terrific, not because *I'm* more terrific or my *analysis* was terrific but because I'm there, where I wanted to be—not just a star, but an *actress*— I'm there, and I could just as easily *not* be there, and if I wasn't there I'd still be sick and hurt and wracked with phobias, analysis or no analysis."

"Okay. Now what about Rog?"

"What about him?"—already on the defensive, voice suddenly hard, eyes turned away from mine—

"You're . . . through?"

"Of course. I'm a bitch, remember? Hippity-hoppety, bed to bed—"

"The assistant director, what's-his-name?"

"Mmmm. Dan Kobrick. And *don't* ask me how come I didn't get analyzed out of my promiscuity. I got analyzed out of a conscience, that's even better."

"Isn't psychoanalysis supposed to reinforce the conscience with the correct materials, not eliminate it?"

"Oh, I was just jesting, silly, mine's still there all right. I can feel it—when Rog used to mention marrriage, and now Dan—my li'l old conscience rears its hoary old head and whispers to me I'm bad, ambitious, faithless, frigid and maritally a bad bargain for any man sweet enough to love me—"

"Rog was sweet to love you?"

"Yes, very sweet, very naïve, and, thanks to me, impotent and a drunk."

"I don't—"

"You don't blame me, I know. Well, I do blame me, you should be pleased I've got that much conscience left. I can't feel love for Roger anymore—all those months of his self-pity and phony boasts removed that once and for all—and frankly I can't even feel much compassion for him, but responsible? Yes, I feel responsible for his problems, they were bad enough when he met me but I managed to make it worse. I'm sorry, Janie—you're his

friends, you and Ed, and you overlook a lot out of loyalty
—but Christ Almighty, try *living* with him sometime, I
wonder if *you* could take it, if *any* woman could—the
continual harangues and demands—"

"Demands?"

"Oh, you know, sex sex sex all the time sex, when I
just plain didn't feel like it. I was tired—my God that
business of rising early and hanging around between takes
at the studio and then repeating your own takes a dozen
times or so until you're hoarse and exhausted, that is
work—and all he did was sleep all day waiting for me
to come home so he could have himself one hell of a bang-
up time every night, prove what a great lover he was or
something—"

"But didn't you just say he was impotent?"

"Oh sure, finally, after I made excuses and refused and
refused some more, and when he got angry about it I
fought back by taunting him, ridiculing him, de-balling
him, I got bitchier and bitchier until I was saying things
I'd even have been ashamed to admit to my analyst. I
don't know—do you find you hurt people almost on purpose sometimes?"

"I used to, often."

"Well, I guess this *was* on purpose, if the purpose was
to get him out of my bed, because pretty soon he was
drinking all the time, he didn't bother me anymore with
demands, he accused me of killing his manhood, I accused
him of being a failure, a hypocrite, a souse—I was a bitch,
I broke him."

"He's not broken, not quite."

"What do you mean?"

"None of your damn business what I mean"—only a
little angry, less angry than relieved; had I perhaps given
him more than I took away?

"Oh Janie"—she looked really hurt; was she acting?—
"Now I've gone and upset you. Now you'll hate me too,
like he does."

"I only hate . . . oh, never mind."

"What? Please."

"Cruelty. Of people, of fate. I hate . . . the shadows."

285

"Shadows?"

"Yes, that's what Rog and I call it. One shadow is falling over this conversation right now, I know it's there, you don't."

"What *is* it?"

"The shadow of necessary deceit. Anything can cause it—a physical impulse, an outgrown friendship—anything which necessitates dishonesty in order to ... to ..."

"To what?"

"To not hurt someone."

"Someone? Anyone?"

"Anyone who ... needs you. There are never very many of those."

"After what I've just told you, I assume I am to regard your comment as a slap in the face?"

"No, I—"

"Or is this your way of announcing *our* friendship is 'outgrown'?"

"By you, maybe. Not by me."

"Not by me either, pal"—she smiled, I did, then both of us burst out laughing—"Wow, I'm all talked out. When we get going we really get going, don't we? It's like we'd just seen each other yesterday and nothing had occurred in between—no Matty, no murder—incidentally, is that why Ed's so much more nervous?"

"What?"

"Cohn's untimely demise—is it his anxiety about Matty's whereabouts that's got Ed a-twitchin' worse than ever?"

"Maybe. Or Roger's condition, maybe—"

"Or yours?"

"What about mine?"

"You're thinner. And you've been out of the picture since Christmas ... no word from you, not a peep. Losing the baby, was that it? Blues got you down?"

"Mmmm."

"Don't want to talk about it, huh? Okay, what about Ed—how did he get the way he is, oh I don't mean how did he get this way *this* time, I mean way back—what's bothering him, what's been eating away at him all his life, the need to succeed? Is he a typical competitive neurotic American like the rest of us?"

"Oh sure, of course. But I suppose it's more than that, I suppose his mother being a beauty and not too bright didn't help much. His father was over at his little candy store most of the time, his mother doted on her handsome only son, maybe he was the outlet for all her affection—you know, the classic case of son-seduction that both of them would be horrified to realize about themselves. She's often told me with motherly pride how she was still putting on his socks for him when he was sixteen —and I married him three years later!"

"Child groom."

"Yes, he rushed into it, all right—we met in September, married on New Year's Eve."

"Met on an airplane, wasn't it?"

"Yep, six minutes out of Denver. I told him he could unfasten his seat belt now, and he said he couldn't because of arthritis of the hands and could I help him, so I was bending over thinking how tragic, such a young boy, when all of a sudden he grabbed my hands in his and squeezed them and started laughing, and so did I, and that was the beginning. We both knew right away it had begun. He kept asking for things all through the trip—coffee, gum, magazines, pillow, my address and telephone number—and then he proceeded to evince much curiosity about the sights down below, insisted I must sit down beside him and peer cheek-to-cheek out the window at the landmarks below that I was supposed to be able to identify but couldn't, I wasn't much of a stewardess—"

"What was he doing in Denver?"

"Oh, some public relations errand for his uncle, he was working for his uncle then, went straight from high school to a job with the clan's plutocrat, Uncle Gus, their pride and joy and only solvent member—"

"*Big* candy store?"

"Owned a string of Manhattan restaurants, then branched out into other areas, nice guy but he was part of Ed's trouble too, I think. All the men in that clan— brothers, uncles, sons—were awed by their rich relative

287

and a little scared, they depended on him and borrowed from him and loved him and hated him, and Ed got mowed under by this male disability right from the start, I guess, since his mother was always implying he should grow up to be a big somebody like his uncle instead of a big nothing like his father. I dare say Ed was already a nervous wreck from the mother-seduction thing in childhood, and then in his teens he lost his father—heart attack—and that must've had much deeper ramifications than the usual grief mixed with Oedipal guilt, it must have been complicated by his having often wished his father was more like his uncle, maybe even wished his uncle *was* his father, wished his father was merely his uncle or his fifth cousin or nowhere at all. His father was a sweet man, Ed loved him but was ashamed of him, then was ashamed of his shame—"

"When he fell in love with you, he was escaping all that?"

"Yes, I used to have a thing about it, used to accuse him of running off with me not because he loved me but just to escape. I'd dwell morbidly on the psychological facts —how I was the exact oposite of his mother, how I came from a comparatively aristocratic and cultured background, how I was the 'older woman' who hooked him before he was old enough to know better—and all these facts would prove to me that he married me for just about every reason but love."

"But you're not older than him, are you?"

"A year."

"Oh boy, big deal!"—through our laughter we heard Ed and Roger coming out of their room; we moved across the room toward the door to the hall, pausing at the mirror for a last check of our lipstick, hair, hemlines, stocking seams—"You must've lied about your age to become a stewardess. Naughty girl, I thought you just told me you hate deception."

"Well yeah, I do, but gee, I'd quit college and I had Greenwich Village room rent to pay and nobody would buy anything I wrote and I couldn't ask my folks for money because they'd wanted me to stay in school and—"

"Excuses, excuses, you could've gotten a job in Schrafft's or something—if you're going to be a waitress why not on the ground, why in the sky?"

"Death wish? Purification, die in flames? Substitute for the Muse, soar high and free? Wish to be male, wear cap and uniform? You name it, clear thinker, O analyzed one."

"Oh, shut up. Maybe you just wanted to see the world?"

"Yeah, I saw Milwaukee and burp cups and Birmingham and burp cups and—"

"—and Ed Thompson from whence cometh the otherwise nonexistent Bruce and Johnny and Terry"—she started to open the door, shut it again for a second, serious now—"Your boys, they came through it okay?"

"Through what?"

"Through . . . their Mommy's long blue funk?"—I didn't answer, and she shrugged, smiling, and opened the door—"Well, anyway, I'm glad you snapped yourself out of it okay. Maybe someday you can tell me all about it"—and we went to meet the other two, downstairs.

Tell her about it? It was hard enough to tell him, across the desk, when he asked me how I saw it now, saw my illness in retrospect—did I understand it a little, fathom what had caused it? As a prospective alumna, could I describe my illness?

"Insanity?"—I watched him get up, watch chain glittering in the sun from the window, watched him adjust the blinds and return to his desk—"It's a bad mood, magnified about a million times. It has all the same ingredients as an ordinary depression—feelings of rejection, insignificance, futility, aloneness—but to such an unbearable degree that they become something quite different, subjectively, become something so alien and inescapable that you know a line has been crossed, and that line is sanity, identity, whatever you want to call it—the line is crossed, you are in a no man's land where you never were before, you are crazy and it is better to be dead than crazy, so all there is left for you is death."

"It's not always like that, you know. There are breakdowns of every conceivable variety. In some the victim turns against himself, as you did. In others the victim turns against another, or many others, society. Some breakdowns contain much less of depression than they do of anxiety—"

"Oh, I know, I remember, that motor in the guts, the fumes of breathlessness, the iron throat and the terror, the terror—"

"The symptoms vary, so do the superficial causes, the immediate precipitating factors, but basically every breakdown has its inception in—"

"Spare me, I beg you. Each of you fellows has his own favorite peg to hang it on. Yours I know, the family romance, etcetera. Sex, death—"

"You find it amusing?"

"Not at all, only old hat. It seems as if I've been hashing and rehashing these matters over with you forever and ever."

"We're just beginning—"

"Maybe—"

"And the shadows?"—he tilted back in his chair as he spoke, puffed on his pipe—"We broke off there last time, as I recall. You spoke of methods of alleviation?"

"Yes. Necessary deceit, it is possible to live with it if I learn to tolerate the little daily lies of social intercourse and to do my best to eliminate the big ones, the whoppers. And the other shadow, the backward one, I can make valiant attempts there too—read, search, try to believe in something outside myself, if I can't acquire faith in God then faith in *something,* in man or nature or art, *something*—"

"In other words, to try? That's all?"

"I haven't finished. Most important about the shadow of necessary deceit is this, I've decided: it pertains only to others, deceit with oneself is never necessary, only comfortable. The relationship one can develop with oneself—the absolute honesty, the brutality, the utter lack of deceit—this can counteract all the interpersonal subterfuge, the—"

290

"Analysis can start the process—"

"—but not finish it, only start it. And the other shadow, the backward shadow of oblivion, that can be counteracted by the . . . the . . . *moments* . . . by certain fleeting *instants*, do you know what I mean?"

"One second of mortal joy is infinitely more to be desired than an endless immortality?"

"Yes! If I can cling to that, *believe* that—"

"Maybe there'll come a time when you can stop all this desperate clinging. But in the meantime, do you see—"

—see that I was cancerous with guilt long long before this hard climactic operative year? Ah yes. I see it all, see the adolescent Janie—murdered, dead, a ghost—and then, at some point, coming back to life but not as herself, reincarnated in the form of a popular college girl, pretty and witty and flippant and cruel. And so on endlessly, until the irrevocable fall: extremes, always extremes—the ghost and the reincarnation, the dead and the alive—back and forth on the tremulous pendulum between gloom and gaiety, between self-love and self-hate, until she "settled down nicely." Settled down nicely? Vomiting her way through three and a half pregnancies, demeaning her husband with sarcasm and flirtations, weeping once a month with sorrow inexplicable—settled down nicely? Ah yes, I see—see she was neither writer nor mother but posed superbly as both: using motherhood as a "way out" of writing, using writing as a "way out" of motherhood, doing neither one well—a double deception of careless neglect—

"And your childhood? Do you see?"

—I see, see I was born of sick parents into a sick house, see the disparity between the public image and the private fact: within the bickering, the recriminations, the violence, the passions, the guilt; without the preaching and the healing, the goodness and graciousness, the father revered and the mother too an angel of mercy. I see, see this fissure between image and fact, see also the Christian themes woven into the fabric of my infancy until that fabric was as smothersome as a shroud: sinfulness, biblical tortures, crucifixion—

"And was it really as bad as all that?"

—no, I was tiny and they were giants, I was already sick and I saw them through my sickness. There were tears but there was laughter too, there was pain but only in proportion to my guilt. I have given no hint of happy times, and there were many. Ours was a house that others loved to enter, it was always crowded—not glancing in the shadows, they found balm there, found Christ there, around the piano singing hymns they did not glance into corners, a parsonage is always very clean. I was too sensitive, too curious, I had an imagination which took stones and made them rubies, took birds and made them monsters, took grown-up tears and shouted words and made of them a hell—

"You forgive?"

—if they can forgive me, then there is nothing else to forgive, they were the children of their fathers, of their mothers, as was my brother, sister, as was I, we are born and live and die—

"And try?"

—they tried, tried harder than most, searched for love and faith and received less than they gave, they were in error and they suffered but they were good—the world will be a little better for the work they did—

"You see?"

—I see, I am not good as they are good, Christian humility is not for me or altruistic dedication, I am not good in their way but I am not bad either, I am not bad to look into myself and question myself, to recognize my selfishness and to accept it, I am not bad because I cannot be their kind of good—

"You believed yourself bad, evil—"

—yes, evil, I killed my fourth child as I had killed my mother's, I knew I had done it before, would do it again —I knew it before it happened, expected it and dreaded it, for I had done it before, had usurped my dead brother's place, by some magic had killed him to be born in his stead, and all my life in my desire for a fourth I desired his return, desired my absolution for his death, but feared too that I might do it again, murder the fourth—

"In the third month of pregnancy you were already anticipating disaster, so you began to hope for a miscarriage, to 'get it over with,' because if it was doomed anyway and would be stillborn like your mother's fourth, why not avoid all those months of nausea and trepidation. You were a murderess, from wishing, so your death neurosis increased until you couldn't sleep. That's what insomnia often is, a fear of death, one transfers the fear of death to a fear of the temporary death that sleep is. You felt you wanted to sleep, had to, but actually you fought it, you expected punishment for your thoughts so you suspected if you slept you would never awake. You panicked—"

—but why then, why just then—

"A reminder here of your childhood, a reminder there —the phone call that woke you, about someone being thrown from a horse, and before that, walking in the rain, in boots—whose boots?—and that whole rainy Sunday before you panicked, wasn't it a replica of your childhood? —the calls from Atkins recreated the parsonage atmosphere you'd forgotten: threat, tension, imminent chaos."

—and in the hospital room later, bleeding, vomiting, and they were kissing and I hated them and I wanted to scream for the nurse and tell on them, I kept thinking they were sneaky and they had no right, they had no *right*—

"And before that, before the abortion, the other hospital room after your insomnia. You knew schizophrenia there, knew the agony of being caught in a dream, so from then on you had a vicious circle to contend with: sleeping meant taking a chance on insanity but *not* sleeping meant taking a chance on panic. You were tortured by the vicious circle, you felt you would become a drug addict or a psychotic, you entered a ritualistic pre-breakdown state so that you were unsurprised at the miscarriage, when you stained in Lisa's apartment you said 'There it goes' because you had willed it so, then you said 'Here it comes' because you knew you must be punished

293

for willing it, and then you achieved a phony calm by divorcing your intellect and emotions until the split between them widened into ... mental illness."

—I see, I see and I know, I know what it feels like, mental illness, it's like a secret room inside your head that you ordinarily didn't use much, before you were sick you drifted into it happily sometimes, you were in a conversation, say, and then you weren't hearing it anymore because you were daydreaming, you were in your secret room, and you stayed there a while, and when you came out a few seconds or minutes later the conversation around you had proceeded to another topic while you were away. You didn't know where you'd been, but you were definitely away, quite literally, "absent-minded"—time went by and words were spoken and you nodded and smiled perhaps but you had not heard anything because you were not there—you were in your secret room. That was pleasant, and familiar, yes—but pretend you don't just wander into your secret room, you're pushed and they lock you in and you can't get out—that's mental illness. It is a terrible room full of torture and death, you claw the walls, then sooner or later you're out—you hear, look around, everything's gone right on outside while you were gone, and nobody even knew you were away—but you knew and yet you didn't, the room is a funny secret when you're healthy in your head and hold a key, you're just a dreamer and a mind-wanderer, but when there's a lock and no key it is horrible—

"You don't lose your mind, you get lost in it?"

—you don't go out of your mind, you go into it, deep deep dark—

"But you find things in there, old mildewed rotten things, poisons, garbage, and each time you emerge, you bring them out and after a while it's airier—"

—and someday it's so aired out you like it again, you go in on purpose and mosey around nostalgically like it's Old Home Week, you've got your secret room back with no doors and no locks and no danger and you can sit down in there and work—

"You are a better person because we talked it all out—"

294

—I am a better person because I have suffered, I made a mountain a molehill, I am surrounded by those who make mountains of molehills, I will make molehills of mountains, I have had practice—

"Ah ha, you are contemptuous now of those who come to suffering after you have left it, you despise the *nouveau* weak—"

—no, no, I remember, I understand, you will never hear me mouth the chidings of the Happy Happy People, not from my lips will any prisoner hear that every cloud has a silver lining, that into each life some rain must fall, that he really ought to straighten up, take hold of his bootstraps, get busy, chin up, listen to the robin how it sings its cheery song—

"You've been there."

—been in hell, yes, been close to death by my own hand, been consumed by ugly hungers and imprisoned in the dark—

"You see?"

—I see, see the strident individuality that hid my other self, hid the crushed-into-nothingness other, hid from myself the knowledge that I had no more emerged from my childhood image of myself than my parents had emerged (or ever will; too late) from theirs—

"And the very old man? The three girls?"

—I see, see the three girls, see since earliest memories the triangle, the trio of my mother and my sister and myself, see that the rivalry between sisters for mother never stopped, became grammar school triangles, high school, college, always two best friends and me, me the central one, the leader, the competed-for, the most-loved—

"You achieved outside your family circle what you couldn't achieve within it. But even within it you never stopped trying, did you. Only you took a devious route. If you couldn't steal Mom from Sis, at least it'd be a cinch to steal Sis from Mom—"

—yes, my first vacation home from college, I'd gotten "glamorous," articulate, my sister idolized me, Mother

295

started feeling left out of our friendship, made kidding complaints about it—

"You see?"

—I see, see that in all my waking and sleeping life the triangle was lurking, ready to gobble me up, to become not only dream but reality—

"And your emphasizing of the blue of your sister's eyes, the blue of hers and his, trying to link them together so you could have your father to yourself, disinherit her, she whose paternal legacy of introversion is as obvious as yours, peas in pod—"

—my dearest friends, she, Ed—

"And the very old man?"

—Mahatma Gandhi, assassinated on my wedding day, my father was too grief-stricken about Gandhi to care about my wedding, as usual something more important preoccupied him, all his emotion was for Gandhi—

"You thought it was Gandhi, even he thought so, but hasn't he always used something impersonal to express his private griefs? Wasn't it always church or world problems which shattered him?"

—maybe he cared—

"He was far from unconcerned. Your imminent loss of virginity was his own loss of virginity all over again. Guilt, fear, shame. The neurotic identifying with his children."

—mother always teased him about Gandhi, "that little old man in diapers," she used to say—

"You see?"

—once when I asked my grandmother what my dead brother had looked like, she said he looked like a little old man—

"If you became a very old man, like Gandhi, your father would love you. If you became a very old man, like your dead brother, your mother would forgive you for replacing him. If you became a very old man you would be too feeble to move, and everyone would have to wait on you and do everything for you, you could be alive and yet dead, a despot and an infant—"

—grandmother said they threw him away, threw away the baby when they found he was born dead, she said

296

they wrapped him up and threw him away, she only said it to teach me a lesson, stop me from asking foolish questions, but I never forgot. I never forgot—

"The package. Death comes in packages, your recurrent nightmare. A corpse is tied up and tossed away. Your first concept of death, a lasting one. And sex in it too, the stick banging you back into the package—"

"Oh, my God"—I burst out laughing uncontrollably—"It's all too pat, I feel like a cartoon, us two talking like one person out of two mouths, one awareness out of two brains, all excited about grandmas and phallic symbols—"

"You've always resented being here, haven't you. You hate that couch, won't ever lie on it—"

"I do resent it, yes, I thought I was strong, it was a big shock to go out of my mind"—laughing—"excuse me, go *into* it."

"People that have reached bottom as you did, they may resent the analytic process but nonetheless they get a lot out of it. They have to: it's a life or death situation. But those who never hit bottom—just have felt in danger or fell halfway—they all too often resent it because it seems to net them such negligible results; not being completely desperate, they could not completely enter the transference—"

"Oh, to hell with transference, all those words, it's all so . . . artificial . . . and . . . pretentious. I'll tell you what *I* think. Those people never suffered enough, they felt a touch of it but not enough, the miracle of rebirth is available only to the dead, not to the half-alive."

"I doubt if—"

"Another thing. If a person goes into analysis gifted or charming, he'll come out gifted or charming. But if a person goes into it untalented or a bore, he'll come out of it untalented or a bore. There might be some little-bitty difference that shows to other people, less affectation in the personality, maybe, but any major change is inside, invisible, just a private little alteration in perspective so you can manage better to . . . to . . . fight off . . . futility."

"Are you afraid?"

"Of what I've been through, the recency of it, the memory, afraid of a repeat performance? Yes, I'm afraid."

"You needn't be. You're past the two most critical points when setbacks most often occur."

"When were those?"

"Well, remember when you saw yourself full-length in the store mirror, just before your Florida trip?"

"Yes. It was awful."

"It was awful because you saw yourself how critically sick you'd been, saw with your own eyes what havoc the mind can wreak on the body. And then, when you started housekeeping again, remember?—no maids, no nurses, all on your own again—you felt—"

"Awful! Awful!"

"Again, it was the 'awfulness' of realization. You could measure the depth of your sickness by the difficulty of resuming the tiniest tasks. You see, in the journey up out of mental illness these are the two biggest hurdles for a patient. You had to realize fully where you'd been, and face it, and then, facing it, you had to conquer your fear and keep climbing out of it."

"And . . . the sex thing. It started so suddenly and then ended so suddenly."

"Ended with the forbidden act?"

"Yes. That's . . . that's all over with, isn't it?"

"Those extremes? Of course. But normality includes physical attractions, you know. Health is not necessarily synonymous with virtue."

—again laughing—"When you say things like that you sound so pedantic and super-enlightened. If I should throw myself at you again, what would you do? I'm not crying this time, I'm laughing, you couldn't stall the issue by dispensing Kleenex."

"Gone the tissue, gone the issue"—grinning, pleased with his little verse, sitting up straight and rustling his appointment-book pages to signal the session's end—"See you Monday?"

"Meanie, you're rushing me out. Have no fear, now that I no longer see you through sick-colored glasses I notice you're not quite my type"—but remembering one more thing I must tell him, serious again—"The other day Ed and I were driving along in the car and his body was quiet, calm, and suddenly I saw tears start rolling down his face. I asked him what was the matter and he answered that there was no 'rippling under his skin,' his nerves were giving him a minute's peace. 'It's such a beautiful feeling,' he said, 'I'm crying because I'm so grateful. I feel so free.' Then I cried too, because I understood how he felt and because I loved him so."

"Most people don't recognize that their freedom fluctuates. I'm impressed that your husband realizes it consciously. Most people, when they get tired or irritable or loud or quiet for no reason, attribute their moods to almost anything rather than the prison of the mind. But it's a blessing, that feeling of freedom, whether or not one is aware of it as such."

"Yes, it is a blessing, but how would *you* know?"—he looked down, stuffing his pipe—"I mean, frankly, it aggravates me sometimes the way you talk as if you know from experience, when obviously you only know from observation, and textbook explanations—I mean, you're obviously strong and solid as an ox, you may be good at charting mental illness but you certainly can't understand it the way *I* do, the way *I* know it—"

"Oh, I know, all right"—he looked up at me with a look I do not expect ever to forget.

"How do you know?"

"Well, you see"—and there was no way of doubting what he meant—"I was there."

TWENTY-NINE

WHILE I was making breakfast Saturday morning the boys were up in Roger's room, watching him don his Martian outfit for his appearance at a local orphanage, an engagement he had set up for today while still in California. I had been surprised when I'd first heard of it the night before, after the theater and over coffee, for I had supposed that during our reunion his time would be our time, without previous commitments interfering in my plans. Now, a disconcerted hostess—when in heaven would he be back? should I still figure on four for lunch or not?—I found myself fretfully banging a pot here and a pan there, quite forgetting in my pettiness that no more than a month before I had entered this kitchen an alien, stumbling on the threshold of reality, and had felt that if only I could make it, just somehow *make* it back to that recollected paradise of sanity, I would be a changed person, utterly transfigured by gratitude, would never never again let any triviality concern, distress or even interest me. And now here I was, slamming a spatula against the sink because of a minor shift in schedule, when I should have been offering up praises that a friend I'd almost given up hope on showed some sign of salvageability, showed in this morning's sudden sobriety, in the unhesitant carrying out of his good intentions, that he could still think of others with compassion and that, therefore, there might also be left in him a thimbleful of fortitude, of pride.

"Mommy, come see." Johnny, breathless, called down the stairs. "He's all ready, I helped him, I zipped him up the back, come and *see*. I'm on one shoulder and Terry's on the other and—wheeee!—he's whirling us around the room."

"Never mind." Roger's shout had laughter in it; maybe our weekend would be fun after all? "We'll be right down, Janie."

But Lisa came in before he did, and, yawning a long yawn as she sank into a chair, said that she'd hoped just this *once* to sleep till noon; she was oh *so* weary, she said, of that 6 A.M. alarm clock on location.

"Since when," I replied, "does a house with three little boys in it contain anything but whoops and hollers from sunrise on? You should've been prepared."

"Oh, I didn't hear the kids. It was Roger who woke me with that yell of his. Ye gods, he's the soul of merriment all of a sudden, from the sounds of it."

"Seems to be"—and then, "Dammit!"—for the muffin

I was buttering crumbled in my fingers, and someone said, "Well, that's the way the muffin crumbles," and laughed.

It was Ed, putting his arms around me and kissing the back of my neck. "You and Roger," I said. "What gaiety this morning. You'd think to hear you two that we'd all gotten more than four hours sleep last night."

"Grumpy dames," he said, sitting down in the chair beside Lisa and sniffing at the stove. "What smells good?"

But the boys were upon us—"Mommy, unknot my sneaker string"—"Daddy, can we go with Roger to the place where the children have no parents, can we go with him, Daddy, can we?"

As Ed explained to them why they could not—they weren't invited, Mommy had arranged for them to spend the day boating with the Silvermans, they'd better hurry up or they'd be late—I finished getting breakfast ready, and just as I put it on the tables (children at one, adults at the other) Roger arrived, resplendent, *M*-chested, a comic-book creature come to life, all muscular, garish, immense. "Away, to Mars," he said, leaping toward the boys' table so that they screamed, and laughed, and an orange juice spilled over.

"Oh, *Roger*," Lisa said, annoyed, but he cut her off. "Ah *ha!* We'll fix that in a jiffy." Putting his head down close to the spreading stain he said, "Fellas, watch me dry it up with my all-powerful antenna helmet," and he aimed the top of his head at the stain, bent over, mock-intent, and making a magic buzz-sound in his throat, while little Terry waited in good faith and in vain for the stain to vanish, and Johnny grinned a grin that was half adulation and half derision, while Bruce—as if by this rejection to reject all the humiliating credulity of his previous years —rose from the table in disdain, saying "I'll get a rag" and got one, and mopped up the mess.

"Thank you, Bruce," I said.

"My pleasure, madam"—sarcastic, spoken with British inflection and infinite disgust (the *children's* table!).

We were still eating when the phone rang for Roger; although we could hear the sound of a voice in the receiver, he listened only and did not respond, and then, abruptly, he leaned across to the buffet while the caller was still speaking and hung up the phone.

"What was *that?*" Ed asked.

Roger didn't answer; he reached for the marmalade but then just held it in his hand, looking at it, as if he were trying to remember what marmalade was for.

At this abrupt change in his demeanor all of us thought the same thing; the single word emerged from each of our mouths at once: "Atkins?"

Roger shook his head.

"Well, for God's *sake,* then"—Lisa had apparently forgotten her promise to "be a lamb" today—"Who *was* it? Some *mystery* woman?"

He looked at her. "Jealous?" he said. Then he laughed; costumed thus, with the joyless laugh barked out as if by mechanical thrust, he reminded me of an amusement-park billboard I'd seen once, seen and heard, for the jaw of a mammoth wooden man had kept opening and closing, issuing forth a fabricated blast of hilarity every twelve seconds or so. Now, still laughing the ugly laugh, Roger got up and walked to the kitchen, then returned with a bottle and, sitting down, poured himself a drink. We all looked somewhere else while he drank it, and his gulping was loud in the silence until Johnny's whisper wafted to us curious and sad: "Bruce, will he get *that* way again?"

"Shut up," Bruce said. He got up and went to the door. "You guys coming or aincha? Can't you hear Mrs. Silverman honking?"

"Terry, wipe your mouth," I said, and he did, and ran out, leaving his napkin in the middle of the floor, crumb-surrounded.

"Have a good day, boys," Ed called after them.

Roger poured himself another drink.

"What's the matter, Rog?" Lisa was controlling her tone of voice this time; I gave her a grateful glance. "Who was that on the phone?"

"Man at the orphanage, Mishter Klem." Already he was slurring his words, as if in perverse anticipation of the drunkenness he had not yet had time to achieve.

"What did he want?"

"You."

"What?"

"Wants you to accompany me. Said he read in the Cedarton *Herald* that you're a weekend guest here too and that the staff's very excited about it and wondered if you might possibly come along so . . . so . . ."

"Yes?"

". . . so the *grown*ups could have a thrill too."

"Oh"—there were looks exchanged between the three of us while the fourth, head back, drained his glass—"Well, don't worry, I'm not accepting their kind invitation."

"Whaddyeh mean, don't worry."

"I mean you can have the"—she didn't say the rest, didn't say "stage all to yourself" because Ed, who had gotten up to go toward the hall for cigarettes, had suddenly, as we watched, stopped and stared toward the front door. I heard a stranger's voice say a questioning word: "Son?" and Ed, still staring, backed up one step so that his hand was not visible to whoever might have arrived upon our doorstep; he waved his hand frantically as if to signal us away from danger.

"Atkins!" This time just Lisa and I spoke together, for Roger was busy with another drink and had not noticed Ed's strange behavior. Now, hearing us whisper and looking up to see our faces, he mumbled, "What? Who—"

"Hello, Matty." Ed was walking forward into the hall, away from us.

"Ed"—but Lisa put her hand across my mouth and whispered "Police!" I just sat, immobilized by fear, not for myself but for my husband, and it was Lisa who reached out for the phone and said into her cupped hands, "Give me the police. Emergency."

"Huh?" Roger looked confused.

"Shsh." There was no sound from the hall. Then, from our lethal visitor, there was a single quiet statement: "I have come for my son." Ed, be careful, I thought. To hell with being brave, be *careful*. And then, strength surging

303

back, I went to Roger and put my hand beneath his arm; he felt the urgency in my touch, for at last he seemed to realize that this was not a scene from *The Martian*—Lisa was *not* a kidnaped girl reporter, I was *not* a Saturn sprite on a spy mission to Earth, he was *not* waiting for his cue to fly, to soar, to slay, to save—and he let me help him to his feet and began to follow me quietly to the dining room's other exit, toward the backyard and comparative safety. Lisa had finished her muffled call to the police and now, slowly, on tiptoe, the three of us held hands as we stole in silence toward the door. A board creaked antique beneath our feet—a cliché of a noise, something straight out of one of Roger's TV films ("Okay, good, it's a take, but tell Max over in sound effects that we'll need a creak, a good big one, right there where The Martian and the two women are fleeing from the madman")—and then we were outside.

"I'll go around front, I'll kill him," Roger said. But he didn't move; he just stirred slightly as if planted there, another peony in the breeze. Bees hummed behind the hyacinth, a kite was in the sky, bobbing briskly.

"I've got to go back to Ed." Why was I so calm, so sure, and why was it not superfluous but somehow essential to notice that the grass still in shadow was tearful with dew, to see the white line of clover like a boundary along the shadow's edge, and, just beyond, the grass three shades greener as it baked in the sun, daisy-dotted. "You two hide. Back there." Behind the birches, the birches that bordered the far bank of the brook. "Go!"

Lisa nodded uncertainly. "But I should—"

"Just hide. Take Rog, that's who he's after. Go!"

"*You* hide. You have kids, you might be—"

"Run!"

I didn't wait to see if they obeyed me. I went back into the house and at once heard the sound of a single voice murmuring, quiet, monotonous. The outdoor light had made me temporarily blinded so that the house seemed dark now, seemed full of dusk at mid-morning, and squinting, I groped my way to the hall. There was a space of maybe six feet between them as they stood facing each other, and at first I could see nothing clearly but the nimbus of sunshine between the door frame and the outline of a man.

"Matty," Ed was saying in a singsong sort of way, "he isn't here, your son isn't here, he isn't here, Matty, isn't here . . ."

My eyes, adjusting, began to take in the scene, began at last really to see the man who had haunted our nights and our days and whom only I had left briefly behind, caught up too completely in my turmoil to know or care about any other peril. He was no longer the black-haired devil of Marianne's Paris, and I had mistakenly imagined him as tall—perhaps conditioned by my husband and even more by Roger, I had become unused to men of average height; too, there was the image one forms of a murderer: huge, hulking, menacing—while the assassin stood frail, gray-haired, seeming almost shy, and except for something he held tightly clenched in his hand, I would have judged him a professor who had lost his way and had stopped, apologetic, for directions. Between his eyes a scowl of slight puzzlement had become part of the skin, chiseled by unreason, but otherwise his face bore no expression, nor his eyes.

"—isn't here, your son, isn't here—"

Did he always purse his mouth like that, as if considering some serious decision? Was it, like his scowl, as much a part of his countenance as his cleft chin, his high forehead, or did it connote a concrete thought within that chaotic mind, a connection, a heard comment and a resulting consideration?

"—isn't here, he isn't here, Matty, isn't here—"

Was he merely brainless, mesmerized by repetition as a brainless fowl can be? And—whether mesmerized or plotting, or crouched like a panther before the spring—did he hear the sirens sounding ever closer down the lane?

"isn't here"—and then the sirens were upon us, and Matty had not moved, had not heard, deaf-and-puzzled had not found his son, and to get the thing from his fingers, as the two policemen held him, Ed had to pry up each finger separately, like leeches.

305

Ed turned from the rigid figure to show me the small bottle he'd taken from him, then placed it on the table beneath the hall mirror. "What *is* it?" I asked, surprised to find my voice still there, quite normal.

"Acid, I suppose." And while one policeman handcuffed Matty the other went to the table, picked up the open bottle, smelled it. "Good guess, mac," he said. "Acid, all right."

Matty stood there. I'd never seen anyone in handcuffs before, not outside the movies or TV; the contraption looked bigger than I'd have imagined, or was it merely that his hands were so slender, so long and slender inside their metal trap and so very very still?

"Where's Lisa and Rog?" Ed asked.

"Down past the brook, I'll get them"—and as I went I heard a voice ask in rapture, "Lisa Maurice? Are you the people Lisa Maurice is visiting?" Ed must have nodded, for as I went out the back door I heard the other policeman say, "Gee, yeah, I read about it too, in the *Herald* yesterday. The Martian's here too, right?"

Yes, The Martian was here, curled in an embryo-curl inside a huge hole the boys had dug in the woods during a digging-for-treasure day the week before. He was whimpering when I found him and Lisa sat on a fallen branch nearby. "We heard the cops arrive," she said, "but he still won't come on up out of there. *You* try."

"It's okay, Rog," I said. "The police have Matty handcuffed. Come back in."

He just kept whimpering.

"Oh, for Christ's sake, let's *leave* him here." Lisa stood up, brushed herself off; I plucked a piece of birch bark from the silk of her peignoir. "He *likes* his grave, it's cozy in there. Come on, Janie, I want to see Atkins before they take him away."

"Don't worry, they'll be sticking around a while. They heard *you* were here. But what about Rog?"

Her glance rode across his huddled form scornfully. "Oh, he'll be along as soon as he loses his audience. Come on"—and she grabbed my hand to pull me across

306

the lawn—no more shadow now, and the kite was a yellow decal flapping loose from the blue-poster sky.

"Did you hear what Roger was saying?" she asked.

"It didn't sound like anything coherent to me."

"Well, you should've heard him before you got there. My God, what drivel. 'Don't hurt my face,' he kept saying, 'don't let him hurt my face.' And he had his hands over his face the whole time so I couldn't make out the rest of the glop he was saying, except something about a window and a crash, yes, that was it, he kept saying 'shouldn't have done it, shouldn't have crashed the window.' Now what could *that* mean?"

"Remember what he told you of his childhood, and you told me; about a dream—"

"I suppose he meant the time Atkins threw the rock through Cohn's skylight, remember? I never realized what an effect that had on him, the rock coming through with his picture on it. Of course, the crash was a shock to us all, but who'd have guessed that—"

"I hope he'll be okay."

"Oh, don't worry. He's a coward, that's all, and I told him so too. He's probably ashamed to face Ed so he's pretending to be drunker than he is. God, what a ham."

"But he seemed so—"

"Where *is* the captive?"—for we were in the house now, and then we were in the hall and there he was, he had not moved, and one policeman was radioing from the patrol car in the driveway while the other one lounged outside, between the artist and his dubious freedom. When the officer saw Lisa he came in quickly, pushing through the door past Matty as one would squeeze against a statue in some mausoleum corridor, and it was obvious that these few moments with Matty had shown him that no flight was imminent here, no welcome relief from boredom, no excitement of pursuit. But a thrill of another kind?—ah, who knew? (hadn't that other actress last year shacked up with a cop on the beat, this very same beat he was stuck with? was not this famous piece of tail similarly available? hell, was there any harm in trying?) —and while Lisa responded warily to his Irish-pixie

307

charms, Ed drew me into the other room a moment, where he explained it to me, what he'd tried to do, and done . . .

"Once when you were at your sickest," he said, "January, I think it was, I overheard you on the phone extension. It was one of those Sundays when you didn't seem to be aware of anything, you were sort of removed, and you were talking to your doctor. You said just one thing, you said 'I have to,' and for the rest of the call it was just him talking and you listening, only he didn't talk anything sensible, he just kept denying what you'd said, denying it over and over in a kind of singsong, like this: 'you don't have to, you don't have to, you don't have to'—and yet it seemed to help, it seemed to hypnotize you into assent, because after a while you said, 'All right,' and he said, 'There, you see, you don't have to, do you,' and you said, 'Not this time,' and he said, 'See you tomorrow,' and that was that."

"And I didn't, not that time or ever, and here I am."

"What?"

"Nothing."

"So, when Matty said just that one thing, I knew I had to keep him there until Rog got out, and I just sort of instinctively did the same thing, tried to hypnotize him with a quiet denial—'Your son's not here, he's not here.' "

"And it worked."

"Seemed to." I noticed for the first time that his face was wet with sweat; he wiped his hand across his forehead. "Where's Rog?"

"Here's me." Roger stood beside us, satin and sequins smudged brown with dirt. He swayed, smiled rather blankly, then moved into view of the front door. At once there was a single sound; it came from Matty, an animal noise, not exactly a sigh and yet not quite a sob, the kind of noise an ape would make, perhaps, upon feeling the ape-equivalent of grief. For an instant his eyes had seen again, seen Roger, seen The Martian, seen his creation, his son, and in the next second his hands came up in front of him locked together and then dropped as he fell back, back from the blazing doorway to the blazing steps, blazing with sunshine and bordered by rosebushes, where he

308

lay, face turned sideward rigid into the roses and his wide eyes full of June-noon unblinking and unfocused and alone.

"Well, well"—Lisa leaned a little against the cop, regarding Roger with distaste; the falling back of Matty Atkins seemed to interest no one—"If it isn't The Martian, come to the rescue in the nick of time."

"Watch out"—Ed guided Roger away from the table toward which he had stumbled, the table on which the acid sat next to a doily my great-great-great-grandma had made. "Spill that stuff on your hand and—pfft!—no hand."

Roger looked at the bottle, then raised his eyes up to his image in the mirror above the table. I wondered if he saw how dirty he was, how covered from head to foot with leaves and mud, but if he saw or cared he did not show it, merely lowering his eyes again and making no attempt to brush himself off as Lisa said, "Well, Mr. Martian, Ed and these two gentlemen have taken care of the whole matter very nicely while you were off in your hole playing dead."

Roger said nothing, and Lisa directed her sarcastic patter now to Ed. "What is it Popeye eats in moments of crisis? Spinach? Yes, that's it, we must have The Martian ask Popeye about that. And maybe Superman could give him a couple of tips too, and Joe Palooka." She laughed, and the policeman too allowed himself an appreciative chuckle. Encouraged, she spat out the name in laughter now as if it were a joke: "The *Martian!*"

"Shut up, Lisa," Ed said.

For a second she swung on Ed in wrath, then suddenly, shrugging, she turned to Roger and continued in her tone of pseudomirth, "I'm *so* sorry," she said, and beside her the policeman ducked his head to smile. "After all, you can't help it if Ed's more of a man than you are."

Roger picked up the bottle of acid.

"How *scary*," Lisa said. "What if he *swallows* it? Tune in next week, folks, and discover how The Martian survives a deadly dose of X2Y64."

"Roger"—Ed started to step toward him, but Lisa

309

laughed. "Oh Ed, wise *up*. I should think an actors' agent, of *all* people, would recognize a bit of minor histrionics."

"Skol!" Roger held the bottle up to his likeness in the mirror. His likeness looked back.

Lisa laughed. "Watch and see, folks. Nothing can kill him—not bullets, not fire, not acid. The Martian's even immune to—"

Roger drank the acid, drank it down.

"Geez, I thought he was *kidding*," one policeman said.

"I guess he wasn't kidding," the other policeman said.

"I guess not."

Abbott and Costello in blue with badges on. And upstairs Lisa weeping on the bed, and on the doorstep, all ignored, a little man who'd had a bright idea.

Look up, Rog dear, with cold corpse eyes, here's someday; and yes, the sun is shining just as bright. Its radiancy invades a million niches while the vacancy of death invades your face. Oh Rog, oh absent friend no longer caring, you lie unsouled and still the sky's so blue. I do not blame you for that twisted smile; your leaving did not even rock the boat.

Death was not grotesque, not immense and overwhelming; it was very small, very simple, trivial really and mundane. Something had become nothing, that was all. Is became was. Presence became absence. He for whom the event held the most vital interest was deprived of participation, but his deprivation mattered no more than one's own. Yes, that was it. It did not matter. Nothing mattered. Nothing had changed. Nothing? Well, oneself, perhaps—imperceptibly, profoundly—the brief iota of grief abruptly tinging one with a more tangible mortality, abruptly shrinking an unpleasant universality into a private painful vacuum where a person used to be.

But now, in this first hour—as monster horror in frantic haste consumed itself—one discovered comfort: found oneself existing inside one's own ephemerality more comfortably, almost smiling in relief, one's natural motions toward oblivion now better accommodated (thanks to the abrupt reduction of another and thus of oneself) inside one's no-longer-so-binding girdle of disbelief.

Who was he? I never knew him. I saw his tears, heard his laughter, felt his body naked on my own—who was he?

That's all he ever asked—know me! know me!

That's all we ever ask.

Someday they'll say: I never knew her. She was my mother, my wife, my closest friend—who was she?

I never knew him. None touch. We try and never touch.

"My fault," Lisa had sobbed later. "My fault, my fault."

"Mine too," I'd said.

"You! He *adored* you, you and Ed, you were the only couple in the world he cared about."

"No, I disillusioned him."

"Not you, never you. Me!"

"Me too."

"No, no, it was me, I did it, I killed him with my cruelty, I killed Roger, I disappointed him so."

"No one dies of that kind of disappointment."

"I killed him—"

"Lisa, he died because he was disappointed, yes. He was deeply disappointed in himself. Nobody ever killed himself for any other reason."

"I did it."

"No"—but why argue, why tarnish her bright pain with doubts, why tell her her memento is a fake? She'll treasure it her whole life long, this spasm: cold-loined, she will convulse her soul with guilt.

It's going away already, the scene inside our hallway, the costumed creature dying on our faded braided rug, his clothes all ripped to pieces by his writhing. It's going away already; having written, I am rid of it, and callous. I tell you of it as I'd tell a dream.

But strange, when I start now to tell you of the others,

311

to tell you of the living-still who'll live perhaps for years, I find it seems more real than all the rest . . .

I sat outside on the steps, while the others were tending to Roger—to roger, that is—doing whatever it is one does to human carrion. Matty never moved (until, later, they moved him forcibly, picking him up all stiff and rigid as I'd once seen a mannequin picked up from a store-window floor, picked up around the fissured waist by a fairy with a mouth all full of pins); he never moved, and the sun was very hot on both our heads. His eyes saw nothing I could see (none touch; we know) and mine saw everything his could not see, saw the kite faltering feebly now above the clump of hemlock on the hill, saw the lawn bereft of any dew, for the dew had all dried up, gone forever the dew from the arid and sorrowless eyes (none touch; we know). There were drops of blood on his collar, just a few, his favorite red, because the rosebush thorns were deep against his cheek. Instead of his feet, his hands were bound, but he did not feel the steel, did not feel the thorns or smell the roses, he did not stir or scream upon his cross. I sat with him in silence and in sunshine; we sat, the two of us, like idle lovers: a pair of lovers crucified by sunshine, and never speaking; for none touch; we know.

THIRTY

"No!"—Bruce's voice came clogged with crying through the crack in the doorway—"No! Go away!"

"Bruce, let me in." He'd heard the news of Roger's death on his way home from boating, he'd heard it on the Silvermans' car radio and, arriving home, had found the house exactly as he'd left it, but with Roger gone and Lisa, and the braided rug missing from the front hallway.

"Bruce"—I'd begun, seeing the look on his face and knowing he must somehow have heard, but he had interrupted me—"Is it true?"

"You mean did Roger—"

"Did he . . . kill himself?"

"Darling, sit down so Daddy and I can try to explain to you how—"

"Why!"—the word had exploded from him as much in anger as in sorrow, and then he'd run upstairs, up to his room, slamming and locking the door behind him.

Now—Ed downstairs with the other two, who were merely bewildered, for how could The *Martian* die? that was *silly!*—I begged again through the closed door, "Let me in, darling, *please*"—and this time he did, angrily, not wanting me to see his weeping, not wanting me to see he needed me.

I sat beside him on the bed, where he had flung himself, face down. The Piper Cub grazed my head, dangling from the ceiling on a string, and along a shelf the other models —boats, planes, rockets, animals—lay in undusted squalor, for Bruce was responsible for cleaning his room, and did it with a brevity unmatched except by that which he displayed at homework. Willie Mays awaited the pitch in a picture above the desk, but beside it that bare nail— what had it held? Then I remembered and looked toward the wastebasket, and there it was—it lay on the floor, frame broken, a single scratch across the *M*-crested chest, and the signature still visible in the growing dusk: "To my good pal, Bruce, from his ever-lovin' Roger-alias- Guess Who?"

After a few minutes I said, "Do you want to talk about it?"

Quickly, belligerently—"No." But, a moment later, voice tight: "I just don't understand."

"It's hard to understand."

"Do *you* understand?"

"I think so."

"No, no you don't, don't pretend"—raising his head now, eyes perplexed in their puffed-up sockets, perplexed and accusatory—"Don't pretend it has something to do with God or Jesus or some dumb thing—"

"No, I—"

"Why? That's all, *why?* Why would he *do* such a thing,

313

how could *anybody* want to do that—to stop *living,* on *purpose*—no, I'll never understand it, never, *never,* not Rog, he wasn't like some poor slob you read about in the newspaper who has nothing to live for or something, he was *Roger,* he was so ... so ... *alive"*—and he broke off, crying bitterly, not bothering now about his shame, sitting up straight with his shoulder pressed to mine.

"I guess he just didn't want to—"

"Didn't want to *live?* But there's *nothing* besides living, there's *nothing.* To *kill* yourself you'd have to be ... be ... *crazy.* And Rog wasn't crazy, you know he wasn't, maybe he was feeling kinda *lousy* lately, but he was still my ... my ... *friend"*—and his head fell into my lap as he repeated—"my *friend.*"

"Someday—"

"Don't 'someday' me, not this time, this is something I'll *never* understand, *never.*"

"Someday I'll try to explain it to you."

"Fat chance!" He sat up, dug his fists into his eyes, sniffed. Then, feeling better, he stood up and tried a smile. I smiled back. *"You'll* explain it"—and this time he laughed, tickled by the absurdity of my pretensions, and got a hanky and blew his nose in it. "Don't tell Johnny I cried," he said.

"I won't."

"What's for supper?"

"Chicken salad."

"With corn-on-the-cob?"

"How did you guess."

"Hey, cool!"

He put The Martian back up on the wall.

THIRTY-ONE

AND the watch chain, the desk, the voice like an echo of my thoughts, an echo or more often an anticipation, the homely, inscrutable face like a haven of safety, my mind

314

stripped bare of fakery, my words unprefaced by caution or motivation . . .

"It's a year now since I got pregnant. Just a year. The longest year."

"What next?"

"Another year. And then another one."

"How will they be?"

"Shorter than this one."

"How will you use them?"

"To be me. All of me."

"All of you?"

"To *use* all of me. Or try to." Two minutes, three. Sixty cents a minute. Stick 'em up, lady—your money or your life. "Thank you for . . . giving me back . . . the world."

"You're welcome, but I didn't—"

"Oh you *did,* you *did!*"

"*You* did."

"Well, anyway, it's wonderful, isn't it? The world?"

"Yes"—smile lopsided, pipe clamped in the corner of his mouth—"Yes, I find it so—"

—and two hours later I was back home in Cedarton, and he was driving to his hospital. On the way his car happened to run out of gas. He stopped by the side of the road, got a gallon of gas from the trunk, began pouring it into the tank. A truck driver happened to glance too long to the left. Veering, he turned his eyes frontward, saw the car and the man beside it, saw him too late. The truck happened to crash into the man, happened to crush every bone in his body, happened to kill him.

I was so silly as a child, screaming when I stepped by mistake on a bug, screaming from what—disgust? pity? identification?

"*Stop* that," my mother would say. "For goodness' sake, dear, it's only a little *in*sect."

—but horrified, whimpering, sickened—"I tried not to—"

"It doesn't *matter,* dear. Who cares about squashing *that* tiny thing. It's only a *bug,* bugs aren't *people,* for heaven's sake."

315

No, bugs aren't people. But people are bugs.

It is as if I had been walking across a bridge, and the river is rough with rapids underneath me, but the bridge is very strong. Behind me is the battleground, before me home country, land of the free. A mine explodes, it shatters the bridge just where my next footstep would have fallen. I stand halfway across a broken bridge, enemy territory at my back, the river bank ahead, yet to be reached. Shall I turn back? Stand still? Can I step across? If I try, will I fall? It's difficult to determine just how wide the gap, just how far I am from solid land. Well, come on, try. Trying, dying—there's nothing else in all the world but birth.

But you shouldn't have done that, you shouldn't have died. It was wrong of you, I can't forgive you, why did you do it?

No one should die. Not unless he wants to.

You haven't treated me fairly, do you hear? Do you hear up there above that implacable ceiling? I resent very much your embezzlement. Where are you hiding it—the jigsaw puzzle with all the missing pieces—where?

Thief, speak. Dawn comes. I sleep.

She slept. Slept, unanswered. But she slept.
Slept? Awoke? Slept again, awoke again? Lived?
Lived! Lived!

It is summer. Ed left yesterday for some Hollywood deal; his wheelings and dealings will keep him busy for a week out there; I stay East this time, stay here and sunbathe and swim and listen, listen . . .
. . . listen to the summer sounds . . .
I hear Bruce playing ball with some friends of his, farther down the beach. I see Terry small and far away, his hooded terry-cloth robe white against a crevice in the jetty—a robber in a cave, a sailor in the brig, a cornered crouching tiger with Noxzema on his nose. He is alone, he is not alone, they have given me a label for him and a

definition and prognosis: autistic . . . dwells to abnormal degree in fantasy, tenuous grasp on reality . . . with treatment, maybe someday; without it, sorry but . . .

Some can't hear, can't speak, don't even seem to see. Their band is half-a-million strong, I'm learning, American child-prisoners locked deep in secret rooms. I am fortunate, they tell me . . . for my child, there is hope.

I wave to him and he waves back; I am as grateful for that wave as I am—from my other two—for hugs and kisses, touchdowns and gold stars.

We come out of the water, Johnny and I, dripping and shivering and rubbing the salt from our eyes. I reach back to quick-twist my ponytailed hair, milking the sea from it, feeling the tickling-dripping-chill along my spine.

"What's that?" my son says, stopping, pointing with his toe.

"Well, it *used* to be a jellyfish."

"What happened to it?"

"It got too far from the water, I guess. Or maybe it got stepped on or something."

Bending down, he regards the phlegmy puddle, formless, colorless, lifeless against the sand. He scowls. "It's sure dead."

"Yep, it sure is."

The tide, advancing, reaches the jellyfish and touches it tentatively before retreating, rippling it into a momentary illusion of aliveness. Johnny's foot moves toward the corpse, pushing the wet sand into a little ridge around it until it lies in an open grave, temporarily protected from the false reincarnation of the tide. "There," he says. "That's better."

It is late in the day, late in August. I say, "Look, sunset soon."

"It's high tide."

"Almost. Hasn't quite reached the seaweed line yet, see?"

"Remember last summer how we found that starfish in the seaweed?"

"Yes, and the conch—"

"Golly, that was a whole *year* ago, imagine. The year sure went by fast, didn't it?"

We have reached our place on the beach. The sunset is starting now, Johnny is building a sand fort. With especially fine sunsets I have to try very hard not to cry. It is going to be an especially fine sunset.

"Does the tide stop at night?" He is seven, his ear puts a perfect shell to shame.

"No. It goes in and out this way all the time, forever and ever."

"Ever and ever? It never ends?"

"Never."

He adds another pailful to the fort. He pats it flat. He smoothes it round on top and adds some pebbles for decoration. They form a mosaic, the more mica-crusted ones meeting the last rays of the sun with a glittering response, and the ocean too is reflecting back the final bright-brave flashings of farewell. The sun lies low in the sky, half into the horizon, but huge, distended, yellow-red, a thyroid orange sinking into the sea. Above it the clouds cut across infinity long and narrow, shallow tapering layers of dying light, clashing their disparate colors in a garish abandon that minute by minute mutes to pastel. "I wish *I* was the tide," he says.

The sun hovers, giving out its last drowning gasps of warmth and glory. Lavender daggers slash across the sky. I lean forward laughing and put my arms around him for a moment. "I'm glad you're *not*. I couldn't *squeeze* you." Then I let him go. We sit separate on our small hot pink Sahara. For just a second or two—long enough for another pailful to be scooped, poured, patted, smoothed—there is a sad sweet hiatus inside me created by the fusion of day with dusk, a fusion, too, illusory (as lines which, formerly distinct, lose their shape against the vast dazzlement of mirroring water) of Johnny's golden shoulder one with the golden ocean beyond us. Then suddenly the sun is gone and I see him whole and real again and beaver-busy, and the hairs on his back form a delicate feather-soft pelt and the way his small sharp shoulder blades move under his skin as he works is unbearably

318

beautiful to see. Seagulls swoop, screech, around us people gather up their blankets, baskets, beach chairs, shovels, dump trucks. Gather up empty Thermos jars of vodka tonics. Gather up packs of cards that pass the time away. Cedarton, boredom, satiety. And here and there, heaven or hell.

"I like the beach best now," I say when everyone has gone and all is still except for the seagulls and the lapping of the tide. "We'll stay a few more minutes. Go round up Bruce and Terry now, okay?"

"First I gotta get a couple more of these smooth kinda pebbles."

"Well, put your sweater on—"

"Nah—"

"Put it on *now*. The breeze is colder and you're still wet."

He puts on his sweater, muttering, then finishes his fort and goes. I love the way he walks, strutting, humming, a tragi-comic transient in damp blue fish-print trunks. After a certain distance he blurs again. Part of the sand. Part of the sky. Part of the sea. The world is turning purple and I watch until it dwindles into gray. Directly above the jetty a crescent moon is waiting for its turn.

ENJOY THESE GREAT
WARNER PAPERBACK LIBRARY
BESTSELLERS!